# In Six Days

**A Tale of Family, Religion, and Sabotage**

*by*

# *M. Quilman*

Cracked Shutter Publishing

In Six Days

Published by
Cracked Shutter Publishing
Lafayette, CO

Cover design by Subsist Studios

Cracked Shutter Publishing - ISBN: 978-1-7358220-1-3

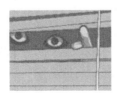

Cracked Shutter
Publishing

FOR MY AMAZING WIFE AND DAUGHTERS...

# IN SIX DAYS

A Tale of Family, Religion, and Sabotage

# Acknowledgement

The author would like to thank all the people who provided support—emotional or technical—to help see this task to its completion. Writing a book is a bit like climbing a mountain without a map, full of false peaks and unchartered terrain to navigate; a tiring, emotional, but ultimately satisfying endeavor. Family and friends who provided a modest suggestion or asked of the book's status, thank you! I appreciate every note of feedback, every word of encouragement. I couldn't have done it without you.

# Major Character List

(in rough order of appearance)

**President Frank Fowler,** aka @PresidentPOTUS.
**Zoe Becker:** Lives in Manhattan, attends high school.
**Heather Danielson:** 60 Minutes producer.
**Ethan Webber:** 60 Minutes journalist.
**Stanley Zivitz:** Zoe's attorney.
**Mo Harbaugh:** former Marine. Currently homeless. Highly religious.
**Ian MacArthur:** Mo's sidekick.
**Sammy:** West Highland Terrier, Ian's sidekick.
**David Becker:** father of Zoe. Former eco-terrorist. Works for an environmental non-profit, Sustainable Pathway Fund.
**Amy (Zimmerman) Becker:** Wife of David Becker
**Yosemite Sam:** Eco-Terrorist.
**Shaggy:** Eco-Terrorist.
**Lorenzo Jamison, aka L.J.:** College friend of David Becker. Former eco-terrorist.
**Reid Johnston (R, TX):** Speaker of the House of Representatives.
**Chad Droburn, Jr. (R, CA):** Congressman, Chair of the Ways and Means Committee.
**Norman Radcliffe (R, OK):** Congressman, Chair of the Energy and Commerce Committee. Has a great chin.
**Ornette Schlesinger (R, GA):** Congressman, aka the Fossil of Congress, Chair of the Science, Space and Technology Committee.
**Landry Muldoon (R, LA):** Congressman, portly Chair of the Appropriations Committee.
**Nathan Culp (R, PA):** Congressman, Chair of the Permanent Select Committee on Intelligence.
**Penelope Archer:** President and CEO of the Faith and Freedom Foundation.
**Graham Bucksworth:** Droburn's congressional aide.
**Dr. Amir Abassi:** College friend of David Becker and scientist with the National Center for Atmospheric Research.

**Shelly Dessev**: Abassi's colleague at NCAR.

**Phillip (Homer) McMannis:** Special Agent with the FBI.

**Sara Roberts:** Special Agent with the FBI. McMannis's partner.

**Sean (Cap) Little:** Special Agent in Charge of the FBI's D.C. office.

**Leun Jiang:** Special Agent in Charge, Department of Homeland Security.

**Nils (Shrink) Jensen:** wildlife biologist, former eco-terrorist.

# Table of Contents

# Act One: Genesis

*One of the biggest changes in politics in my lifetime is that the delusional is no longer marginal. It has come in from the fringe, to sit in the seat of power in the Oval Office and in Congress. For the first time in history, ideology and theology hold a monopoly of power in Washington.*

- Bill Moyers, award winning journalist, 2004

## Chapter 1. The Tweet

*Un-American eco-terrorist #ZoeBecker will rot in jail until she dies. Unless she gets the death penalty, which I fully support. #DeathPenaltyforZoe*

@PresidentPOTUS, June 3, 2017 07:22:47

Within 24 hours, President Frank Fowler's tweet garnered over nine million likes and was retweeted about 51,000 times.

## Chapter 2. The Interview

Later that day.

The commotion frayed at Zoe's nerves: industrial size cables, high-intensity video lights, production crews, lawyers, prison guards. An unceasing buzz. Her head throbbed as the chaos pulsed around her like moths circling a flame, electrons orbiting a dense nucleus. A nucleus with a throbbing headache. She wore a bright orange jumpsuit, her new identification in black lettering over a chest-high white rectangle: 79370-022.

Outside, the throngs continued on. Six weeks long, they've camped, sang songs, screamed in protest. Detractors and cult-like fans on opposite sides of the entranceway, just past the double rows of metal barriers and concertina wire added in makeshift fashion. A sign of the times.

The unlikely home of America's most notorious teenager, the Metropolitan Correctional Center, was the lower Manhattan tentacle to the Federal Bureau of Prisons. From a distance, the dun-colored facility could be mistaken for a hastily-designed office tower or a 60s era medical facility ripe for modernization. But the grimy twelve-story structure, the former home to John Gotti, Bernie

Madoff and El Chapo, Al Qaeda operatives, international drug dealers and gang leaders, was now the inner-city domicile for Zoe Becker while she awaited trial. Zoe and her defense team took weekly, highly-guarded trips across the Manhattan Bridge, the ugly step-sister to the famed Brooklyn, to battle prosecutors over jury selection, material witnesses, and admissible evidence in Federal District Court. Down the hall and three floors above, her father, David Becker, sat in a very similar cell of his own until his release on house arrest a few days ago. The trial was scheduled to begin in one week.

The country waited, glued to their TVs. They gathered in bars and paused at the airport, unwrapping the plastic from their overpriced sandwiches, cutting their flights too close. CNN's ratings shot to OJ levels. Servers on Twitter shut down from the overload of traffic, argument and counter-argument. The yawning fracture across the nation's landscape—red vs. blue, smooth vs. chunky— widened in subsidence. The President tweeted daily, complicating the jury selection process. "Zoe Becker is a traitor to this country!" screamed one man into the reporter's camera outside the MCC's walls.

Inside, on the seventh floor, Zoe watched from the corner next to her graying lawyer. She clutched a chamomile tea with both hands to reduce the shudder.

Heather Danielson barked at a production crew of two dozen. "The interview starts in 5 minutes!" The cafeteria of the correctional facility's only female wing had been transformed into a makeshift studio. Another dozen or so, guards in standard-issue garb—white uniforms, black patent leather shoes, walkie talkies, billy clubs, Smith and Wessons—looked on stoically from the cafeteria perimeter, avoiding her gaze. An uncommon pre-trial conversation awaited. It would air the next day, Sunday, the 60 Minutes broadcast expected to reach an audience of about 100 million, nearly ten times its normal size. Zoe heard the rumors, some calling it a desperate attempt to portray a criminal as a misunderstood teenager, a confused child, angry at the state of her country. "Ethan, are you ready?" the producer asked.

Ethan Webber, 11 years as a journalist for the famed TV show, another 20 plus in the industry before landing the coveted spot, hunched over in one of three plastic chairs at the center of the room, studying his notes.

"I want camera one here pointing at Zoe from a low angle," Danielson shouted, reining in the chaos. "Camera 2 for Zoe and the lawyer straight on. And camera 3 on Ethan. Places everyone, please!"

Producer Danielson turned to Zoe, motioning to the chair. "We're ready for you, honey."

Zoe and the attorney stood up. She floated above her body, appendages numb, a surrealistic echo in her ears. Stanley Zivitz, an expert in criminal defense, was paid from an anonymous donation if he agreed to cut his fees in half to $450 per hour. He took the offer readily. They sat in unison, Zoe right, Stanley left, and traded assuring glances. Days of practice were coming to a head.

After an initial greeting, Webber took his seat opposite Zoe, forestalling eye contact, rumpling his prepared questions one last time. He was more handsome in person, she decided, but not in a jerky way. The lights turned on, massive 800-watt bulbs slung from a skeleton of steel, wheeled forward to perfect the mood.

Pinkish chafe marks, silhouettes from the handcuffs worn during regular transporting, hung like bracelets around her wrists. She gathered her hair, brown with blond highlights, into a quick knot, and looked past the giant lights to discern the production crew. *Was this a good idea?*

"And we're live in six, five, four," Danielson counted the remaining numbers with fingers and thumb in silence. Her free hand pointed to Webber as the camera's red recording light came on.

"Zoe, thank you for being here."

"Thanks for having me."

"You've been in jail for six weeks. How are you faring?"

"OK. Nobody bothers me."

"It's been rumored you have some guardian angels here at the Metropolitan Correctional Center. Is that true?"

"Yea, that's true."

"And that the other inmates ask you for autographs."

"That's true too."

"Outside, can you hear them?" Echoes of shouts and airhorns, muffled but unmistakable, filtered through the prison walls. Webber pointed to a small TV monitor to Zoe's right as it flickered on. "This is a live picture," he explained. The crowds outside, factions separated by the jail entranceway, came into view. *Free Zoe. Arrest the King of Clubs,* handheld signs read that warm night in New York, just a mile or so from where she grew up. "There are people out there, shouting for your release."

The camera panned west along Park Row, the name far more glamourous than the non-descript six lanes of poured concrete affronting the southern Manhattan prison. Across more rows of metal barriers and a cordoned off no-man's land, the opposition crowd, even larger and louder than her supporters. The posters all read the same three-word phrase: *Lock Her Up!* "And others," Webber commented, "for your life imprisonment."

"It's kinda crazy," she admitted.

"In some ways, you've become a cult hero. Was that the intention?"

Zoe hesitated to let the anger diminish. She practiced this very moment, word for word, with Zivitz for the last week or more. But now, most of America was watching, or going to in another 28 hours, give or take. She gathered her hair. Webber noticed her tattoo: listening quietly from behind her left ear, Buddha holding a blue-green earth.

"N... No," was all she could muster.

"But you planned all along to expose the King of Clubs? Isn't that right?"

Zoe shook her head, not sure how to respond.

"Excuse me!" Stan Zivitz stood up and blocked the camera, searching for Danielson, the 60 Minutes producer, between the lights. He pushed his wire-rim glasses back into place, sat down, and gestured to Ethan Webber. "I'm sorry but Ms. Becker is not here to talk about the court case or the King of Clubs or offer any admission of guilt."

Zivitz corralled his gray hair into place, down towards his dandruff-flecked suit. "We agreed to the ground rules. You wanted to introduce Zoe to the American people. That's why we're here."

Webber looked back at his notes and tried again. "Zoe, can you take us back? How did you first become interested in protecting the environment?"

Zoe paused, looking over the edge of an imperfection in the concrete floor. Her lips quivered with response. "Where do I start..."

# Chapter 3. Let There Be Light

April 4th, 2017. 63 Days before the 60 Minutes Interview

The old Tacoma pulled across the large abandoned lot, about a hundred and fifty yards from the dealership, one of the biggest in northern Pennsylvania. The truck's rear pointed toward the over-priced SUVs and new pickups, more than twice the Tacoma's in size and cost. The mutant offspring. Two men got out wearing baseball caps, cheap sunglasses, fake mustaches, and rubber gloves. Ten minutes to three a.m., the mischief hour. They took expected precautions: splattering the license plates and other markings with mud; parking under Interstate 79, outside the reach of the security cameras. The hotel, 30 miles away, was paid for in cash. Actually, everything was cash, about $16k to cover the expenses as needed, pulled out in bundles of old 20s from the gym bag they kept under the Westie snoring in the backseat.

They moved quickly, cracked open the rear hatch, gently enough to avoid the squeal, and plucked four large bottles of propane. Nodding to each other, they hustled to the auto dealer, staying low, moving silently. A siren wailed in the distance and they paused for a moment, half-way to their destination, contemplating abandoning the plan, hauling ass out of there before it was too late. They searched the horizon. The city glowed dimly from the distance. The siren? It seemed to be moving away from them.

"Not us," Mo shrugged, crouching on the lightless blacktop. "Probably a junkie."

"Bad night to be a junkie," Ian surmised.

"Why do you say that?"

"Looks like rain coming in. Shelters will be full."

"Come on," Mo replied in frustration, "we got work to do."

They ran the last 75 yards, a propane IED per hand—20 lbs. of fuel each, stolen from the metal cage outside Home Depot a few miles away—and hid between two gigantic Ford F150 Raptors. MSRP $52,855. Plus options. They kept cover in the shadows. Away from the light. Away from the cameras.

The men dropped off the payload and turned, shuffling back to the Tacoma in silence to grab one more canister each. "You look real stupid in that get-up," Ian said, motioning to the fake mustache falling off Mo's lip. Mo pushed it back on, over his own thick facial hair. Ian nodded and held back his snicker. They scampered back to the dealership, Mo in front, Ian shadowing.

Bent over, hearts pounding, they caught their breaths in the cool air pulling off Lake Erie just a couple miles away. Mo yanked off his cap and wiped the sweat from his clean-shaven dome. His bulbous browns glinted in the faint light between the vehicles. His beard, long and dark, fell like an angry hornet's nest halfway down his oversized frame. Ian cast a twitchy air like a small car that idled too fast.

They searched back for the lone 2002 Tacoma. The old gal, in Impulse Red with matching bed cover, seemed tiny parked in the abandoned lot. Just beyond, the highway underpass. The egress route. Mo picked up a few things before the Marines gave him the boot. Even at this ungodly hour, traffic raced ahead, fighting for position to nowhere. In the distance, a siren wailed, streetlights flickered, dogs barked at shadows.

They caught each other with that look they gave. "Let me guess," Mo whispered, his Louisiana drawl covered in Spanish Moss and crawdads. "You havin' second thoughts."

"How'd ya know?" Ian said, catching his breath. "If I wasn't blowing them up, I'd love to have one of these puppies."

"First things first."

"Sure Shaggy knows what he's doing?"

"Well, he paid us up front. Besides, I was always a Toyota man. Now hush up," Mo whispered in frustration. "And don't say no names."

Ian covered his gasp as if he could undo the words. He wasn't much of a criminal. Without any gainful employment or a roof of his own, a prior meth addiction that knocked free an incisor and a bicuspid, you could say he was more of a wandering soul, a scuba diver in the dumpster of life, rummaging for something interesting to do, a little spiritual guidance, and a few dollars in his pocket. On the other hand, Mo spilled with consequence. The years of mishap and misdirection, he realized one day, were all pointing him to a higher purpose. Despite all of the ancient teachings, mankind evolved into a rude guest that puts his muddy boots on the coffee table of the earth, dirty dishes piling up in the sink, sitting at the Lord's dining table with unwashed hands. A terrible sin in need of rectifyin'.

Mo produced a box from his pocket: threaded bolts with large hex heads. He gestured to a propane bottle. "Every other truck. Pull off the plastic coating, wedge a bolt into this here brass nozzle, spin the tank until the bolt catches, and then unscrew this metal valve," he explained, demonstrating along the way. Mo rotated the large tap, the gas hissing forward a few seconds, before closing it again.

"Got it," Ian tried to reassure him.

"Then slide it right under the gas tank. And don't forget all them plastic bits," he said, maintaining eye contact through the budget shades.

"Yea, yea, yea - no evidence."

"A good rule no matter where you are in life." They held their gaze, seeking an answer to the unspoken question: *should we do this?* A turning point they could never reverse.

"I still think you look stupid in that disguise," Ian offered, breaking the tension.

"Not as bad as you," Mo retorted and coughed into an oversized fist. "Terrorist? You got some nerve." They let out a big laugh before silencing each other in the shadows. "Y'all ready?" Mo asked.

"I'm not sure. This could go down real bad."

"Don't overthink it. Just be in the moment."

Ian grabbed a propane bottle and scampered to the truck parked on the far side. "Don't overthink it, just be in the moment," he repeated the mantra.

They wedged the bolts like pins reinserted into hand grenades, spun the propane canisters until the threads caught, shimmied under the trucks and their 36-gallon fuel tanks, and unscrewed the valves. Pressurized gas collected below two F150 Raptors. 450 horsepower each. Snarling twin turbos. 0-60 in 5.7 seconds.

They stood quickly and searched for onlookers. A chronic bark in the blackness filled the space between heartbeats. Heads nodded in agreement: *first truck, done.*

They grabbed another propane tank apiece and ran, heads low, to their next targets. Ian selected a white F250 Limited with heated leather seats, adaptive cruise control, 48-gallon fuel tank, 15 miles to the gallon, MSRP $39,000; Mo a Ford Expedition with extra tow capacity: 9,200 pounds.

"Look at these things," Ian stopped, peering inside the vehicle, the truck so tall and Ian relatively short, he had to get on his toes to read the window sticker. "Leather seats? Apple Carplay?"

Mo tried to ignore him.

"And they want $2785 for some Platinum Ultimate Package? Some fuckin nerve."

"I swear to God," Mo stammered, as he clambered under the Expedition, "y'all gonna get the platinum package with an incendiary in your brain."

"Real nice," Ian muttered to himself, wrestling the propane tank into place, spinning the valve open, the distinctive sound of gas escaping. The men held their breath, grabbing the last canisters. Two more victims. For Mo, a GM Suburban with seating for nine. For Ian, a Ford Super Duty F350 King Ranch with Kingsville Antique Affect Leather Bucket Seating Surfaces. He wasn't sure what that was but he wanted it. Badly. They worked in silence, too distant to banter. Pry open, wriggle under, and spin. They found each other in the darkness, signaled all clear, and ran back, silently through the shadows.

Halfway back to the Tacoma, on the abandoned lot, Mo threw two playing cards on the ground. Both, the King of Clubs. Ian looked at him and shook his head, not sure the difference between righteousness and greed.

Sammy watched from the truck interior, tongue out, head tilted, groggy from his slumber. He barked as they approached, paws—one still bandaged—up on the seat rest.

"I'll put that dog down in a heartbeat," Mo said without emotion.

"He'll be good," Ian promised, motioning Sammy to shush. The dog wagged his tail but offered no guarantees.

They pulled a dropcloth out of the pickup bed, laid it quickly on the ground, and grabbed the utensils. For Ian, a Colt AR-15 from a softshell case designed for easy access. Just need the ammo and someone to pull the trigger.

Mo opened an oversized hard shell Pelican case to find the metal beast in matte black. The .50 caliber, Barrett M82. He pulled the pieces from the precision-cut foam, clicked the upper barrel and lower stock pieces together, inserted the cross pins, opened up the bi-pod legs, and pulled back the spring-driven bolt carrier. He didn't bother with the suppressor, it only cut the decibels by a third; they were sure to attract a lot of attention either way.

They stared down their scopes and eyed their targets: 20-pound propane tanks, gas pooling dangerously underneath six pickups and SUVs.

Ian chortled at the massive rifle in Mo's arms, nearly five feet in length. "Over-compensating for something?"

Mo ignored him. "You loaded incendiaries, right?"

"Yours are just tracers, not incendiaries."

"Jesus Christ!"

"Which one you hittin'?" Ian changed the subject.

Mo answered as he practiced the sweep of his rifle. "Mine are left. Y'all's are right. Go left to right. One bullet each. One shot, one kill,"

"One shot, one kill," Ian repeated the sniper refrain.

They stuffed silicone plugs in their ears, then muffs on top. The explosive force out of a .50 caliber could ring eardrums for hours after, if not permanently. "Make sure ya actually hit a propane tank," Mo offered sarcastically.

"What?"

"Never mind."

Mo switched to hand signals, counting down with fingers and thumb. Ian nodded with confirmation. They plucked their triggers in unison. Tracers flared across the parking lot, arcs of light in search of destiny. Two propane tanks exploded immediately with gigantic force, fire and detonation pouring out. A slight pause before sonic pulses hit them in repeating waves.

"Holy shit!"

The weapons reloaded automatically, hot shells flying. They refocused on the next propane tank. Mo didn't need to, but waited.

"Fire when ready!" he yelled.

They shot another round. The propane tank under the Expedition hesitated as if contemplating where to send the shrapnel before flames slithered across the row of vehicles, instantly melting tires onto wheels. Ian's target, the white F250, sat silently, eerily quiet amid the chaos a few feet away.

"I knew you'd miss."

"Fuck you."

Ian repositioned his rifle, wrestling the weapon and his adrenaline like a Boa Constrictor in his arms. Seconds ticked loudly. Firing again, the tracer round pierced the dark abyss. The F250 hopped sideways and rotated, spinning into the truck next to it, flames shooting in all intervals like compass bearings.

Smoke filled the wide abandoned lot, a violent echo rolling toward the men. The guns sent violent ends to the last two vehicles. Windshields shattered, glass ricocheting in all directions.

Distant lights flicked on, sirens pulsed closer.

The men scurried, tossed the weapons in. No time to dismantle. They pulled up the dropcloth, closed the Tacoma bed. "Hurry! " Mo hissed. "Get all the cartridges." Ian scampered in the dark, counting seven shells. Two more gas tanks from adjacent vehicles blew in succession sending giant fireballs into the night sky, waves pulsating across the tarmac. They jumped into the Tacoma, Mo behind the wheel. He spun the truck toward the carnage, shadows and light throbbing across their faces.

"*Then God reacted, 'Let there be light'; and there was light,*" Mo whispered, his focus soft.

"What?" Ian asked.

Eyes glowing with bonfire, Mo continued with awkward calm. "*And God saw the light, that it was good; and God divided the light from the darkness.*"

Ian stared back in silence, sweat glistening off his forehead, silty dust attached like powdered sugar on a doughnut.

Mo pulled out of the abandoned lot, gave Ian a knowing glance, his voice rising with intensity. "*God called the light Day, and the darkness He called Night. So the evening and the morning were the first day.*"

He sped the Tacoma north two blocks, under the highway, left at the on-ramp, onto the interstate, accelerating quickly to 85, frenetically passing the other traffic. They whooped as the Tacoma headed south. It was 2:58 a.m. They didn't stop for 4 hours and nearly 300 miles.

# Chapter 4. News in NYC

April 4, 2017. Later that Day

Four hundred and thirty-two miles east southeast, a digital video recorder clicked to record at 6:00 p.m. Within a second, the hard drive whirred to full speed.

David Becker came in about 45 minutes later. Ascending the fourth-floor walk-up in lower Manhattan tired and beaten from the day, the week, the year. 600 days of insanity. The election and presidency that would exhaust a nation. He panted, pulling large grocery bags up to the kitchen counter.

He clicked on the TV and started the DVR at the top of the broadcast, just like every other day. Wesley Brandt, too handsome to take seriously, jumped into the day's news.

*"The White House claims invisible drones are circling Washington, D.C., searching for an opening into the Lincoln bedroom. President Fowler continued allegations he and staff have been spied on by the drones, most likely of Chinese or alien origin, although no evidence has been brought forward. Across the country, dozens of lawsuits have been filed against the President to stop his travel ban on countries ending in "stan." In New York, Media Conglomerate Incorporated Chairman Lewis Liebner faces new sexual discrimination charges. And in Pennsylvania, a Ford dealership was attacked in the dead of night. Good Evening and welcome to CBC News. I'm Wesley Brandt."*

Becker put the groceries away, still exhaling 11 hours of emails and a brief that was filed in the nick of time, the culmination of three weeks of frenzied work at the Sustainable Pathway Fund. The news filled the void, a blurry soundtrack to the anxiety-riddled times. The new top 40. He found it best to keep moving. Make dinner, do the dishes, grind up a bud and fill a small pipe to unwind from the day. He took a couple of quick hits, careful about the dosage. A little bit takes the edge off. Too much, and his depression would magnify.

"Hey Pops," Zoe entered, slamming the door shut and throwing the jumble of keys 15 feet in his direction.

"Jesus!" Becker jumped as the metallic thud landed on the kitchen island, pushing a loaf of bread to the floor. "Don't do that!"

"Sorry," she offered, a bit tickled. "Good throw though, huh?"

"Yea, impressive."

Becker gave his daughter a hug that lasted a bit too long, one of the few remaining antidotes to the lunacy.

"I think I'm taller than you," she said, breaking the awkwardness.

"That's impossible!"

"Let's see." She had them stand back to back. Now nearly 5'8", just an inch shy of the old man as he balled up over the years. "Not quite," she reported.

She pulled her light brown hair behind her shoulders, exposing the tiny Buddha and earth tattoo behind her left ear. Mama, she called it. Full lips and a wide smile. She wasn't the rail-thin kid he was expecting; the curves of a young woman were becoming apparent. The midriff and ass cheek-bearing shorts of middle school gave way as well, replaced by flowy dresses, embroidered blouses. Bell-bottom jeans were back. *When did that happen?* Becker wondered.

Wesley Brandt and his CBC colleagues continued in the background. Angry crowds gathered at airports to demonstrate against the travel ban from "stan"-ending nations. Chaos across the country.

"Ugh," Zoe garbled, dropping her overloaded backpack to the floor, flopping on the couch. "Can we watch something else?"

"It's good for you," Becker replied, walking into the master bedroom. He molted away his work clothes as a lizard sheds his skin. Dress pants, sport coat, button-down shirt. A return to normality. "Like eating your vegetables," he yelled into the living room. "How was school?" Something about kicking ass in math but probably failed the Spanish quiz she forgot to study for.

"Dad!"

"Yea?" he shouted back with concern.

"I forgot to tell you..."

"Yea?"

"You know my friend Hannah?"

"The redhead?"

"No, she's Korean. Anyways, she has turned into such a drunk. You know we got fake ID's right?" Becker grimaced, not certain if he knew that. "Well, we got this huge bottle of wine. Hannah drank most of it. Anyway, that walkway on the Brooklyn Bridge?"

"Uh-huh," Becker muttered, entering the living room, muscles contracting in preparation.

"Yea, the far pillar might reek of puke for a while."

"Just great."

"You wanna see my ID?" she offered enthusiastically.

"Not bad," Becker surveyed the plasticized picture and non-believable information. "You're from El Paso?"

"I figured my Spanish might come in handy since I'm so close to the border now."

"Smart."

"*Si senor, inteligente*," she poked at her temple for emphasis.

Becker had given up punishing Zoe years ago. *The kid lost her mom, for Chrissakes*, he'd argue with the mirror. For better or worse, Zoe shared more information than the old man bargained for. The ragers, the LSD, fooling around with the guy whose name she forgot. He tried not to prune his face during the colorful yarns. *When she needs me*, he convinced his reflection, *she'll trust me to help her*. In truth, he could barely care for his own shit let alone another living thing. The plants were on life support, the experiment with tropical fish long since concluded. He was flailing between meds, his rants a run-on sentence playing in his head.

*"In Erie Pennsylvania, six propane tanks were exploded under pickup trucks and SUVs. Neighbors described 50-foot flames and thick smoke blanketing the area."*

"I haven't seen the new Game of Thrones yet," Zoe declared, picking up the remote. "Probably more interesting than the real world."

"Don't touch that! I'm watching it."

"I thought you hate this guy. Isn't he the fluffball?"

"Yea, but something just happened. Just watch." Becker grabbed the remote and hit the 10-second rewind button.

Smoldering inky plumes, firefighters hosing down burnt vehicular skeletons, filled the screen.

*"The blaze got so hot, windshields and tires melted. The owner of the Pennsylvania dealership says at least 15 vehicles were damaged, valued at roughly one million dollars."* Brandt cocked his head at awkward angles for emphasis, his hair motionless. *"Erie Police Chief Warren Post offered a statement earlier today."*

*"At approximately 3:00 this morning, Erie Ford was attacked,"* Chief Post explained, cameras climaxing in the background. He flattened his walrus mustache, pushed his wire-frame glasses back to their appointed location. *"We're investigating the matter, inspecting video footage, conducting door to door interviews. If anyone has information that may be helpful, please call the Erie Police Department."*

*"Chief Post!"* a reporter blurted out. *"Dana Klingman with KCBC-Erie. Were there any claims of responsibility?"*

*"No,"* he explained. *"No one has come forward about the attack."*

Klingman chimed in again. *"Were authorities aware of any threats?"*

*"No, we hadn't received any warnings."* the Chief replied, glancing around the room.

*"Sheriff, Dana Klingman with KCBC-Erie again, do the Police consider this an act of terrorism, and if so, will you seek assistance from Federal authorities?"*

Zoe grabbed a Coke from the fridge and sat back on the couch like a twisted ficus. "Dad..."

"Uh-huh."

"You know anything about that?"

"No," he reacted distantly before turning to the insult. "Why would I?"

*"At this juncture, we do not consider this an act of terrorism,"* Chief Post explained, scanning the room. *"The FBI has offered their assistance but this is a local investigation until further notice. Any questions from other reporters?"*

The press core became distracted, checking their cell phones. Notebooks were closing, equipment re-cased. An elementary school was under lockdown, someone suspicious tried to enter the building. Potential active shooter. Next story.

Wesley Brandt broke in. *"When we return: a tiny superhero in California is protecting the environment, one lemonade customer at a time."*

Becker turned the TV off, took another hit from his pipe, and pulled at his dark curls, detached with thought.

Zoe picked at her lower lip. "Do you think Earth Liberation Front is active again?"

"Who knows — it could be high school kids."

"Dad, those were NOT high school kids. The most vandalism my friends could pull off would be breaking into a construction site, smoke weed, and spill the bong water."

"Maybe you're right," he wondered, opening the fridge, hoping dinner would make itself. He grabbed a beer instead and cracked it open. "Honestly, it's what we need right now. A wake-up call." He sucked the foam before it spilled over the can and released a belch. "Or something."

## Chapter 5. Becker

About five months earlier. November 8th, 2016. Election day.

"Damn it," David Becker whispered well before the sun pierced through the windows of 22nd Street. Once the Ambien receded in his bloodstream, it practically jarred him awake, like clockwork. 4:20 every day. Strange coincidence for a stoner. It was only getting worse too, leading up to the election, impossible to tell reality from hallucination, it all a nauseating carney ride.

Sometimes he'd take another half Ambien and lie to himself he'd moderate his use next week, make up the shortage before the monthly allotment ran out. Or simply barter with the man upstairs and fabricate how he was about to get his shit together, be a better person if only they could agree to the terms and conditions.

Even as a kid back in Philly, sleep never came easy. In his 20s, it was Nyquil, then Lunesta, then Ambien, interspersed with sleep clinics, melatonin, to and fro to that wacky acupuncturist, her bottles of allergens and reflexology maps of the human body, searching for his kidney meridian. Now, back on Ambien with a 50/50 chance of getting a half-decent night's slumber. The fog usually lifted by the morning's second dose of coffee but it was a turntable, like one of his scratched records on the old player in the living room. He could never step off.

Growing up he was relatively happy if not a bit klutzy, the spastic sibling to the family athlete. The cartoon character. The Ozone Ranger, earning that label in college. Dad coached all the little league teams he never participated on, except the one time, in the stratosphere bored out of his mind in left field, the ping of the aluminum bat calling him back to his home planet, the ball and his attention arriving at the same time, passing his glove, smacking him right in the face with the force of a small asteroid. Benches cleared, his Dad carried him back to the dugout so he could ice the alien egg forming on his noggin with the few cubes remaining in the cooler.

"Damn it," he muttered again, definitely audible, the record still skipping in place. Even after successfully haggling with his maker, he'd squander the extra hour conjuring the frustration and boredom of another day on this plane. Another day with his boss, Joel, frantic convulsions and all. Another day waiting in line to buy overpriced groceries kept fresh in plastic that would never disintegrate, the material finding its way to the ocean, teaming up with the Great Pacific garbage patch. Floating, expanding in perpetuity. All cause he wanted a fucking yogurt parfait for breakfast. Another day fighting his way uptown, wedging himself into an overcrowded subway car, out into the noisy street where the smell of gasoline and bagels sold from impatient men inside tiny metal carts filled the air. Another day sitting in that chair, battling every rearguard attack. All for what? Going backward, our society was.

Becker took to cycling and hiking instead, recoiling from team sports the way a snake hisses when passed, too close to the trail. A sport that brought him closer to nature, on his schedule, that was more his style. If he could find the time, get the hell out of New York, that is. It was the only reliable remedy, really. Better than the therapist's couch or the prescriptions across the no man's land in the cabinet. He always hated those anyway, the cure worse than the disease.

He frittered in bed as the traffic and dogs and construction pulsed back to life, deliberating existence under a Fowler presidency and his favorite methods of suicide. Perhaps a quick jump in front of a bus. The #35 up 2$^{nd}$ Avenue seemed to get a lot of speed around 29$^{th}$ street. Or maybe he'd call on the soldiers of opioids, leftover after that nasty fall on the ice, his elbow shattered, and whatever else he could find defending the back of the bathroom vanity. *Sir, Yes Sir,* they salute from behind the talcum or the hydrogen peroxide, ready for duty, whenever he opens the cabinet door. A revolver seems more appropriate, somehow. But he can't do it at home where Zoe would find him. It would ruin the apartment, where men in white jumpsuits had to clean bits of brain off the walls. They'd have to follow up with a quality primer and then match the paint perfectly and fade in the color or it would be obvious something awry happened there. No. He'd have to go somewhere upstate, to a nice wooded area. The state troopers would locate the body, four of them carrying the blanket-draped stretcher out of the woods, their large flat-brimmed hats covered in plastic to stay dry in the cold morning drizzle.

His funeral was a quiet affair, tasteful of course. His brother and elderly father came up from the Philadelphia suburb where Becker grew up; the locals at the diner who congregated after Sunday morning bike rides around Central Park; L.J., of course, his best friend since Redwood State, getting high watching cartoons when they weren't cramming for an exam or causing mischief for the loggers. And poor Zoe. First, her mom…

Becker's phone vibrated, mercifully, with a text. He raised the needle on the record player, spinning silently, interrupting the morbid tale playing in his head.

*Check your emails!*, the text from his boss, Joel, read. 19 messages amassed for him since he left work last night: Frank Fowler drew eerily close in the polls, and anything could happen. He pondered if he had pulled the trigger last night, somehow, and was quickly chaperoned to hell. He opened his bedroom door, surveyed the apartment, caught his reflection in the hall mirror, and convinced himself he hadn't.

He scanned the email thread: a long exchange between Joel and other attorneys at the Sustainable Pathway Fund they toiled at. A Fowler Presidency and Republican stranglehold on Congress could mean a return to the stone ages. Everything they fought for was up for grabs: land protection, air quality, water quality, species protection, parks and wilderness.

Becker could only shake his head at the irony that was the modern Republican party. They claim Lincoln as their founder, but that was only due to a strange fold in time and space, the parties flipping in perspective decades later. Instead, they had evolved into Lincoln's polar opposite, something akin to the Southern Democrats of his day, avoiding the natural truths of slavery's evil behind arguments of state's rights, commerce, property, and the good book. Becker—still in his underwear, scratching his nuts—stewed at it all.

"Better get the day started," he muttered to the awful looking dude in the mirror. A dissonant buzz, as if mosquitos annexed his ear canals, whined in the silence. He'll have to continue the disquiet from the shower. He waited for the water to warm, stripped his underwear and t-shirt, and sank under the showerhead, the third-best anti-anxiety money can buy. Make that fourth best. At least he and the country were in sync emotionally. Well, maybe not quite.

When his good friend Amir Abassi died mysteriously back in July, Becker fell into a deep declivity in the earth. Hygiene became optional, irritable the new standard. Most people follow a consistent path: youthful distrust replaced by portfolio returns and kale. For Becker, the opposite was true. The kale endured but his cynicism only grew, contempt launched into the upper atmosphere where it would cross paths with his attention in left field that day the alien egg formed. Perhaps, something profound transpired in that fateful moment, synapses rewired, his outlook forever cockeyed, assimilation traits knocked loose. His poor daughter—the only family he really maintained—too often in earshot as he ranted about the system, the money that rusted our democratic machine.

He told the police he and Abassi talked just weeks before. The potential break-in. The confidential computer models. The contentious—some would say, irresponsible—results. But the coroner confirmed what it appeared to be: suicide by hanging. A call to Abassi's doctor back in Boulder confirmed he was depressed and well-sedated, Celexa and Prozac found in his bloodstream. No sign of forced entry or struggle inside the room. There was a small amount of toxin, 0.2% by volume, in his blood, but that can occur naturally from eating shellfish. According to the police, it was an open and shut case.

Becker soaped his pits, his throat tightening, uncertain of his own sanity. He missed his Amy, the spoon in bed, like a serving of sedatives, calming his nerves, helping him discern reality from illusion. That grounding laugh of hers. How could she and that fucking cancer expect him to raise Zoe alone? It's hard enough as it is, the deep dung that teenagers can get into. Plus the job, the boss's abrasive orders, the shit show this country was becoming, *about to become*, if his worst election fears turned real.

He shampooed the remaining curls on his head, reviewing each memory like a decaying film strip from the silent era. He even contacted the FBI a few months after Abassi's death, but the file never received any attention. They determined the case a matter for local police. No jurisdiction without contradictory evidence. Closed. The country had more important things on its mind, the chaos that is election season in full swing. He mentioned his theory—the one about the sex scandal—as if the Feds could take him seriously after that delusional hypothesis. But he wasn't crazy, he insisted, soaping his nuts distantly.

## Chapter 6. Inauguration Day

73 Days later. January 20, 2017.

Two figures met at The Market Tavern, an Irish pub, a block from New York's Penn Station, the city's main stop along the Northeastern rail corridor.

Shaggy arrived at 11:25 a.m., a few minutes late. Getting out of the station and over to the tavern, another 10 minutes. Yosemite Sam was already there, typing nervously on a cell phone, twisting a lip into taffy under the Jameson's Whiskey sign. Shaggy entered, walking past the long dark bar and dozens of beer taps, wearing a hat with a large American flag waiving across the front.

"Nice touch," Yosemite Sam laughed.

They agreed to this time and place using encrypted WhatsApp, signing in only as their code names. Cartoon characters would be appropriate, they agreed, given the zany caricature the country had become. *No names, real or coded, in person. And never meet in the same spot twice.*

The bartenders and waitstaff were setting up for the lunch hour. Three guys, locals in Giants jerseys, sat at the bar getting a headstart on the day, arguing about whether the coach should be fired, if the offensive line needed gutting. An older couple sat toward the front window, eyes glued to the closest television.

Shaggy leaned in. "The timing could be better."

"It can't wait any longer," Yosemite Sam responded.

The pub's eleven large-screen TVs were tuned to the same event: Frank Fowler's inauguration. Ten days before the election, Samantha Barnstable appeared poised to be the first female President of the United States. But when it was revealed she hung her own laundry, pictures of old underwear and socks flapping in the breeze, her lead narrowed in the waning days of the campaign. Even with a popular vote shortage of almost 3 million votes, Frank Fowler won the electoral college, 304-227, and was about to become the most powerful person on earth. Shaggy and Yosemite Sam watched the TVs in depleted silence, mouths agape.

"But will it help our cause or hurt it?" Shaggy whispered.

"There was a murder, you know," Yosemite argued, eyes bulging with intensity. "People need to know."

Shaggy gazed around fretfully. The bartender surveyed their direction as he brought ice up from the cellar. Shaggy was older, maybe in his 50s, with a knack for staying out of jail, although that hadn't been tested in a while. The moniker seemed to fit, the disheveled wanderer, the weak beard, cajoled into solving mysteries. Yosemite Sam, more radical and enraged, wanted to go in with guns blazing, take no prisoners. Consequences, schmonsequences.

The young waitress disrupted the tension. "Are you here for lunch?" she asked, blowing aside a few strays of straw-colored hair. The aroma of the kitchen wafted past the swinging doors. Two fish and chips, a Coke for Yosemite Sam, a Guinness for Shaggy, minding the bartender as he shifted his attention, cleaning glasses on the far side of the bar. The waitress turned to put the order in, out of earshot.

Fowler's speech painted the country in the bleakest palette possible, as if starting from dystopian bottom. *"Our education system, mismanaged and over-budget, leaves our brilliant children devoid of wisdom. Do they even teach U.S. history and science anymore? I don't know."* The bar groaned in pain.

"Remember how this got started?" Yosemite asked.

"Not completely," Shaggy admitted, most of it a blur.

"You said the movement had stalled. That young people need to carry the torch."

"Yep, that's true."

"But it can't be random acts that don't seem to connect."

"Yep. That's true too," Shaggy agreed. "Has to be a good story, something you'd binge on Netflix."

Yosemite Sam spent months pouring into the research, creating the plotline, a narrative worthy of Shakespearean tragedy. "The FBI is gonna solve the murder for us."

Shaggy hesitated and leaned in low. "After ELF, the Feds have labeled this shit as the highest security threat. We could go to jail for a long fuckin time." Shaggy lifted his flag hat to wipe the sweat away. The bartender gawped the tension in the back corner.

"We knew all this from the beginning. Besides, you don't have to take the blame. I want to know who's on the ground?"

"I want separation of powers," Shaggy argued. "I'm not bargaining with you. You came up with the plan. It's solid. You're Vice President of Strategy." Yosemite Sam smiled. That sounded good. "But I'm Chief of Operations. I handle the crew."

Yosemite Sam chewed on a thumbnail, nervously thinking of loose ends. "Where'd you meet these guys?"

"Church."

"Really?" Yosemite snickered.

"Not the kind of church *you* go to."

"I don't go to church, remember?"

"Well, not a normal church."

"A church for terrorists?"

"Something like that."

"Oh my god," Yosemite Sam hooted a bit too loudly, "we're in trouble!" The older couple rubbernecked from the front of the bar, but agreeing with the sentiment, turned back to the broadcast.

The TVs' talking heads announced the ascendancy of Frank Fowler, President of the United States. The Giants fans booed like a pick six in the wrong direction and ordered another round. Plus shots.

"So, how long till they're ready?" Yosemite Sam solicited.

"Two months."

"Two months?!"

The rubberneckers craned from the front again. Shaggy whispered into a concealing beer glass. "The folks in the field have to get organized, cash out the crypto, buy the toys. These things take time."

They sat up straight as the waitress brought the fish and chips and paper napkin-wrapped cutlery. "Careful, the plates are hot."

"Thanks," they replied, salivating at the fried bouquet.

Yosemite Sam held Shaggy's gaze and conceded.

"OK. Two months. Hold onto your ass, America."

# Chapter 7. I Hate this City

April 4th, 2017. The day Erie Ford is attacked.

After fighting off Republican challenges to environmental protections all day, learning of the attack in Erie Pennsylvania, opening a beer, and contemplating the demise of the western world, David Becker turned to Zoe and asked the infinite question of parenthood.

"You got homework?"

Zoe snorted something unintelligible, typed a message on her phone, scanned Snapchat for updates. Bestie Amelia posted a video, her dog in an epic battle with the vacuum cleaner. Ex-boyfriend Travis searched their circle of friends for some molly. A party to end all parties was on the horizon.

"I have a little work myself," Becker offered, hoping that may prompt her. He walked into the back study, a rear nook to the 22$^{nd}$ Street apartment he inherited from his grandparents where they and other immigrants toiled as seamstresses or butchers or bakers, their shops just below, the smell of blood and yeast wafting up through the floorboards. Now it was worth a couple million, way beyond his current means. *Strange how that happens*, he thought to himself, pausing before the fluted millwork around the door to the study.

Zoe was a city kid. A little edgy, comfortable in her own skin. She propped herself on the couch and perused the artifacts on the white shelving unit extending the living room wall, stopping at her favorite photo. "I love this one of you and mom."

Becker opened his laptop slowly, every motion a little too deliberate. A tinnitus buzz—cymbals shimmering with déjà vu— filled his ears.

"Yea, me too," he called back. He knew the one she meant: he and Amy in the forest, surrounded by other beatniks and hooligans, illegally camping for weeks to slow the loggers, for a slim chance to save the old-growth timber—its existence measured in centuries, if not millennia—and everything it represented. Becker, only 20 at the time, looked straight at the camera, clear-eyed, curly dark hair framing a sly smile. Amy looked at him, her almond eyes beaming at the young man she would marry, his goofy sense of humor mixed with an infectious dose of rage. She wore a wonderful grin, as if laughter was about to spill out.

"This one too," Zoe pointed, her mouth agape at the astonishment of seeing herself in diapers. In a dark wood frame, the happy couple giggled. Late summer rays eclipsed a background of Central Park and a baby carriage, as Zoe—six months old, lying on a blanket under an old oak—jerked at mom's long brown hair, squealing with delight.

She examined the bookshelf as an archaeologist, centuries from now, might. *Highly intelligent,* the archeologist calculated, *given the lack of evolved thought back in the 21$^{st}$ century.* She studied the baseball that bounced fortuitously at a Yankees game; a hookah, the spoils of a shopping raid she and her Dad led on an outdoor Tel Aviv market; the dust-covered record player and assorted albums, mostly classic rock that faded from popular culture like a Cheshire cat vanishing onto the page. Somehow, Amy's ABBA LPs endured.

*Books are the most telling,* the archaeologist explained to the lecture hall of students: the titles, the relative placement, the organization by size. Rage of a Dying Planet, Monkey Wrench Gang (with author's inscription), The People's History of the United States, the Invisible Man, nestled against the entire collections of Kurt Vonnegut and John Irving. Another shelf, travel guides from vacations realized or not: France (check), Israel (check), Portugal, Peru, Thailand, Alaska (all unchecked). Just above, history, Becker's favorite subject. At least, until recently. Tomes on the founding fathers, Truman, Lincoln, de Tocqueville's Democracy in America, the beacon for the world to follow. Bottom left, law texts, mostly unopened since Becker passed his LSATs 20 years ago. Bottom right, court documents from a recent filing to force the U.S. Government to recognize carbon dioxide as a pollutant. Zoe took it all in, wondering its pathway to this time and place.

"We should go on another trip," she tendered to the old man.

"Yea," Becker agreed, pulling at a few remaining curls like the stray strands of a sweater. The screen's reflection bounced off the magnifiers he initiated a couple years back, his eyesight decaying in lockstep with the federation of body parts he dragged into the shower every day.

"Maybe China. Someplace really far away." Zoe faced her phone the way a puppy looks into a mirror. "Hey Siri, what's the farthest spot from New York City?"

"I found an article on the internet," Siri answered.

"Australia. Hey Dad..." She rolled a cigarette of loose tobacco. "We should go to Australia. Dad?" she prodded him out of his daydream.

"Yea?"

"You're just staring at your computer screen. Did you forget how to turn it on?"

"Very funny," he turned to her. Sitting in the old couch, orange shafts of sunset behind her. The room wasn't large but the tall ceilings gave it a scale that Becker always found comfort in. He looked at her more closely, studying. *I did ok raising that one.*

She pulled it to her mouth and drew a puff.

"Are you smoking?" he asked stupidly, the answer pretty obvious.

"They're organic."

"I don't give a shit!"

He turned back to the laptop, powered it on. In the screen's reflection, he caught her flipping him the bird. "I saw that," he revealed.

"Impressive," she admitted and drew in another puff, calculating the angles and distance of the image back into the living room, damn geometry, the residue of freshman year, still taking up space in her brain. Compared to pre-calculus, that at least seemed useful. Spanish was a disaster. Who could tell if it was subjunctive or pluperfect? Her brain barely functioned in English. But she loved literature: Swift's Gulliver's Travels, Vonnegut's Slaughterhouse, Toni Morrison's Bluest Eye. A well-crafted story, something to get lost in.

And then there was science, her curse or inspiration, depending on when you asked. Chemistry was impossible, even for a kid personally motivated to cure cancer. Biology, unwrapping that formaldehyde piglet day after day, just too gross to think about. But environmental sciences, ecology, how it all fit together. It was simultaneously fascinating and infuriating. Late night papers on carbon cycles, toxins that concentrated in the food chain, the earth's dwindling biodiversity. She even joined the Climate Club at school, but quickly succumbed to exasperation, their efforts a micro-drop in an ocean-sized bucket. Her anger could seethe to the surface at times. Once the nicknames in school caught on, she hid her fury, wrapping it up and sticking in her pocket, not to be shared. It even kept her awake sometimes, lying in bed, speechifying to the dumb galoots running the country with head in sand, avoiding all responsibility. She'd stare out her bedroom window, over the neighborhood air conditioners convening in the back lot, a last hit before sleep to calm the nerves, hopefully drifting off to a good book, a distraction from it all.

Zoe watched her Dad from the living room and drew a puff, worrying about the geezer, idling in front of his computer. He hasn't been the same since Abassi died.

Sirens and horns, the cacophony of rush hour, frayed his nerves. "Jesus Christ," he screamed in frustration, bulling his way into the living room, the smell of cigarettes in the air. "Are you still smoking that thing?"

She pulled it to the other side of the couch, blew the last remnants into her sweatshirt. "No, I put it out."

"You're a terrible liar." He walked past, opened the window sash, and searched for the culprit. "I guess that's a good thing. Good liars make awful children."

Zoe smiled and pulled the cigarette up from its hiding spot, taking another drag. *Lying is one thing,* she surmised. *Acting is a whole other.*

The traffic backed to 2nd Ave, drivers laying on their horns, their only recourse. A delivery truck double parked and pulled its back door high. Clif bars and Wheat Chex for the corner store. An SUV clogged the other lane as two women said their goodbyes. Becker leaned out the window.

"Shut those fucking horns up!" he squawked, a parrot with temporary madness. An African man driving an Uber looked up at the fourth-floor window, shook his head and recommitted to his hooter, willing the traffic forward.

"Hey!" Becker screamed again.

"Dad!" Zoe butt-in with embarrassment.

"Look at these people," the African man hollered back, his red and green soccer shirt belying his origin, gesturing to the cars ahead. "They have no sense."

Becker scanned the bottleneck. SUV Lady got out to hug her friend, plan lunch for next week.

"Lady!" Becker screamed at her. "Do you mind moving your effin car?!" SUV Lady searched her surroundings in confusion, finally finding Becker in the apartment window.

"Dad!" Zoe tried again.

"You're causing a giant traffic jam! The noise is killing us up here!"

Zoe muffed her ears.

The woman waved apprehensively and ducked back into her SUV, safe from the arrows volleyed, the nut job archer leaning out the fourth-floor condo still visible in her side view as she pulled away. The traffic advanced slowly.

"I hate this city," he said and shut the window.

"You need to get high or something," Zoe suggested.

"I am high!"

"Well, maybe prescription drugs." She raised her phone to her lips. "Hey Siri, what are the most common drugs for depression?"

"Here's what I found" Siri responded.

"Let's see," Zoe read, "Abilify, Adapin, Anafranil..."

"Yea, I've tried all those," Becker countered. "Come on, let's go get some dinner. My treat."

"Of course, its *your* treat. I'm only 17."

"Yea, I know. But it makes me feel like I'm being generous."

They walked out of the apartment, down the oval stairway that centered the building. Mrs. Goldberg's cats were whining for dinner and a movie blared from the Scot's apartment as they passed. Zoe liked to pull wide on the old wooden banister as she turned back down another flight across the Victorian tile floor, past the wood detail of the walls covered in innumerable layers of paint, scuff marks, and more paint.

Through the double doors and side panels of translucent glass block installed for security a decade ago. Down the few steps to street level, the April chill hit their bodies. Becker and Zoe pulled their jackets tighter and leaned in together, holding hands as they walked.

"Maybe we should move upstate. You know, up along the Hudson. I love that area."

"Oh Jeez," Zoe responded. "Here we go again."

"I know, I'm a broken record." Past a flower shop and a popular Thai restaurant, clanging over the metal trap doors that provide access to the shop basements.

"You want Thai?" she offered.

"Look at that line. Let's go over to 3rd Ave, there's a new vegetarian restaurant around 19th."

"Only if they have shrimp," she rejected. He looked at his progeny, confused. They stopped at the crosswalk, waiting for the signal to turn. Car headbeams pierced the twilight. Zoe paused, not sure if she should bring it up again. "So, what do you think about that thing in Pennsylvania? You know, with all the pickups vandalized."

"What d'ya mean?"

"You think it was political?"

"Could be."

"You think it'll... make people talk? About what they drive?"

Becker looked up and down 3rd Avenue, the flood escaping Manhattan, bumper to bumper, six lanes of drivers jockeying for position. The streetlights offered a silhouette of the eternal story: driver upfront, single passenger in the back, inching across the city, locked into place like a jigsaw, exhaust pillowing out from each wheeled contraption. Becker shook his head.

"I doubt it. Nothing can get us out of our complacency."

Zoe examined the traffic, calculating. 20 cars in each lane. Times a couple hundred blocks, by a dozen avenues, hundreds of cross streets... And that's just Manhattan. Her head spun. "How about Chinese?" Becker pointed to the Jade Dragon sign in Fu Manchu lettering. The décor was standard – decades-old dark paneling covered with cheap imports from Chinatown: a calendar with pictures of the Great Wall and other famed landscapes, faux bamboo, plastic statues of Buddha and Confucius. But the food was always delicious, overwhelmed plates of shrimp and pea pods, ginger-garlic beef and fresh broccoli. Plus, Becker's favorite waitress worked there. Empress, they liked to call her. Those cheek bones, that delicate smile conveying *this is your food*, when she carried a tray piled high, a sinuous sweep of steam like the white clouds escaping a locomotive back when such things had a real romance to them.

"Perfect," she radiated. "Let's get more than we need and bring home the extra."

"Deal." He opened the door.

"Thank you, kind sir," she over-articulated with British accent.

"Quite welcome, my lady," he added a Cockney twist.

Becker exhaled deeply before entering the restaurant. *Time to relax.* He flinched when two drivers vying for the same spot blared horns like dueling jazz musicians, offered middle fingers in vain combat.

Zoe peered back at Becker, stiff with tension. She nudged his elbow forward and motioned to the elderly hostess for a table. "He needs some alcohol," she said.


## Chapter 8. Protest at Fowler Manor

Becker and Zoe passed back through the doors of Jade Dragon, out to the cool New York City air, too few leftovers to take with them. Should have put the chopsticks down 20 minutes earlier.

Instead, they were uncomfortably full. The city washed over them. The traffic. The horns. They drifted north past the smell of fruit and newly cut flowers from the corner store patterned over garbage ready for nightly pickup stitched over falafel and baba ganoush from the ever-present Hallal food truck, its small generator idling loudly.

"Protest at Fowler Manor?" Becker asked.

"Let's give that fucker a piece of our mind," Zoe agreed with a smile, stockpiling her hair behind an ear, exposing Mama to the April night, the budding shoots of spring, the random vibrancy of the city. "You wanna walk?"

"It's like 30 blocks. Let's grab a couple of city bikes."

"Not in the dark. Scares me too much." She asked the operating system for exact measurement. "Hey Siri, how far is Fowler Manor?"

"I found two Fowler Manors," Siri explained. "Which one?"

"Jesus," Becker said impatiently. "Let's just take the subway."

"Ok, the subway," she settled.

Three children ran in front of a Muslim couple. The little one, maybe 3, stumbled over the cracks in the sidewalk. The father uttered something in Arabic. The kids stopped to barely listen and then ran forward again, the universal testing of autonomy. Becker smiled as they passed. They crossed a few blocks west to Park, two more north, and scrambled down the familiar steps. A mother carried a stroller and baby out from the void.

"A train's coming. Hurry, Dad."

Becker fumbled for his pass card, searching the rubber wallet affixed to his cell. "It's in here somewhere."

"Come on, old man!" The subway pulled in with a giant gasp. The doors shuttered open while the intercom officiated. "23rd Street Station."

He skimmed the plastic key through the metal scanner and the turnstile spun free. Zoe grabbed his hand, jerked him through the train doors before they shut tight.

"That was close," she exclaimed.

"You know they come like every four minutes."

"This train has special karma."

Becker looked up. A young couple watched a cell phone video together. Tourists studied the subway map on the train wall. Others sat silently, their stories held in secret. "I guess."

The screech of the steel wheels foreshadowed each stop: 28th Street, 33rd Street. Then the hubbub of 42nd. A three-piece band played funk. A few paused before flipping quarters into a sax case and getting on the train. Someone sold pretzels warmed over hibachi grill. A city within a city.

They held hands and quietly took in the setting. "We'd be so bored upstate," Zoe decided.

"Boring sounds ok sometimes."

"Not for me. That's how kids get in trouble. *Boredom made me do drugs*," she droned with Reefer Madness affect, arms stretched forward, eyes like saucers, zombie style. She dropped her arms and the accent. "At least until I go to college."

"It's a deal," he agreed. "You go to college. I'll sell your bed and move under cover of night." They shook hands, ending with a pinky pull, the bond now sacred.

"You know, your gonna need me back for the holidays."

"That's true." He put his arm around her, closed his eyes. The thought of her not around scared him to death. Becker lost track of time, swallowed in the surf of the train's sway.

"51st Street Station," the announcement said over the whine of metal on metal, the train hissing to its stop.

"This is us," she said excitedly, "come on." They rushed out, up the steps, west to 5th Avenue.

A muffled din grew as they drew closer. Fowler Manor, part of the President's vast real estate empire, was now a transmuted fortress. Concentric circles of steel barricades created a moat around the building, oversized police vans as sentries. Across the street, about a hundred people gathered around. Many held signs. *Die Frank Die,* read one simply.

Zoe joined the chant as they worked through the crowd. *Hey Hey, Ho Ho, Frank Fowler has got to go. Hey Hey, Ho Ho...* "It's smaller than it used to be," she shouted above the noise. "I was here a couple of days ago. Its already waning."

"People have to go back to their lives at some point," Becker noted.

Young couples, children on their shoulders, looked onward. A Hispanic family held signs, their dread poorly concealed under halfhearted smiles. A woman in headscarf was even less successful, and wept openly, the chin of her hijab damp with tears.

"They just need a call to action," Zoe offered.

Becker pondered the scene like a cloud contemplates the horizon. He felt something like the hand of God on his shoulder, a calling from above.

"Becks. Becks."

Becker turned with confusion to find L.J., his best buddy since college. They embraced, sharing a laugh, the night's protest all around.

"L.J.!" Zoe screamed with excitement as she reached up for a hug. Zoe patted his afro. "Wow."

"Old school, right? I started picking it wide, just like college."

Becker asked him how he was. L.J. pulled at his light soul patch of a beard and smiled the whitest teeth in New York. "Still fighting the good fight."

L.J. turned to Zoe and gave her a knowing smile. They had a special bond, those two. When Amy's cancer got real bad, L.J. would take little Zoe to the park or wander through the outdoor bazaar in Union Square at Christmastime. Sometimes they would get awkward glances, 10-year old Zoe pulling on the L.J.'s tall black frame, leading him through the windy lanes of merchant's tents filled with handmade jewelry and caps and scarfs.

Just a year ago, L.J. himself fell ill. Terrible headaches, vision blurred, the corner of his mouth numb like the paint of a portrait melting off. He had a stroke. A small one, luckily. He called a cab and got himself to the hospital before any real damage set in. Becker and

Zoe would bring in soup or a seafood stew, Cataplana, they learned to make watching Anthony Bourdain visit Portugal.

L.J. seemed to make a full recovery. But lately there was a slight awkwardness when Becker and his hoodlum college comrade would catch up. They'd meet in Little Italy, halfway to Brooklyn where L.J. called home, for linguini and mussels and a bottle of red. They hadn't seen each other in a while, too many deadlines to meet, errands to get done. A strange distance between them.

A lone voice cried out from the crowd. "Frank Fowler, where are you?" The assembled laughed and watched the heavily guarded building for an unprovided response.

"How's work?" L.J. asked Becker as Zoe wandered off into the masses.

"It's insane. Like this," Becker gestured to the throng. "Our new President is set on destroying the EPA from within. Eviscerate every protection put in place."

"Zany times," L.J. agreed, shaking his head.

Becker waived his schnoz back and forth as well, then changed subjects. "We're gonna see you in a few days?"

"The seder?" L.J. replied. "Yeah, I come every year."

Zoe, holding an ice cream, returned to Becker and L.J. in the crowd. She passed it forward for L.J. to share. "Mint chocolate chip?"

"Thanks," L.J. said, wiping the excess off his nose.

"See that thing in Pennsylvania?" she asked.

"The auto dealer?"

"Yeah."

He drew up a cautious smile. "Crazy, huh?"

"It could be in our screenplay," Zoe suggested, referring to a little project they shared.

"We should write it in," L.J. agreed and turned sheepishly back to Becker.

Zoe handed the ice cream to her Dad, measuring his gaze. Becker measured hers right back, rubbing the dissonance in his ear drums.

"You want some, Dad?" she asked.

"Sure," he shook his head and took a bite, crunching into the cone. He tried to ignore his last thought, the one about their conversation. The past year was peculiar in so many ways.

# Chapter 9. The Ralston

Ten months earlier. June 2016. Specific Date and Time Not Recorded.

"Gentlemen, welcome to the bachelor party," Reid Johnston, the Speaker of the House, declared. The line, delivered with his usual impish smile, was followed by a great bellow that could be heard by the well-heeled waitstaff, in their pressed white uniforms, just outside the oak paneled room. They carried in *hors devours* of caviar and melon wrapped in overpriced meats.

"The last time you got married," shouted his good friend, Chad Droburn, Jr., "California was hit with 8 inches of rain! I hope this marriage is easier on our economy." Again, the laughter echoed from the back room.

"That second wife was wicked. Wicked, indeed," Johnston agreed, releasing a big grin into the room. Having won 11 consecutive terms to Congress, and for the past four years, the most powerful man in the lower chamber, he had carefully honed his sense of timing like a well-sharpened axe. "Democrats," he would quip, "have too much sense to argue with a real Texan." That was a sure winner.

Reid Johnston was a big barrel of a man with large ears, too many teeth, and a pinkish caste that burned bright as a police siren after 15 minutes in the West Texas sun. Surrounding him that night were five of his fellow Congressman, great men all. Chad Droburn, Jr., California's senior representative, chaired the Ways and Means Committee and was indeed witness to the great California flood of 2004, just days after Johnston wed wife #2.

"I remember the first time I met her," Droburn offered. "I figured, Reid - he must've broke right thru the condom to marry that one!"

The laughter grew a few decibels, giving pause to the tourists and businessmen mingling in the grand foyer of the Ralston Hotel. Tall marble pillars compete with ornate tile work above and below. Just off the corridor between the lobby and the main dining room, a small hallway led to a large private room with detailed plaster decoration and oak-paneled walls.

A waiter entered with two bottles and an ice bucket atop his tray. "More Bourbon, Sir?"

"Keep them coming until we say stop," Johnston replied, his toothy grin showing ear to ear. He offered a wry smile and clinked glassed with Droburn, his foxhole buddy in the war zone that is the U.S. House of Representatives.

Droburn shot back a proud nod. He had jowls like a basset hound, flapping in dismay when his portfolio took a hit or someone from Massachusetts held the House floor. His dark eyebrows matched his shock of hair and permanent five o'clock shadow. "To third wives," Droburn offered the group, "may they never share stories with the other two!"

Four additional men joined the toast: a handsome cleft chin, Norman Radcliffe of Oklahoma; an ancient relic, Ornette Schlesinger of Georgia; a Cajun parade float, Landry Muldoon of Louisiana; and an anxious, blue-eyed Pug of a fella, Nathan Culp of Pennsylvania. Each chaired powerful House committees of their own. They raised their glasses. "Hear, hear!"

Waiters brought in a poker table and rearranged the stuffed chairs.

"To the distinguished Texan," Norman Radcliffe, the photogenic clef, toasted. "Good luck. You'll need it."

The men raised their glasses with pride. "To Reid," they shouted in unison. "Cheers!"

Speaker Johnston beamed with gratification. "Gentlemen."

"Long as we're here, we might as well play a little poker," Old Man Schlesinger, the Fossil of Congress, chimed in.

"Might as well," the portly Muldoon agreed. He pulled poker chips and cards from his briefcase.

They first met for cards and other distractions, as it were, nearly three years ago to the day. The events were arranged by the Faith and Freedom Foundation, an organization so powerful it could raise millions in donations for favored candidates or crush its opposition with a coordinated attack of doubt and rumor. Representatives slipping from core values were subdued by a sub-sonic blast, every source of media weaponized, quickly replaced with more loyal proxies.

Ornette Schlesinger disrobed his jacket and placed it on the back of his chair. The old warrior preparing for battle. "I've lost a lot of money in this room," he reminisced.

"It's Landry's fault," cried out Radcliffe. "The son of a bitch never loses!"

The monthly Ralston meeting was the most powerful game of chance in D.C. Only six people were invited, their combined supremacy rivaled the President and his cabinet. Perhaps even bested. As long as Republicans remained in majority, that is. To assure that, the Foundation painstakingly finagled Republican control for 9 straight sessions through clever gerrymandering, thinning of voter rolls, and good old-fashioned fear tactics.

"OK, Gentlemen," Schlesinger took charge. Ornette Schlesinger was the longest serving member in Congress, 44 years and counting. His frail body was topped by a small melon of a head, an oversized mouth and gray eyes magnified by coke bottle glasses. "Put up your $300."

They pulled wads of bills from their pockets bound by rubber bands and metal binder clips. "Landry, count the money," Schlesinger continued, "I don't trust these SOBs." They all laughed. Landry counted the money.

Radcliffe passed out the cards, face up, to the other players. "First King deals."

"First King deals," they agreed.

"4, Jack, 8, 9," Radcliffe announced as the cards emerged from the deck. "King," he said as the next card skidded to Reid Johnston. "Mr. Speaker and almost-not-a-bachelor, your deal."

"OK, hand the cards over." Johnston stared into the cut-crystal patterns of his glass. "A good quality bourbon should have equal parts smoothness and heat."

"Yea, just like us," jostled Landry Muldoon, 315 pounds of crawfish etoufee. "Go ahead an' deal."

"We've done some great work here, haven't we?" offered the Speaker, a nostalgic bead of sweat dripping from his nose. "Killed at least three swings at a carbon tax, sent another twenty enviro bills into foul territory."

"Those dang liberals never learn," someone yelled in. Bellyaching laughter followed.

"I remember our first toast." Johnston looked into their eyes as he spoke. "Penny Archer was here. She suggested we continue to meet, for the good of the country."

Penelope Archer, President and CEO of the Faith and Freedom Foundation. She ruled our nation's capital with an iron fist, a nefarious overbite, and a feverish enthusiasm for sequins. She'd open the poker games with a short welcome and a designated agenda of the Foundation's legislative priorities. For special occasions—perhaps a fire drill of a bill requiring quick defeat, a birthday, or in the present case, a bachelor party—she may hire a few young ladies to keep the gentleman company.

"The Club of Kings, she'd refer to it," Nathan Culp chimed in, nervously pushing his glasses into place. "American royalty. For the good of the country."

"And then I said, that's too vain, too European," Droburn threw in. "Since we love poker, we switched it, made it the King of Clubs."

"And there you have it. Now, stop waxing poetic and deal already, Reid," pleaded Schlesinger. "It's almost past my bedtime." That one produced a large howl of amusement.

"Lets start with Omaha," Johnston said, sliding four cards face down to each player. "High, Low. Use two and *only* two from your hand, three from the board."

"Shit, we've been playing Omaha for years," Muldoon complained.

"Yea, then why does Culp always use three from his hand?" Their cheeks glowed as they laughed, almost in pain, the bourbon only deepening the hue. He turned to the first player. "Your bet, Landry."

"Five," Muldoon tossed a red chip into the center.

"In," they all recited, one by one, adding chips into the pot.

"Pot's right," Johnston announced. All square. He discarded one to the side and laid three community cards in succession, *the Flop*, turning them with suspense: 3 of diamonds, six of clubs, and... the Jack of Diamonds. Radcliffe, your bet."

Norman Radcliffe was distracted with his phone. Frank Fowler, the likely Republican nominee required the liberal press to cover his rallies from inside cages, to be heckled by the angry mob like prisoners on their way to Medieval gallows. He was frightened and envious at the same time.

"Radcliffe?"

"Ten." Radcliffe distantly tossed a blue chip to the center. The remaining players called the bet.

"Pot's right" they called. Six players still in.

Johnston threw another discard to the side and a fourth community card on the table. *The Turn*. He flipped it over. A four of diamonds. Possible straight. Or a flush. Or a real good low.

Schlesinger added another $20. The room grew quiet as the center pile grew tall. Six men, glaring from acute angles, evaluated who was for real and who was just hanging around with nothing better to do.

Johnston slid a last discard to the side and laid the final card, *the River*, face down. The table watched in anticipation. "Gentlemen, now that I have your attention, I want you to know about an insidious enemy saying dangerous things under the banner of a federal research agency."

"Jesus Christ, Reid!" Muldoon's Louisiana twang cried out.

"Are you familiar with Dr. Amir Abassi?"

"Will you throw the card, puh-lease?"

"I will," Johnston held firm. "Penny wants to send a clear message. The federal payroll is not a bully pulpit."

"Yea, yea. They always have our support. Now, turn that card over."

"Culp, I'm gonna need your leverage with immigration. This Abassi, he's Iranian. Here on a work visa. Muldoon, Appropriations needs to bring the budget hammer on Commerce and this National Center for Atmospheric Research Dr. Abassi works for. This crap could cause mass hysteria."

"Agreed," they all nodded in approval.

"I powwow with Archer tomorrow morning," Droburn offered.

"Good," Johnston pursed his lips in approval, turning back to his hand.

The gentlemen ignored the knock at the door, the cards dominating their focus. "Just place it on the side tables," Johnston ordered.

"We can place it on the side tables, but we're gonna need more attention than that," the sultry voice responded.

Their gaze altered fields to find three young ladies in short-cut trench coats and fuck-me pumps. Johnston realized his mistake and shot up from his chair. "Excuse me. I, uh, we didn't see you come in. Did we boys?" Heads bobbed in agreement, mouths ajar. A large pile of poker chips provided was one thing, beautiful hookers a whole other.

"We're from Paradise," a long-legged ginger cooed, loosening her waist belt to reveal an endless thigh wrapped in day-glo bikini. Wars were fought for far less. "We thought you might like some company."

The Congressmen stared, lips quivering with chromosomal yearning. Paradise, the famed escort service, almost as storied as the Ralston, brought in some of their top talent: two petite brunettes and the ginger, at least 6 feet tall in her sexy heels. "Now, who here is the lucky bachelor?"

"Gentlemen," Reid announced, "tonight's poker game is adjourned until further notice."

## Chapter 10. Chad Droburn, Jr.

The next day.

There is a saying in DC, that a Congressman is only as good as his personal secretary. Or at least there should be. Hell, I might start it myself, Chad Droburn, Jr. thought to himself, tilting in the entry to his office reception, Kentucky bourbon still escaping his pores.

Margaret Jimenez looked up from her desk, manilla folders lined and orderly, ready for the Congressman's modest review and minimally-informed decision. "Sir, you look awful."

"It was a helluva night, Margie, I gotta tell me, I mean, you. I-gotta-tell-you," the Californian practiced his enunciation as he admired the framed photos of himself with icons of the Republican Party.

"The poker game, Sir?"

"We had a little bachelor party for Reid as well. Poor bastard." He squinted at his favorite picture on the wall, shaking hands with Nixon. Young Droburn, in jacket and tie, fresh out of middle school; Nixon looking aged, steeped in isolation and anger. Simply unfair, the way we treated him.

"Did you have a chance to go home and clean up?"

"This is cleaned up," Droburn responded with disappointment, smoothing his graying temples.

Margie crumpled her features. "If you say so, Sir."

He eyed another picture, just above, with Ronald Reagan. *What a proud day.* He checked his watch. His Chief of Staff should have been there already. "Where the hell is Bucksworth?"

"He's at your 9:00. With Penny Archer from the Faith and Freedom Foundation. You told him it was urgent."

"Of course," Droburn offered slowly.

"He said you called last night as the poker game was ending. Something about—don't piss Reid off."

"Of course." He turned back to the picture with Reagan: at the President's ranch, in western attire, Ronnie looking a bit past and to the left of the camera. *Sounds like something I would have said.*

The interior door to Droburn's office opened. Graham Bucksworth—tall, handsome, an eager head of hair—emerged with his usual Aussie cheer. "...no worries, you'll have the full support of Congressman Droburn."

"Excellent, we always appreciate our allies in the right places," Penny Archer replied, exiting the conference room with an enthusiastic laugh.

Bucksworth noticed Congressman Droburn. "G'day sir. Figured you'd be a bit dusty this morning..."

Droburn slanted an annoyed eyebrow.

"Just having a chat with Ms. Archer... of the Faith and Freedom Foundation."

Penny straightened one of the framed photos. "Graham and I had a very agreeable discussion regarding the *science* coming out of our research institutions."

"Excellent, excellent," Droburn responded. "Graham, you go above and beyond for Ms. Archer and the Foundation."

"Of course, Sir." Bucksworth replied, forcing a smile.

Penny straightened her impossibly blond mane and pulled this morning's Washington Post from her purse. She wrestled the paper along its folds into submission. "Have you seen the latest broadside?"

"*Tipping Point Research Ignored by Congress,*" Bucksworth read aloud, following with his pointer digit.

"Read it," she encouraged. "It's... It's quite disconcerting."

"*An extraordinary threat undermines our planet and our society. Alongside the changing climate, a quieter but just as insidious peril lurks. Our oceans and seas – the original source of life on Earth – are under continual stress. The hazards include increased acidity, rising temperature, and pollution from a wide array of sources. Countless species, our food supply, and humankind itself are at risk.*

*This is not some distant future. We've lost 25% of our reefs already. Another two-thirds are at a critical juncture. Phytoplankton, the planet's largest source of oxygen, are shrinking from acidification and pollution, impacting the entire food chain.*

*I have developed a powerful computer simulation, the first of its kind, to incorporate these effects into a single model. The seas could be lifeless in a few short decades. Destruction of ocean habitats threatens nearly every country in the world—hundreds of millions of people—with starvation and massive displacement.*

*Please help spread the word to our "leaders" in Washington, D.C. The relationship between humans and the planet should not be viewed as a trial-and-error science experiment, one that could go horribly wrong for humankind and all that is under our stewardship.*"

Bucksworth paused and looked up from the paper.

*Dr. Amir Abbassi*

*Boulder, Colorado.*"

"Wow," Droburn responded, his jaw hanging in ire. "And this man works for the Federal Government?"

Archer threw up her hands. "Exactly! Finally, someone gets it. Original source of life?  Has he even read the bible?"

"Nothing but scare tactics," Droburn added.

"He needs to be stopped."

Droburn chewed on his lower lip, thinking on his feet. "We begin budget discussions in a few weeks. Muldoon heads the process. Should be able to give Commerce budget numbers a good tune-up."

"Excellent, Chad."

"Perhaps a special rider on climate analysis... require prior Congressional approval." He swept his hand across an imaginary billboard. "*Saving the American taxpayer from unnecessary spending.*"

"Yes, well done," Penny responded behind a contorted overbite.

"Sir," Bucksworth interrupted, "the Research Priorities Enquiry is next week to guide the nation's federal agencies. Dr. Abassi is scheduled to testify on the Mars program."

"Well, we certainly don't want him testifying." They paused in contemplation.

"I could get him removed from the testimony schedule," Bucksworth offered.

"That may only raise his profile."

"He could exploit it for more attention," Penny agreed. "There's a bigger issue, here. Isn't there?" she asked rhetorically. "That a federal scientist, let alone a foreigner from Iran, of all places, can use his position like..."

"Like a lectern," Droburn suggested, involuntarily twitching at the thought. As a child, Droburn would fidget through the Pastor's endless sermons until his father's powerful flick snapped him to attention.

"Yes, a lectern," Penny agreed.

"It's reprehensible," they nodded in unison.

"Ungrateful is what it is."

"He needs to be taught a lesson."

"I'll talk to his boss."

"Perhaps there's a mix-up in immigration?"

"His wife is from Iran too."

"That's a shame."

Bucksworth thought for a second. "He could still protest from Tehran. Embarrass the party."

"You're right, Graham. We need something more... persuasive."

# Chapter 11. Doggie Delay

March 15th 2017. Five days before the first scheduled event.

The phone was under the pillow when it buzzed, awakening Shaggy, always the light sleeper. 5:30 a.m. Shaggy opened WhatsApp and logged in. Secure.

Yosemite Sam: *Are the guys ready to go? It's been two months.*
Shaggy: *They need more time*
YS: *???*
Shaggy: *Something about the dog.*
YS: *Seriously?*
Shaggy: *Surgery on his paw, I think*

A long pause, Yosemite Sam not sure how to respond: *These guys for real?*
Shaggy: *Don't have a lot of options.* Another pause.
YS: *First target ready?*
Shaggy: *Sent all your instructions. Transferred the $$*
Yosemite Sam looked at the calendar and calculated the timing: *Start on April 4*
Shaggy: *U sure?*
YS: *Yea, the 4th. Its perfect actually.*
Shaggy: *OK. I'll tell them.*
YS: *Hold onto your hat*
Shaggy: *You too*

They wiped their conversations clean, logged out, and closed WhatsApp on their phones. They each stared at a bedroom ceiling, uncertainty the only certainty. In unison, each took a big hit of weed: Shaggy, half a joint on the bedside table; Yosemite Sam, a small bong on the dresser. They exhaled towards their respective windows, the smoke percolating in the early morning light, their minds rambling over common terrain. *Is a crime that exposes a crime any less criminal? Do these end-to-end encryption apps really work?*

## Chapter 12. A Bridge Too Far

April 8th, 2017. Four days after the attack on Erie Ford.

"Damn middle schoolers," Zoe complained, cleaning up where a crash of boys rearranged melted cheese and drizzled Coca Cola into modern art on Table 14 at D'Antonio's on Avenue A. *New York's Best Pizza*, the sign in the window claimed unconvincingly. The art project, a rendering of a boy and his dog, showed some talent, she had to admit. She wiped it clean and moved onto the next table.

Her phone buzzed in her back pocket.

*Wanna grab dinner?* the text from Dad read... *Meeting L.J. for a bite*

*Sure*, she wrote back. *Time?*

*7?*

*My shift ends at 7*

*Ok. 7:15*

Her boss, Roberto, gave her a sideways glance. Tables 3 and 4 were a mess, a line of customers to the door. *Anything but pizza*, she texted back quickly.

At 7:00, she removed her apron, threw it in the laundry pile underneath the time clock, said goodbye to Roberto and another co-worker, and checked for messages.

"Jade Dragon again?" she muttered under her breath. "This city has 10 million restaurants," only slightly exaggerating, "and he goes to the same one every week."

Zoe stepped outside and exhaled into the dark night—strangely quiet for New York—exhausted and satisfied. She walked north counting her share of the cash tips. $28. A little pocket money. There would be more in the paycheck next week. After the cash and credit card tips were added, she averaged about $19 / hour. *Not too bad*, she figured, *for a high school kid*. Enough to grab dinner or a movie, hang with her friends, and avoid touching the investment money her grandfather gave her.

When Grandpa Max on her Mom's side died about three years ago, Zoe inherited $125,000, cashed after a property sold, and the funds split among her and a few cousins she never talked to. She bought some index funds, her Dad convincing her they were a good investment with low fees, with about half the money. The other half went into an alternative currency that was still relatively unheard of: BitCoin. Zoe and Travis were just wide-eyed middle schoolers when they saw a totally awesome movie about hacking and scored free tickets to a coder and hacker convention. Malware, trojan horses, and everything to stop them. Travis and his friends coded and searched PirateBay and other barely hidden sites for the next killer virus. But that year, the talk of Hack NYC, a summit of 1200 geeks and coders, was all about crypto. Alternative currencies. The new, new thing. Zoe bought at less than $90 a coin, before the insanity. It closed today at $1,175. And ninety-five cents.

She kept it hidden, away from Dad, still pissed he was shut out of Grandpa's will. Besides, he never grasped Bitcoin anyway. *Why would anyone trust that? And how the hell did it work?* the geezer would ask. But Zoe was fascinated by it all, the complex network of computers, solving equations to earn a diminishing supply of coin over time, causing the currency to increase in value as it became more widespread in use. It was a safeguard as dictatorship sprouted in every corner of the globe. Mr. Bartram, her civics teacher, engaged the inattentive teens with pop quizzes and Socratic discussions on the spread of dangerous authoritarianism. Russia, China, Turkey, Syria, the Philippines. Maybe the U.S. was heading in that direction as well. Recent events highlighted the nation's vulnerability to technology, our inability to discern fact from fiction. Rush Limbaugh and InfoWars, useless Facebook posts, misinformation. It was all consistent with the pattern, Bartram explained. Zoe agreed, wide-eyed in the front row. The dangerous place this country was heading in. Bitcoin made as much sense as anything else, maybe more. Left on 9th Street. She loved the independence New York gave her. Just 17, she could navigate as she pleased, get anywhere with a subway pass and her wits. Freedom most kids would kill for. North on 2nd Ave.

Zoe spotted giant high rises in the distance sprouting up around Central Park. Ridiculous toothpicks jutting into the sky, condos priced at $100 million dollars or more, the buyers only part-time residents. Wealth for flaunting. The excess left her nauseous, her head shaking in disgust as she approached a young man lying on the sidewalk, his dog at the extension of a leash sniffing the Starbuck's threshold for an offering. Alms for the poor. And their pets. A sign at his feet: *Need Bus Fair. Every Bit Helps.* She crumpled two dollars into his cup and kept a quick pace, hoping not to make eye contact.

She had a unique sense of fashion: knit tops pulled over dresses, purposely mismatched socks, a hat from another era. Or she'd sew the faux fur hood and cuffs from a bulky coat onto a crushed velvet jacket. Her feet usually filled Chuck Taylor's or Doc Martens. Somehow, it always worked.

She crossed the other side of 2nd Ave, then west on 19th, passing a corner deli with blueberry muffins the size of a potted plant and a construction site where hard-hatted men lowered miles of cable into an underworld labyrinth, bathed in floodlights fit for a UFO abduction. Another store dedicated to mannequins of every size, shape, and color. Bizarre. Only in New York. North on 3rd Avenue.

She stopped at the Jade Dragon, aromas of sesame oil, shrimp, and pork filled the air. *We just ate here 4 nights ago*, she smirked.

The old hostess with paper-thin skin greeted her again. Zoe found Becker and L.J. seated in the front, commenting on New York as it passed by. Her Dad looked relaxed, thank God, laughing with L.J. at some craziness in their day. Even at 5'8", her hug only came to L.J.'s shoulders. She turned to Becker, weary from a long day at the screen, and gave him a big squeeze. "Hey, Dad."

"Good shift at work?"

"Yea. I'm starving though."

"Jade Dragon will do something about that."

She turned to L.J. and whispered past her knuckles. "Someone has the hots for a certain Chinese waitress."

L.J. laughed.

Empress walked to the table. Tall with angular cheekbones, a pony tail of dark hair that bounced when she walked. Looking up from her notepad, she recognized Zoe and Becker. "Oh, you're back again, huh?"

"Yea," Zoe laughed. "We're back again."

Becker gave her a parental glare. Zoe returned with a teenage version. Empress handed out menus. The boys ordered beers, Zoe a Coke.

"How's school?" L.J. offered some small talk.

"Pretty good. Mostly As and Bs."

L.J. leaned back and recalled how he hated high school. College was his ticket out of Ohio. Hell, he never learned how to take notes or prep for an exam until Redwood State. Empress brought the drinks over.

"I'm not even going to college," Zoe argued, "so it's all kinda pointless." She stared at her knife, a porcelain cat, paw swinging in time, refracted in its length.

"Ready to order?" Empress asked.

"Whoa, whoa," Becker cried out. "Not going to college? Where'd this come from?"

"I'd like the shrimp and garlic sauce," L.J. requested. Empress repeated it back.

"Well, the world's turning to shit, right?" Zoe argued. "*We're screwing the only planet we have!*" she mocked him, hands gesticulating. L.J. leaned back, enjoying Zoe's performance.

"Yea, but...," Becker stammered, then gazed at the waitress. "What do you like?" he asked, negotiating for more time.

"What are you in the mood for?"

"Something with a lot of vegetables." He turned to look at Zoe. "Just cause I say the world is turning to shit doesn't mean I'm suggesting you just flush the toilet." He shook his head, unhappy with the analogy.

"The eggplant is good," Empress explained, leaning in to turn the pages in Becker's large menu. A stray from her ponytail landed on his shoulder.

Becker didn't move a muscle, his nerve endings at full attention, as he copped the world's lightest feel. "Eggplant can be greasy. Is it cooked in a lot of oil?" he said turning into the shiny dark of her hair.

"No, it's delicious."

"Hmmm," Becker thought out loud.

"Oh Christ, Dad!" Zoe barked. "You've been eating Chinese food for 50 years. Just order!"

"I'll have the eggplant," he closed his menu in embarrassment.

"You like it. I promise."

"I like it already."

L.J. turned a knowing stare to Zoe. "I see what you mean."

"Very funny," Becker responded, his attention fading as Empress walked away, past a portal of beads hanging in long strands, into the steamy kitchen where she snapped out the orders in Chinese. Swift moving men cooking in the distance snapped the orders back, a blur of nightly commotion.

"Let's talk about Earth First!" Zoe changed subjects with a mischievous smile.

"Now that's an 'Oh Christ,'" Becker responded.

L.J. howled. "Where do we start?"

Zoe took a swig of her Dad's beer, eyes lighting up, like a child watching popcorn pop. "Same place as always. You guys met at Redwood State. And then the whole Williamette Forest thing."

"Yeah. Your Dad and I, we lived on the same floor," L.J. explained.

"We both hated our roommates," Becker recalled with a smile, surfing the creases of his memory bank. "Mine was a drug dealer. Weed, cocaine. I don't think he even attended Redwood State."

"And mine was pretty flat out racist," L.J. chimed in. "He kept asking me if I filled out the questionnaire correctly, as if there was some big mix-up and they roomed him with a black guy." While they laughed, Becker stole his beer back from the underaged.

"And there was this one dude who was really committed," L.J. continued. He'd hang on the quad with pamphlets. Old school college environmentalism."

"Yea. Nils Jensen," Becker said. Zoe stole another swig of beer while he time travelled.

"Yea," L.J. agreed. "Shrink, we used to call him. He was messed up and brilliant all at the same time. But we really dug his message. We went to a few meetings, joined a weekend retreat. They took us to the Cutting Edge where the loggers halted, quitting time Friday afternoon. On one side, centuries-old trees. Beautiful, primeval. Heaven on earth. Then, on the other, a hellish wasteland. Absolute devastation. Not a tree left for miles. They were letting big logging corporations just..." he searched for the word with a pang still fresh in his gut, "exploit it for profit. That's how Shrink explained it. That really hung true with us."

"It's still true," Becker agreed and grabbed his beer back from Zoe, took a big swig, their eyes smiling with agreement. They loved when L.J. could add a spark to their nightly routine.

"So, Becks, or Ozone Ranger, as we liked to call your Dad back then – he starts going to all the meetings."

"Ozone Ranger. That is perfect for you, huh Dad?"

"L.J. was there, too," Becker laughed. "And Shrink and Danny. They became our family."

"Not like you, man. You got really into it." L.J. then turned to Zoe. "There was a very nice little lady that got his attention, if you know what I mean."

"I know what you mean," Zoe agreed, grabbing Becker's beer for another swig. "He doesn't even like eggplant."

"I love eggplant!" Becker defended himself, the laughter echoing. He grabbed the beer once more and realized it was empty.

"So Nils develops this plan. Since the trees can't speak, we will speak for the trees," L.J. says theatrically, his hand pointing to the air, eyes bulging for effect.

"He's good," Zoe said.

"The best," Becker agreed.

"'If you want the trees," L.J. continued "you will have to knock us down too. And we go in the dead of night and create this blockade right in the logging road. The press came. We made national news. Unfortunately, the cops come and arrest us pretty quick. But your dad and the lady get really into it. Supporting the tree-sitters, monkeywrenching the earthmovers, hammering spikes..."

"Lorenzo!" Becker scolded him by his real name.

"It's true."

"I already know, Dad. I've seen all the old photos in your closet."

"Not tonight. A bridge too far."

"Awww. I want to use it for our screenplay." She swept her hand in the air as if modeling an all-new cleanser. "Eco-Terrorism, the Musical."

"You'll have to Google it."

"Anyway," L.J. continued, "your Dad and the pretty lady really got some quality time in. He had the big L." He formed the letter with his hand then drew a heart in the air. Zoe responded with a snort-laugh.

"That lady turned out to be your mom, by the way."

"She was gorgeous," L.J. assured Zoe.

"Yea," the Ozone Ranger said, time traveling again.

"Yea," Zoe agreed. She was just 8 when her mom first fell ill to the adenocarcinoma. Not even 12 when she died. Either in school or upstate riding horses at Aunt Joanie's during summers, Zoe was sheltered from a lot of the suffering. She could still recall the sweet pungent aroma of straw and dung and the countless hours brushing the horses clean after a good ride when her parents arrived, her mom sick from the radiation, needing help to get out of the car with her oxygen mask that late summer afternoon. Zoe hadn't seen them since June and her heart fell when she realized, probably for the first time, that her mom was dying of lung cancer.

"So, did you stay in the group? Earth First!" Zoe pulled them back, drying her eyes.

"Well, Mom got into law school back here in the city. At Fordham. I needed another year in Oregon. But I was in love, didn't even want to finish." L.J. held up a big L again. Zoe's smile lit up. "But Mom convinced me to. I followed her out to New York City, somehow got into law school a few years later, and the rest... is history."

Empress portalled back through the beads, a tray at her shoulder, steam billowing up and curling behind her as she positioned dishes on the table. "Eggplant for Mr. Indecisive," she said, situating the dish in front of Becker.

"History?" Zoe questioned. "What about me?"

"Shrimp and garlic sauce," Empress placed a dish before L.J.

"Smells delicious," L.J. offered.

"Well, yea," Becker corrected himself. He bit into a cube of caramelized eggplant, still swirling with heat, "...that changed everything."

# Chapter 13. Pass That Over

Two days later. Six days since the attack on Erie Ford.

*Roast Lamb by Laura Rege.*

Becker repositioned his laptop, close enough to read, distant enough to survive his cooking.

*Preheat oven to 450º and place oven rack in lower third of oven. In a small bowl, mix together garlic, rosemary, thyme, and 1 tablespoon oil and season generously with salt and pepper. Rub all over lamb.*

*In a 9"-x-13" baking dish, toss potatoes with remaining oil and season with more salt and pepper. Place lamb on top of potatoes and roast until internal temperature reaches 145º, about 1 hour.*

*Let rest 15 minutes, remove twine, then slice roast and serve.*

Simple as could be. Unfortunately, Becker could still fuck it up. *How did Amy make it seem so easy?* he wondered. The doorbell rang.

"Honey, can you get that? The kitchen is burning down."

"I doubt that." Zoe rolled her eyes, sulked off the couch, and feigned excitement as she opened the door. "Hi Pop Pop! Uncle Steve! Come on in." Her grandfather crept forward, cane in hand, and embraced Zoe with an erudite kiss on her forehead. Zoe got her height and blond highlights from Pop Pop. The schnoz too, unfortunately, never missed a generation. Uncle Steve, an older, rounder version of Becker, entered, hugged his niece and brother, and shrugged off the drive the way a convict removes his prison garb for the last time.

"You grow every time I see you," Pop Pop said to Zoe.

"I think you're shrinking, Pop Pop." Becker eyed the teenager with condemnation. She averted his stare and hung the coats in the closet.

"Hey Dad," Becker offered from the kitchen, "how was the drive up?"

"It took half an hour to find parking," Pop Pop complained. "Could've walked here faster." Now they all rolled their eyes. Becker gave his brother a clandestine smile.

"Welcome to New York City," Becker summed up, "the city that never sleeps or parks without discussing it. Everyone will be here in a few minutes. We've got lots of good food and..."

"How long is this going to take?" Zoe blurted out. "I can't take one of those three-hour seders."

The air left Becker instantaneously, his shoulders dropping to the floor. "Don't listen to her," Pop Pop offered.

"Thanks, Dad. The whole thing takes like thirty minutes," Becker lied, "if everyone pays attention." The living room was rearranged for the holiday. The sofa pushed aside, three small tables and a large tablecloth formed a makeshift slab in the center of the room. Mismatched plates and glasses. Zoe folded cloth napkins origami-style. Eight chairs and place-settings. Plus one for Elijah, the prophet, in the corner. No room at the main table. Sorry, Elijah.

Within half an hour, the remaining guests filed in. L.J. took the subway from Brooklyn; Josh and Cathy, friends from high-school, from the upper west side; and Mrs. Goldberg, now in her 70s, practically interrogating Becker until he invited her, walked up from Apartment 2D. Josh noticed L.J. looked tired. "Thanks for asking," L.J. replied. "I haven't been sleeping well."

"Hello everyone!" Becker announced loud enough to get their attention. "Welcome to Passover 2017," and motioned to take their seats. Zoe angled next to Pop Pop, got off a quick snapchat, and started the timer on her phone. Becker saw he was on the clock, paused, and practiced the breathing techniques his psychiatrist taught him to reduce stress. "Tonight," he attempted enthusiasm, "we retell the story of how our ancestors escaped slavery in Egypt." Becker thumbed through the Hagaddah, looking for familiarity. "Now, how does this work?"

"Oy," Zoe said in frustration.

"You start in the back," Josh laughed. Becker got it wrong every year.

"OK, first thing we do is wash hands. I'll get the pitcher." He poured water over their digits into a metal bowl and awkwardly passed a dishtowel to dry themselves.

Steve, bored of the process already, leaned into L.J. "What are you up to these days?"

"I'm an EMT. Drive the ambulance," L.J. whispered back.

"Interesting."

"Yea. I like it. And I work for a church on the west side. I run their soup kitchen a couple days a week."

"Feeding the homeless?"

"Yea, homeless. Also, we take meals to indigent around the city."

"You know," Josh jumped in, "the last thing we need is to feed the homeless. Its more humane not to feed them."

"Oh, Christ," Becker garbled, "here we go."

"Studies show it doesn't really help them."

L.J. expected to have this conversation. Again. He coughed into his elbow, everyone waiting on his words. "So, we should let them starve?"

"If they want to be fed, they've gotta be on their meds. We've gotta see you take your meds." Josh's wife Cathy smiled at Becker apologetically.

"The next step in the Seder," Becker labored for control, "is the bitter herbs. Take a piece of parsley, dip into this bowl of saltwater representing the slaves' tears, and eat that." He passed the bowl around. Becker read the accompanying prayer in phonetic Hebrew, glad he didn't butcher it too bad.

"That's not what my faith would tell me," L.J. turned back to Josh. "Or yours. That's why you have the empty seat for whats-his-name."

"Elijah?"

"Yea, Elijah. Doesn't he appear as a homeless person? Someone in need of a good meal?"

"Yea, I remember something like that," Becker concurred, pleased with this segue. *Things really do come full circle.*

"No, that's not true," Josh broke their bubble. "Elijah was a prophet. He conducted miracles. Almost exactly the same story as Christ. He even rises from the dead for judgment day."

Becker attempted to raise this seder from the dead. "The next step is to break the middle matzoh. We have three on this plate..."

"What I don't understand," Pop Pop started at L.J., "is how Jews became the enemy of Christians."

"Oh, Christ," Becker muttered. Every seder, friggin chaos.

"I mean, Jesus was a Jew," Pop Pop continued. "Mary and Joseph, Jews. The apostles, all Jews. All of them, kikes."

"Christ, Dad!"

"And yet, anti-Semitism is as high as ever."

"I don't know, Mr. Becker," L.J. said politely. Becker gazed over, eyebrows contorted. *Sorry about the old man.*

"Jesus was mad the money changers were using the temple to conduct business, right?"

"Dad…" Becker tried to chime in.

"That's because you couldn't bring Roman currency into the temple, so they exchanged it for Hebrew currency…"

"Dad."

"Because Jesus is mad they're ruining his religion. He's a teacher, a rabbi. Mark and John, they refer to him as rabbi. But he's mad at the old guard, the top brass in bed with the Romans. Big Brother. You know about Big Brother, right Mr. L.J.?"

"Dad!" He finally got the geezer's attention. "We all know about Big Brother! Unfortunately, you're off by a few thousand years. We're telling a different story tonight," pointing at the table prepared for Passover.

"OK, boss," Pop Pop liked calling his son.

"So, where were we?"

Zoe giggled to herself as she checked an incoming Snapchat, took an off-angle selfie, Pop Pop and the candles as background, and sent it back.

"Zoe!" Becker screamed.

"Mr. Becker," L.J. whispered to Pop Pop amid the stoppage. "Did you know your son is investigating a murder?"

Becker shook his head, wondered if they'd ever finish this damn seder, and held back a smile. "Not really, Dad. Don't listen to him."

L.J. leaned in further. "Our friend from college, Amir. He was a scientist. He died under mysterious circumstances. The police say he committed suicide, but Becks, er Dave, thinks it may have been a murder."

"Wow," the table said in unison and drew in a bit closer.

"Yea, Becker talked to him the week before," L.J. said over the candle flicker. "Then the morning of his public testimony, they find him hanging from his own belt."

"And now," Zoe added, eyes lit with animation, "he thinks that sex scandal and the emails on Wikileaks are all connected." The table looked at Becker and then back again at Zoe. "And Dad says Congress is involved, like a big conspiracy."

Cathy said out loud what everyone was thinking. "Dave, are you keeping up with your meds?"

"Yea, I'm on my meds," he said defensively. "Are you?" She returned a sneer poorly masquerading as a smile.

"L.J. and I are writing a screenplay about it," Zoe added proudly, she and her co-author sharing a glance.

Uncle Steve nudged a knee under the table, finding Zoe's. "Remember that vacation when your Dad left his wallet on top of the car? You should put that in the screenplay."

"Or that trip we took to Utah and he ran out of gas in the desert?" Zoe shared with excitement.

"How bout the time he tried to give your mom's dog away to a homeless guy?" Cathy joined in. "He always hated Snickers."

Becker rubbed at his temples, stirring the anxiety cauldron, the ring in his ear at full symphony. Perhaps he should become a monk in one of those stone fortresses, commit to never speaking out loud again. Or run away to the circus, hide behind clown makeup. *Do they still do that?* Perhaps a timely step off the curb as the #35 is heading down 2nd Ave. He'd have to check the schedule.

Three hours later, they finished the Seder. "The lamb was delicious, David," Mrs. Goldberg thanked him. "He was sacrificed for a very good cause." She pulled him to the side for some privacy. "David, if you're not feeling well, my husband Morty, God bless his soul, was a therapist. I learned a lot. We should talk..."

"I'm ok. Thanks for asking."

"Cause when I found you on the roof. I was looking for Angel."

"The one with the stubby tail?"

"No, that's Whiskers. Or maybe you're thinking of King James. He has a greenish coat. Anyway..."

Becker decided to change the subject. "I'm ok. I just wanted to see the view up there."

"In the freezing rain?"

"I'm on excellent medication. I'm OK, I promise," he guided her to the door, thanked her for coming, and started the extrication. As much as he loved seeing everyone, he enjoyed getting rid of them even more. They filed passed, L.J. the last to say goodbye, bringing Becker in for a firm embrace.

"I'll walk you down," Zoe said, recalling a detail they should add to the screenplay.

\*\*\*

Seventeen hundred miles away, a red Tacoma pickup drove the backroads of west Texas, staying off the Interstate. Two men and a dog, tired from a long drive, noticed the oil derricks and drill pads becoming denser, the air more pungent. They got out to stretch their legs and take a leak by the side of the road.

# Chapter 14. The 50

A few hours after Becker's Passover dinner.

"You're just spotting tonight," Mo reminded Ian before he could pull the AR-15 out of the old Tacoma bed, worn clean of paint. Mo noticed Ian's disappointment and tried to reassure him. "That thing is practically useless from here."

Ian tucked the AR back to its corner as the engine ticked away, cooling off after sixty miles at breakneck speed on the West Texas bi-ways.

The moonlit sky was wide open, the infinite patchwork quilt of the Milky Way above. The two men worked silently, setting up quickly under their headlamps and the light of the quarter moon. Mo checked his watch, hidden in the hair of his large forearm and straggly beard. 23:45. Still on jarhead time. Fifteen minutes left to the day. Should be enough.

They peered across the valley from atop a low rise. Oil drilling dotted the landscape in all directions. A peculiar fog settled. Mo coughed into his sizable fist as the fumes collected in the back of his throat.

About an hour ago, the Tacoma rolled gently out of Stay Awhile RV Park on the New Mexico border. The other tenants were bedding down for the night, generators humming away, TVs blaring inside RVs. The Walking Dead, Hannity ranting on about Samantha Barnstable or some other Democrat. No one seemed to notice that site B52 cleared camp at an awkward time, wheeled slowly, without much ceremony, into the darkened night.

Ian set up the scope, spread the tripod feet, removed the lens caps, adjusted the dials to hone in on the target. A tattered strip of cloth cheaply assessed wind direction and speed. At the center of the optics: the target, floodlit in unearthly aura. Steel pipes emanating from a plane of concrete. Wheeled valve controls the size of extra-large pizzas regulated the flow. Silvery tanks wide enough to house village elders held oil and water condensate of increasing purity. A 20-foot pipe stood on end, like a cigarette upright on its filter, flames and oily smoke endlessly pouring out the lit end. Underneath the concrete pad, 30 ventricles sucked hydrocarbon out of the earth. To the left, a row of stainless-steel transport trucks.

They dressed in black, faces covered by baseball caps, cheap sunglasses. The fake mustaches were abandoned; it was irrelevant for Mo and it made Ian chuckle uncontrollably, punchy from lack of sleep. As they spread out the tarp and laid out the inventory, Sammy watched from the back, vision blurred from the Benadryl Mo added to a sausage slice. He wasn't taking any chances tonight.

Mo opened the large Pelican case to find the M82. "The Seventh Trumpet," he gleamed under his breath. He clicked the stock and triggered handpiece together, opened the bipod legs, checked the chamber and the safety. "You got my magazine?"

"Loaded," Ian whispered back, handing it over, heavy with copper-jacketed lead. "Incendiary tracers," knowing Mo's next question.

Mo locked the magazine into place, contorting his face as if he could reduce that ominous sound from bouncing over the valley below. He looked at the weapon, the aerated guard rail, the fluted 29" barrel terminating in a noble arrowhead, the heavy gauge steel wrapped in diamond fashion over the precision recoil and ammunition handling system. The Staff of Moses, the power of lightning in his hands.

Back in the early '80s, young entrepreneur Ronnie Barrett of Tennessee created a breakthrough in weaponry, *the first recoil-operated, semi-automatic .50 caliber rifle designed for long-range anti-materiel sniper activity*, the official marketing would say. It was a revolution in muscle and weight, capable of hitting a torso at over a mile, pierce thru half-inch armor, and burden a soldier with only 35 pounds. Barrett Firearms Manufacturing was borne. The company's first major sale was for 30 rifles to the Swedish Military in 1989. The U.S. Army tested it in Operation Desert Shield and Desert Storm in 1990 and '91, and formally adopted it thereafter as the M107.

The civilian M82 is, for all intents and purposes, just as powerful as its military sibling. Of course, any weapon can fall into the wrong hands. For one particular .50 caliber rifle, passing through west Texas in April, the Year of the Lord 2017 (or Passover 5778, depending on when you started counting), its ownership changed hands one night a few years prior. Unfortunately, the original and law-abiding owner spent far more on the gun than the safe he kept it in. The cheap steel walls were cut through in about 20 minutes by burglars coveting the weapon and the silver bullion rumored to be kept there. The powerful M82 traded hands a couple of times before a man named Jarrett Jacobs, mostly flannel and oversized sideburns, bought it from a neighbor in his Missouri trailer park, evading the federal registry due to a string of burglaries in his late teens.

Ian zoomed in through the spotting scope. "We're about a kilometer," he guessed from the maps they studied the night before, looking for a good vantage point. "That's a thousand meters."

"Yeah, I know." Mo searched his rifle scope and ignored Ian as best he could. He placed a small dense pillow under the rifle butt, rotating it to get the weapon to the proper angle.

A Barrett M82 can cost up to $9,000. Add good quality optics, in this case, a Leupold 4x29, and a silencer, the tag can easily reach 15 grand. Luckily for Mo, Jarrett Jacobs ran into money trouble when his truck broke down and Jarrett Jr. fell off a swing and nearly split his head wide open, and had to sell the rifle at a rock bottom price: $2900 cash money, no questions. "Comes with two hundred rounds of ammo too," Jarrett convinced him.

"Slight wind blowing right to left," Ian said as convincingly as he could, looking down at Mo in prone position. At 6'3", 250 pounds, Mo and the large weapon nearly filled the cloth tarp.

"Yep. Should pull and drop about 36 inches," Mo calculated. "I'll make the adjustment. Gonna hit that middle condensate tank first."

"Got it," Ian agreed, visualizing the moment through the scope. "Should blow the other two."

"Then that pipe coming out of the pad."

"Got it."

"Then the fuel trucks," Mo explained as he practiced a leftward swing, every millimeter of movement exaggerated in the powerful optics. He'd love a good laser scope to help pinpoint the targets or a proper wind-speed calculator, but couldn't chance stepping back into an FFL dealer, back on the grid. Too dangerous at this point, he figured. He dialed down the zoom a bit. 23x should do it. Make it 24.

Mo pulled the recoil lever as smoothly as he could, like the gate latch after sneaking home from a night out with his buddies, Ka-Clink, before letting it slide forward with deliberate quiet. Ka-Clink, it locked into place. Ian eyed an extra bullet in his hand, the last pulled from the metal ammo can. The projectile extended an inch over the edges of his palm. "Jesus, it's like a missile."

Mo checked his watch before the point of no return. 23:52 and one second. Two seconds. Three. He had calculated the tempo and rhythm of the relevant steps: get to the spot, hit the targets, break it down, and get back to the highway before midnight. They were behind schedule.

"Slow breath out," Ian coached.

"Shit, who here is the ex-Marine?" Mo muttered under his breath, as he donned the earmuffs, and positioned again. Through the nasal passages, a warm breeze on his trigger finger. Tighten the orbit, the target passing back across the scope's center guide marks. One last breath out, and a trigger pull. The first sound here, on the tarp, above the acrid valley, through the silencer like a giant tree felled in the wilderness. The tracer extended to the middle condensate tank. The empty shell grasshoppered out, steaming with explosion.

A kilometer away, the bullet pierced its target, a perfect inch-wide aperture, a caterpillar through a leaf, vapors escaping. The explosion, a brilliant flash, the holding tank now an oversized grenade, a slow-motion ballet of anarchy. Then it hit them. The sound. BAM. **BAM.**

"Holy shit," Ian pulled back, the detonation weaponized through the spotting scope.

Mo edged the rifle the width of a mouse's tail, just enough to bring the oversized pipe, periscoping out of the concrete pad, into view. He pulled the trigger before the target scittered past and got lucky. The arc of the tracer created a perfect line before fizzling out an instant before contact. Then, the explosion, twisted metal in the air followed by successive sonic crashes.

Ian searched the horizon with more excitement than he could remember.

Mo swept the rifle to the left, overshooting the distribution trucks by 50 yards. Back again like a pendulum passing its center. His orientation was confounded in the chaos. *Where the fuck did it go?*

He zoomed his optics out, found the target, zoomed back in, slowed his breathing, reduced his heart rate. He pulled the trigger. A small pile of dust kicked up.

"About 10 feet low," Ian said, following the tracer.

"Damn gravity."

The target pulsed out of center, Mo's heartbeat now a 1970s discotheque. He fought it off, re-tightening the orbit, past the pancake batter-smoke, the trucks coming into clarity, the background blurring with anticipation. A last breath out. Squeeze of the trigger. The recipient ass of the distribution truck spilled liquid fuel and vapors. A miniscule lag in the incendiary before white sparks spit out in all directions.

The truck lifted like a misfired Saturn rocket. Heat flashes strobed the night sky. Smoke filled the valley floor like cheesy rock concert staging. "Fuck," they both gasped.

Ian broke down the spotting scope and balled up the tarp.

Mo collapsed the .50, into the Pelican case, and crammed it in a corner of the truck bed. He got behind the wheel, rambling the checklist in his mind. "Shit, the sign!"

"Fuck the sign!"

"It's important!"

He searched the truncated floor behind his seat. "Excuse me, Sammy," and produced a mallet and a dowel from under the sedated pup. A single playing card was nailed to the top: the King of Clubs. He drove the dowel into the sandy soil then wiped it clean with a rag, praying he rendered the fingerprints useless.

He spun the truck around and drove like a bat out of hell, back over the dusty road, past the innumerable pumpjacks and gas flares, the flat expanse of western Texas. Back to the interstate, to disappear into the wilderness of society.

\*\*\*

Zoe couldn't sleep that night, perhaps too much horseradish on top of the Passover fixins. She rolled a cigarette and stared out at the back alley behind 22nd Street, waiting for a sign. Something. That things would be ok. Or not.

# Chapter 15. Ian

Moments after the second attack.

The smell hit Ian first. An unexpected bile. "Gosh darn it, he's puking back there."

"I knew I smelled something," Mo rolled down his windows, the dog's stench swirling with dust and the noxious residue of ordinance on the wind as they barreled down a west Texas dirt road in the first minutes of the day. They sped past corn and cotton and sorghum, whatever that is. A farmhouse awakened in the night, bedroom lights flickering on, dogs barking at the sudden confusion of detonation and illumination rippling across the valley.

"I told you not to give him Benadryl! It makes him puke every time," Ian complained.

Mo focused on the dirt road, headlights off, faint moonlight bouncing off the crops that lined the byway. Gravel flew as the truck slid into each turn, the intersection of physics and worn shock absorbers. "Trying to drive here!"

Ian wrestled the dog from the back to clean him, thankful the Westie was too tired to snip at him. "It'll be ok," he said reassuringly.

The Tacoma hit a series of deep ruts, earth kicking in all directions, Sammy bouncing off Ian's lap.

"He really stinks. Would you mind placing him in the back seat?" Mo asked with unnatural calm. He skittered to a stop. An intersection, two unpaved gateways. Dust encircled the truck like a witch's cauldron. "Which way? IAN, WHICH WAY?!" Ian tossed the dog into the back and grabbed the map crumpled at his feet. "163! South on 163," he pointed right at the shot-gunned sign and Mo drove off again, hitting the truck's top speed. "In a couple of miles, east on Interstate 10," Ian navigated above the roar of the engine, tires bobbing off the washboard surface. To the north, distant sirens and approaching helicopters, searchlights piercing the toxic soup that hung in the dark sky. The enemy has awoken.

They drove for hours, took in a quick respite behind an abandoned trailer so Mo could rest his weary rods and cones, start again. 251 miles southeast of Barnhart, on I-10 or parallel side roads, east into Texas hill country, he finally felt comfortable enough for a pit stop. No sense getting caught on a random video camera before necessary.

They changed out their hats, donning straw ones from the back seat. Ian checked himself in the side view mirror. "I'll get something to clean that up," as he walked Sammy on a knotted leash to the convenience store.

"I'll fill the gas tank," Mo replied.

As Ian guided the old dog through the door, right front paw still bandaged, he noticed a crowd milling around the cashier. He looked over a man's shoulder and quickly recognized the carnage on the small TV in the corner, live scenes of an explosion in the Permian, just a few hour's drive from there.

"I told them they're getting lots of impurities in the gas," one old-timer complained. "The processing is done half-assed."

"That ain't no accident," another responded. "Looks like arson to me."

Ian watched, mouth agape, not sure what would be more suspicious: going about his business or standing there awkwardly. His hollowed-out eyes were framed by cropped black hair, dark brows, and dark bags. He noticed people rarely took to him until he gave a wide grin so long as he could obscure the gaps where his teeth went missing due to the meth addiction and all. He often practiced in the mirror, testing combinations of facial muscles to get the smile just right, imagining saying hello to the pretty girl he would marry one day. "Just watching," he said when the cashier asked if he wanted to make a purchase, wondering what the weird little guy with the dog was smirking at.

When Sammy pulled him by the leash over to the snack aisle, Ian figured that must be a sign from above, so he just shook his head at the news like the other convenience store customers and searched for the pretzels with the peanut butter crammed inside.

He could recall, like it was yesterday, when his 4th Grade teacher told his parents what a promising student he was. "But he likes to horse around in the back of the room," she explained, "always finding a way to get into trouble." Before you know it, he was skipping 8th grade with Billy Ryan, playing in the abandoned mill not far from his house in Duluth, Minnesota. Once he realized he'd have to spend the equivalent of three straight summers to graduate high school on time, he figured the hell with it, and packed all he had in the old Datsun his Dad rebuilt for him. Out of Minnesota. New adventures on the horizon. Things looked ok for a while, that year and a half, hauling fracking fluids around the Bakken of North Dakota. Was even dating a nice woman he met at the county fair, shooting 11 toy ducks on their endless conveyor belt, winning an oversized blue dog-like creature she was perplexingly taken with. But when the meth got a hold of him, it never let go. A downward spiral took it all away: the job, the girlfriend, the dog-like creature. Gone, just like that. He got back in the Datsun and continued on until it finally eschewed necessary parts just south of the Georgia-Florida line, muffler and busted hoses lining the road. He was proud of himself that he never took to heroin like some of the other homeless guys in Jacksonville. He hated who he had become but always said he wouldn't change a thing if he could.

He finally got clean in New York City after he found a bus pass just lying there next to an old pizza box under the bridge he called home for seven weeks. It was providence, he figured, a sign he still can't explain. A few days later after arriving, Ian Michael MacArthur found himself getting a hot meal in the basement of Holy Redeemer Church on west 39th Street in Hell's Kitchen when a large bearded man asked him if the seat across the table was open.

"I'm Mo," the man said.

"Ian," he replied with gap-tooth smile.

Ian was captured by Mo's intensity, his knowledge of the world, the stories. Ian couldn't quite explain it, a void somehow filled, a thirst quenched as he befriended the man, his impenetrable facial hair swaying with comedy and tragedy. If Mo came up with it, Ian figured it was worth listening to. Mo inspired him to wean from the meth with the good book and maybe a shot of tequila to get past the irrepressible cravings, transforming to a life of more-or-less sobriety.

They spotted Sammy eating out of a sideways-leaning trash can in Central Park. No tags. Another sign from above. They adopted the dog on the spot, baptized him in Turtle Pond, and designated him as Sammy, the name of Ian's imaginary friend when he aimlessly wandered the wheat fields surrounding Duluth on late summer afternoons, wondering what he'd be in life.

Days later, they strolled into a pet store and bought a bone-shaped silver tag for the grand sum of one dollar. Sammy, it said, and provided Mo's cell although it only worked when he kept up with the payments. They had to hide Sammy in back alleys, underneath heavy coats. No pets allowed in homeless shelters. But it was all worth it. Ian loved that canine more than anything on God's green earth.

He squinted at the Westie, panting in the convenience store, the pup motioning to the leathery treats the way pups do. Ian patted him on the head, and picked up Sammy's selection.

As Ian returned to the Tacoma, rug shampoo, K-9 Chews, and peanut butter-filled pretzels in the bag, Mo was reading from the bible, his large finger sweeping over the text as he muttered the scripture. "Where the hell you been?" Mo asked.

"I got a little lost," Ian explained, cleaning up the vomit in the back seat.

"Lost? It's only a hundred feet away."

"Not that kind of lost." He finished scrubbing the back carpet as best as he could given the circumstances, sat back in the passenger seat and buckled up, still contemplating right from wrong and his choice of snacks.

"Read this." Mo handed him the book, verses highlighted in yellow and pink. Ian never liked to read in public and would often complain to Sammy, his imaginary friend, about the embarrassment of stuttering the passage his teacher selected for him as the prettiest girls in class rolled their eyes at each other at the front of the room. Mo pointed to the line where Ian should start.

'We give thanks to you, Lord God Almighty, who is and who was, for you have taken your great power and begun to reign. The nations raged, but your wrath has come,' Ian read slowly.

"They're talking 'bout God's wrath," Mo explained as he pulled out of the truck stop, back onto the highway. "And the nations, that was Rome. Big brother. Jesus and his disciples, they were all anti-establishment SOBs, if you know what I mean. Keep going," Mo encouraged, "you're doing great."

'and the time for the dead to be judged, and to recompense your servants, and the holy ones,' Ian read, uncertain what the words meant.

Mo pointed to the page and joined in the reading, full-throated in his deepest baritone.

'AND THOSE WHO FEAR YOUR NAME, THE SMALL AND THE GREAT ALIKE,' they read together, Mo now excited by the oration.

A monster pickup, tires fit for a bulldozer, filled the rearview mirror. Mo tried to ignore it but was unsuccessful. He checked the speedometer—80 in a 65—and gestured in the side view for some personal space. But the wheeled beast pulled tighter, nearly touching the Tacoma's tail. Mo swerved into the right lane. Oily black plumes billowed out of the monster truck's modified exhaust. Rolling coal, they call it. The driver sat several feet above and offered Mo and Ian his middle finger. Mo returned the favor, his voice now booming with sermon as he and Ian read the next line as one. *'AND SHOULDEST DESTROY THEM WHICH DESTROY THE EARTH.'* Mo imagined lifting thousands to their feet inside a great hall filled to the brim. Instead, his only flock was inside the Tacoma that day. Ian's eyes lit up as the meaning washed over him. Sammy, too, felt the electricity, and barked for attention, wagging his tail as Ian pet his head. *'And shouldest destroy them which destroy the earth,'* Mo re-read for emphasis.

"Revelations," Ian muttered, turning the bible over in his hands, adding the "s" even though it wasn't there.

"Book of Revelation. Do you know the word for revelation in Greek?" Mo asked, always the teacher.

"I don't think so," Ian said, not sure of anything anymore.

"It's apocalypse. An unveiling of things not known. Apocalypse just means a revelation. To bring the truth to light." Ian smiled awkwardly, not sure how to respond, and contemplated the turns his life had taken. Providence continued on, traveling east on Interstate 10, passing San Antonio, headed for Houston and beyond.

\*\*\*

David Becker jarred himself from a nightmare in the wee hours of the day. Zoe was banging around the kitchen before the sunrise. The smell of roast lamb still permeated the apartment. The loop of a conversation played in his head. It was Abassi. Becker couldn't make out what was real and what was not.

# Chapter 16. Dr. Amir Abassi

Mid-July, 2016. Nine Months Earlier.

Darkened office lights cascaded toward Abassi, whiling away at his machine.

"You headed to Rita's retirement party?" someone asked through the cracked door. He peered over his glasses, a bit overwhelmed, and found Shelly Dessev's friendly face.

"Maybe," Abbasi said hesitantly. The scientists from the National Center for Atmospheric Research shared an eastern descent—he Iranian, she Indian—and a natural comfort to their collaboration. "I have to get these simulations set up for the weekend. Don't drink all the beer, ok?"

"It's a deal." She smiled and walked away.

Two miles up Table Mesa Road, 700 feet aloft where it sits on a perch like a church gargoyle, NCAR overlooks Boulder, Colorado. Way to the south, the high-rises of Denver poke through a dejected gray haze.

NCAR researchers analyze weather and greenhouse gasses, chemistry in the atmosphere and oceans, fire patterns in an evolving climate, particulate concentrations and resulting lung disease, feedback loops that could intensify the worst effects of climate change over the next decades. Amir Abassi, Ph.D. toyed with the final computer settings, prepping a batch of runs over the weekend. Artificial light refracted off his glasses, caught in an endless loop between machine and operator, whichever one was which. Since his simulations require 31 hours on the agency's powerful supercomputers, errors equate to lost time and research. Abassi was fighting the clock. Of the day, the year, the decade. The powers that be will not loosen their grip on the status quo easily.

For fifteen years after earning his PhD at Cornell in physics, Abbasi worked at NCAR on a wide range of issues. Formerly trained in planetary physics, he focused his doctoral thesis on sunspots, small dots of intense magnetic activity on the sun's surface where it cools below 4,200° Celsius, relatively frigid when compared to the average 5,500° C surface temperature of our sun. Part of an eleven-year cycle, reaching its peak at the Solar Maximum, some claim sunspots—not human-induced carbon emissions—are the cause of our erratic climate.

Upon first arrival, Abassi was ecstatic to join NCAR. But his curiosities morphed with the Earth's warning signs. Funding dictated the analysis and an uncomfortable phone call from Washington could kill a controversial project. Abassi's interests and research overlapped less each year, two lines on a chart diverging across the X-axis, time.

For the past two years, since he first spoke out, he was relegated to UC-14-381: An Examination of Atmospheric Differences on Nearby Planets: Mars and Venus. Abassi hated UC-14-381. *Absolute kossher, bullshit*, he muttered to himself. *It's all mind games, trying to make me quit*, as he reformatted data to upload from one model to its successor, clicking through steps he had perfected over the years. "Congress just pretends they are planning for the future!" His hands and Farsi contorted in the air.

"Excuse me, Sir," the woman asked in a newly-arrived accent, pulling off her headphones, interrupting the podcast. She wore a blue apron and pushed a large trash can on wheels. The cleaning crew had begun their nightly chores, emptying the wastebaskets, vacuuming the short-pile rugs.

Abassi looked up sheepishly. "I was... its nothing."

"No problem," she said, grabbing his wastebasket to dump the contents. "You should go home to your family."

"You're right," he agreed, head still rotating side to side, a metronome of argument with a faceless enemy at a consistent 4/4 time.

As Abassi hit Run, the screen log offered the first modeling step: *Collecting Inputs*. There was always time for UC-14-381. Mars and

Venus weren't going anywhere. Tonight's simulations would be a different matter. Something a bit more dire. Over the past five years, Dr. Abassi built and improved a powerful series of models regarding the earth's oceans. The cornerstone to our planet, the seas were heating, losing oxygen, becoming more acidic, and turning into a dumping ground for all manner of our waste. *If the very chemistry of the oceans is altered?,* Abassi's real passion, *what impact could that have on all marine life? On all human health?*

Forget the atmospheric conditions of Mars or Venus, in order to indulge the inane fantasies of Congress and billionaires, with what? To escape from Earth? For them and a very short list of beautiful people on the friends and family plan? *Ahmagh hā.* Idiots. Every pound of payload into space costs $20,000 or more. It was all a diversion to rationalize the status quo. "Why don't we take care of this planet since its, you know, blessed with liquid water and an atmosphere!" Abassi screamed, the sound pinballing off the empty laboratory corridors. He listened for the cleaning woman, praying she turned her headphones up.

His ocean research had a legitimate birth, funded by the Department of Commerce, the primary backer to NCAR endeavors. But in their unbridled wisdom, someone in the District of Corruption objected. After an initial report, the effort was folded and Abassi bounced from one irrelevant project to another. Now, he was relegated to the bane of his existence, UC-14-381. Luckily no one paid too close attention, and Abassi logged his ocean analysis, gobbling up computing requirements, under the idiotic Mars effort.

He stood up to leave, go back home to Maya and the kids but recent events were gnawing at him. He removed his coat, closed the door, and picked up the phone.

"Hello," someone answered across the country.

"David?" Abassi asked, his voice like a car rolling over gravel.

Becker was still at work. "Amir? I was just thinking about you."

"Is this a good time to talk?"

"Hold on." Amir heard his friend close the door. "What's up?"

Amir Abassi and David Becker met as freshmen in college at Redwood State, sharing the bathroom at the end of the hall and observations about the hot girls in cutoffs walking the manicured pathways. After one such incident, Abassi wandered into the wrong building, dumbstruck with love or something similar.

They became fast friends, got stoned, turned Hendrix up to 11. Even went to an activist meeting or two together. But when Abassi got three Bs, a C, and an incomplete to finish his third semester, his parents nearly yanked him from school, sent him to work in Uncle Mohammed's shop selling rugs and backgammon sets in Tehran's Grand Bazaar. His strict Persian upbringing required far more obedience than western kids like Becker and L.J. He was expected to get a Ph.D., like his father, smile through an arranged marriage, set in stone since he was thirteen, and produce lots of progeny to continue the tradition. He buckled down, cut out the parties, dove headfirst into the chemistry lab, occasionally sleeping next to his experiments and research papers. After Redwood State, he got his Ph.D. at Cornell, following his assigned pathway. But a nagging disappointment of not deciding his own fate trailed him like a shadow.

"Dave, I think I'm being followed."

"What? Where are you?"

"I'm in Boulder. Prepping for next week. I testify in a House science subcommittee for the Research Priorities Enquiry."

"Yea?"

"Officially about atmospheric conditions on Mars to support a NASA station. So stupid. But I'm gonna raise my unofficial research. About my ocean models. We're on a collision course. I believe it with all my heart."

The friends hadn't talked since 2014, when it was first reported the Great Barrier Reef was dying. They were incredulous, each needing someone to talk them off the ledge. On the phone for hours, they finished a six-pack between them, and bemused where things were headed.

"What happened?" Becker asked him.

"We were broken into. I think."

"You're not sure?"

"They didn't take anything. The kids left the backdoor unlocked. There was no forced entry. But it was clear someone went through our things. And my computer keeps getting attacked. I get phishing scams all the time."

"Well," Becker consoled him, "that's pretty normal."

"Some people really hate my research." NCAR, funded by Commerce, was subject to Energy and Commerce Committee oversight. Committee Chair, Norman Radcliffe himself, called NCAR management screaming with threats of tightened funding, stricter supervision. Then all of a sudden, Abassi got an ominous note from Immigration Services: there may be a problem with his visa. Abassi shared the myths he had heard: the country's power brokers tossing policy proposals and poker chips onto a felt-lined table, to be haggled over bourbon and cigars in smoke-filled back rooms. The nation's investment in scientific research had become barter props, whole agencies potentially eliminated, researchers dispersed.

"You think they're trying to scare you?"

"I made some enemies with that Post editorial."

"I saw that. You really believe it?"

"It requires some negative feedbacks. But, it's a distinct possibility. The oceans are a mess. Red tides. Acidification. Pollution in the farthest reaches."

"It's frightening," Becker agreed.

"Current models only look at these things in pieces, as if they're unrelated. Mine is the first to look at the interactions, the multiplicative impact. You know, Dave, our warming models were all too conservative. It's happening way faster than we thought."

"I know," Becker muttered.

"They were politicized. The IPCC is a consensus bureau. Any nation with oil or gas interests can hold back the results, tone down the language so it's more politically palatable."

"But the message is too dire?"

"Or I'm the wrong messenger."

"You are kind of obnoxious," Becker laughed.

"I know. I might get fired. If I do, I'd lose my visa." Even though he's tried for decades, Amir was never granted U.S. citizenship. Too many holes in his U.S. residence. Back in the 90s, he returned to Iran for over a year when his Dad fell ill. A couple years later, Iran called again. This time, to get married in the arranged courtship to Maya, a beautiful girl from a well-respected family. "My citizenship has taken forever." He could hear Becker shake his head at the complexity. "Maya and the kids could get deported. It's scary. I'm..." Abassi was whispering, nearly in tears. "I'm on anti-depressants."

"Well, so am I. Half the country is, Amir."

"No, you don't understand. A lot of them."

"Maybe there's something here at Sustainable Pathway Fund. You'll find someone to support your visa," Becker said. "If the government wants you to stay in line, they'll probably keep your position. You're more dangerous if you're unemployed."

But Becker wasn't buying it. "Don't be so cynical," he countered. "Those are just paranoid tales."

"You're right. I get anxious sometimes. It must've been growing up in Iran. People would just disappear. Speak out against the government. You might go out to the store and never return home."

"It'll be ok," Becker tried to sound confident. "This is America."

Abassi thanked his friend and suggested they get together. Becker should come out to Boulder, the Republic, escape the rat race back in New York City.

"I'd love that," Becker said, and hung up with a quiet hesitancy.

***

Zoe was watching reruns when Becker walked in, dumbfound, stammering about an old friend. Some guy named Abassi. She was on summer break: sleeping until noon, picking up extra shifts at D'Antonio's, hanging with friends. It was the first time she noticed him pawing at his ears, trying to get the sound out. She checked his temperature while he nursed a beer.

# Chapter 17. Imperfect Vessels

July, 2016. Five days after Abassi called Becker.

Penny Archer was reviewing the week's agenda in bed, the room ornately accented in Louis VXI style, embroidered drapery, matching wallpaper and bedspread. At 11 p.m., she picked up her cell phone and made the call she was contemplating all evening.

"G'evening," Bucksworth overindulged his Aussie accent, as if to lighten the mood.

"Graham," she answered. "Thank you for taking my call."

"Happy to, Ms. Archer," he lied. He knew not to call her Penny on the first reference no matter how many times she requested it.

"Please, call me Penny."

"Of course. Penny."

"Our friend, Dr. Abassi, is at it again," she said, navigating to the heart of the matter.

"I saw. He's going to testify on his research. Turn it into a circus."

"It's not even sanctioned," she countered. "He's using government property to conduct his own personal agenda. What happened to the immigration status?"

"We're working on it. He has to be fired for cause first." He breathed heavily into the phone. "It's taking more time than I thought."

They say money can't substitute for taste. Nothing could be more true for Penny Archer. Squeezing into jeans stretched Saran Wrap-thin, the dye job way beyond credibility. And then there were the teeth, the disorderly collection of enamel. The Archers, millionaires many times over, could certainly afford braces. But 13-

year-old Penny was riotous, the metal work worse than torture. Regardless, first-born Penny was raised to succeed. Offered the best schooling at Choate, then Georgetown for business then law. She ignored the naysayers, determined to prove her worth through the important works of the Faith and Freedom Foundation, and plot her enemy's demise.

"Would you mind paying him a visit?" she asked playfully, twisting a platinum strand in her fingers.

"A visit?"

"Just a little reminder. Of the order of things. Perhaps he will see that testifying could be considered... unpatriotic." She could hear the hesitation in his voice, the lack of clear response. "Graham, the Congressman placed your talents at my full disposal."

"I'm not completely comfortable..."

'*Rulers do not bear the sword for no reason. They are God's servants, agents of wrath to bring punishment on the wrongdoer,*' she quoted. "That's from Romans."

He stammered, unconvinced.

Penny kicked off her sneakers, still disrobing from her nightly walk to the  Capitol, her source of inspiration.  Such a beautiful building, it's religious values clearly enshrined among its artwork and design. Inside the famed structure, Penny would make her way to the Rotunda and find *The Discovery of the Mississippi*, a glorious retelling of de Soto's declaration at the mouth of the mighty river. Priests accompanying the explorer gloriously hold a crucifix in place, clearly declaring the young nation a Christian one. Penny would then search out IN GOD WE TRUST sculpted over Emancipation Hall or a relief of Moses over the gallery doors of the House Chamber, staring in awe.

"Graham, did you know Moses killed a man?"

"He did?"

"An Egyptian who was brutal to a Jewish slave. So Moses murdered him, buried him in sand, and fled. But God still spoke to Moses and asked him to free the Jews."

"I didn't know that."

"King David broke half the commandments and is still considered a great leader. God understands — if you're doing His important work, it's ok to bend the rules." She searched the silence for an acquiescent reply. "Jesus has brought us here for a reason. The President, the Republican leadership, they were chosen to lead our great nation."

"Droburn was chosen?"

"Sometimes God selects imperfect vessels to conduct his work. It wouldn't have happened unless Jesus wanted it to." Bucksworth's hesitation was audible. Penny decided to change subjects. "Do you know Radcliffe's intern, Paul Anderson?"

"No. Should I?"

"He's on the Foundation payroll. Very loyal. Give him a call. You two will really hit it off."

"Of course, Penny."

"It's probably best if we keep this formal."

"Ms. Archer," he corrected himself.

"Thank you, Graham. God appreciates all your contributions."

"That's..." he searched for the words, "reassuring."

"Good night, Graham."

"G'night, Ms. Archer."

# Chapter 18. Delivery

Two days later.

About a week after he called Becker, Amir Abassi checked into the Biltmore Suites hotel around 4:00 p.m. The establishment offered none of the luxury amenities one could infer by the regal name. Instead, Abassi found stained carpets, the metal piping of a retrofitted fire suppression system overhead, and a toilet that flushed in perpetuity. He removed the lid and fiddled with the mechanism. He called the front desk again, asking if someone could fix it, but was not expecting a satisfactory response.

Abassi returned to the mosaic of information spread out on the floor before him. Tomorrow morning, he would testify. One chance to get the message through.

72 hours earlier, he was called to the most prestigious corner of NCAR. His manager, Center Director, and an assortment of agency Vice Presidents were present, stern looks across the board. Congress was threatening budget cuts. People's jobs, their livelihoods, were on the line. His trip to D.C. was canceled, he was told. If he wanted to go, they couldn't stop him, but it'd be on his own dime. He left the meeting shaken but determined, and rebooked another hotel room, possibly the worst in all of D.C. At least it was close to the Capitol, he reasoned, as he typed in his credit card information.

Another hour passed in a wink when he heard a knock at the door. Finally, someone to fix that toilet. Abassi reviewed the information at the peephole: an impatient Asian man through the looking glass. "Who is it?" he asked

"Chinese foo," the man responded in thick accent.

"I didn't order any Chinese food," he offered the dirty rug a confused stare. Had he forgotten? It *was* a long day.

"You company order for you."

"My company?"

"Yeah - you colleague, let me see... Shelly. She order for you, says worry about you."

"Shelly ordered for me?"

"Yea, Shelly! She order for you!"

"It does smell delicious."

"Shrimp and Vegetables. And Spicy Scallops with Ginger," the delivery man told him.


He opened the door and let the delivery man in, setting the bag on the table next to the plastic room keys.

"Thanks," Abassi muttered, ready to close the door.

"Tip?"

"What?"

"Tip? They pay no tip," the delivery man said.

"Oh. Ok." Abassi rummaged his pants pockets until he found a crumpled up one and some coins. "Sorry, it's all the cash I have." The delivery man looked at the meager gratuity, shook his head, and muttered something in Chinese as he left.

Abassi opened the bag. As the aromas hit the ol' olfactory, he realized he hadn't eaten in hours. *That was thoughtful of Shelly,* as he opened the styrofoam boxes. Steam poured out and collected under him, the succulence filling the Biltmore Suites to its implied grandeur. He found disposable chopsticks, opened them up, and snarfed up a scallop. They forgot to leave a menu, he muttered to himself. Carrying the carton back, he sat on an old stuffed chair and labored over his notes and computer. The scallops were so hot, he could barely get them in his mouth. He shoved another one in, stood up, and raised his right hand.

"Do you swear to tell the truth, the whole truth, and nothing but the truth?" Abassi asked the man in the mirror, designed to make the room look larger. He turned back to the cheap furnishings, now reporters with oversized cameras, the hideous vase a collection of microphones.

"I do," he answered back, proud of his bravery. "Your honorable Congress..." He stopped to correct himself. "Congressmen and Congresswomen, it's an honor to stand before you..." One more try. "I would like to thank the honorable men and women of Congress to allow me to testify before you today." That was better, he agreed, turning back to his reflection.

A twinge in his stomach and Abassi winced. Suddenly, he fell to the floor between the chair and the bed, the taste of vomit in his mouth, his head weightless and spinning out of control. He reached for his phone, but never found it.

\*\*\*

The next afternoon, a chambermaid opened the door to Biltmore Suites room 207. She screamed, slammed it shut, and ran to the elevator. 20 minutes later, the D.C. police ominously pushed the door ajar and found Dr. Abassi hanging from his belt, tied to the fire suppression's iron pipes. A coat hanger was repurposed to shore up the extinguisher system, supporting the man's weight. The stuffed chair was kicked over a few feet away. He never showed for his testimony in the morning. Instead, he swung slowly hour after hour, his neck stretched grotesquely from the leather strap. One cop looked at the other. "Better call the coroner, just to make sure."

# Chapter 19. Soft Shoe

April 11, 2017. The morning after the second attack in West Texas. Washington, D.C.

Sara Roberts waited in the lobby a few feet from the insignia in the buffed marble floor: scales of justice atop a red and white-striped medallion encircled by thirteen stars and gold ornamentation. On top, it read Department of Justice, On the bottom, Federal Bureau of Investigation. Across the middle, a banner waved: Fidelity. Bravery. Integrity.

"Where've you been?  We're gonna be late," she said with frustration, scrutinizing her watch for extra seconds in the J. Edgar Hoover Building in Washington, D.C.

"Sorry," McMannis said, out of breath. "The metro broke down again. Fuckin' nightmare."  He eyeballed his watch. "We've got 4 minutes."

"That thing is slow. It's 7:58. We've got 2 minutes. Come on," she said, and they went into a full sprint. Down the hall, up the steps, left, no this way. It's right.

They composed themselves and opened the door. Cap looked at his watch as they entered awkwardly.

"Just made it, Homer."

"Yes, Cap," Phillip McMannis responded. The strap of his briefcase caught on the doorknob. His partner, Sara Roberts, worked to get it free.

"Roberts, we don't have all day."

"Yes, Sir," she said.

Cap pushed the door closed and locked it behind them. Special Agents McMannis and Roberts arrived at the team meeting dead last, as usual, and took the first open chairs available. McMannis straightened his combover, now teeming with sweat.

"OK. Let's get started. McMannis, Roberts: you're familiar with the Ford dealership in Pennsylvania last week?"

"Yes, Sir," they answered.

"They're at it again. Rural Texas. This time, oil and gas facilities. Potential eco-terrorism." Cap turned on the overhead projector, flipping through images on his computer. "April 4th. Erie, Pennsylvania. Six propane tanks jammed open and hit with high-powered rifles from 150 yards." Pictures of hulled-out pickup trucks from Erie Ford, blackened and twisted metal frames. A mass of melted rubber, steel, glass, and plastic.

"We found .50 caliber and AR-15 leads in the propane tanks and under one vehicle. It's with ballistics, but the heat incinerated them pretty good. Probably not much to work with."

"Yes, Sir," McMannis said, peeking out from his feverish notes.

"It's all in the file, Cap said reassuringly. Special Agent in Charge (SAC) Sean Little ran the FBI's D.C. office. Everyone knew him as Cap, short for his former rank in the Army. Shaved head, muscular, no-nonsense. He rolled up his shirt sleeves ensuring everyone caught sight of the scar when the IED hit the Humvee, and the firefight ensued right there in the public market, bullets ricocheting off the cobbled street before it jogged left following the ancient urban layout. Captain Little pulled two buddies out of the carnage to give them a proper burial before getting his own ass out of there in one piece.

McMannis watched as the scar moved involuntarily. "How are the two incidents related? Sir?"

Cap flipped through the slide deck, stopping at a picture of playing cards inside a plastic evidence bag with FBI markings for date, time, location, and internal serial numbers. "This seems to be their calling card. The King of Clubs. Two were found in Pennsylvania. In Texas, about sixth-tenths of a mile from the target, another card was found. Wanna guess which one, Homer?"

"King of Clubs, Sir?"

"Good guess. It was nailed to a dowel and hammered into the road shoulder. It appears to be the vantage point they attacked from." Cap Little clicked through more pictures, now from the Texas incident. Exploded vessels and piping like soldiers strewn across the battlefield. Burned out delivery trucks.

"I've never profiled eco-terrorists before, Sir," Roberts mentioned.

"I know," he answered. "But Jacobs retired last month and Galbraith got himself shot while hunting a few weeks ago. Now, his ass is full of buckshot. So, the case is yours. Unless you want to go back to murders in RV parks?"

"No, Sir," McMannis jumped in quickly before his partner could object again. "We'd be happy to take this one."

"Pennsylvania," SAC Little explained, "appeared to be a local event. The Pittsburgh field office is leading the site analysis. But now we have a pattern across two major regions, so it's come to HQ. As I mentioned, we're short-staffed among our profile group, and folks have been called in overtime to handle background requests for Fowler's..." he paused, suppressing his gag reflex, "...for the President's administrative posts. I've assigned you as the Case Agent."

"Case agent, Sir?" McMannis stammered.

"Yea, don't screw it up and make me look bad. Coordinate with Ernest Frohm from the Dallas field office."

"Yes, Sir."

"Get on it. We're already way behind."

"Yes, Sir." The agents were confused whether to stay or go. When Cap turned his back, they slid out the door. McMannis knuckled the elevator call button, caught Roberts with a wry smile, and tapped a light soft-shoe into the elevator, excited for the opportunity.

Perhaps out of sheer luck or dumb coincidence, domestic profilers McMannis and Roberts were somehow assigned to the HQ Building: the J. Edgar Hoover on Pennsylvania Ave. For McMannis, the placement meant moving Julie and the kids and buying into an overheated D.C. housing market. The pay was only marginally better than the detective job back home. He asked to stay in Chicago. They gave him D.C. instead. Roberts asked for Philadelphia. They gave her D.C. as well, forcing her to leave little Charlie with Grandma back in Philly, battling the hellish traffic on I-95 for three-plus hours during the odd weekend off. But the wisdom of, and loyalty to, the Bureau is not to be questioned.

McMannis rationalized the D.C. placement, imagining an occasional elevator with top brass, an opportunity to get noticed. But it never worked out that way, his cases barely rising above *who cares?* And then, out of nowhere, like the last cherry on a slot machine, a terrorism case falls in their lap. A chance encounter to lead a national pursuit. He was elated, except for the fact he had to deal with Page.

Four floors down, McMannis and Roberts got off the elevator. The Dungeon. Formally known as Records. It smelled dank, the lack of sunlight immediately noticeable.

"Did you put a request in?" Page asked in his usual surly manner, barely looking up from his screen, dark hair hanging in his face, dozens of Fanta Orange cans stacked on his desk, his girth overwhelming the unfortunate chair assigned to him. Two cans fell to the floor exposing his nameplate: Laurence Page, Records.

"No, we just got the case, and came straight down," Roberts explained. "We're just getting up to speed."

"Yea," McMannis said as he threw a concerned gesture in Roberts' direction: *share less with the basement dweller.*

"You guys are lucky," Page commented.

"How so?"

"I heard Jacobs was forced into retirement. I'm guessing sexual harassment."

"Huh," McMannis looked over at Roberts, wondering if he's ever crossed the line, an inappropriate joke perhaps, or an overextended gaze as Roberts bent over in tight-fitting pants or knotted a dark bun of hair around a pencil during a late-night case review.

"Yea, huh," Page agreed as he piled three cardboard boxes full of files onto an adjacent table. "Cap told me you'd be coming. This should get you started," he offered before waddling back to his chair. "I'll have more for you in a few hours."

"OK. Can you send it up to Profile?"

"No. We're short-staffed. You'll have to pick it up yourself."

"Great seeing you, Page," McMannis responded sarcastically, picking up two of the boxes. Roberts grabbed the third.

"I miss you already, Homer," Page countered.

"It's Special Agent McMannis."

Page gulped a Fanta Orange and stared back as McMannis and Roberts got in the elevator. Once out of earshot, he responded.

"Whatever."


# Chapter 20. Reporting from West Texas

"Shit, it's crappy outside," Becker was talking to no one in particular as he pushed thru the apartment front door, wet and frigid, underdressed in a suit jacket and baseball cap. Nature was not cooperating. 45 degrees and slanting rain. He should have looked at the forecast this morning. Instead, he woke up late and ran out the door with spring fever. Returning in the evening, grocery bags in purplish hands frozen to monkey paws. He squinted past the hat pulled tight over his watering eyes, placed the bags down, and shook off the cold wet.

Zoe didn't bother looking up. Lying on the couch, homework and social networks competing for her attention. Her hair was piled haphazardly atop, dark wontons under her eyes, sweatpants and a dirty sweatshirt to match. The house was a mess, table and chairs barely cleared from last night. "You alright?" Becker asked, putting the groceries away. "You look like crap."

"I haven't been sleeping," she explained.

"School ok?"

Zoe feigned focus. "Math sucks."

"Yes, it does," he agreed, putting the groceries away.

"I can't solve these damn quadratic equations." She pulled the device to her lips, the amber light glowing brighter.

"Wish I could help."

"Then I have a big report on fossil fuel use for Environmental Science. Did you know greenhouse gas emissions have barely budged in over 30 years?" White plumes escaped her mouth. "They predict annual emissions will be exactly the same as 1990."

"Yep," Becker replied, the statistics all too familiar, pulling the compost bin to the fridge for efficient transfer. He tossed soggy spinach into the can, limp celery, and multi-colored cream cheese. His head popped out when the realization hit him. "I thought I said no smoking in the house."

She blew another hit in his direction. "I'm vaping."

His head bobbed in modest defeat as he went back to work, scoffing at the zucchini, now liquefied and pooling at the bottom of the vegetable compartment.

"So, I look like crap?" she questioned.

"No, I mean..." he said, discarding fur-covered olives. One bounced out as the compost skied past the too-small container. *Got it*, he muttered proudly, under the kitchen island, scofflaw olive in hand. He glanced back at Zoe and offered his palms to the ceiling. "Sorry... but it's true."

"I had a big fight with Travis. He says the breakup was my fault."

"Oh, the boyfriend." Becker nodded, the universe recognizable again. "You broke up?"

"Well, I don't know for sure."

"How long were you together?"

"We've been friends forever. But dating? Off and on for nine months."

"Hmmm. Welcome to relationship-land. It'll be alright," he dug deeper into the meat tray, pulling items of uncertain provenance. "No one stays with their first anyhow."

Becker turned on the TV, menu'd through the DVR recordings, and began the nightly ritual.

*"Good evening, I'm Wesley Brandt with CBC News."*

"How does he keep his hair so perfect?" Becker wondered aloud, trying to connect with Zoe. She didn't take the bait, nervously eyeing her phone instead. Becker went back to his task.

*"Today the Republican Senate confirmed the nomination of Susan LeBlanc as head of the Department of Energy."*

"Booo," Becker's voice echoed inside the fridge. He pulled out some lemons, now lime green in spots.

*"Ms. LeBlanc is the President's astrologist and cat-sitter. Critics claim she has no knowledge of the Department's focus: our nation's energy and nuclear weapons production systems. Nonetheless, the Senate confirmed Ms. LeBlanc's nomination on party lines."*

"The whole thing is a joke," Becker hollered past cartons of OJ and almond milk. No one was listening. Budweiser? How'd that get in here?  He found a Sam Adams behind an empty jelly jar and cracked it open. He looked back at Zoe, still lost in thought. "Everything else ok?"

"Should I just break it off with Travis completely?"

"Wait till it gets really painful," Becker advised as he sucked the foam from the bottle. "How bad is it, 1 to 10?"

"10 being painful?"

"Yea."

"I'd say… a 4. Or a 5."

"That's not bad. Most marriages start at 4. You contemplate divorce at 7. Cheating at 8. Murder at 9."

"Great, I can't wait. How 'bout you and mom?"

"We had some 9 moments," he said admittedly. "Some awesome moments too, of course." He gave a distant grin. "You and Travis argue?"

"Yea. I want to smoke and talk. He wants to drink and have sex."

"Sounds insurmountable," Becker replied, squinting back at the broadcast. "You should stop bathing and get a dog," he suggested. He searched backed for response. "Looks like you're half-way there."

*"In rural Texas, in what appears to be a potential terrorist activity, an oil drilling and processing system exploded, sending a giant fireball into the sky. The area is part of the Permian Basin, the most productive oil region in the U.S."*

"Very funny," she snorted, lowering the TV volume with one of the remotes stuffed in the couch cushions. "But *can* we get a dog? I saw the cutest puppy at that shop on 9th Avenue."

*"On the ground is CBC reporter, Angela Butler,"* Brandt continued, his audience barely paying attention.

"I stepped into that one," Becker muttered, imagining his punishment: 14 years of scraping dog shit off the sidewalk, daintily carrying turd-filled plastic bags in search of a trash can breaking the horizon. The crime: one hurtful joke. He raised the volume again.

*"Thank you, Wesley. I'm in Barnhart, Texas. Just before midnight last night, authorities believe, there was a coordinated attack on one of the area's many production facilities. Behind me, you can see smoke still rising from the damaged pipelines and nearby infrastructure. Those trucks,"* the camera focusing on the smoldering shells, *"carried fracking fluid and other flammable liquids. Local Police and federal law enforcement are investigating the matter."*

Zoe assumed the role of strangers on the street, leaning down to pet the imaginary beast. "Oh, what a good boy. What's your name? Dad, I know," she offered excitedly. "We can name him... Martian!"

"No thanks."

*"The damage appears to have been delivered by a long-distance weapon,"* the correspondent, explained. *"Authorities believe this could be the work of a new terrorist organization."*

"I know, we'll name him Asteroid," Zoe suggested, thumbing the remote between the couch cushions, the TV distancing itself. She jumped up and nervously rummaged the hall closet. There used to be an old tennis ball in there.

"Watching a lot of science fiction lately?" Becker questioned.

"Still not interested." Becker adjusted the side buttons on the idiot box, increasing the volume, only partly to fight off the puppy advances.

*"Just last week, an attack on a Pennsylvania car dealership left over a dozen large pickup trucks and SUVs were damaged. Wesley, as far as we know, no one has taken responsibility for either attack."*

"What about Ribbit?" Zoe's eyes lit with excitement, returning from the closet hunt unsuccessful. "A dog named Ribbit? That would be so cute. Come here, Ribbit,"

"It doesn't matter what we call him. If I have to clean up his puddles around the apartment..." Becker walked closer to the screen, taking in the wreckage. The footage panned. Firefighters hosed the final flames, a spaghetti dinner of twisted metal piping, a swirl of noxious fumes painting an early sunset of purple and black.

"You were saying," Zoe reminded him.

*"Angie Butler, reporting from West Texas."*

*"Thank you, Angie."*

Becker finished his thought as if the lines were fed to him. "I'd... commit hare kare like a Japanese warrior defeated in battle."

*"When we come back, a nun who coaches basketball for orphaned kids with a pretty good hook shot of her own."*

Becker hit the power button. The TV went black. "Wow, that's amazing," he exclaimed.

"I guess," she agreed succinctly. "What about it?"

"I'm not sure." Becker tugged at his earlobe, went back to his computer, and started typing.

# Chapter 21. Agent McMannis

Two days since the attacks in west Texas.

McMannis opened the suburban door, mayhem just over his shoulder. "Jesus, Julie," he barked back inside, "can you get these kids to bed?"

"Easy Homer," Sara Roberts said in the spring evening, dismay and chuckle spilling out. She was in jeans, a white blouse and hoop earrings. "You gonna let me in?"

"Sorry." He pushed a Big Wheel and some naked barbies out of view. The modest house a train ride away from D.C. was a stretch when the McMannis family bought it six years ago, just before the twins arrived. 16 months later, Rosie showed up, and they're busting at the seams.

Roberts craned her neck into the kitchen. "Hi Julie, how are you?"

Julie McMannis was washing dishes, earbuds in, singing out of key. Away from the tumult. "Hi, Sara. Working late, huh?"

"Yea. Can't talk about it though."

"I understand. *Official business.*"

"How's Rosie..." she stalled as Tommy and Phil Jr. tore after their little sister, Nerf guns in hand, a satanic wail resonating through. "...and the boys?"

"Still awake," McMannis answered, piercing his wife with an indignant eye. He scooped Rosie out of harm's way. "I'll save you." He kissed her brow, handed her off, and shook his head with exhaustion, happy to leave the chaos behind.

McMannis led Roberts to a back room, the *magnum opus*. She took in the landscape. Florescent tube fixtures hung unevenly from cheap chain. The far wall, a caffeine-inspired fluster, a mosaic of photos, articles, post-it notes. Connecting it, multi-colored string theories of personnel, actions, tactics, and philosophies. He turned up the space heater and closed the door.

"I converted my garage," he explained. They stepped over boxes of FBI records, piles of books. Two long folding tables supported stacks of paper; half a century of eco-terrorism evidence amassed. Empty coffee cups and a trash can full of bar wrappers competed for space.

"Been busy?"

"Cap Little hates me," McMannis shrugged. "I have to nail this one or I'm gonna be sent to records purgatory with Page."

"Don't be so paranoid. He hates everyone."

"You know anyone else he calls Homer?"

"No," Roberts agreed. "You better nail it."

After earning his bachelor's in criminal justice, Phillip McMannis thought his career was headed towards social work or bail bonds. Luckily, he met the girl of his dreams, or at least someone with deep family ties in law enforcement. Julie was the daughter, granddaughter, and sister of Chicago policemen. She hated the idea of her husband joining the force but he needed a job with health insurance. So he used his wife's connections and earned a coveted opening. The local beat was drudgery and he passed the detective's test as soon as he was eligible. It turned out his college education was a valuable supplement to his work, and he became the Chicago Police Department's top-rated investigator.

Eight years ago, at 35, he applied to the FBI and joined their Profiler department to find patterns across cases, clues in personality tests. But he never quite found his own footing at the Bureau, always a minute late to the morning briefings, less organized and disciplined than he pretended in the vetting process. Five years later, Roberts joined right out of graduate school and was teamed with McMannis as Unit 7 in the department, handling low-level cases: unsolved murders, missing teens, the leftovers after units with more seniority picked the good ones. The hours can be insane, the secrecy continuous. But there was an addiction to the culture.

"The movement starts decades ago. Greenpeace was the first formal entity," McMannis said as he pointed to the montage of photos and colored thread: green for Greenpeace (of course), red for Earth First!, yellow for ELF, blue for unaffiliated attacks. "Some of the founding fathers, here," he explained. Roberts studied the black and whites of Robert Hunter, Paul Watson, and others aboard a rusted tub docked outside Vancouver, Canada. The faces are laughing; harmony before the unexpected tumult ahead of them.

"It's 1971, the height of the cold war, and the U.S. government's planning a massive nuclear test on Amchitka Island at the western edge of the Aleutians." What started as close-cropped nostalgia, the 60s exploded like a firecracker in America's pocket: Vietnam, civil rights and civil disobedience, the Watts Riots, Abbie Hoffman and the Yippies, bedlam at the Democratic convention, MLK and RFK gunned down in less than a season. By '71, we lost Janice and Jim and Jimi to overzealous self-medication and scores of thousands in a place most Americans never heard of to fight communism on every front. Nuclear testing was another cornerstone to that effort, and the Feds and their scientists were planning a massive detonation on Amchitka Island, as far west as America gets, to test their latest toy and send a message of strength and determination.

"Alaska?" Roberts inquired.

"Yea. Practically Russia by then. These Greenpeace guys charter a tiny vessel, barely seaworthy," McMannis laughed at the amateurish effort. "It was supposed to be passive resistance. *Bearing witness,*" he finger quoted the air, "so they could impede the nuclear tests, afraid it may cause earthquakes, tsunamis. The whole world is watching. But they never make it that far, and the nuclear detonation goes as planned. Despite failing, they return to a hero's welcome, you know, sticking it to the man, half of Vancouver on the dock waiting, children holding signs, music, donations, the whole thing. Mid-70s, they take on the whaling industry." He points to another picture: rusting Soviet whaling ships surrounded by a crimson sea, a firehose of blood pouring out the overflow port, as blue and sperm whales were dragged into the vessel's hold for sawing and deboning. Another picture of Greenpeace members on small rubber rafts—Zodiacs, used in World War II—maneuvering in-between the whalers and their objective. "It was pretty fanatical at the time."

"I read it changed the way society views whales and whaling."

"Probably would have happened anyway," he rationalized.

Roberts held back a smirk. "But is it relevant?"

"Not likely. But you never know. Anyway, their success becomes a burden. At least 15 other groups co-opt the name GreenPeace. Internally, a fight for identity breaks out. Should we be conservative or radical? No one's really in charge. The group's a mess."

"Huh," Roberts mumbled, peaking at her watch.

"In '75, Edward Abbey writes the Monkey Wrench Gang. It glorifies eco-sabotage, or eco-tage. It becomes a tome for the movement." McMannis fingers the archaeological dig following a red tether. "1980, disillusioned Wilderness Society employees, an ex-Yippie, and a cynical BLM manager form Earth First!. In 1985, they create a blockade to the Williamette National Forest in Oregon, a BLM area set for logging. Essentially, a bunch of idealistic hippies."

"Maybe."

"Well, the Feds come in and eliminate the blockade in a day. So, they resort to more extreme tactics: tree stands, chaining themselves to redwoods and bulldozers, destroying equipment, spiking trees. By the late 80s, there's a clash between mainstreamers and more radical members, no real leader to define the mission."

"Sounds familiar."

"Yea, practically same story. There's a split in 1992. More militant members start the Earth Liberation Front, ELF."

"I read the file, Homer," she scolded, then found his disappointment. "Sorry... Phil."

"It helps to hear it again," he justified. "ELF spreads. Germany, Netherlands, Russia. They're in 12 countries. They vandalize McDonald's. Hunting towers in Germany and Netherlands. Pretty low-level stuff."

"So, Oregon is the epicenter here in the U.S.?"

"Yeah - starts with logging. They burn down a ranger station in an Oregon forest, the feds considered complicit in crimes against nature, I guess. On Columbus Day, 1996, they graffiti a McDonald's and another building. '504 Years of Genocide'. It was 504 years since 1492, and Columbus landing."

"I can do the math," she says.

"The bureau has tags on many of the key actors from that time. I asked Page to work up current bios anyway."

Roberts is exhausted. "I've gotta pack for Texas. We've got an 8 am flight."

McMannis ignores her and continues the history lesson he's gorged on all day. "Then the ELF gets busy. From '97 to '09, the FBI cataloged at least 87 separate events. They burn a new massive lodge, still under construction, at Vail, release minks and ferrets in Wisconsin, destroy a lumber company in Oregon, blow up a timber research facility, torch some pickups and an SUV in Pennsylvania."

"Pickups and SUVs in Pennsylvania? Like the first attack?"

"Yea. Back in 2003. But the guys charged with that are clean. First thing the bureau checked – they've relocated, have full alibis, lots of corroborating witnesses."

"Would have been too easy."

"Anyway, the FBI gets a break in December 2005. We arrest six individuals. One of them commits suicide. A couple of them help finger others. Most notably, Daniel McGowan gets 7 years and $1.9 million in fines. He was released in June 2013."

"Really?" Roberts asked, the suspect now obvious.

McMannis shakes his head. McGowan is the most-watched man in America. Clean as far as the FBI could tell. In fact, since 2009, not a single crime has been claimed under the ELF banner. The Kings of Clubs playing card didn't match any profile in the FBI's terrorism database. No initial leads.

"Did you work up a profile?" he asked her.

"First draft," she caveated before opening the file. "White males and females, 20-35, college-educated, not religious, underemployed, spend time outdoors, and have a history of activism." Roberts showed McMannis the computer printout, statistical analysis of each characteristic.

"That narrows it down."

"Yea," she scoffs, "if it's even accurate."

"Will help to get on the ground tomorrow."

Echoes of bloody murder drew closer. Phil, Jr. burst onto the scene with a deviant laugh, Nerf gun in hand. PJ hid behind the office door, planning his ambush. Twin brother Tommy, also armed to the teeth, was in hot pursuit.

"Tommy!" McMannis screamed, the inevitable chaos crystal clear. Suddenly, PJ snipered from his blind, the Nerf bullet finding the crinkle between Tommy's eyes. Tommy flung like an Olympic diver; a perfect back gainer, two and a half twist. The folding table and large file stacks never had a chance, the paper and hours of work flying in all directions.

Steam blew from McMannis's ears. "Julie!!"

"I better get going," Roberts said as she slipped out, a wry smile on her face, the carnage still audible in the crisp April night until the car door closed tight. She drove the quiet streets, back to her garden apartment in D.C., a short burst of giddiness escaping as she recalled that perfect moment of hell on Homer's face. Then it washed over her and the distraction turned somber. At a light, Roberts hit her speed dial's top number.

"You're calling late."

"I know," Roberts replied. "Can I talk to Charlie?"

"I finally got him to bed."

"Please Mom," Roberts cried. "I need to hear his voice." When she cracked the door, the boy was wide awake, hoping the late-night ring was the one he was waiting all day for.

"Hi, Momma!"

"Hi, baby. Are you being good for Grandma?"

"When are you coming home?"

"Soon, sweetie. Real soon."

# Chapter 22. Wheels in Motion

Shaggy's phone buzzed with a text.

"Fuck." Sleep had finally come. Turn over, fluff pillow, ignore. Incorporate into next dream. The phone buzzed again. "Fuckin' Fuck." A new message in WhatsApp. Shaggy logged in.

His eyes needed extra time to focus, discern reality from dream, contemplate the possible scenarios.

Yosemite Sam: *See the news?*
Shaggy: *Yea. Pretty cool*
YS: *Didn't mention the cards*
Shaggy: *They will*

Both deliberated, bathed only by the light of a phone in a darkened room.

Shaggy: *Can this wait?*
YS: *They scattered them, right?*
Shaggy: *Yeah – as instructed. Feds will figure it out*
YS: *Georgia next*
Shaggy: *Yep. Sunday*

Yosemite Sam paused, not truly certain of the security.

YS: *See you*
Shaggy: *Night*

# Chapter 23. Just Warming Up

The next day.

Phillip McMannis and Sara Roberts pushed past the congestion, the unmistakable sound of airport commotion, flight delays, unintelligible messages overhead. They flashed their badges and ID cards and were placed through an alternative screening process.
"I hate commercial flights," McMannis complained. Roberts rolled her eyes. *Yeah, you mentioned.*
Reagan National to San Antonio. They settled into their flight. Roberts opened her laptop, initiated the FD-302, other paperwork.
McMannis conjured on a thumbnail. "I was thinking about the King of Clubs."
"Domestic or international?"
"Looks domestic. International targets are higher profile. New York City. Planes. The Pentagon."
"Right." She paused for a second. "Do you think they're connected to ELF? Last known activity in 2009?"
"That's a long quiet period," he agreed. "Why resurface now?"
"Sleeper cell? A lone wolf with the same philosophy?
"ELF was always lone cells acting on their own. No central strategy or control. But attacks were followed quickly with a press release through a third party."
"The King of Clubs?" Roberts wondered. "Something in those playing cards."
McMannis had to admit: he was off-base when first meeting Roberts. *Cute girl*, he remembered thinking. *Probably not too bright. At least she's got a great ass.* After two weeks, he felt like the ass. She was bright. Hard-working and selfless too. She could also outrun him in a heartbeat. And somehow, managed to take care of herself, her mom, and little Charlie. *Where was the father? A busted condom?* He tried not think about it. It seemed to cross the line.

They touched down in San Antonio and headed to the cluster of rental car companies.

"May I help you?" the red-vested agent asked.

"I'll take the biggest thing you've got."

"We have a Chevy Suburban."

"Perfect," McMannis said, signing the paperwork. He avoided Roberts' stare until answering the obvious question in her head. "I'm not pulling in with a Ford Focus or some econobox. Frohm will be there, local law enforcement."

"So?"

"You don't get any respect in one of those."

"You *do* realize how stupid that is?" she asked. "You think Frohm will respect you if you're driving a Suburban?"

"I didn't say *that*."

"But he won't think you're a pussy?"

"Exactly."

"Men are so stupid."

"No argument."


The problem with Roberts, Homer thought to himself, is she looked great even before 8:00 in the morning. It made it difficult to keep his mind completely on the work. The errant brush as they clicked their seatbelts in place, the banter, the friendly jousting. He and Julie used to banter like that, before the kids and the mortgage and those Christmas trips back to Chicago to see her over-sized family, their number and pant size growing in every family portrait.

Three hours and twenty-three minutes, Google Maps tells them, if they take Texas Hill Country Trail to I-10 and then north on 163. The undulating landscape gave way to pancake-flat, trees to sparse shrubs. The oil rigs, however, grew taller and denser. Gasses were flared.

"Looks like the apocalypse," McMannis offered.

"Smells like the apocalypse."

"Smells like money."

"It's making my eyes water."

White piping popped out of the earth like prairie dogs testing for predators. Valves and cylinders, unmarked boxcars. Had McMannis and Robert been there about 36 hours earlier, they might have spotted Mo, Ian and Sammy hauling ass in the other direction.

They pulled into Barnhart, population 110, where they met the local sheriff, Special Agent Frohm and his cohorts from the Dallas office, refilled the tank, emptied their bladders, and grabbed some cheap snacks: mountain dew and pork rinds for him; vitamin water and kale chips for her. Back in the car, they followed the sheriff south on 163 and onto a dirt road.

"What were you talking to the gas station attendant about?" Roberts asked him.

"He was telling me about Barnhart. Used to be the largest cattle delivery spot in the country. Decades ago. Now it's all oil and gas. They use so much water fracking, that all the wells in town dried up a few years ago. The town and businesses have to truck water in now."

"Wow."

"Yea. And for every barrel of oil generated, they create another two to five barrels of *produced water*. Essentially, briny H2O full of chemicals. They have to pipe it out of here or dump it in lined pits. Most of the oil drilled from here actually goes for export: Asia, Europe, even the Middle East.

"You got all that information buying pork rinds?"

"Not bad, huh?"

After 10 miles of dust and rut, the convoy pulled to a low rise that overlooked a valley of drill sites. The initial gratification of escaping their cars quickly vanished, defending their noses as foul air hit their nasal passages. The sheriff pointed at the blackened site past a bandanna gas mask. "We calculated the shot: .61 miles."

McMannis grimaced behind binoculars, the wreckage still smoldering in the distance. "Find any shells?"

"None yet."

Ernest Frohm held up a plastic evidence bag. "Here's the playing card. It was hammered into the dirt here. You could drive past it for a week and not know. Some men drilling a new rig spotted it."

McMannis and Roberts took pictures, examined the card and dowel in their evidence bags. The Dallas agents completed tread analyses and soil samples. They searched miles of road for shell casings. Didn't find any but did recover some dog shit. McMannis placed it in an evidence bag. In all, it took four and a half hours.

Roberts looked at the sun, low in the sky, checked her watch, and broke the news to McMannis. "We're gonna need to stay the night."

"I figured. There's probably something in Odessa. Probably an hour away. Sheriff, can I borrow those binoculars again?" McMannis exhaled with concern.

"Homer, you ready?" Roberts asked him.

"Almost," he said, lips contorting in mental calculation.

"What's wrong?"

"Sheriff," McMannis pondered. "What's the value of the destroyed property?"

"Well, we haven't calculated all the rebuild costs..."

"Roughly."

"Let's see. Three separator tanks, piping, labor. Plus, all those trucks, the lost fracking fluid. I'd say 'bout ten million dollars."

"Why?" Roberts asked. "What are you thinking?"

"Well, even at $10 million in damage, that's still a pretty small site. We could've driven by it a dozen times and not paid particular attention to it."

"Yea? So?"

"Well, if they can hit targets like that, they can hit just about any site in the country."

"You think they're just warming up?"

McMannis pulled the binoculars down and handed them back to the Sheriff. He walked back to the Suburban and opened the door.

"Yea. That's exactly what I think."

## Chapter 24. Little Lion Man

April 14th, Good Friday. Four days after the attack in west Texas.

Zoe rang the Tribeca bell unannounced. Amelia's voice came through the intercom. "Hello?"

"It's me. Can I come up?"

"Sure," Amelia responded and buzzed her in. Her single mom was still at work, Dad across town in his bachelor pad.

Zoe entered the apartment like she's been there a million times, crashing in her bestie's room watching Criminal Minds or fuming late night about parents and boys. "Do you wanna get drunk?"

"I've got homework," Amelia shrugged.

"It's Friday, ya know."

"I know, but I'm behind in my science project."

"Me too, actually." Zoe's backpack thudded the coffee table. "Do you mind if I hang here a few days?

"No problem." Amelia put up some hot water for ramen, their favorite meal. She pursed her lips in Zoe's direction. "Everything ok?"

"My dad is off his meds or something."

"Your dad's funny."

"I guess." They opened textbooks and pulled out vapes, completing a practiced correlation. They studied for the time it takes to buy a slice of pizza before Zoe burst into anger. "I can't believe how we treat endangered species. Like it's just ours to play God with."

Amelia changed the subject, touching Mama behind Zoe's ear. "I love your tattoo. I wanna get one just like it. Does she give you peace and tranquility?"

"Not exactly," Zoe smirked.

"We should get matching ink. Maybe butterflies on our butts."

"I guess."

"Oh, I know! A Ms. PacMan but she's really a yin-yang symbol."

"I'm not sure..."

Amelia paused between slurps of noodles. "What's up with you lately?" she asked.

"What do you mean?"

"You've just been acting really weird."

"I don't know. Just feeling really stressy," Zoe offered.

Amelia dug into her mom's liquor cabinet, finding a cheap bottle of red in the back. She opened it and handed Zoe too generous a pour. She put some music on and before another slice could be served, they were over-singing Mumford and Sons' Little Lion Man.

By the time Amelia's mom came home from her nursing shift, Zoe was crashed in her bestie's bed, science book parted on the floor. The crinkled page was open to a morbid graphic, members of the animal kingdom, great and small, lost since the dawn of man.

# Chapter 25. Keep Up the Good Fight

Becker counted the pills as they spilled onto the herringbone tile. Now seemed as good a time as any. Five milligrams each. *20 should do it*, he narrated. *Make it 25, just in case.* He palmed the tinny buzz in his ears, the mosquitos apparently propagating, louder than any rock concert he could remember. *And chop them up in little pieces, so they hit the bloodstream quicker. No time for the body to reject them. Should take about ten minutes. OK, make it 30, and put it in a hot tea.* He got to his knees and found his reflection over the bathroom sink, hoping to reason with the lunatic screaming in his skull.

He groaned to his feet and hunted the apartment for validation. He rifled the back of the closet to find his anxiety treasure chest: an old shoebox hidden under out-of-style sweaters and wide, patterned ties of yesteryear. Inside, pictures of Amy and L.J. fighting the power, tripping in the forest; a pamphlet from the early environmental days; his grades from junior year, barely nudging his 2.8 average. A chuckle escaped as it all floated back to him.

Becker selected a major before even arriving at RSU, it all too clear computers were the future. Trouble was, by second year he hated the things, the bane of his existence, the root cause of night after sleepless night in the Comp Sci lab. All that time learning Pascal a waste, only a teaching language; he'd have to learn a million other tedious computing dialects in the real world. But mainly, it was the removal of it all, the hollowed-out souls staring in the dark at blinking screens. Where was the connection to nature, the planet? *That* real world.

Luckily the cute chick in Assembly Language kept him amused. "Zimmerman," he acknowledged her in class. "Becker," she acknowledged him back, her lip curling a bit in the corner. Her computer skills sucked almost as much as his, but he liked her company, giddy with exhaustion, late-night pizzas to keep the neurons firing a bit longer.

"There's an interesting meeting," Amy mentioned one full moon, both skulls lowered in coding position, an unused terminal between them.

"Yea?"

"It's an environmental group. Earth First! I think they're called." He looked over and saw her almond eyes smiling at him.

"Sounds cool." Anything, he figured, to spend more time with her.

They met in a darkened town park, a few other aimless recruits milling about, and followed a fading flashlight to an old prospector's cabin in the woods. It was just an introductory presentation, around campfire, the advocates sizing up the trainees' sincerity. True bona fides were down the road with tests of increasing loyalty. Becker spent half the time listening, the other half finding the flame flicker in Amy's eyes.

By the time he got back to his room, he was downright smitten. He'd construct excuses to go past her dorm, bump into her at a party, and finally found courage at the bottom of a fourth tequila shot one night. The relationship blossomed and they were joined at the hip. Or the pelvis, as the case may be. But when they got into that fight, drunk on sun and grain punch, ruining a killer party at a buddies' lake house, and then didn't talk for three weeks, it practically eradicated them both. It wasn't a perfect fit, that's for sure. There was volatility and a perfect loop of infinity to some of their arguments. But it was a love worth fighting for.

That summer he and Zimmerman drove up the coast, navigating narrow 101 past the massive logging trucks filled to brim, their Civic shuddering in invisible wakes. They camped on the beaches of Olympic National Park, blue-green waves tumbling into rocky sea stacks, walking for miles in one direction, then the other. They played in crystal-clear tide pools till sunset, cooked dinner by firelight, and sang songs till dawn. Not a hint of humanity as far as the eye could see, and the place couldn't be more perfect. Then they kayaked around the San Juan Islands near the Canadian coast. Becker and Amy tested the sea skills they learned reading  an old boating manual as rumors of orca sightings sifted through the windowed ferry cabin. From there, the Olympic mountains, snowball fights on the receding glaciers, the photos never doing justice to the majesty. They drove back to school tired, filthy, and more determined than ever to make a difference.

It was Natural Resource Economics, actually, first semester junior year that changed David Becker's perspective forever. The wilds were full of market economy. Supply and demand. Populations of predator and prey in a continuous tangent wave, a capitalism of life and death. Unfortunately, market and natural economics exchanged different currencies. Societal assets didn't properly appraise, couldn't properly appraise. Tragedy of the Commons, he dedicated his term paper to, when a resource was available to all without governance to allocate it for the long haul. There were plenty of examples to draw from: the atmosphere as a sink for man's waste, the seas a source of sushi until the last tuna is fished.

By junior year, their rank in Earth First! grew to something akin to corporal. Rallies in the forest, pictures with Edward Abbey after he signed Becker's copy of Monkey Wrench Gang. He and Amy tested the law and their bond, an eco spin-the-bottle. Truth or dare. The blockade on the forest road, practically goading law enforcement to arrest them. Playing lookout while Nils Jensen sugared the gas tanks of giant earthmovers. Then, the direct involvement, with a large hammer in hand, 12-inch nails in the other, spiking the trees they loved more than themselves, a gift of Russian Roulette for the lumberjacks and mill workers if they didn't heed the warnings. Once he crossed that line, sleep wasn't the same, interrupted with sweaty outbursts, pools of fear sopping the sheets, waking up in the small college apartment he shared with Zimmerman, his heart running a continual 100-yard dash. The police came by twice, even got a permit and turned the apartment inside out that one time, Becker and Zimmerman watching, handcuffed on the floor.

It was too late for Becker to change majors. Besides, he wasn't great at economics or anything. The next class was a disaster, barely passing, the text filled with indecipherable equations. He'd stay the course, finish the friggin Comp Sci. Amy switched majors, Sociology, somehow graduated on time, and moved to the city, to Fordham Law. Becker followed once he could scrounge up enough credits, to New York and law school as well. They were gonna figure it out together or die trying. A few years later, the wedding was small by any standard, the two of them at City Hall, only the judge, bailiffs, and a few other couples in line to congratulate them.

They honeymooned in Florida. It never sounded too impressive to their families, but they loved St. Augustine, America's oldest city, founded by the Spanish in 1565, more than half a century before the pilgrims took all the credit. The architecture, the massive stone fort, the Spanish Moss-covered Anastasia Island, all just a modest pedestal above sea level. Amy and Becker knew it could be gone in the instant of a decade or three, climate change and rising saltwater pushing it to the brink, to be swallowed one day.

Becker recalled the night Amy wore that white number that tied behind her neck, the candle flicker throwing prisms of red wine across the newfound tan of her shoulders. Dinner was followed by sex in the ocean, the newlyweds ecstatic to have crossed the threshold together.

By the time Zoe came along, the Beckers had gone full adulthood, eager for sippy cups and diaper changes. Their former lives were a distant memory, crimes limited to overdue electricity bills and stealing the neighbor's paper. She entered the world healthy and full of curiosity. A dervish in training pants, an all-consuming ball of flesh and piss and vinegar.

Becker closed up the shoebox and rambled back to the bathroom to find the cabinet doors ajar, the pills spilled across the herringbone tile. He reached for his phone and called the one number he could think of.

"Thanks for coming over," he exhaled 30 minutes later.

"No problem."

"I... I just need some company. And Zoe is non-existent these days."

"I'm here for you, man." L.J. stepped into the apartment, dropped his backpack, and folded his long arms over the short Jew as if aliens from distant planets were learning to embrace. L.J. scanned the apartment as he entered: floor grit noticeable underfoot, the Passover table as he left it days ago, an impromptu laundry pile in the living room, the counter speckled in coffee grinds.

Becker plopped on the couch and babbled an explanation. He was a pitchfork-wielding peasant fighting off a blitzkrieg. The President and his cronies were laying siege to every environmental protection: Bureau of Land Management and EPA rules designed to limit releases of methane; vehicle efficiency requirements; controls to prevent another Deepwater Horizon, the largest oil spill in human history.

L.J. wandered to the coat closet, found a broom and dustpan, and went to work.

"I don't know what's up with Zoe. I haven't seen her in days," Becker complained.

"Well, teenagers..."

"She can be really distant sometimes."

"I was the same in high school. Spent weeks on my friend's couch. Only went home to grab some fresh underwear."

"Me too," Becker admitted apprehensively.

L.J. motioned the broom and Becker lifted his feet. The prize: large bunnies of dust, errant snack mix, the cap of a now-defunct marker. He pulled it to a tight pile and gathered it in the dustpan. L.J. stood up and noticed the long-ignored titles on the extended shelving unit.

"You read all those?"

"Nobody reads books anymore. But once, sure, maybe."

L.J. pulled out Monkey Wrench Gang, searched behind the cover, and found the inscription. *To Dave, Keep up the good fight. Ed Abbey.*

"That was pretty cool, meeting him."

"Changed my life," Becker agreed, glancing him a knowing smile. "Tell me more about this screenplay," he suggested.

L.J. dispatched a laugh. It was nothing, really, just a way to poke at the election, all the insanity.

"Sounds fun," Becker confessed. "Maybe I can read it..."

L.J. wiped the counter. "Actually, Zoe has it."

"That's funny. She said you have the latest version."

"Maybe I do," L.J. suddenly recalled, his sponge corralling a herd of bread crumbs near the toaster. Becker thanked his friend, mentioning the craziness of his week.

"No problem," L.J. assured him.

"But it's all in there?  Abassi?"

"Yep," L.J. said with some reservation.

"The congressmen?"

"Yep."

"The sex scandal?"

"You gotta have a sex scandal, right?" L.J. reasoned. "Wanna watch TV?"

Maybe L.J. could stay for a movie, Becker suggested. Raiders?

Too long a commitment, L.J. smiled. How 'bout a Seinfeld on the DVR? The friends cracked a beer and watched re-runs, the zany foursome betting who could go longest without masturbating, Kramer losing in mere minutes. Before he knew it, the show was over and L.J. had to get home. Becker was alone again, the dust bunnies imperceptibly growing back to full size, the strange buzz of silence returning to his ear, a fold in time without the benefit of recollection. He couldn't remember what day it was, or even what he had for dinner. There was something about the screenplay Zoe and L.J. were writing together. It seemed so familiar. If only Becker could clear the fog of his own medication.

# Chapter 26. Through Thick and Through Thin

Late July 2016, One Week After Dr. Abassi Died

Just blocks from the Capitol Building, in a stately rowhouse, Ornette Schlesinger donned thick black frames to check his messages. "Damn them," he muttered under his breath.

Schlesinger shared the D Street residence with Landry Muldoon, Reid Johnston—the gregarious Speaker of the House, and other members of Congress, names withheld for discretion purposes. Monthly rent for Schlesinger's large bedroom, access to the grand dining room and kitchen, laundry and cleaning amenities provided 6 days a week by a live-in maid: $650 per month. Approximate market value: $4,900, all a supportive thank you courtesy the Faith and Freedom Foundation. He did have to make his own bed on Tuesdays, the maid's day off.

Roommate Landry Muldoon settled next to him, the leather couch creaking in dissent, and raised a concern, his accent drawn in Louisiana butter. "I see the Foundation is hosting a poker game at the Ralston tonight."

"Those dang fools have gotten themselves into some real trouble."

A few hours later, diminutive Schlesinger and massive Muldoon, guised in rain coats and dark glasses, quietly entered the ornate Lancaster room of the Ralston Hotel. Unnoticed, thankfully. Nathan Culp was waiting inside.

"You two look ridiculous," Culp commented.

Schlesinger found Culp from behind his Coke-bottle lenses and muttered something disapprovingly. He removed his overcoat.

Muldoon walked to the side mirror, produced a comb from his pocket, and straightened his coif. "Let us now praise famous men," Muldoon said, to no one in particular, as he aligned the last strays in the mirror.

"Ecclesiasticus, I believe," Schlesinger followed, guessing the origin.

"The old man is good. He knows his bible," Muldoon bellowed, pointing a portly finger, his mood lifting. "Even the Apocrypha. Impressive." He placed his briefcase on the table, opened it, and pulled folders aside: the pending farm bill, the quadrennial military analysis, air pollution legislation in need of derailment. Even before the unfortunate demise of Dr. Abassi, the Congressmen had an uncommon bond, a collective purpose.

Ornette Schelsinger looked on, waiting for his task, as Muldoon unearthed the cards and poker chips. Ornette organized the chips in colored stacks: blacks, $20; blues, $10; reds, $5.

Handsome Norman Radcliffe and Speaker Johnston entered next arguing about the Redskins terrible year, as choreographed, navigating through the kitchen via the back alley, also as choreographed. They closed the large wooden door and turned to the others, tension hanging like a wet cloth over a prisoner's waterboarded face.

"Where's Droburn?" Johnston barked.

"He'll be here."

"He better."

"The real question..." Nathan Culp suggested, "where is Ms. Archer?"

"Penny will not be joining us," Chad Droburn answered, his five o'clock shadow forty-eight hours past due, as he made his way into the poker room. The palace interior. "She ordered us rack of lamb and all the trimmings, so practically as good."

"We are going to be rack of lambs to the slaughter," Culp erupted with intensity.

"As a lamb to the slaughter," Ornette Schlesinger offered, "Isaiah 53:7."

"Not now, Ornette!" Culp screamed back. "Not tonight."

They were interrupted by the first servers, trays loaded heavy with Chateau Lafitte '87, shrimp cocktail, oysters on the half shell. The wait staff placed the appetizers down and paused at the discord. They had served the congressional poker game for several years, always a jovial event, tipped incredibly well for a few hours of service. The staff's only requirement: discretion. Johnston shooed the waiters out and closed the door.

The Congressman stood in silence, measuring each other's gaze, a ring of gunslingers in search of a twitchy finger.

"What the hell happened?" Culp whispered tensely.

Muldoon ambled to the trough and started grazing, washing oysters with the Lafitte. "Representative Culp," he bellowed, coming up for air. "Your decorum is unbecoming."

"Decorum?!" Culp's eyes bulged to the edge of his wire-rim glasses, his hair thinning as they spoke. "Gentlemen," Culp reminded them, "we have a dead scientist on our hands."

The men placed their bundles of cash and sat at the poker table. Only Johnston offered a shrugged response. "Things got a little out of hand."

"Out of hand?"

"They were only trying to scare him."

"Scare him? He was found hanging from the fire suppression system."

"It was officially ruled a suicide. The coroner confirmed it."

Culp was incredulous. "It looks quite suspicious. What if someone was caught on camera? Droburn, what happened?"

"My man Bucksworth and the Foundation's intern were handling it," Droburn said between gulps of bourbon. "But it went awry."

"Awry? So they came in like thieves in the night, and what? What happened?"

"Thessolonians!" Ornette was on Bible Jeopardy fire. "Like thieves in the night," he repeated and raised his hands in glory, giving Muldoon a high five.

"Schlesinger!"

"Gentlemen," Radcliffe tried to ease the tension. "I suggest we do not waste this lovely occasion." He placed his hand on Culp's shoulder. "Nathan," he offered, "we will get through this. Through thick and through thin, right?" Old Man Schlesinger bit his tongue even though he knew the answer.

"Through thick and through thin," they all repeated. Just then, the waitstaff opened the door cautiously. Johnston waived them in. Plates piled high with rack of lamb, brushed with olive oil, rosemary, and garlic, grilled to perfection. They placed the steaming plates in front of the Congressmen. Sides of hot rolls, roasted asparagus, and red jacket potatoes topped with whipped butter.

"Pard'n my reach," the large Muldoon stretched across the table. The men paused for a moment, salivary glands firing, as the lamb steamed up. They dug in with abandon, complementing the meat, the '87 Lafitte, the buttered red jacket potatoes.

All but Nathan Culp. The Pennsylvania congressman sat staring, flipping the lamb onto its side, turning the potatoes over and over. Beads of sweat conjured on his forehead.

"It's a sin to waste food," Schlesinger prompted him.

"It's going to come out," Culp insisted.

"That reminds me," Muldoon agreed. "We should get some doggie bags for the leftovers."

"We're doomed."

"Nathan," Reid Johnston got his attention, looking deep into his soul. "Can you pass the asparagus?"

Old Man Schlesinger sipped his bourbon between bites and found Culp behind thick glass. "And please shut up," he chastised. "You're ruining our meal."

# Chapter 27. Sammy

Skirting Houston and its tentacles of development, the red Tacoma swung south to Sugarland and Pearland then back north and east on I-10 again. At Beaumont, a hard right, south to Nederland and Port Arthur. Tall marsh grass and oil tanks competed for attention. At the Gulf of Mexico, they crossed the state line and turned left onto Louisiana 82, due east along the coast. The Cajun Riviera. Modest dwellings painted salmon and robin-egg blue propped on 10-foot stilts. RVs lined up along Brant Street, a stone's throw to the beach in Cameron.

"Good to be home," Mo said as he drove past slowly.

"How far is your sister from here?"

"Couple of hours, if that."

The boys needed to stretch their legs, find a bathroom, wash off the grime. Unfortunately, there were not a lot of public resources, as it were.

"We'll have to use the ocean," Mo surmised. "You got swim trunks?"

"Think I left 'em in Pennsylvania."

"Well, it's pretty quiet here," he said, parking across a deserted section of road, far from prying eyes. The haze offered a welcome relief from the midday sun.

Mo excavated his body from the driver's seat with a familiar groan playing accompaniment like a foghorn in the distance protecting the tankers from grounding. Ian pried his seat forward. Sammy jumped out, raised his right hindquarter, and offered his name, rank and serial number to the low scrub by the side of the road.

The men dropped down to skivvies, ambled across route 82, another patch of scrub, and then a thin sugary beach that marched closer to the road every year. A low wood and wire fence protected the ocean lazily as if the guards have given up. Ian picked Sammy up, placed him on the sea-side of the barrier, then carefully stepped over himself. "Don't get your bandage wet now," he instructed. The dog pretended not to listen, moseying the water's edge.

Mo's large frame stepped over without much hesitation. He let his drawers fall to the sand and waded in.

"Jesus, Mo," Ian searched nervously east and west on 82 to see if cars were coming.

"The human body is to be celebrated, Ian," Mo countered, now knee-deep. "In its natural state. As God created us."

"I guess." Ian stepped slowly into the water, wishing it was warmer. "But I'm keeping my underwear on."

"Suit yourself," Mo said, stepping further out, the water slowly obscuring his privates.

Sammy ran from the wave's low break, unsure of its intention. He had never experienced the ocean but immediately took to it, the way dogs do. He ran along the shore on a quest. A bark in search of a reason. Always the explorer, Sammy was. Six months ago, bored as Shakespeare in the Park droned behind him, he wandered from his owner. Pizza, his snout counseled him, was in striking distance. Maybe dessert too. Instinctively, he turned away from the policeman, over a schist outcrop, one of many in Central Park. Out of sight, on the run. Now, new masters to ignore, at the southern edge of landmass, he rifled east along the Gulf of Mexico in search of his destiny.

Ian followed Mo further out. Like Sammy, it too was his first experience of the ocean's splendor. The light sting of saltwater reminded him of a cut on his ankle. A silvery shad, once thick in these waters, scurried out of the way. With each step, an inch deeper until he met Mo where the water splashed at their rib cages.

"Feels good, huh?" Mo proffered.

"Yea, once you get used to it."

Mo dove into the water gracefully, his ass bearing witness to the Louisiana sun as it melted the haze and offered its warm embrace. He stayed low to the bottom, swam back, and grabbed Ian's ankle like a beast from the watery deep. He resurfaced to see his friend's reaction.

"Don't scare me like that!"

"Ya gotta get your head wet."

"I... I ain't a good swimmer, Mo."

"Here, I'll hold you. You just drop your head back. Just trust me." And Ian did, leaning back awkwardly until the cool water found his hairline.

Farther up the beach, Sammy found something of his own: a dead crab pushed past the whitewash. He darted at it and pulled back, testing its powers, barking a mystic language he believed all animals, dead or alive, communicated in. He decided he needed a sidekick of his own, and adopted the crab for safekeeping, something he liked to do back then, before he met the men who brought him here. As far as Sammy could remember—and comprehend one thing from another—he lived in the suburbs of a large city. Snarling at that loud contraption that made the grass shorter, baying at the window when that man in blue brought the letters every day. The world was a confusing but wonderful place. Upon the ding of the toaster completing its mission, he'd pounce on anything in range including his poor submissive brother, like a prizefighter coming out for the final round, his owner punishing his behind in response.

Then one night, in the park, Hamlet annoyingly questioning to be or not to be, Sammy's life changed drastically. Tangling with his brother, wine and pasta salad tumbling across the picnic, Sammy was released from his leash amid cries of frustration. He wandered from the rage in quest of food and affection. The last of sunset disappeared and everything was painted in an unfamiliar hue. In the distance, he recognized a trash can leaning with goodness, its contents overflowing like a cornucopia, and rummaged for sustenance. An unaccustomed hand startled him, but it quickly found the places that made Sammy happy.

"What's your name?" the human asked him before removing the strap about his neck. "What a good boy you are," and he kissed Ian's face for the first time. And just like that, he belonged to another human. Two humans, in fact. More confusion and wonderment. The smaller one offered food, so Sammy went to him with hunger. The larger one, discipline, so he slept at his feet. They gave him a new name, scribed on shiny metal in the shape of a cartoon bone, and from then on he answered to it: Sammy, uncertain to its meaning.

Sammy barked at a wave when it came higher than the others, bewildered. Then from above, he felt another unacquainted hand...

"Have you seen Sammy?" Ian wondered, looking back at the beach.

"Not lately," Mo replied, still rejoicing in the waters, when a thought drifted across his mind. "Don't say nothin' about Pennsylvania and Texas to Jenny when we see her. Or the 50. Nothin."

"I won't. Jeez," Ian said defensively.

"We're just on a little trip. Wanted to see where I grew up, is all."

"Don't worry. I *ain't* stupid."

Mo stayed silent, uncommitted to that statement's accuracy. Just then, a squad car pulled slowly down Louisiana 82. The vehicle stopped and the cop gave a quick pull of his siren to get the men's attention. Thirty yards out, waist-deep in the ocean, at or near naked, Mo and Ian gave each other an uncertain glance. Nowhere to run. Caught with their pants down. They waded slowly back to a well-fed cop, his brows askew with reprimand, uncertain whether to raise their hands.

"No swimming here, boys."

"Yes sir," and they walked back the shallow shores, Ian in his wet cottons like a sodden loincloth, Mo in all his intended glory.

"And definitely no skinny dipping," he raised a hand, obscuring Mo's birthday suit from view.

"Yessir," they answered, wandering onto the beach. Mo's beard dripped with seawater as he struggled with his Fruit of the Looms.

The cop gave them a cockeyed stare, straight into their souls. "You boys lose your way?" He walked back to the squad car, steel cage separating the rear compartment.

Ian walked forward in mild panic. "We ain't done nothin'. Maybe there's a fine we can pay."

The cop threw them a look as if Mussolini asked St. Peter to get past the pearly gates. He opened the black and white's back door, the one emblazoned with shield and Louisiana's silhouette. Mo bowed his head in submissive guilt, visualizing his future: roadside cleanups in striped pajamas, shiv-carrying enemies hiding in the laundry, a meatless gruel somehow called pot roast.

Just then, Sammy jumped out and the cop's face converted to something approaching a smile. "This your dog?"

"Sammy!" Ian ran forward and offered his hand over the low wire fence.

"Don't want nobody stealin' a nice dog like that."

"No sir," they wheezed.

"Lucky for you boys, the only thing I hate more than skinny dipping hippies like y'all, is paperwork. Nasty stuff."

"Yessir."

The cop looked around to take in the scene. There were reports of vagrants in the area, illegally camping on private property, disturbing the law-abiding folk. The dirt-encrusted Tacoma sat across the street, Texas plates barely visible behind the muck.

"Is that your truck there?" he asked, picking Sammy up with a friendly scratch under the muzzle.

"Yes sir."

"I'll just stick him in there, seeing he doesn't have a leash and all."

Mo, paralyzed with dumbfound, watched the cop waddle across narrow Louisiana 82, Sammy under his arm, when it hit him. The debris from weeks of accumulated travel, the .50 in the Pelican, the AR in the soft shell, the case and a half of ammo, the short red duffel with wads of cash under the driver's seat, a stolen license plate or two, maps of Pennsylvania and Texas—notated and highlighted with strike directions and egress routes, the paramilitary library on the rear floormat: *The Guerilla Sniper Tactics Handbook*; *The Complete Illustrated Handbook of Survival*; and *Left of Bang: How the Marine Corps Combat Hunter Program Can Save Your Life*. It was all a prosecutor's dream, the jury needing the duration of Johnny Cash's Folsom Prison Blues to consensus around life sentences.

The men jumped over the low fence and bare-footed the hot asphalt just before the officer could open the door.

"I'll take him," Mo wrestled the dog away. "He's got an awful mean streak."

"Seems real friendly to me."

"Nearly bit a child's finger off one day," Mo's eyes bulged with emphasis.

The cop looked at Sammy, his tongue panting with faux innocence. "Best keep him on leash then."

"Yessir."

"You boys have a good day."

Mo and Ian redressed in the low scrub and got back in the Tacoma. The cop out of view, Sammy on his lap, Ian opened the glove box to find a flask of Tequila. He took a swig and handed the bottle to Mo. "That was close. What would you've done if he opened the door?"

Sammy, too, was curious and awaited the answer, tongue out, left ear drawn high. Wedged under the windshield, Mo found his bible and flipped the pages for guidance. "Well on one hand, we're told: *Put your sword back in its place… for all who draw the sword die by the sword*. That's from John."

"Uh-huh," Ian and Sammy replied, still tremoring with baptism and near-ensnarement.

"On the other, *Praise be to the LORD my Rock, who trains my hands for war, my fingers for battle*. Psalms, 144."

Mo started the Tacoma and headed east to Jeanerette, his roots, as the party deliberated in silence. As far as Ian and Sammy were concerned, that sure didn't answer the question. In fact, the thought of turning that page downright scared the bejeezus out of Ian.

And Mo? He still had some explainin' to do. Did the bible preach vengeance or mercy? Retaliation or forgiveness? It depends where you open it, he figured. But for now, he just drove. The backway, past the Cajun Riviera and the wildlife refuge as the sun's declining vector shimmied off the grass, the land and water as continuous as could be. Burnt orange filled his rearview mirror as he nearly caught up to his past.

# Chapter 28. The Old Oak

Saturday, April 15th. Five days since the last attack.

Before bestie Amelia could arise, Zoe tiptoed out of the bedroom and down the stairs, onto the streets, as Tribeca lazily woke to a Saturday, barely a siren in the distance.

Walking north up the west side, she spotted the entranceway to the High Line. What was once an elevated rail line had been converted to a calming pedestrian oasis above the city. Stopping at a picnic bench, she rummaged through her backpack, found some foiled chocolate and fig bars well past their due date, and had an impromptu breakfast, there overlooking West 14th Street, next to the old train tracks the High Line was constructed from and flower boxes filled with natural grasses. She could still see her breath in the morning cool, looking east, a blushing sunrise cascading down the shop windows.

Six years ago today, her mom passed. Zoe can still remember the moment: her dad answering the 3:30 call, a 4:00 a.m. Uber back to the hospital, her mom's vitals crashing without warning. Amy was dead by the time they arrived, the goodbyes and *I love you*'s thoroughly incomplete. Zoe just cried, inconsolable for days.

She found her vape in her backpack's front pocket and stared at it, knowing what her dad would say. "Mom died of lung cancer and you're going to put that shit in your body?" *Mom died of lung cancer and she didn't even smoke, so what's the point, old man?* she argued back in her head. She tossed the vape back in her bag and shook her head in frustration.

A text from Dad came through. He suggested they stop by the crypt where mom's remaining ashes sat. A barely-noticeable plaque commemorated her existence in the smallest way imaginable. Some visits, they could barely find her. It was all too depressing that a life's mark on the world could be summed in the engraving of 6"x12" piece of granite. *Amy Lynn Becker*, it read, *1965-2011. Loving Mother, Wife, Citizen.*

Zoe ignored her dad's text, shook off the guilt, and kept moving, finding a strange newness in the architecture, facets she never noticed before. Her Chuck Taylor's carried her north when several important facts dawned on her. First, that chocolate. The stuff at the bottom of her backpack? Apparently, that was laced with weed. Pretty strong stuff too, based on the way her feet flopped on the ground, like a seal clapping for attention before a throng of theme park tourists. And that way she could serpentine past the other New Yorkers, banking into turns, hands extended like wings on a fighter jet. Not exactly what she was planning on for today, but worse things have happened.

Next, she realized, she wanted to be under that oak, the large-limbed beauty in Central Park where at just six months, she squealed on the blanket and pulled at her mom's locks. The one they'd picnic under time and again, and finally scattered most of Amy's ashes. When that hit her, the wings folded in, the walk became more purposeful.

Up 10th Avenue, the energy of each city block pleated onto itself. Cuisine, fast and slow, from every corner of the globe. Starbucks and shoe stores. Diners and massage parlors. This one used to be a book store, that one a pharmacy. Down 39$^{th}$, she saw a familiar face walking out of a small red-brick church called Holy Redeemer. It was L.J. She'd recognize that tall black frame a mile away, let alone across the street.

"Hey," she said.

"Hey," he replied, peering over his shoulder at the church, then down the street, and finally back to his favorite teenager.

After a quick glance to see if it was clear, she crossed to his side. "What are you up to?" she asked.

"Just helping with some deliveries. Big weekend for us. Good Friday yesterday. Easter coming up."

"This is the church, where you work?"

"This is it," he said. He noticed that look on her face. "What?"

"I don't know, I just pictured it differently."

"More radical?" he laughed.

"I guess so." Zoe imagined the parishioners, lining up for the Eucharist, a sacrament, a sip of wine, and a hushed whisper of rebellion. She hesitated the way a deer pauses in the woods, ears elevated for the sound of distant footfall. "Mom died today. Six years. I'm walking to Central Park. You wanna join?"

He took her in cautiously, the way he does. "Sure."

They found themselves telling stories, like the first time L.J. had to change Zoe's diaper, the item bloated with pee, poop seeping out the leg gatherings. He still had nightmares about that one, he chuckled, Zoe snort-laughing in response. It reminded L.J. of Amy's hoot, so unpretentious. The conversation segued to Amy's pecan pie, probably the best in New York. L.J. could see the sadness creep up on Zoe's face, and asked if she was o.k.

Zoe shared that she was really high from the chocolate, deceived by its innocent appearance in the morning light.

It reminded L.J. of the Oregon woods, where he and Becker and Amy first consumed marijuana other than by smoking it. He knew Zoe needed his company, the moment heightened and fragile, an emotional high-wire act.

Solace, Zoe would find, came once the din of 59ᵗʰ street faded away, the sound and smell and enriched oxygen of Central  Park embracing her fully.  They located the old oak, just under the ESSEX sign protecting the greenspace, along the windy path. Light filtered through the budding leaves, and they found a patch of grass in the sun, dry enough they decided, to take it all in without getting damp rear ends.

Zoe stared at the tree as if it communicated through dimensions, somehow personified everything that is good. She pulled a few daisies, placed the bunch next to the oak's trunk, and sat back next to L.J. He held her hand and she quietly held back her tears. Her lips quivered, first in sorrow, then with anger so pure it could tumble the walls of Jericho.

"You see that thing in Texas?" she asked.

"I did," he responded.

"Those bastards are gonna pay," she said, still staring at the old oak.

# Chapter 29. Wikileaks

September, 2016.  About two months after Abassi died.

"Congressman, Congressman!"

"No questions now. I'll have a full statement later." Photogenic Norman Radcliffe pushed past the crowd of microphones, hoping to skirt the Capitol's open hallway where the press gathered for crumbs of insight from their elected leaders. The heat from the camera lights, the adrenaline, four cups of coffee by 8:30 a.m., constant meetings since a 3:30 a.m. wake up call. The Oklahoman perspired from every pore. His tie askew, bags under his eyes, teeth still not brushed, he was poorly prepared for the storm to come.

"Congressman!" someone yelled. The press saw blood. They had a monster on their hands, a gift from God, the holy grail. "Sir, when did you hear about the email leak from Paradise, the escort service?" Radcliffe pressed on. Another reporter jumped in. "Congressman, how often did you visit prostitutes, Sir?"

Unwavering to his destination, staff of nine in tow, he sliced through the crowd.

"Does your wife know?"

"Will she be asking for a divorce?"

Radcliffe recalculated, fists clenched, not sure how to react. With denial? An unconcerned laugh? Violence? Hours of prep were about to go up in flames. His staff nudged forward but his feet anchored him, like an unnecessary mob boss, as if in concrete. His voice frogged up with excess mucous, beads of sweat fell from his chin. "Now, hold... hold on!"

Cameras clicked, high-powered lights came to life, the world zoomed in on the Representative, the Chair of the powerful Ways and Means Committee.

"Congressman Radcliffe will make a full statement shortly. Until then, no further questions," Leah Hand, his Chief of Staff barged in. A bulldog in a business suit, perfect legs in knee-high stockings, Ms. Hand's momentum carried the legislator and his team headlong. "Congressman, this way," she motioned, thru the House rotunda, beyond the press access point, past the stone-faced Capitol police.

A few last questions while the Congressman was in earshot.

"Sir, did you use campaign funds for your visits to Paradise?"

"Congressman Radcliffe, do you know of other politicians that use escort services?"

"Congressman! Congressman!"

Radcliffe paused as he gazed back at the throng of reporters, lips quivering with revenge. Leah Hand swooped in again, steering him to safety. Down the hallway, past the portraits, famed assemblymen of yore, where Radcliffe fancied his picture sharing the esteemed marble walls with Thomas Jefferson and Henry Clay. *Now what?*

"It'll blow over," Radcliffe offered his staff procession.

"Maybe hell will freeze over," Leah Hand offered back, avoiding the Congressman's gaze.

House Majority Leader Reid Johnston was waiting in his office. Radcliffe led his cohorts in, his skin a greenish hue. "Jesus, Norman," Johnston said, "you're 45 minutes late."

"We were strategizing with major donors," Leah Hand offered. "The Foundation is available with resources when called."

"It's all over the news," Johnston thumbed through three TV screens against his office wall. The Echo Chamber, he liked to call it. The staffers pulled chairs around, frankly discussing openings on the Hill, how this scandal differs from the Jessica Cutler disgrace of 2004, the Spitzer disaster in 2008.

"Shhh, y'all," Johnston hushed, turning up the volume as CBC News filled the room. Daytime anchor Dan Blackburn:

*"According to our initial review of the seventy thousand emails placed on Wikileaks, the clientele of Paradise included at least two Congressmen—Republican Norman Radcliffe of Oklahoma and freshman Democrat Nicholas Constalletti of New Jersey—numerous foreign diplomats, and several famous businessmen. With us is Washington, D.C. correspondent, Jacqueline Ingram."*

The screen split in two, adding Ingram in foreground, Capitol dome in background.

*"Jacqueline, what can you tell us about the emails?"*

*"Dan, there were literally thousands of exchanges between the escort service and their clients, mostly very cryptic, sent from anonymous email accounts. But two Congressmen transmitted the emails from their personal accounts, providing damaging insight into their sexual activity."*

The anchorman could barely contain the smile on his face.

*"So, we only know of two Congressmen? There could be more?"*

*"Yes, that's right. As the press and the public digs into this scandal, it could go deeper... er... things are still unfolding quickly. It*

*does appear that Congressman Radcliffe was quite taken with one escort he refers to as Desiree."*

The room gasped. Radcliffe dug his fingers into his scalp, blood rising to the surface. "How is Fox News handling it?" he blurted out, urging a channel change.

"Shhh," House Leader Johnston silenced him, pupils bulging with intensity.

*"That's extraordinary, Jacqueline,"* the CBC anchor responded.

*"Extraordinary indeed, Dan."*

*"When we return, more on the Paradise Sex Scandal..."*

# Chapter 30. The Apology

Three days after that fateful revelation, when news of scandal opened wide on the prairie of American media, the starting gun to constant chatter from every corner of the cable box and Twitter influence, Becker yawned with exhaustion and searched for additional flecks of disgrace in the gold pan of his cereal bowl at the kitchen counter on 22$^{nd}$ Street. That morning, in his bathrobe, crumbs of sleep still in the corner of his eyes, he raised his right hand, pointed to the TV and hit the power switch on his remote. As the screen came to life, the colors saturating, the volume awakening like the first birds testing the sunrise, Congressman Norman Radcliffe stepped to the microphone.

Radcliffe's wife stood stoically to his left, seemingly holding her decorum. The children, off to her side, held still as well in uncommon torture. To Radcliffe's right, his Chief of Staff, Leah Hand, fellow Republicans, well-wishers and campaign boosters, vigilantly balancing somberness and defiance. The staging, the choreography, now set. Queue the lights.

"Fellow Christians, members of the public, family, friends, colleagues," Radcliffe paused with well-practiced humility, scanning the distant shores of familiarity among a blank sea of eyeballs. "I want to take this opportunity to apologize for my transgressions, for any humiliation I have caused, any disappointment I have created." *Good start*, Becker thought to himself.

"I am a very lucky man," Radcliffe continued, "my beautiful wife and children supporting me in my time of need." Radcliffe looked down momentarily, his wife's knuckles turning white, a freshly manicured thumbnail jammed into opposite hand, nearly breaking skin. He soldiered on.

"To my fellow Republicans by my side, my dear family, neighbors and constituents, sharing their mercy with me, from the bottom of my heart, I thank you. As the Apostle Paul spread the teachings of Jesus Christ, he wrote an epistle—a letter—to the Ephesians. In the letter, Paul said Christ commanded: 'Be kind to one another, tenderhearted, *forgiving* one another, as God in Christ forgave you.' And so I ask of you, please forgive me, for I have sinned. I am but a humble man who seeks to serve."

The uncertainty in the room was palpable, the gathered bewildered. *Was that it?*

"Thank you, very much," Radcliffe clarified. That *was* it. He and his supporters conducted a sharp right face, dual file configuration worthy of a Marine unit. Exit stage left. Leave no man behind. The audience stunned, the press disoriented; they could barely fire off a question.

"Congressman Radcliffe, can you offer the identity of Desiree?"

He leaned back to the microphone, still working on his egress. "I'm sorry, no questions at this time."

"Sir," another reporter shot in, "should Polly Townsend go to jail?" *Madam* Polly Townsend, that is, the now-infamous former prostitute and proprietor of the Paradise Escort Service. She had more dirt on D.C. than a gravedigger, which is exactly how Congress saw Polly if they weren't careful.

No response.

"Sir, did you use campaign funds for your visits to prostitutes?"

No response.

"Do you plan to resign?"

Again, nothing.

"Congressman, one of the emails indicates the bill was paid for by a third party, someone named P A."

Radcliffe stared back, a deer in the headlights. His family and colleagues stood in mid-step, stage curtain half parted, uncertain whether to keep time with the Congressman or leave him to fight the enemy alone. The room was dead silent. He made his way back to the microphone awkwardly, leaning in from the side as if afraid of its power. He opened his mouth to answer but only a loud shriek of feedback filled the void.

Becker watched eagerly from the kitchen counter, the press conference getting more interesting.

"The Congressman has not seen the email you are referring to," Leah Hand strode in, the Lone Ranger, the Army Ranger, knee-high stockings still standing at attention, and took control of the situation. "We're reviewing the emails and will come back with a statement on that particular message. Thank you for your patience and respect for the Radcliffe family in this difficult time."

One week later, Radcliffe's junior aide Paul Anderson resigned in disgrace. A nondisclosure agreement and six-figure sum were transferred to the young man in the form of a scholarship, tax-deductible of course. Paul returned home to complete his undergraduate degree in Religious Studies from the University of Notre Dame. He has not made a public statement since.

The country moved on. There was an important election to follow. Samantha Barnstable could be America's first female President. 228 years. Can you imagine?

For Norman Radcliffe, it was a very large bullet dodged, an unexpected hole in his trousers the only apparent damage. He had his own election to worry about. Sure enough, his wife and children watching vigil from his side, he campaigned with forgotten vigor across central Oklahoma, claiming he was a better man for falling as he did, with renewed purpose to his work.

# Chapter 31. The New Project

September 2016. One week after the Apology that subdued the Paradise Sex Scandal.

The TV was on, textbook in her lap, snoring out loud, when Becker ran thru the door, keys on the kitchen counter, jacket off, sleeves inside out, draped over the kitchen barstool. "Hey," he said.

Zoe stirred awake, cushion crease lining her face. "Hey yourself. What's all the excitement?"

"Got a new project."

"I didn't know you could move so fast."

He scurried to the back office, opened his computer, and flicked it on impatiently. Most days, Becker entered the front door with the enthusiasm of roadkill. Today, his butt was on fire. "How was school?" he asked obligingly. "11th grade. Big year."

"Don't remind me." Zoe wandered to the study, leaning on the door jam. Curiosity kills the teenager. "Everything ok at work?"

"Yea. Not really work-related. More of an extracurricular thing." Becker scratched his head and rubbed at his eyes, the mating call before research.  Becker waited impatiently for the computer to boot up. He offered Zoe some small talk to pass the time. "So, first weeks of the semester?  Any classes you hate yet?"

"Just one."

"That's not bad."

"The others ok?" Becker asked, eyes affixed to the booting screen, searching for the knife edge between parenting and annoying.

"I guess. I joined the Climate Club at school. We're gonna put on a play about the planet."

"Interesting."

"Not really. It's pretty frustrating actually. As if that's going to do anything," Zoe scoffed. "So, tell me more about this *project* of yours."

"You know the sex scandal?"

"Yea."

"Well, all those emails are on Wikileaks."

"Really?" She retrieved a barstool from the kitchen and shoved a little space for herself, elbowing Becker over. He paused to give her a contorted look, opened up the Wikileaks page, and scrolled down to find the Paradise Sex Scandal. File size: 3.2 GB. 72,000 emails. Zoe's eyes widened like the archeologist in the living room. "Cool."

"Really cool," Becker agreed. He clicked on the link, then another, the hard drive coming to life with the sound of a massive download, a Hoover of information. Becker watched the icon spin, the percentage bar rising.

"I'd love to get more of those Congressional bastards."

"Well, time's a-wasting," Zoe said, searching the screen for a riddle's answer.

Becker chuckled at her impish curiosity. "Ok, let's start from the top." He opened the documents: cryptic conversations, dates, anonymous email handles. This is going to be harder than he imagined. BearHug was a frequent solicitor - who could that be? He liked tiny girls, less than 100 pounds, no tattoos.

Another customer, ATLAS: *Katrina begs for it. Is she available?* ... *Sorry, Katrina doesn't work here anymore. I'm sure Amber will beg for it too*, the escort service offered back.

"Wow," Zoe said, enjoying the moral deficiency in others. "Men have a lot of issues."

"You have no idea." He searched for the Democrat, Constaletti, and found 17 emails. There are six types of sexual addiction: biological, psychological, spiritual, trauma-based, intimacy anorexia, and mood disorder. Constaletti had at least three of those on any given day. He was a junk-food junkie in a candy store. Or perhaps more accurately, a sex addict in a whorehouse, hundreds of miles from home.

He searched for other patterns, names he could decipher, code words used frequently. Out of the seventy thousand emails stolen from Paradise, five were written from or to Radcliffe's personal account, the first on February 11$^{th}$, 2016.

*Please tell Desiree I had a wonderful time last night. Flowers on the way.*

The other four were written on the same day: June 20, 2016:

Radcliffe: *Big celebration tonight.*

Paradise: *We have a couple of girls to help relax.*

Radcliffe: *Three should do it.*

Paradise responds again: *Enjoy. Bill clear per PA.*

"*Big celebration tonight,*" he repeated. "There's a familiarity in those words. They know each other well. Then, *Bill clear per PA.*"

"Yea," Zoe explained, "it was his aide, Paul Anderson. Haven't you been watching the news?"

"Yeah, I watch the news. It just doesn't make sense. Why would you have some college kid purchase hookers for you?"

Zoe shrugged. "People do stupid things sometimes."

"True, that," Becker practiced his street cred. He found the clock on his phone, exhausted. 10:30 p.m. "Where did the last 3 hours go? I'm headed to bed, kid."

"Yea, I should get back to my math."

"Christ, I'm a crappy parent." Becker surmised, suddenly remembering Zoe may have homework. He crawled into bed, took an ambien, and fell asleep still fully dressed.

\*\*\*

A rapid-fire burst. And then another. Becker finally recognized the jackhammers, ricocheting down 22$^{nd}$ Street before the sunlight could warm the asphalt.

"Fuck!" Becker ran out of bed, still not quite awake, and miscalculated the door jam, his right shoulder banging into the molding. "Fuck!" again he let fly. It was a two-fuck morning. So far. "Zoe!"

She startled awake, confused. The laptop fell to the floor.

"Jesus Christ," he screamed at her. "You never went to bed?" He spotted the construction crew from the bay windows. Normally, he would curse them. Today, he thanked them silently.

"Dad."

"Come on, get dressed." Becker stammered back to the bathroom, closed the door, and turned on the shower. "We're both late!"

"Dad?" Zoe said louder.

"Honey, just get ready for school."

"I was searching the emails."

"You find anything?" he asked with a hint of optimism.

"Not really."

"It was a stupid thought. OK, see you tonight."

"Love you."

"Love you too," Becker said under the showerhead, still contemplating.

\*\*\*

There wasn't much there. Paul Anderson took the fall and went back to Notre Dame, practically a hero to his fraternity brothers. Congressman Radcliffe apologized, again. In fact, he employed a jovial approach, poking fun at himself and his own misgivings. *God's still working on this subject*, he would laugh out loud on the election trail. It almost made others confess their own sins, right there in the ice cream parlor or wherever he happened to be stumping. His wife forgave him. At least in public. And his children appeared indifferent, Snapchatting at their pre-scandal rate. His congregants were only slightly mortified, the liberal edge calling for his resignation. But he did not concede, and the affair seemingly blew out of the American conscientious.

For the next six weeks, Becker sifted the entire catalog: 72,017 emails. He searched for connections and patterns. It was a jigsaw puzzle without borders, a universe still expanding. But for the beleaguered environmentalist the hours spent were a slight reprieve from the election coverage, the country a stowaway on a rocket to an inter-stellar asylum, a place where rational discussion is turned on its head, down becomes up, inside becomes out. Democrats and Republicans were speaking different languages, perceiving color and shapes, light and shadow, fact and fiction in wholly unique ways.

# Chapter 32. Gone Phishin'

Two months later. Wednesday, November 9, 2016. The Day after Election Day.

Becker rose from bed at the crack of dawn, having slept not a wink, a horrendous pit in his stomach. A song he couldn't name played weirdly in his head. It was as if he was incredibly high, which he was.

Frank Fowler was going to be President of the United States. Could that be true? He decided to stay up all night and smoke every grain of weed he had. It wasn't exactly helping. Nothing could. The pot, of course, was just an excuse, his alibi for the raw tonnage of depression that weighted his bones, compressed one vertebrae into another. The world wasn't losing its mind, he could rationalize, he just had a wicked buzz on.

He got to work early, reviewing the state returns: Fowler took Michigan by the daily attendance at a country fair; Wisconsin by the audience of an indoor tractor pull. Nationally, Fowler garnered 46% of the popular vote. Barnstable, 48%. Doesn't matter. The rules are the rules.

Congratulations and cries for one-way tickets out of the country poured across the internet. For the left, it was a giant gravy boat overturned on the Thanksgiving table, the oversized bird still frozen, the oven not working, half the country awkwardly grimacing at the table. For the right, it was a last-second touchdown, winning the big game, carried off in the arms of cheerleaders. Christmas, Hannukah, Kwanzaa, Thanksgiving, and the rise of the Lord Jesus Christ on Easter Sunday all rolled into one. Big business was elated. Wall Street came on itself. The Dow was up 257 points the first day.

Penelope Archer, President and CEO of the Faith and Freedom Foundation, was on the morning talk show circuit glowing over the historic come-from-behind victory. Becker streamed it on his computer. He closed his door and turned up the volume, nausea be damned.

"Why is Fowler so popular with the Christian right?" the interviewer posed. "He's had multiple wives, lots of apparent philandering. Why do conservatives claim him as their own?"

"The President will protect the sanctity of life, and finally rid the country of Roe v. Wade."

"It's all about abortion?"

"Not only. He will stamp out corruption."

"Maybe," the reporter pruned skeptically.

"There will be a cleansing of the Temple."

"A cleansing of the Temple?"

"Yes. A shakeup. A renewal of Christianity in the country."

Becker turned off the video in disgust. *A cleansing of the temple. Puh-lease.* When did lying, conning, and blaming everyone else become Christian values? Maybe the unsatisfied graduates of Fowler Academy knew? Or the hundreds of contractors not paid for services rendered to one of Fowler's corporations.

His scalp twitched with thought. The Paradise emails. There was an anonymous chain, *what was it?*

He opened his laptop, placed it next to the larger machine, multitasking the rest of the day. Luckily, his boss Joel was occupied with donors and interviews for a position protecting endangered species in Africa; someone skilled in biologic sciences, tribal negotiations, and international sanctions.

By 5:00, Becker was dying to get out of that chair, his ass sore from the hours stuck to it, the Dockers tag indented in his backside. He grabbed some takeout from the hot trays at the corner deli and dashed back into the apartment.

"See, I told you," he shouted, pointing at the laptop screen as Zoe spooned out chicken and peapods. *"Please send one of your lambs over tonight.* Here's another. *Two lambs for KOC poker Wednesday."*

"So?"

"Lamb is biblical."

"Again, so?"

"Two other emails mentioned them as lambs."

"Dad, you're not making any sense."

"Remember this email? #25246. Paradise wrote 'Bill clear per PA.' We wanted to know who the hell PA is, right? Supposedly, it was Paul Anderson, Racliffe's intern." His eyes lit up with excitement.

"Yea, he admitted it," Zoe reminded him. "He had to pay a big fine and everything."

He explained his theory. The one about the mythical poker game in DC. About Amir, his good friend. The strange call. The calamity he spoke of, and how dangerous some circles found his rhetoric. *Then, suicide just before his testimony? What if he was murdered?*

Zoe gauged the sanity behind her Dad's eyes. For years, the death of her mom hung like a sopping rain, no visible line between cloud and earth. He had retreated into the apartment, lost contact with friends and neighbors he pretended to like, cut out the weekend rides through the park. "I think I'm coming down with something," he'd complain frequently, but it was depression, she diagnosed from her TV training. Now, he was a bit manic in the other direction, perhaps even delusional. "Dad, are you still seeing Dr. Feldman?"

"You think I'm nuts?"

"Some people think your... a bit unstable."

He cursed Mrs. Goldberg, the old cat lady, under his breath and carried on, flipping through pictures collected from the internet. Congressional fundraisers, conservative confabs, ribbon cuttings, the congratulatory applause of a bill signing. From the evidence presented, Norman Radcliffe was a man about town: on the podium; in the interviewee's chair; with gin and tonic in hand, milling with important people in the grand lobby of a grand hotel.

With flip-art repetition, additional forms became more familiar. A woman, hair an irrepressible color of golden flax in the sun, a tight-lipped grin to cloak an unflattering smile. Still, there was an important air to her presence, centered, deferent ears turned her direction. With Radcliffe at a prestigious symposium. At a benefit with Speaker Johnston. The peaks of Aspen gleaming in the background, a large Republican caucus gathered around Penny Archer for the Faith and Freedom Foundation's annual retreat.

"These folks are the largest donor to the Republican party," Becker explained.

"So?"

"So, what if PA is not Paul Anderson? What if it was actually Penny Archer?"

"It doesn't make sense," she refuted. "Why would Anderson say it was him?"

"Maybe he was paid to."

Zoe looked unconvinced. She read the anonymous emails again. *Two lambs for KOC poker Wednesday.* "What's KOC?"

"I'm not sure," Becker admitted. "But I tracked everything Radcliffe does on the Science Committee. He doesn't make a move until the Foundation tells him to. If only there was a way to be sure."

"What are you suggesting?" Zoe asked suspiciously. Becker took another bite of Szechuan vegetables and contemplated the answer in his prefrontal lobe.

She prompted again. "Dad?"

"Travis knows how to hack someone's email, doesn't he?"

"I'm trying to avoid him at the moment. Besides, isn't that illegal?"

"It could be. If you get caught," he spoke a bit distantly. He blurted it out, that thing in his head. "Do you know how to do it?"

"Yea," she admitted. "It's kinda easy, actually." She sipped at a Coke, reflecting. A curl of interest rounded her lower lip, the fantasy of exposing Congress baked into her marrow, spoon fed along with strained peas at six months, a dip for her chicken fingers at year five. She typed the address of a dark web site: PirateBay. A laundry list of malware, credit card numbers for sale, viruses to destroy an enemy's hard drive, spy on your neighbor. She clicked on a phishing app. "So, we send this to her from an anonymous email with a RAT."

"A RAT?"

"Yea, a Remote Access Trojan. She'd have to click on a link or somethink. Then we could get access to her hard drive. Her IT folks will probably shut it down quickly."

"Could we get caught?" Becker asked, surprised by his own lack of boundary.

"We can't use our regular internet provider. Could be traced back to us." She closed his laptop and grabbed a coat. "Come on. I know a place."

\*\*\*

Dozens were snapping selfies on the broad stone steps facing 5th Avenue. "Please don't sit on the lions," the police officer told two college girls as a third took their picture. More steps up the grand entrance, a toddler cried as his ice cream toppled from its cone, melting under the frieze above the wide doors: New York Public Library.

Becker and Zoe passed the famous lions, up the marble steps, and entered the building.

Inside, the marble continues. Massive vaulted ceilings, the patterned chisel-work of master craftsmen, ornate Beau-Arts style. Past tourists endlessly pouting into their cameras, up a flight of stairs that overlook the entranceway and then another, wandering into expansive reading rooms, stately gold lamps along solid wood tables, arched windows, too congested with tourists and researchers alike. Back to the first floor, someplace less crowded: the DeWitt Reading Room, generous windows interspersed with frescos of a young, optimistic America adorn an intimate corner of the building.

"Try to look normal," Zoe murmured under her breath, finding two chairs overlooking 5th Avenue. Becker pulled his computer out. Zoe spent the next fifteen minutes anonymizing the machine, she explained as she typed, removing identifying codes and other tracing abilities built into the laptop's software. Back onto PirateBay, she downloaded phishing malware designed to set up a trojan horse behind the Foundation's firewall. If only they could get Archer to click on a link.

Becker shot her a contorted look.

"You started this," she defended herself. He decided to keep quiet. "Hackers just like to pretend," Zoe explained, "like they're in a movie battling government overlords."

"Uh-huh."

"They build these tools as if they're gonna get back at their enemies. But it's usually just to screw with each other. Travis broke into his buddy's computer and then posted naked photos he took of himself. It was pretty hilarious," Zoe chuckled.

"Uh-huh," an overwhelmed Becker muttered.

"We need to put together an email she'll click on. Something to start the RAT."

"Like what?" he asked.

"Something that gets her excited."

"How bout from the NRA?"

"The National Rifle Association?" Zoe grabbed an image of the NRA logo, and made it look like letterhead. "OK, now what?"

Becker dictated.

*Dear Colleague,*

*The National Rifle Association appreciates your consistent support. Our freedoms are under constant attack by the liberal media, activist judges, and the Democratic party. Help protect our constitutional rights.*

*Please join our new campaign: the Framer's Pledge, designed to support Congressmen committed to American freedoms as our founding fathers, the framers of our liberties, intended.*

*Join the Framer's Pledge today.*

*Thank you,*

*Wayne LaPierre*
*President*
*National Rifle Association*

Zoe typed it up and inserted the malware program to the hyperlink embedded in the email. They contemplated the letter, father and daughter together.

"Where will the email come from?"

"It will say NRA in the subject line but the actual address will be random. It calls a server in Russia to fire it back to the U.S." Zoe described the process: if Archer clicks on the link, a text will come through Tor, a secure platform. Archer will only see 'Link broken,' but it will give them access to her hard drive, behind company security. "Bail me out if I go to jail?"

"You're a minor," Becker reminded her. "Bail *me* out when *I* go to jail?"

"Deal." Their hands met for a shake and a pinky pull, the eternal oath, there at the New York Public Library. Zoe hit send.

Becker muttered with psychosis and stood nervously.

Zoe pulled him back into his seat, whispering with intensity. "I just got a text from Tor. Archer's computer is open. We probably only have a few minutes!"

They ignored stares from corners of the small reading room. Zoe opened the laptop again, and logged into the Faith and Freedom Foundation's computer. Penny Archer's screen opened before them. She searched the file directory.

"Something with poker," Becker suggested.

"Nothing comes up."

"How about paradise? Escorts?"

"Still nothing."

"Of course, she's not that stupid."

"Aces?"

"Nothing?"

"How about Kings?" The search came back with a file.

"A spreadsheet! It's called King of Clubs."

"KOC?" Becker wondered. She opened it and found six names down the left column. To the right: state, district, and committees led, followed by current activities, active bills in various subcommittees, Foundation donations by the tens of thousands.

"Chad Droburn, California..." Becker read across the first line, smudging the screen with his pointer. "I recognize this legislation. Democrats tried to monetize greenhouse gasses. I wrote a supporting affidavit. It was killed in committee."

"Do you know these other congressmen?" she asked. "Reid Johnston?"

"He's the speaker of the House."

"Landry Muldoon from Louisiana? What about Norman Radcliffe?"

"He was the one caught in the Paradise Scandal. These are the most powerful men in Congress."

"What about Ornette Schlesinger?"

"That old fossil. There hasn't been a piece of environmental legislation he hasn't tried to kill."

"Nathan Culp from Pennsylvania?"

"Can you download it?" Becker asked.

"It's not letting me. I'll take a screenshot," she said, capturing the computer image. She rifled through Archer's emails.

"Search for Abassi," Becker suggested. 11 emails popped up, all on the same thread, dated July 25th, 2016. "Holy crap!" Wayward pupils from across the reading room sniped in their direction. They ducked their heads, eyes fixed on the display.

"That's just after Abassi was found dead," Becker whispered.

"They're between Penny and someone named Graham Bucksworth." Zoe read the thread, starting from the bottom of the email chain. "What the hell happened?"... "There was an OD. Too much in the scallops." ... "So?" ... "We had to go to Plan B." ... "I know the coroner. Will make a call." ... "That will help." ... "Stay out of sight." ... "Headed on vacation." ... "Back to Australia?" ... "Yes." ... "Perfect. Stay out of sight."    Just then, Zoe's laptop went black, the connection terminated.

Penny Archer returned from the bathroom and noticed her computer acting strangely, files opening on their own. Type filled the search bar: A... b... a... s... s... i... A thread with Graham Bucksworth unveiled itself, the cursor bouncing across the messages. Archer ripped the ethernet cord out of her machine as realization of the hack washed over her.

Zoe closed up the laptop and leaned into Becker's ear. "Let's get out of here."

# Act Two: The Two Witnesses

*Whether or not he is manipulated by propaganda, advised or equipped by outside experts, or armed by an external sponsor, when he fights in his hometown or local hills in defense of traditional identity, he is a formidable opponent.*

- The Accidental Guerilla, David Kilcullen

# Chapter 33. Undulating Conveyance

June 3rd, 2017. Day 134 of the Fowler Presidency.

Except for the disorganized, muted chanting outside the Metropolitan Correctional Center in lower Manhattan, the prison cafeteria was dead silent. Twenty-five members of the 60 Minutes crew and a dozen well-armed guards watched the girl at the center of the room. Zoe's throat was bone-dry, desiccated by the powerful lights hung a few feet away, an hour of tears finding the edge of her jowls.

Ethan Webber, the journalist, waited patiently for Zoe to regain her composure. "You lost your mom when you were only 11?"

Zoe nodded, no sound escaping. She recalled the photograph in the living room, her mom and Dad just old enough to be burdened with thunderclouds of cynicism, fighting the power in the wilds of Oregon, falling in love with the eternal peace of a place untouched by man and each other. Or the one where they're peering over their baby daughter in Central Park, giggling back as she tugged at mom's brunette locks, lying on the blanket in the grass as late afternoon sun kaleidoscoped through a maze of oak limbs and leaves. She could almost imagine being that little girl, looking up at her young parents who were beaming back at her, marveling at what they had created.

"Zoe," Ethan tried again, "what was the last memory of your mom?" Zoe shot from Central Park to the hospital bed at Sloan Kettering Cancer Center, the undulating conveyance in time and space making her slightly nauseous. She covered her mouth and let out a little belch.

"She was really weak. In the hospital, dying from a disease she never should have had," Zoe offered, defeated, her eyes fixed on the wormhole in the prison's thick concrete flooring.

"Do you think, if she hadn't died, your path might have been different?"

Zoe trumpeted silently before releasing a light chuckle. "I don't know, she was pretty radical." The camera crew laughed uneasily in solidarity. "I have this vivid memory – my mom was making signs and organizing, volunteering for the Earth Day celebration in New York City. She was on the phone for weeks, planning, copying leaflets, that sort of thing."

"Was she optimistic she could make an impact?"

"She was at the time."

"How old were you?"

"Maybe eight. Everyone said it was a big success. Thousands of people turned out and they raised money for Nature Conservancy and the Wilderness Society, sent letters to Congress. Really made a difference."

"You must have been proud of her."

"I thought it was the best thing ever. But by the next month or two, she was really..." Zoe searched for the word.

Webber waited patiently.

"Just sad, melancholy," Zoe continued. "I asked her what was wrong. She was gazing at the traffic in all directions from our apartment, mumbling about some endless war in the middle east. Earth Day was gone. *What was it all for?* my mom asked." The room fell silent. Another tear made a path to her lip. "But she fought within the system," she admitted. "She got a law degree. My Dad too."

"But you didn't think that way?  To fight the system from within?"

Attorney Stanley Zivitz waved his arms in protest, trying to slow the conversation.  Zoe answered the question anyway.

"No. I guess it's ironic."

"Ironic?  How so?"

"Teenagers are really impatient. Even though we have the most time to fix something."

"Why's that, you imagine?"

"Cause we have to live with the other people's decisions, I guess."

"You wanted to change the world?" he fed her the tag line, the teaser they'd use to plug the episode that would air across the globe tomorrow.

Before Zivitz could stand and stop the interview, Zoe agreed. "I wanted to change the world."

"And what happened next?"

## Chapter 34. Mo

The day before Easter. Five days since the second attack.

"Let's go. Let's go, little fella." Mo nudged him again. Still no movement. He grew a few shades paler as morbid thoughts bounced around his head, a pinball with no exit. "Ian, wake up! Ian!"

As if jolted by electricity, eyes still closed, Ian torqued into the air. "It wasn't me! It wasn't me!"

"Ian," Mo tried again, "wake up. You're having a bad dream!" Some mornings, it can take Ian nearly 10 minutes to discern dream from reality and back again, the two swirling together like icy Minnesota streams that feed one another and then encircle him, unable to cross for fear of falling in. "Pack up your stuff. We've got a big day."

Ian scanned the room and the pullout bed he was on, confused by his surroundings. Mo's sister, Jenny, could be heard arguing with her husband. "They're leaving today, ok? So just relax. And please feed Tanner a normal breakfast," as she passed the crying toddler off. She broke into the living room hesitantly. "Ian," she offered in a deep twang, "it was nice meetin' you and all. Don't listen to everything my brother tells you – he was dropped on his head while he was still formin. Understand?"

"Yea, I do. Thanks, Jenny."

"You sure you boys won't stay for Easter tomorrow?"

"Mo says we gotta get back on the road," Ian said, looking at Mo for reassurance.

"I got a double shift today at the supermarket, so I probably won't see you for a while."

"It was nice meeting you," Ian said. He stood up, still in his underwear and an old t-shirt, and embraced Jenny. He tried to recall the last time he had a good hug, other than from Mo, of course. Jenny then gave Mo an awkward clutch, one that only estranged siblings could share, their bodies a bit rigid with battle scars of bathroom torment, high school embarrassments, holidays gone wrong.

When Ian heard Jenny start the engine and the baby carried off to the other side of the house, he figured now was as good a time as any. "Mo, I've been thinking."

"Oh no. Not again, Ian."

"I don't know if we're doing a good thing here. Listen, I don't need no money. Well, maybe a little bit to get back to Duluth. But you can keep most of it. You don't really need me, anyhow." Ian cowered a bit, his face folding in fear, not sure what his large friend would do. He would swear he actually saw smoke coming from Mo's ears in that moment.

But then Mo turned to him, smiled, and asked if he could show him around the property since it was his boyhood home and all. Mo grabbed his bible, gestured for Ian through the small kitchen, and out the back door. The sun was rising up the over the Louisiana bayou, lighting the sky a brilliant pink and orange, turning a few wispy clouds into cotton candy. When the screen door slammed behind them, two large Ibis flew off from the culverts that watered their crops, intersecting above and below the horizon with each flap of the wing.

"I used to play in the swamps, just a few miles from here," Mo explained. "I was Huck Finn on the Mississippi Delta. I could catch crawdads all day long or bring home a basket full of fish for Momma to fry up. It was beautiful."

Ian smiled at the thought of that, unconcerned about the toothless gaps. "It still is," he reminded Mo.

Mo looked over the perfectly flat expanse. One day, when he and Jenny were still in middle school, he convinced her to join of one of his little adventures. They "borrowed" a little rowboat with an outboard motor from Mr. Cutler down the road, ran out of gas, and got so lost in the wetlands, it took the Coast Guard two days to find them. They were covered in sun blisters and vomited for days, sick from drinking the silty water. Jenny was so mad, she didn't give him a Christmas gift for years.

Once their parents died, he said she could keep the house they grew up in. "I'm headed into the U.S. Marines," he said proudly, screwing on his new cap like a true jarhead. But when Katrina hit and flooded out the region and he was dishonorably discharged for drug possession and disorderly conduct, the shit kind of hit the fan for both of them. Mo Harbaugh, too proud—or too embarrassed—to hang around southern Louisiana, drifted north in his only real possession, a 2002 Toyota Tacoma, lucky just to be employed most months of the year. He worked on the coal handling system at a large power plant in Georgia but found the early shifts did not fit his hangover recovery schedule and was asked to move on. That's ok, the coal dust irritated his lungs anyway, the result a nagging cough in the mornings to this day. He drifted again. And again. And eventually found himself in New York City, of all places, working as a short-order cook in a restaurant before the kitchen caught fire and he was forced to sleep and accept meals in the basement of Holy Redeemer Church on the west side of Manhattan. He found a friend he didn't know he missed, the Bible, and started internalizing his life and the strange pathway it had taken him on. One day, he stumbled across an unfamiliar chapter in the Book of Revelation and realized his fate. God was whispering in his ear all along.

"This part of Louisiana is special. Really special," he broke the silence, mostly the good memories bubbling to the surface. "But we're losing the very ground we stand on. Louisiana is disappearing.

16 square miles a year. That's most of Manhattan, just lost to the sea. Man's ignorance. His stubbornness, that's what it is."

"Mo, I still don't like what we're doing."

"If sea levels rise like they're predicting, most of this great state could be underwater..."

"At first, I was excited but..."

"Florida, too. Gone. Forever wiped off the map. What do we tell future generations?"

"I mean, I do love explosions and everything but..."

"Let me share something with you, Ian, before you make up your mind."

"What if someone gets hurt?" Ian said as he searched for Jenny's husband and the baby. He drew close to Mo. "Or we end up killin' someone?"

Mo ignored him and thumbed through the book for a dog-eared passage.

*'The earth is defiled by its people; they have disobeyed the laws, violated the statutes and broken the everlasting covenant. Therefore a curse consumes the earth; its people must bear their guilt. Therefore earth's inhabitants are burned up, and very few are left.'*

Ian's gap-toothed grin was absent, his throat full of hesitation. "The folks I know are good people."

"Isaiah, 24:6," Mo explained, as if that might persuade him.

"But what does that have to do with us?"

"Ian, we are the witnesses."

"The witnesses?"

"That's right," he flipped the soiled pages again. "It's all here. Book of Revelation. Chapter 11."

*'And I will appoint my two witnesses, and they will prophesy for 1260 days, clothed in sackcloth.'*

Mo gestured to the dirty jeans and Iron Maiden t-shirt Ian wore. Mo wore fatigue pants and a t-shirt from Holy Redeemer Church, also in need of detergent, water, and some gentle agitation. When Ian returned an agreeable nod, he continued.

*'They are the two olive trees, and the two lampstands and they stand before the Lord of the Earth.'*
Mo turned back to assess Ian's comprehension. "That means they shine a light on the injustices of man, the covenant of protecting the earth," he interpreted. "They fill the lamps with the pressed oil from the olive trees."

Ian tilted his head in silent contemplation the way a field mouse surveys the dark for the ominous flap of a barn owl. Mo continued on.

*'And if anyone tries to harm them, fire comes from their mouth and devours their enemies. This is how anyone who wants to hurt them must die...* Blah, Blah, Blah. Here we go... *And they have power to turn the waters into blood and to strike the earth with every kind of plague as often as they want.'*

Mo flipped to the book's title page. "New International Version. Beautiful translation. Modern but still consistent with the original Greek."

Ian grimaced. "See, that's what I'm talking about. I don't want to hurt nobody."

"We're not going to, Ian. God is just asking us to protect the earth. The Temple Mount."

"But what about *devours their enemies*?"

"Well, our enemies are just the inventions of man, the puppet masters. The two witnesses are the ones thanked by Jesus for destroying the destroyers of the earth."

"They are?"

"Yea, remember the passage I asked you to read. It's just below in Revelations 11," Ian squinted and recognized the highlighted verse. Mo closed the book again and embraced Ian under his wing. "This is what Jesus wants. The two witnesses shall prophesy for 1260 days, clothed in sackcloth. Besides, they started this fight. We're just ending it."

Ian's grin slowly came back. Providence continued to call, the way he figured it. He shrugged towards the back door. "OK, I guess. Where we headed?"

"Central Georgia. Should be there by nightfall. Just in time."

# Chapter 35. Easter Sunday

April 16, 2017. 7:15 a.m. Juliette, GA, about 22 miles northwest of Macon.

Oily black pillars of smoke and steam billowed in the distance, still over a mile from the largest coal-fired power plant in the United States. Two hundred-foot smokestacks, eerily inactive, frame the ominous smolder, steam clouds rotating upon themselves, like the unnecessary gears of a Rube Goldberg machine. Fire trucks rushed past, sirens blaring, forcing Special Agent McMannis off the narrow, forested road.

He pulled the standard-issue black Suburban to the first checkpoint when powerful floods blinded him in early morning haze. McMannis approached, his partner and the other FBI agents in the vehicle. State troopers, their eyes barely visible behind flat-brimmed hats, asked for I.D.

"F.B.I.," he said authoritatively, hoping to roll right through. The ad hoc gate stayed immobile. McMannis hit the brakes.

"I'll need to take a closer look at those badges," the trooper said. After inspection, he told them to park just beyond the checkpoint. The main parking lot was full of company personnel trying to get the plant operating again. Most of Georgia was still dark due to those dang nut jobs.

McMannis drove in as far as he could but the road was choked with large SUVs parked askew. "Why can't Federal agents park like normal people?" he asked.

"They'd make terrible valets," Roberts agreed.

The smoke had a distinctly metallic taste and burned at the FBI agents' throats as they trotted towards the wreckage. Like the anxious freefall when sleep first embraces, their lives can be

interrupted without warning. Agents learn to sleep lightly, eat
quickly, shower without getting wet, dress without thinking, feed
the kids, take a crap, masturbate, fully prepared for the familiar buzz
of their cell. For McMannis and Roberts, it was a phone call from HQ
at 3:45 on Easter Sunday. An hour later, they were on a Bureau
LearJet to the Middle Georgia Regional Airport in Macon. As they
flew in, the entire region was covered in darkness requiring the
pilots to land under backup lights powered by emergency
generators. They met seven additional agents from across the
Homeland Security network, piled into three identical Suburbans
and barreled to Juliette, only to be stopped half a mile away, the
roadway so congested they'd have to hoof the rest.

Sara Roberts hoped to be in Philly by now, making the few hours'
trip up from D.C. early enough to wake up Charlie on Easter morning,
capture that look of confusion and pure joy he gave. Instead, she
was running toward a smoldering veil just ahead, sweating in the
Georgia humidity as the sun rose.

Law enforcement descended on the power plant: local police,
county Sheriff, state troopers, Homeland Security, U.S. Marshalls,
Bureau of Alcohol, Tobacco, and Firearms. And now the FBI had to
elbow in to calculate jurisdiction and priority to the evidence.

"Excuse me. Agents McMannis and Roberts at the FBI," he
flashed his badge to the first person who made eye contact with
them. "Who's in charge here?"

Deputy Lockhart from the local Sheriff's department was
pointing people in various directions. "Homeland Security is up
ahead - the guy in the law enforcement jacket."

"They're all guys in law enforcement jackets."

"The, uh, little Asian guy, Sir."

"Thanks."

They found Homeland Security Special Agent in Charge Leun
Jiang barking orders to subordinates. Barely 5'0", a slight pudge,
shaved head atop a broad face, he could be confused with the life-

size options at the local Build-a-Bear store. Until you actually meet him. Jiang, in his mid-50s, gave them an impatient exhale, traded business cards, and shouted orders to his men.

"We're with Behavioral Analysis Unit of the FBI," McMannis explained, "working on the King of Clubs investigation. Can you brief us?"

It was his fourth briefing in the past 30 minutes. Probably another five to go today, given it was only 7:15 in the morning. "Agents, this is the largest power facility in the country. It was knocked out of commission by large explosions in its transmission network and a central steam loop, causing cascading failures and wide-scale blackouts across the region. Three men were hurt, one was taken to the hospital with second- and third-degree burns. No fatalities."

"That's good," McMannis replied as Roberts pulled him aside, workmen waiving in large utility trucks, sirens spinning silently atop.

Leun Jiang quickly corrected him. "There's a lot of pissed-off people around here, so be careful about your qualifiers, Agent."

"Yes, Sir," McMannis recoiled. They walked closer to the debris. Shrouded in smoke, steam hissed as firemen doused the area. Blackened transformers, burned up utility poles, contorted valve pipes. "Did they leave a calling card?"

"We're still searching the perimeter. It's several miles long," Jiang responded. He led Roberts and McMannis inside the administration building, now a makeshift homeland security headquarters, to a sizable conference room, large maps on the wall and splayed on the table. Roberts assessed the room: dozens of agents, mostly alpha males, filing in and out, unintelligible chatter from wireless radios and conversations in the corners.

Jiang introduced McMannis and Roberts to the plant manager, William Kernon. About 65, his thick white hair buzzed to a flattop, Georgia Power embroidered into his standard-issue blue button-down, Kernon looked like he has spent most of his life at the plant. And he had, learning one position and the next until he eventually was asked to supervise the whole operation.

"The first explosions happened here at these large transformers," Kernon said pointing at the map lying on the table. "They seem to have hit three of them in a row, according to some of the employees on shift. Bam! Bam! Bam! Then they shot out a large steam pipe here, causing the injuries."

McMannis nodded, awed at the enormity. "What's this mountain?" he asked, pointing at the map.

"That's the coal pile," Kernon explained. "The rail line brings it in from the east here. Five to six trainloads a day, each with about 100 cars. Over a mile long."

"Wow."

"It's a real sight. Normally, when this place isn't full of sirens and FBI agents," Kernon joked, "it's humming with coal loaders, the sound of the furnaces reaching 1500 degrees. It's the largest electric generating station in the country. 3,500 MW." They nodded at the scale. "It's got every damn pollution control imaginable. Why anyone would want to destroy a perfectly good power plant..." The old-timer took off his orange hard hat, his hand shaking to wipe away two tears coming down his cheek. "I'm sorry," he continued "I've spent my whole at this plant. 42 years."

"And this lake here to the south?" Homer asked, hoping to break the awkward pause.

"That's the cooling water. Lake Juliette."

"They could have fired from across," Roberts suggested. "I bet the calling cards are over there somewhere."

"That's over a mile."

"How big were those transformers?"

"About the size of a bus, standing up straight."

"They've got incendiary ammunition," Roberts said, staring at the map. She looked up to find McMannis and Jiang listening. "Could easily knock those out."

"And anyone can get these guns?" Kernon asked. "That doesn't make any sense."

"No, it doesn't," Jiang chimed in. "We don't make the rules. Just enforce them." He changed the subject, wondering about the blackout. "Isn't backup generation available?"

Kernon explained that a sudden outage of a large plant can cause massive shifts in voltage, disrupting everything in its path like the torrent released by a burst dam. The walkie talkie squawked. Then a voice came through the rasp. "We've found a calling card." A noticeable cheer from the corners of the room, a bit of good news. "It's in a mile marker. No 28.3 on Dames Ferry Road."

"That's the other side of the lake," Kernon pointed at the map. "I guess those guns can shoot that far."

35 SUVs knotted on the stuffed access road, causing a traffic jam over to the location. Roberts shook her head. "By the time we investigate this, they'll be in Mexico." The long line of vehicles pulled up to the agents who called it in. A King of Clubs playing card was wedged into the bolt atop a metal mile marker.

"What the fuck is that supposed to mean?!" Jiang screamed to the other agents. McMannis and Roberts stayed silent. Too early to speculate.

"There's no clear shot from here," Jiang countered. "Goddamn it. You fuckers listen to me," he screamed at anybody in earshot. "I want tire tread analysis of every dirt road in the area, I want video of every vehicle from every goddamn source within a 100-mile radius. Search every goddamn text, email, Facebook post, whatever, for power plant, Robert Scherer, coal or planet. Are you reading me?"

"Yessir," they answered in a collective moan.

"Get me the Goddamn bullets from the burned-out transmission system and run ballistics."

"Yessir," the low response came again.

"Well, get moving, God damn it!" Agents scurried in various directions, photographing the scene, barking orders at respective underlings.

"You two," Jiang snarled, pointing at McMannis and Roberts, "you're profilers?"

"Yes sir."

"What the fuck are we dealing with here?!"

McMannis bullfrogged his cheeks out wide and glanced at Roberts. "We're gonna need a projector. There's a lot of info to cover."

Jiang shook his head and walked back to his Suburban. "I'm gonna need some more fuckin' coffee."

# Chapter 36. Conference Room

An hour later, 50 law enforcement jackets crammed the admin building's conference room designed for 20. Another 50 crawled the grounds searching for bullet casings, tire treads, video camera feeds. Any clue they could find.

"Pipe down, everyone," the diminutive Leun Jiang said with authority. "Hey, in the back," he tried again. "I need everyone's attention at the front of the room." Still, commotion. SAC Jiang of the Homeland Security Department opened the heavy glass conference room door and slammed it nearly to shatter. The room flinched in unison. "Pipe down!"

He stood on a chair and paused, drilling eye contact into his subordinates. "Better. Since there are power outages over most of the state, it's a shit show getting back to regional HQ in Atlanta. And Georgia Power has emergency gensets and satellite communication, so this is home base for the next 24 hours. They are not happy about it, but have told us they will accommodate every need they can."

Jiang glanced at McMannis and Roberts. "Agents. It's your show."

McMannis hooked up his laptop to the projector. "You wanna lead?" he asked under his breath.

"Sure", Roberts whispered back. "Thanks." After a quick review of her notes, she scanned a room full of blank stares. McMannis gave her an affirming nod.

"I'll refer to the activists," she started, "as the King of Clubs. That is their apparent calling card, but they have not self-identified as such. That's an important difference to nearly every historical attack. No formal responsibility taken. No messages scrawled, no press releases, no manifestos. A very different approach than previous groups: Earth First!, ELF, Animal Liberation Front, etcetera." The agents scribbled quickly in their notebooks.

"But these are clearly eco nut jobs?" Roberts heard from her left.

"There is a consistent environmental theme here. Large pickups in Pennsylvania, something an ELF cell targeted directly before. But the method and mode very unique. High powered rifles to initiate the explosions." Roberts flipped through pictures of the attack on Erie Ford then advanced to a map, highlighting the sites with a green laser. "That was followed by oil and gas drilling in Texas. Again, explosions set off with high-powered rifles. And now coal-fired generation in Georgia."

She thumbed through a montage of historical sabotage: the Vail Resort, million-dollar homes burnt during construction, animal testing labs, timber industry offices. Then chaotic images of a street riot, shattered windows, police formations holding back the mob, shields and truncheons in hand.

"Of course, anti-establishment movements go beyond eco-terrorist activity. About 500 activists were arrested at the riots in Seattle for World Trade Organization meetings back in 1999, nicknamed the Battle of Seattle," McMannis added. "The most militant was referred to as the Black Bloc, after their attire." The chaotic images played to a soundless conference room.

More slides, dozens of mugshots, fading with age. "We're tracking down every individual directly connected to environmental or anti-government activism to the mid-80s." Another hundred mugshots, the images indistinct but the message clear. Many possible suspects. Next slide, same thing. And another. And another. On the last slide, among the other grainy pics, a few college kids from Redwood State: a dopey looking Becker and his girlfriend, Amy Zimmerman.

"We have a hundred agents conducting interviews in the field," Roberts continued. "Agent McMannis and I have interviewed dozens of potential suspects directly. But so far, the clues don't point to any one individual. As far as we know, there's been no known reference to the King of Clubs in prior terrorist or anti-government activity. This appears to be a new movement with new methods of terrorism, organization, and communication. Our profile analysis suggests young to middle-age males, ages 25-39, disillusioned, high probability of former military, most likely Caucasian, moderate to high intelligence. Still a work in progress as we collect data from this most recent attack."

Jiang interjected. "If the profile suggests males 25-39, why go back 35 years of potential leads?"

"One, just covering all bases," Roberts answered quickly. "Two, older leads could be organizing, funding, providing equipment, shelter, etc."

Jiang nodded in agreement. "And three?"

"Three, the profile is just a best guess at this point."

"Any standout leads so far?" someone asked from the back.

"I'm afraid not. Investigation of indirect affiliations continue. We may have to go back further in time, to the 70s during the early days of Greenpeace."

Three agents conferred in the back room, covering their cell phones as they argued, pointing at laptop screens.

"Gentlemen, what the hell is going on back there?" Jiang asked.

"Sorry, Sir," one of them responded. "Our analysts have turned up a video sighting of an old red pickup in the vicinity at about 2:45 this morning. Image quality is poor but it appears to be two white males. And a small white dog."

"Make and model of the pickup?"

"Looks like an older model Toyota. A Tacoma."

"Plates?" Jiang asked back. The pause only made him bark louder. "Any license plates, God damn it?"

"Looks like Texas plates, Sir," as the three agents pointed to the video feeds and whispered back to each other.

"An old red Tacoma. There's probably a couple million of them on the road. Get the Texas Rangers on it. I doubt they were dumb enough to use their own license plates, but it could work." He found Roberts again at the front of the room. "Agent, you may continue."

"Thank you, Sir. The only real tie so far across the attacks is the King of Clubs. Sometimes one and sometimes two. Since the sites are all over the country, there could be a hidden meaning." The room rasped with confusion.

"The attacks also appear to be escalating," Roberts continued, "in property value and scale. Larger targets, wider audience." She displayed a map of the attacks. "The first attack—vehicles in Pennsylvania—caused about a million dollars in damages. The second—oil drilling in Texas—ten."

"And if the station manager is right," Jiang interrupted, "this could be a 100 million dollar write off."

"Yes sir. They're increasing by orders of magnitude. Next one could be worth a billion."

"Jesus," Jiang muttered. "They've already got half the southeast out of commission with a blackout."

Roberts flipped to the subsequent chart.

"This map represents additional sensitive targets across the country. Electricity production: green triangles. Gas and oil production: red squares. Refining and pipelines: yellow circles." The map grew in complexity until state boundaries could no longer be distinguished, all definition covered in overlapping color and form.

"Christ," the room muttered at the immensity.

Two officers barged in, panting with effort. Everyone stared as they caught their breath. "SAC Jiang..." They found the firing site and retrieved a cartridge, a .50 caliber. "I've never seen one in real life," he held up a plastic bag with the shell casing evidence. "It's even bigger than I thought."

"Excellent. Get that to ballistics, pronto."

"Yes sir. It was down one of the dirt roads that lead to the man-made lake." They gazed at the map on the conference table, and point to a finger of land stretching into Lake Juliett.

The plant manager used a shaky hand to measure the distance—his palm to the tip of his middle finger equaling the distant shore of Lake Juliette to the transformer bays—then laid it over map's scale. "That's 1.2 miles."

"Fuck," Jiang burst with exasperation. "Clearly they have a military background."

"We believe so, Sir," Roberts agreed. "The first attack was about 150 yards away. Anyone could have carried that out. Second attack was about six-tenths of a mile, requiring some precision and training. And now almost double that. These weapons can hit larger targets up to 1.5 miles. Maybe two depending on the size of the target."

"So, we have to protect every sensitive target across the entire country with a radius of two miles?" Jiang asked. "Narrow down the possibilities, agent."

"Yes sir."

"We'll have a draft priorities list for you today," McMannis added.

"Good. Do we know when the next attack will occur?" Jiang asked. The room was heavy with apprehension.

McMannis walked to the whiteboard and started drawing a grid. Across the top row he added S,M,T,W,Th,F,S. The days of the week. In the next row, the third box from the left, he put a star and the number one. He came down a row on the grid, over one column to the left, drew a star and the number two. Down another row, over a column. Star. Number three.

| S | M | T | W | Th | F | S |
|---|---|---|---|----|---|---|
|   |   | ☆ 1 |   |    |   |   |
|   | ☆ 2 |   |   |    |   |   |
| ☆ 3 |   |   |   |    |   |   |
|   |   |   |   |    |   |   |

"Attack number 1: Tuesday, April 4. Attack number 2: Monday, April 10th." He looked up to confirm he had everyone's attention. "Attack number 3: Sunday, April 16th. Easter Sunday," McMannis noted.

"Every six days," Roberts whispered, her face growing pale with realization.

McMannis moved over to the last column, drew 4/22, and circled the grid square.

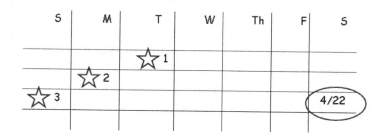

"Saturday, April 22nd. Earth Day." He scanned the room to make sure everyone was listening. "The country will be attacked in six days."

McMannis placed the cap on the marker and walked back to his chair. The room fell silent. Then into chaos.

An hour later, frenzy reached every corner of the plant, agents hunting down leads, hectic searching of databases, controlled chaos at any available desk. McMannis and Roberts took over a middle manager's office, placing calls to New York and Africa, of all places. It was the middle of the night when his call to Africa was returned.

# Chapter 37. Price of Admission

Later, Easter Sunday.

The Tacoma was covered in dust from the last twenty-five hundred miles and three corners of the country. They stopped at a nondescript gas station, four miles off the highway, the older looking the better, pausing only long enough to refuel, take a piss, grab a couple of pre-wrapped sandwiches, a body bag of pork rinds, a six-pack of cheap beer, and two large mountain dews. Mo waited behind the wheel while Ian paid.

"Breakfast of champions, huh?" Mo mused.
"Pork rinds can keep you alive forever. Where are we?"
"Kentucky, I think."
"Right, Highway 119. I got us located on the map," Ian measured the distance from Joliet, Georgia on the tattered atlas. "Probably did 400 miles since this morning."
"Yeah, my back is killing me," Mo stretched out with a groan. "Just don't turn on the cellphone."
"Its been dead for two days."
"Good. We'll charge it up near St. Louis or so. Just need a cheap hotel and a shower. You stink like a Georgia swamp."
"I thought Georgia smelled pretty good."
"It don't smell good on you."

The Tacoma turned over. Mo put it in reverse, peering across the road, pondering for a moment as a refracted sunbeam caught his eye. He shifted the truck back into place, never taking his eye off the blaze of color, and turned the ignition off. "There's a little church across the street."

"Yea, so?"

"So, today is still Easter. And I figure it can't hurt to have a quick conversation with the Lord. Maybe He'll give us some guidance." They tied Sammy to a metal signpost and opened the weathered door fronting a low-slung, cinder block building, the windows decorated with stick-on stained glass.

"Methodist, perfect," Mo surmised. "Aren't you a Methodist, Ian," he lowered his voice, a few remaining parishioners scattered in the pews.

"I'm not sure what I am," Ian responded. "I spent more time avoiding church than I did attending it."

"Can I help you?" the man asked, a white collar underneath his flannel shirt. "We've already completed our formal service."

"That's ok, Father. We just wanted to say a few prayers."

"I'm a minister in training," the man said gently. "You can call me Pastor Ray," as he shook their hands and guided them closer to the alter. "It's a special day, isn't it? Today, our Lord Jesus Christ rose from the dead and ascended to heaven."

"What chapter and verse would you recommend, Pastor Ray?" Mo asked.

Ian cocked his head starboard, surprised there were options.

"I like John 3:16," the Pastor responded.

"Thank you." The men entered the church, eight pews on each side of a center aisle denoted in old, red carpet. Tears in the drop-ceiling panels offered views of pink insulation underneath the popcorn surface. At the front, on top of a low stage, sat a large wooden cross, a metal lectern, and an old stand-up piano. "Tasteful," Mo whispered to Ian.

They sat in a middle pew on the right, picked up a bible, and opened to John. Ian waited patiently as Mo thumbed through. "Let's see," he pulled on his long beard "3:16."

*For God so loved the world that he gave his one and only Son, that whoever believes in him shall not perish but have eternal life. For God did not send his Son into the world to condemn the world, but to save the world through him.'*

Ian pruned with bewilderment. "What about Revelations and the Two Witnesses?"

"What about it?"

"Well, don't they contradict each other?"

"Ian, it's an old book. Not every word is gonna agree with every other." A siren wailed in the distance.

"Then how do you know..."

"I'll read you one of my favorites," Mo countered, ignoring his question. "Here it is:

*'But ask the beasts, and they will teach you; the birds of the heavens, and they will tell you; or the bushes of the earth, and they will teach you; and the fish of the sea will declare to you. Who among all these does not know that the hand of the* LORD *has done this?'* That's from Job. What do ya think?"

Ian looked around nervously, the siren growing. "I think we should put some miles on."

"Sounds about right," Mo agreed. He laid the bible on the pew, thanked Pastor Ray for his guidance.

As they unmoored Sammy from his anchor, an ambulance drove by at full speed, the siren's wail and pitch pushing them back into the church door. The breath left them quickly, life-size rag dolls remaining where they stood. They pulled their hats lower, got back into the Tacoma, drove out of town, talking about how much they liked Pastor Ray.

They roamed the byways, rolling and verdant, farmers' outbuildings leaning in the wind. Oaks and red maples leafed out in the spring, pollen floating like a rug beaten in the first cleaning since winter released its grip. West on Kentucky 80, past Manchester and London, the northern edge of the Daniel Boone National Forest, a thousand shades of green, the road so quiet, so peaceful, Ian was sure they were lost. North to the Indiana-Illinois border, the landscape transforming: straight lines, right angles, and productive. West on 50, the corn already knee-high. Fifty miles outside the city, the nervous energy of society enveloped them across multi-laned asphalt. Mo, listless and bleary from the day, steered clear of the rev and horn blasts as best he could.

Just off the highway, at a sleazy motel on the north end of St. Louis, the boys and Sammy fell into twin beds, the smell of Carpet Fresh layered over cigarettes and fast food wrappers.

"Let's put the news on. See what's up." Mo said as he grabbed the remote. He brought the cheap flatscreen to life and flipped past the latest in blender technology, interminable daytime drama. Then, the authoritative voice of Wesley Brandt...

"...we're following a nationwide manhunt for eco-terrorists, now referred to as the King of Clubs for the calling cards left at three separate attacks across the country. The latest, at the nation's largest coal-fired power station."

Ian jumped off the bed, spilling Sammy to the floor, appendages spreading in astonishment. He picked the dog up apologetically, held him over his head, and whispered intensely to his partner in crime. "We're on TV, Sammy!"

"Georgia Power crews are scrambling to fix the plant and transmission lines fried in cascading failures in the attack's wake. The utility indicates it will take several days to fully restore power throughout the region."

Seeing their efforts broadcast across a nation renovated Mo and Ian's perspective. They cracked a couple of beers, propped their feet up, and settled into new-found gratification.

"We cut now to downtown Atlanta where a rally is taking place. Hundreds of protesters have taken to the streets at the courthouse. Two groups—for and against the King of Clubs—are engaged in dueling rallies, only police barricades to separate them."

In a cheap hotel room just north of St. Louis, beer cans we're being emptied, high-fives exchanged.

"Damn," Ian said. "We've created a friggin controversy!"

"We've created a movement you son-of-a-bitch!" Mo shook his little friend. "A revelation."

"*We now turn to Special Agent-in-Charge Leun Jiang of the Department of Homeland Security,*" Wesley Brandt continued. "*Welcome to the program.*"

"*Thank you for having me.*"

"*The whole country is in fear. What is the state of the investigation?*"

"*We're throwing every resource we have for this nationwide manhunt. We're currently searching for two persons of interest.*" He offered a picture of the suspects, grainy but still effective: Mo driving, Ian and Sammy in the passenger seat. Both men wore Houston Texans caps and cheap sunglasses. "*If you've seen these men, please call the FBI hotline.*"

Silence hung over the motel room. Ian surrendered his hands in the air. "That's enough for me. I'm out!"

"Ian, we have to finish the job! We're only half-way."

"For what? $10,000? For life in federal prison?"

Mo looked sheepishly at the stained carpet. "Ian, I've been meaning to mention somethin'. You see... I told you we got $25,000 for the two of us, right?"

"Yea, I remember. I'll take my money now, thank you."

"Well, we actually got more than that."

"How much more?"

"Like fifty more." Ian's eyes protruded from their sockets. "But we have expenses. The guns, gas money, hotels and such. Your cut is really like $30,000. Not bad for a few weeks work, huh?"

Ian smiled at the thought before quickly changing his mind. "It still ain't enough. My brother makes more than that one season crabbing up near Alaska."

"Didn't he almost die doing that?"

"Yea, but he ain't going to jail."

"You're right," Mo agreed. "We tell Shaggy. The price of admission just changed. We want another $75k for the next job."

Ian shook his head and thought about it for a while. "That sounds about right."

# Chapter 38. Visit MuyBuenaVista

*To the complete LOSERS who are terrorizing the great people of #USA, you will hang from the highest trees in the world (which may be at the beautiful #MuyBuenaVista Golf Club and Resort). The un-American King of Clubs will be in jail soon! Pathetic!! #Visit MuyBuenaVista.com*

@PresidentPOTUS, April 16th, 2017 03:45:01 pm

\*\*\*

Late Sunday afternoon, Zoe left a handwritten note for her Dad. *Headed to Hannah's. Phone has been quirky. Love you. Z.* And drew him a smiley face.

Zoe walked behind her apartment building, grabbed a large brick lying in the alleyway, and dropped it on her phone. The force created a massive crack in the face. She picked it up and texted Amelia.

*Hey*

*You coming over?*

*Be there in 20.*

*CU soon* 😊

It still worked. She stuck the phone inside a Faraday cage, a lead-lined case that eliminated tracking, and walked to the subway.

# Chapter 39. Monday

April 17th. Five Days to Earth Day.

Mere ticks after the bell rang, Zoe scurried down the hallway, quick stop at the locker, shoved it close before the cascade, past the three sets of double doors and the newly installed metal detectors at the Rachel Carson School of Science and Technology. She two-stepped the stone stairs, out into the clear spring day. Through the earbuds and the Led Zeppelin mix her Dad made for her, she could hear him calling her name.

"Zoe! Zoe!"

*Fuck,* she mouthed, then turned to face him. "Hey, Travis."

"Hey," he said as he ran to catch up.

"I didn't see you there." She looked around nervously, searching for witnesses to the awkward exchange as other teens poured out of the high school.

"I texted you a bunch," he filled the silence.

"Aren't we broken up?" Zoe argued. When he looked around for onlookers, she returned to her long-legged pace, turning north on Columbia.

Travis ran to catch up, panting again with exertion. "That wasn't my idea."

Zoe paused, nodded in disbelief, and returned to her trot, tinged with new-found anger. Across Houston before the light turned, left on 4th Street. She had bigger fish to fry. "It doesn't matter. I've just been really busy."

Travis struggled to keep up, knotting himself in two slobbering bulldogs causing problems at the end of unattended leashes, their owner distracted with an Instagram feed. "Too busy to text?" he asked.

"My phone is busted," she said, displaying the evidence, a crack spiderwebbing the screen. "See? It's super fucked up."

"That sucks," he agreed, scuttling to avoid three skateboarders. "River is having a big party on Saturday, on his dad's property up-state. 35 acres. It's gonna be a rager."

The idea of getting wasted with her friends crept up her spine settling in the crevices of a smile. It's been way too long, hiding in the shadows. "Sounds fun," she admitted, slowing to take in his gaze. But then it all came back, like it was yesterday…

The open flirtation with those two chicks at the movies, that other bitch in his fourth-period chemistry class, the overall lack of commitment.

"Are we boyfriend / girlfriend?" she asked one night after he snuck into her apartment, blotto after breaking in that beautiful new bong purchased in Chinatown. Don't creak the door, get out of the kitchen, you're gonna wake my Dad, laughing to her room just down the hall as the old fart snored, knocked out once the nightly dosage kicked in. They had sex and Travis passed out, mumbling something about not wanting to get too serious, taking most of the bed, forcing Zoe onto the couch where the early construction woke her up.

Then, she was back, turning away, navigating the city. *I can catch the light across Avenue C if I hurry.*

"Stedman is going to have molly," he pleaded once more, knowing the drug's power to keep her laughing until dawn.

"Friday?" she asked.

"Saturday. It's gonna be awesome."

"Earth Day," she muttered to herself and turned to him. He *was* pretty cute: those friggin blue eyes, the fiendish smile behind the weak teenage beard. *Damn it*, she hated herself. "Is Amelia going?"

"Yea. She can't wait," he guessed but was probably true. Zoe and Travis shared a group of friends in the 11th grade, the usual trouble makers. They were grounded by the shithole that their planet was to become in their lifetimes; by the all too common threat of some undersexed, over-video-gamed teenage boy with access, somehow, to a small arsenal; of their friends Domingo and his sister Seche, now shit-scared as the President tweeted nightly of immigration roundups, the DREAMers never attaining their citizenship even though they knew them since kindergarten.

But mostly, they liked to party, avoid parental conversations about college, and Snapchat off-center pictures, barely visible from the corner, purposely awkward. Maybe they'd add purple dog ears or a flowered crown or use the filter that makes you look like the opposite sex version of yourself. *Amelia made the ugliest boy ever,* the giggling lasted 10 minutes, drunk on a cheap bottle of rosé, followed by one of Zoe's famous snort-farts.

The thought of blowing off some steam sounded therapeutic. Maybe River will run naked through the mud again, like last year. Or that time the bonfire almost lit the garage and his dad's old Camaro on fire. "Wait a minute," she stopped, "how you getting home?"

"We're gonna crash there."

"So you can get some?" She quickened her pace again, under the construction scaffolding, atop wood planks where sidewalk existed just last week. She avoided the bag lady, not committing to Travis as his agenda comes to light.

"It'll be chill. We've got lots of blow-up beds. We'll just crash and make a big breakfast."

"Ok, I'm in," she said, her face widening with a far-away smile. She held up her phone again, blaming it for any perceived rudeness. "I have to get to work."

"Awesome," he said, the realization of accomplishing his goal dawning across his face. "I'll contact you through Amelia?"

"Perfect," she agreed, a last turn to see him bounce across the street as if he lacked a destination.

\*\*\*

As she entered the apartment, quiet guilt greeted her. Her shift wasn't until tomorrow. She turned on her phone, cracked but still functional. Now she was alone, the thought of homework like climbing a sheer wall. Even with the endless honking below, three construction sites and 2 dogs barking in earshot, the apartment hung with deafening silence.

She flicked on the TV, the usual crap. Day-time soap operas. *Barbara, how could you?* Click.

Cheesy confrontations on stage. *He cheated with her little sister!* The audience called for a fight. Click.

*The latest in non-stick cookware, now at an insanely low price!* Click.

A bottomless argument about sports. Click.

*The King of Clubs knocked out power across the southeast. A giant manhunt is underway...*

She stared at the TV and contorted her lip with fury. "They started this," she whispered to an empty room.

# Chapter 40. Oceans

November 2016. About six months before the attacks.

Less than two weeks since the election, another eight or so before Frank Fowler would be sworn in as President, and Zoe's dad was bordering on zombie status, ODing on Fuckitol. He inhaled the news, 24-7, as if a toxic cloud settled on a pastoral village, normality evaporating with the morning dew as the sun rose again over the landscape, never to be the same again. *Our election was infected by foreign interference, intelligence tactics to sow systemic anguish and confusion.* Fowler, the beneficiary, claims it never happened. Zoe encouraged her dad to turn off the TV, his phone, all of it.

She never brought up the phishing exercise, breaking into Faith and Freedom Foundation's computer. Neither did he, too embarrassed by his lack of parenting, as if he could ignore its existence away. Instead, they dove into Abassi's research. But it was all so alien: the language, the equations. Becker contacted Shelly Dessev, Abassi's co-author. Yes, it was true, Amir was working on groundbreaking models. And yes, Amir's wife and kids were quickly emigrated out of the country and back to Iran. It all seemed so wrong. But, herself on a 501C Visa, Shelly didn't want to ask a lot of questions.

After three unanswered emails, Shelly finally agreed to meet David Becker from New York City. But only in person. "I don't trust technology anymore," she explained.

It made sense to Zoe, Shelly's paranoia; she read about the meta data that can be collected—every call, text, email, post and reply. Who contacted whom, time, duration, location, internet node. It was all accessible to the CIA, the NSA.

"I'll be back in a couple days," Becker assured his daughter.

"No, *we'll* be back in a couple days," Zoe stated as if fact. Becker didn't argue with her.

They met in Boulder, agreeing to an old coffee and book shop on the main drag, Pearl Street. Angled sandstone peaks guarded the college town. They found the old brick structure a few blocks west of the bus stop, wheelie bags in tow. Worn wood flooring and slow-moving fans atop the tall ceiling put Becker at ease. He guessed when he saw a woman of eastern Indian descent standing nervously near the door.

"Shelly?"

"Yes, hi."

"David Becker. Thanks for meeting us." Shelly offered him a quizzical look. "This is my daughter, Zoe."

"I read your papers with Dr. Abassi," Zoe said as she shook her hand, attempting to remove any veil of threat. Then she confessed. "I couldn't follow all of it. But I got the gist."

Shelly had delicate features, high cheekbones behind chai-colored skin. She offered only awkward quiet while they waited in line. Zoe noticed how much longer it took than in New York but figured maybe that was a good thing.

"You were focused on ocean health?" Becker prompted the scientist.

"That's right. We were." They found an old booth in the back, the fabric and springs long past their engineered lifetimes.

"And that was controversial?" Zoe asked.

"Not just because of the research, but the way Amir wrote about it. The way he talked about it," Shelly responded, choked up, a hint of Indian accent coming through. "The papers you read were all modified by management. They always toned it down, added scientific complexity to dilute the message. Amir would speak at rallies, post provocative replies on the web. And then the Washington Post editorial."

"That probably didn't make him any friends."

"It seems to be when things really changed."

"But it's possible?" Zoe asked, the research so improbable. "The results?"

"The oceans absorb about 40% of the $CO_2$ we emit. That changes the chemistry of the water in several ways. Mostly, the $CO_2$ reacts with water molecules, $H_2O$, to form carbonic acid. $H_2CO_3$. Hydrogen ions break off and acidify the ocean." Zoe and Becker gulped coffee and information, larynxes scaling up and down.

"Sorry, I'll go slower," Shelly offered.

"Please."

"The oceans are dying. They're more acidic, hotter, de-oxygenated, more polluted. We've seen red tides grow. Millions of people, hundreds of millions really, will be affected. Since industrialization, surface waters have increased 30 percent in acidity. That makes it more difficult for corals and shelled organisms to form their exoskeletons: mussels and other bivalves that filter the water, clean our estuaries and bays. Then you add higher temperatures, more pollution—all those are stressors on the system. We're seeing the effects already. Coral reefs are bleaching, lifeless. It's happening all over the world."

"Holy shit," Zoe muttered under her breath, stewing over the power of the revelation, that we could be playing Russian Roulette with the seas, with the planet, with our own future. *Could the geeks back in Climate Club even imagine?*

"Amir's models were really unique," Shelly continued. "Plastics have a magnifying effect, essentially poisoning the most important algae we have. Prochlorochoccus."

"What?"

"Prochlorochoccus. It's the most abundant algae in the oceans. It produces 10% of the world's oxygen. And they're shrinking in size and productivity. It's all a beautiful web. And humans are spiders, benefitting from the weave. But we're pulling the web apart, strand by strand."

"And Amir was becoming more agitated," Becker added.

Shelly nodded but couldn't speak. A tear found her upper lip. "Sorry," she stammered. "I miss Amir so much."

"Me too," Becker stammered.

"NCAR management saw the value of his work but were caught in between, fearful of budget cuts. So, they would give him something else to work on."

"Was he too aggressive?"

"Maybe. We had some huge arguments about it. But to Abassi, the conservative perspective was to do no harm until we better understood the impact. It's not some far-off potential threat. It's here and now. Unfortunately, that rhetoric got him killed."

"You think he was murdered?"

Shelly looked around the café, assessing each table, not committed to answering out loud.

## Chapter 41. More Dog Food

Yosemite Sam was at work when a pocket buzzed. Not one of those phantom buzzes, when it just travels down your butt, muscle memory or something. Yosemite looked at the phone to find a new What'sApp message, then glanced around a bit nervously. It was Shaggy. Time for a bathroom break.

Shaggy: *The dogs want more food*
Yosemite Sam: *Shit. How much?*
Shaggy: *$75 worth*
YS: *Ok. I have it*

Shaggy: *Really?*

Finger nails were bitten on both ends of the conversation.

YS: *Yea*
Shaggy: *No more crypto*
YS: *Damn dogs*

The bathroom door turned. "Taken," Yosemite Sam yelled out.

YS: *Gotta go*

Shaggy messaged Mo back. More dog food on the way. Mo was lying next to Ian in a cheap hotel, watching Star Wars. The original. Ian's seen it 20 times. Good against evil. Mo just shook his head as Chewbacca picked off another galactic fighter. The good guys never win *that* easily.

# Chapter 42. Calling All Kings

That night, the KOC reassembled at the Ralston, upstairs in a private room Reid Johnston booked a few hours earlier. Two bottles of Bourbon sat on the side liquor stand, seals intact. With extra precaution, they filed in, through the kitchen and rear entranceways. Reid Johnston stayed in the private suite for the afternoon, avoiding his residence or the Capitol's public spaces where the press gathered looking for red meat of one kind or another.

The powerful men looked at each other with furrowed brows, jowls puffed in indignation.

"Did you get a call?" Johnston asked.

"They came to my Goddamn house in Georgia," Old Man Schlesinger responded. "My wife was there, for God's sake," shaking his head in disbelief. "I took the first plane back to D.C."

Culp spoke up. "They knocked at the residence on D Street. Questioned me for half an hour."

"You didn't tell them anything, did you?"

"Of course, not. The F.B.I. is on a need-to-know basis."

Landry Muldoon cracked the first bottle of Maker's Mark with outrage.

"Gentlemen," the lone female voice rose up, requiring attention. Penny Archer greeted with freshly dyed hair and extra sequins. "Before we get started, let us pray."

Archer bowed her head and spread her hands in the room's large interior. Landry Muldoon lowered the Bourbon and joined the circle. The others followed, clasping hands. "Heavenly Father," she began, "give us the strength to wade these turbulent waters, to find resolve in your wisdom, your guiding light."

"Amen," the men replied in unison, ready for a stiff drink.

Archer's head remained genuflected, her focus intense. "Jesus," she began again, "our Lord and savior, protect us from those who would cause us harm. We are but your servants, your army of righteousness."

Schlesinger peeked under one eye, unsure of the sermon's status.

"*He who does not enter the sheepfold by the door, but climbs up some other way, the same is a thief and a robber. But he who enters by the door is the shepherd of the sheep. To him the doorkeeper opens, and the sheep hear his voice.*"

The Congressmen prayed for the prayer's termination.

"Amen," she said.

"Amen," they concurred.

"Beautifully done, Ms. Archer," Landry Muldoon broke the silence. "Do I recognize Luke, Chapter 5?"

"Matthew, 14:3?" Droburn guessed.

"John, Chapter 10," she corrected them.

They nodded in agreement. *Of course.* Schlesinger kicked himself for slowing up in old age.

"What is it supposed to mean?" Culp asked nervously.

"It means," Muldoon explained, "act natural, dammit. The shepherd doesn't sweat nervously, like you Nathan. He walks into the barn naturally."

"That's right," Schlesinger agreed.

Muldoon opened his briefcase and pulled the chips out, handing everyone their stacks. Penny Archer joined in, her first tourney in over a year. Just like the good old days.

After an initial game of seven-card draw, Norman Radcliffe pulled in his winnings. He assembled his chips in color-coded stacks and broke the awkward pause. "We gonna talk about why we're really here?"

Commotion from all directions. Reid Johnston raised his hands for order. "Gentlemen," he paused before correcting his mistake, "and Penny, of course. It appears we have a serious problem." They nodded in unison. "Three attacks have been made in our districts. The F.B.I has been asking questions, wondering if we have any insight."

"Of course not!" they all agreed.

"So… we play cards?" Landry Muldoon asked, squinting at his last hand, assessing a late fold. "There's nothing illegal about that."

"Well," Nathan Culp stammered. "We have a card game called the King of Clubs."

"A term of affection for our little get-togethers," Reid Johnston clarified. "I recommend we keep that fact to ourselves. It could confuse the manhunt." They nodded in agreement, Droburn's jowels swinging with approval. Johnston paused and stared at Culp, waiting for the other shoe to drop. "Out with it, Nathan? I can see the wheels turning behind those beady little eyes of yours."

Nathan Culp stood up, calculated the distance to the entry door, and decided not to run for it. He spied the liquor cart, walked over and poured himself a bourbon. He slugged the drink, getting most in his mouth, and sat back at the poker table. "Whatever became of Dr. Abassi?"

"Dr. Abassi," Penny Archer waded deep into Nathan Culp's blue eyes, "met an untimely demise. Like many of you, I was so saddened by the news. He was a brilliant scientist. But he died of natural causes." She bowed her head and crossed her chest.

"I thought he hung himself."

"Yes, that's what I meant. The coroner confirmed it."

"The important thing," Johnston chimed in, "is that we don't know anything about the King of Clubs. We have a poker game among friends. Nothing more, nothing less."

"An informal gathering," Radcliffe agreed. "Stay the course. Now, let's play cards."

Muldoon handed the deck of cards to Chad Droburn, the basset hound's turn to deal. "They're shuffled."

Droburn kept his gaze on Norman Radcliffe and reshuffled the cards, over and over, just staring at his KOC partner.

"He said they're shuffled, Chad."

Droburn kept rearranging the cards, shaking his head in disbelief, before pointing a meaty finger back at handsome Radcliffe. "It's your fault, you son of a bitch!" and he lunged across the table, Radcliffe's lapels in his fists, drinks upended, poker chips flying to the floor.

"Jesus Christ!" Johnston cried.

"You used your Congressional email to contact prostitutes?!" Droburn screamed. "Your goddamned Congressional email?"

"Chad, Chad!" Johnston screamed. "That's Armani. You'll ruin his jacket."

"His jacket?! He'll ruin us all." The table skidded sideways and overturned as Droburn and Radcliffe grappled into the window's heavy drapes, thudding to the floor. Geriatric gladiators in fierce battle. The others pried them apart.

Droburn wiped the snot from his face as he faltered to the corner. "It's all there, on Wikileaks. My aides did a thorough search of every email from the Paradise scandal," he straightened his tie, glancing at the others in the room, his chest heaving in despair. "Its only time until the press figures it out."

Penny, on her knees, toweled up the spilled drinks. She cried out. "Gentlemen, please!" She straightened her mane as she rose to her feet. "Even if our colleague from California is right, so some Congressmen were at a party with prostitutes. There are far bigger sins in the world. We can get past this."

"We *can* get past this," Reid Johnston agreed as they picked up the table and chips scattered across the room. He brought his fingers together to a fist. "As long as we stay united. Our bond to one another is the most important thing." Cliché but effective.

"And these eco-nazis are caught before they do any real damage," Radcliffe added.

"Amen," they replied in unison.

Penny exhaled deeply, sat down at the table, and bowed her head. "Perhaps we should pray again," she suggested, extending her arms in each direction, "...for the capture of the terrorists."

"Agreed," the men said as they rejoined the table.

"And for Dr. Abassi," Penny Archer explained. "We will pray for his soul." Repentance on the cheap. They bowed their heads in silence.

# Chapter 43. Sara Roberts

Since graduating from Quantico a little over a year ago, the initiation process that altered her life in every imaginable way, Sara Roberts participated in exactly three social activities. First, the weekends getting back to Charlie and her mom. The five-year-old grew taller and mom a bit shorter every visit, it seemed. She'd hug them deeply and dive into a big plate of homemade ravioli, famished from the drive up. They'd play games until Charlie fell asleep on top of the Clue board or sacked out in the stroller, and she'd kiss his forehead, hug mom and drive back down I-95, white-knuckling past the fender benders and near misses, falling back to her apartment before starting the week all over again.

The second was that quick fling with the guy upstairs, the one with the Porsche. He came on strong but faded once he knew the complex life Roberts led, fidgeting at the thought of weekends in Philly visiting a geriatric and a multi-racial kindergartner.

Her third social activity was on April 17th, 2017. After a grueling overnight in darkened Georgia, a few hours' shut-eye in cots lining a power plant administrative building, she and McMannis flew back to D.C., worked all day in the Strategic Information and Operations Center, the fretful nerve center and were now getting loaded.

"Excuse, excuse me," McMannis stuttered to the waitress. "She'll have one more."

"Don't listen t' him," Roberts mumbled. "He's trying t' get me fired."

The waitress looked back blankly, breaking down the adjacent dirty table. "So, which is it?"

Roberts looked back and nodded to the waitress. "Nother 'Rita. Coin style. Rocks n salt," she instructed in a Philly way of cutting words Smithereen short, covering up a little belch.

The FBI profilers slouched in a booth at a local watering hole a few blocks from the SIOC, the massive facility used to coordinate response to the 1995 Oklahoma City bombing and the 9/11 attacks: walls of computer screens, 500 analysts tied to every corner of the globe.

It's been 10 days of near-constant work, on the road, banging their heads against the wall, the only solid clue a cryptic King of Clubs stuffed into the bolts of a mile marker or nailed to a dowel and hammered into the dirt beside a road-side attack site. The agents needed a drink. Or maybe three. Roberts motioned to her partner, now at the bottom of his beer. "I ain't the only one gettin wasted."

McMannis tilted his empty beer glass to the waitress. "Another Scofflaw." Maybe one more and he would solve this case.

"A Scofflaw. Coming right up," the waitress said, turning back to the bar. *Keep those tables ordering. Or turning.*

Roberts contorted an eyebrow, her face rubbery from the tequila. "That seems to suit you."

"A couple of *Feds on the Rocks*," he countered.

"A round of *J. Edgar Hoover's* for my friends," she snorted. "Hold the dress." They slipped deeper into the booth. 19-hour days suddenly got to them, alcohol the only appropriate antidote. Roberts straightened up, scanned the bar, hoping not to be spotted in this condition. "Think Homer, think!"

"Let's review what we have."

"OK, every six days. King of Clubs. It's got bible written all over it. The creation story."

"Isn't it seven days?"

"Well, He rested on the seventh day."

"I went to church," McMannis snapped in defense, then muttered to himself, "...once. Not my fault Dad was an atheist..."

Roberts shrugged him off. *He's in his own head.* "Well, Catholic School may be finally paying off for me." She leafed through a bible plucked from the bedside drawer of a west Texas hotel. *Thank you, Gideons.*

The waitress came back with the drinks. "Third Margarita's the charm," she calculated as the lime-salt combination tunneled her cortex. "That's better. Let's see. Book of Genesis is 50 chapters. Each chapter is 20 to 30 verses. That's up to fifteen hundred verses. Could be anything. Between the old and new testament, there's 66 books in total," Roberts rambled. "These nut jobs hear God when they flush the toilet."

McMannis didn't pay much attention. *She's in her own head.*

Sara Roberts had an edge, a mix of schooling by street and classroom that McMannis slowly realized as an asset to their team. After she was caught stealing her father's cigarettes and smoking behind Sal's Pizza, her parents scraped together Catholic school tuition: Little Trinity through 8th Grade and then Holy Flower High School, girls only. "You'z just a number in a public school," her mother would tell her. "It's a factory there." Roberts always hated the name, Little Flower, and once punched Luke Franini right in the

face for saying she would lose her flower before she graduated from
Holy Flower. It took Franini 45 minutes to get the blood to stop
flowing and his nose angled left thereafter. He flinched when she
walked by, all 5 foot 2 of her, most waking hours hands clenched in
fists.

Looking back she had to admit, Holy Flower was probably the
best choice for a Northeast Philly girl in need of some discipline, and
she would have thanked her Dad over and over, except he passed
before she got the chance. A heart attack, right there at the family
picnic celebrating Columbus Day with all the Italians on her mom's
side of the family. They thought he was just kidding around, like he
always did. But the heart attack was real, and he pulled an entire
platter of burgers and hotdogs right off the barbeque as he tumbled,
mustard and relish splattering on the patio of gray stone half of
Philadelphia is built from. Roberts' life was rotated, as if on a wheel,
in a new direction. She was supposed to follow her Dad into law
enforcement, walking the local beat. But it felt too small, all of a
sudden, Philadelphia. Hanging out at Five Points with her friends,
arguing about who has the best cheese steaks and whether or not
the Eagles should retire Randall Cunningham's number. She would
go to college, like her mom always dreamed of for her. Maybe it
wasn't that crazy. Except for the Franini incident and that time she
rammed her car accidentally into an ambulance—D for *drive,* R for
*reverse*, her Dad would tease her before his untimely demise—her
high school experience was pretty good. Solid grades. Two years
working at the Humane Society. A year and a half really, but how
would those college admission people really know. Plus she ran
track, one of the fastest middle-distance runners in the state that
year. Roberts wanted to clear the state boundary, even the east
coast. Try something new. But then Dad died her junior year and
mom was alone—immobilized with ghostly familiarity. Her radius
contracted dramatically. When Villanova offered a scholarship, it
was a no brainer. She outkicked the coverage. Nova, a notch below
Ivy League with kids twice as smart as her. It made her nervous as

hell, now up against Asian girls with perfect SAT scores and geeks who slept in the computer lab.

Fortunately, the Criminology major came naturally to Roberts, a mixture of sociology, data analysis, and legal studies. Plus, she loved the basketball games, screaming from section 319 with her roommates, the whole college showing up when Big East giants Georgetown and Seton Hall came to town. She graduated Cum Laude by the skin of her teeth, 3.5 on the dot. Unfortunately, the FBI's requirements were more than she could offer, and her application and resume were never considered.

Another problem was little Charlie. Named after her father, the child started to show senior year at Villanova. She did everything she could to hide the fact, baggy sweats and all. Charlie's father, LaShaun Tyler, Nova's starting point guard begged her to get an abortion. He was good, but not NBA good. How could he afford it? But it was against her faith, she argued. "It would kill my mom on the spot," and she told him he didn't have to help raise the baby.

They moved back in with mom, her and mulatto Charlie, and joined the local force. She could barely afford a new crib and clothes for the baby, never mind a decent vacation. It was enough to keep every guy in Philadelphia from not calling for a second date. She applied again to the FBI, and for the second time, her application never got much notice. If Sara Roberts was being completely honest, she was more than a bit resentful toward Charlie, her mom, the Catholic Church, and everyone else in the tri-state area.

Roberts saw only one pathway out: more education. She went back to Nova, nights, and got her masters in Psychology with emphasis on criminal behavior, the curriculum self-designed. She cobbled three student loans and maxed out the credit cards. Third time's a charm, she bemused, and sure enough, the FBI finally took notice and gave her the call she had always imagined and would never forget.

Now, she was profiling the most important case in the country, but had to crack it, had to prove to Cap and the other muckety mucks upstairs—and perhaps most importantly, to herself—that she had what it took. That it wasn't all for nothing.

"So, Genesis," Roberts drew in some margarita and read from the opening chapter. "First, the creation story, 'let there be light and He creates day and night. Then Day 1 seems to start, and God creates the sky and separates the waters below the sky from those above the sky. Don't ask me what that means. Day 2, He gets really busy and creates land that separates the waters, and the plants and fruits and seeds. That's a good day. Day 3, He puts the stars in the sky and seems to re-create the light which I thought was already created... Seems like He could have gotten more done that day. *Whatever.* Day 4 He'z creatin the birds and all the fish and tells them to be fruitful and multiply. Day 5, we're onto wild animals, the cattle, and everything that creeps along the ground. I guess they didn't have a word for insects yet. Day 6, God creates humans in His image, male and female, and gave them 'dominion over the fish of the sea and over the birds of the air and over every living thing that moves upon the earth.'"

"Wow."

"Yea, we're in charge of everything."

"That was a mistake. Has He seen what we did with New Jersey?"

"I'm from New Jersey!"

"I thought you're from Philadelphia?"

"I am. But we go to Jersey shore in the summer. Anyway, that's just Chapter 1. Then he makes man out of dust, names him Adam, gives him the Garden of Eden, then gives him a wife, Eve. Except that Eve talks to serpents, the serpent tells her to eat some forbidden fruit, and she causes the original sin."

"Women," he shakes his head.

"So, they're cast out of the Garden of Eden and they have to toil in the fields, cause they didn't listen to God."

"The same thing happened to me in ninth grade, I swear." McMannis rubs his head. Beer and bible studies do not mix well. "Where does Noah come in?" his curiosity got the better of him.

"Let's see," flipping through the translucent pages, pausing to lower the margarita in the glass. "Not till Chapter 5. 5:32. Noah was 500 years old when he has children. Shem, Ham, and Japheth."

"Some names."

"Chapter 6," she flips the pages, her eyes wide with excitement as if hearing the story for the first time, "God tells Noah the world is evil and he better get started with the Ark." She looks McMannis in the eye. "At this point, he's 600 years old."

McMannis pulled from his beer, hoping there was knowledge in the foamy head. "OK, Roberts." His head is starting to throb. "Where does that get us? What about the King of Clubs?"

She shakes her head. "We ain't turning up zilch. There is a book called Kings. In Christian bibles, it's split into First Kings and Second Kings. It's Old Testament, ancient history of Israel. King David passed the torch to Solomon. He built a temple to house the Ark of the Covenant. Unless it's really coded, it's not in there."

"Sounds like a dead-end," he suggested.

"Agreed. Let's focus on the attacks."

"Great." His side of the analysis. "Three separate attacks across the country. We spoke to local law enforcement in all three. Nothing. Never heard of King of Clubs, received any threats, or seen eco-terrorism before. No one bragging on social media."

"What about internet traffic?"

"Good question. We have seen a lot of suspicious Google searches from New York City, lower Manhattan region. We're cross-referencing with our prior activities list."

"Interesting." Roberts pulled at her forehead as she spoke. "There's gotta be something that ties those sites together. Too far away from each other not to be coordinated."

"Agreed. Clearly going after fossil fuels."

"Clearly."

"Growing in size."

"Yep."

"All three are Republican districts. We spoke to each Congressman today. Let's see," he said, pulling out his notes.

"Nathan Culp from Pennsylvania, Reid Johnston from Texas. He's the Speaker. And Ornette Schlesinger from Georgia. 44 years in the House."

"44 years? How old is he?"

"As old as the hills."

"Are they connected?"

"Well, they caucus together as Republicans, of course. They all participate in a Republicans for Commerce caucus."

"Probably most of the Republican party participates in pro-business caucuses. That can't be it."

They stared at each other in silence, confused. McMannis's phone buzzed. Leun Jiang was calling. *Quick, sober up.*

"Agent McMannis," he answered.

"Agent, this is SAC Jiang. We've had a little break in the case."

"Sir?"

"Analysis division took a range of spectroscopy tests on the playing cards. We didn't find any fingerprints."

"Sorry to hear, Sir," McMannis offered. "We'll get something on them."

"Yea, my point is, the cards were stuck in a book. Analysis found page imprints on the card from Georgia. It was in a bible."

"The bible," McMannis replied, pointing to a snockered Roberts. "We're digging into that now."

"They were reading from Book of Revelation. Chapter 11."

McMannis thanked him and hung up. Roberts flipped through the bible quickly till she found the correct page. "The Two Witnesses."

"Two Witnesses?"

"Yea. Let's see..."

*'And I will appoint my two witnesses, and they will prophesy for 1,260 days, clothed in sackcloth... If anyone tries to harm them, fire comes from their mouths and devours their enemies...'*

"What does it mean?" McMannis questioned.

"I think it means they see themselves as prophets with..."

"With what?"

"With the power to strike the earth as often as they want."
McMannis shook his head. "Fuck."

# Chapter 44. Tuesday

April 18th. Four Days to Earth Day.

Mo looked at the dashboard. 191 thousand miles. *Mostly highway*, he could convince a new buyer one day. "I'm gonna miss the ol' gal."

"She's not going anywhere," Ian sneered.

"I know. But it won't be the same," Mo said, a little misty-eyed, wiping the drainage from his nose.

"You're a piece of work, ya know that." Ian shook his head in disgust. "You care more about this truck than Sammy, or me, or your sister. Or anybody."

Mo surveyed the Tacoma—his home, off and on, the past nine years. Only 7 dents, and none bigger than a dollar bill: front bumper, a perfect indentation from the chain he had to drive through after getting locked in a parking lot on account of that problem with the bill. The broken ends of the chain dug parallel scratches into the right quarter panel like cat claws on a sofa cushion. Rear bumper, partially hidden under the sticker, running over those belly button-high shrubs when he and his friends made themselves at home partying on a yacht, hauling ass before the cops busted them.

Mo wanted to argue but figured Ian was probably right. That truck had more soul than any living thing, as far as he could tell.

They pulled behind an old strip mall, abandoned for better real estate in a larger mall, which was abandoned itself as the shopping public discovered the awesome, brutal efficiency of Amazon, retail stores displaced in its wake. This was all quite fortunate for Mo and Ian that day. The space between the loading docks behind the abandoned Gap and Blockbusters proved a perfect venue.

Mo produced two plastic bags full of supplies, purchased earlier this morning. One large roll of blue painter tape; two rolls of brown masking paper, 18 inches by 20 feet each; one bag of rags; eight cans of Krylon white primer + paint. Two steps in one, Mo played his own salesman, in the Home Depot aisle, trying to look like a perfectly normal guy.

"First, we clean the truck real good, get all the dirt off…" Mo muttered, contemplating all the ensuing steps. The men wet rags with the last of the water they had and wiped the dusty Tacoma clean. Don't bother cleaning the wheels, Mo instructed. More rags for the dry cycle, and she was ready for Phase 2.

Thorough taping and masking is critical to any professional paint job. Mo learned that during the five and a half months he worked at Maaco while passing through Bethesda, Maryland. It was unfortunate it didn't work out; he liked the friends he made there, those nutjobs. But Enrique was dead shit serious about collecting on his gambling debts, and Mo busted out of town before the sun ever peaked thru the winter sky that day.

They papered the windows and bumpers, taped it tightly where the grill met the headlight, the rear hatch met the bumper. Mo pondered the after-market bed topper in matching Imperial Red, destined for an all-white rebirth. Too late to change now. "You better switch out the license plates," he told Ian, shaking a can of paint in each hand, the metallic balls bouncing in the cylinders like a washing machine filled with marbles, he recalled with an awkward smile.

Half an hour later, the paint was sputtering out of the last of the spray cans. "Should've bought more, dammit," Mo muttered to himself, eyeing the vehicle's coloring. Ian walked up, a big grin on his face. "What are you so happy about?"

"Nuttin."

"You changed out the plates?"

"Just like you told me. They were on a Tesla."

"Good," Mo said, calculating on his watch. "We'll give it 15 minutes, then start pulling the tape and masking paper."

"It was the best license plate I could find. Perfect, really."

"Mm-hmm," Mo responded as he contemplated the new color palette. *Should've gone with black for the topper.* Finally hearing the words, Mo pinched his eye sockets nervously. "What da ya mean, the best license plate you could find?"

Ian held up the new plates and shook with giggle. "GAZ SUX. That's funny, right?"

"You stole vanity plates from a Tesla?"

"Yea," Ian chortled. His face dropped when he saw Mo's eyeballs pop, like a night lemur high on devil worship.

"You FUCKIN idiot!"

"What?" Ian shrieked in confusion.

"What's easier to spot: some random number assigned by the DMV, or a truck with GAZ SUX for plates?!" Ian didn't bother answering. "Go back and change it out again, Numnut. And don't get fuckin' caught!"

"You don't have to get so mad," Ian bruised. He grabbed the screwdriver and stole away again, paper bag in hand, in search of the truck's new identification.

Mo unwrapped the Tacoma, pulling it clean of the masking paper and tape. It's unveiling in pearly white. He grimaced at closer inspection; based on the angle and the bounce of waning light on its surface, it looked as if a third-grader painted it, a moth-eaten coat, specks of Imperial Red shining through. *No one will notice*, he tried to convince himself. He was hunting through the spray cans for a last spritz or two when Ian sauntered back, unsure which facial expression to wear.

"Temporary plates," Ian said as he pulled them into Mo's vision, chest high, a shield if necessary. "They ain't got no number. I got two of them from the front of two different cars, just like you told me, so people don't realize they're missing."

"Temporary plates, huh?" Ian cowered as Mo approached, towering over him. "You're a genius, Ian McArthur!" Mo said and bear-hugged the air out of Ian's lungs.

Suddenly, a panic attack came over Mo: while he was playing *Better Call MAACO*, he may not have been perfectly clear with Ian.

"What happened to the Tesla plates?" he asked over Ian's shoulder. Ian struggled to answer. "You didn't put them on another car, did you?"

"IAN?!" Mo finally released him. Seconds ticked away like eternity.

"They're in the bag."

"Thank God."

"The Tesla was gone. So, I just kept them."

"That's ok," Mo sighed relief as he collected the dirty rags and empty spray cans, filling the Home Depot bags and flinging them into the covered truck bed. "Give me a hand with this," he instructed as they rolled up the brown masking paper, splattered and tassled in blue painter's tape. "We'll find a way to get rid of this shit when we get a chance. Hop in."

"Where we going?" Ian asked.

"Somewhere in Oklahoma. Let's meander up north for a day or two first. I want to make sure Shaggy makes the next payment."

"Yea," Ian agreed, "let's meander up north. Stay outta sight." They looked at Sammy when he barked in agreement and jumped into the uneven-white Tacoma, feeling pretty good about things.

# Chapter 45. L.J.

Lorenzo Stephen Jamison. Born May 13th, 1965. 44 days older than Becker. Place of birth: Columbus, OH. L.J., the middle brother. The peacekeeper. He always knew he'd have to see Columbus in the rearview if he was gonna do anything with his life. It wasn't hardcore, but L.J. had witnessed some things. Shit went down. Like the time baby bro D'Marco found himself with a bullet hole in his thigh. Never did figure how that happened, D'Marco's stories a leaky sieve. L.J. got so sick of propping his ass up, he figured he'd yank the crutch all the way to Oregon. Redwood State. *He'll never find me there.* But it was really those trees, so fuckin green. A cajillion acres of wilderness in what? 90 minutes? Plus, the cuties strolling the manicured campus, the tales of epic bashes, classes in twelve thousand subjects. Yea, his life was about to change, big time. *Buh Bye, D'Marco.* Sure, he'd be the third black dude on a campus of 7,500. But, so what? He had a chill way that worked across worlds. More worlds than most RSU frosh ever encounter. Becker, especially, the Jew from the suburbs. Christ. But that didn't matter, he and the goofball fell in pretty quick. "What the fuck is wudder?" L.J. teased Becker's Philly accent on their first encounter.

"Mr. Jamison?" she asked with a knock like it meant something.

But he wouldn't have guessed in a million years, back then, when he and Becker first met in the dining hall—before the first acid trip, laughing all night under the stars, or the blockade at the Williamette Forest—that he'd be there, inside the door. That strangely authoritative way they knock, Federal agents, on the other side. Just like in the movies. But there he was. And here they were. Looks like a balding thick kind of dude on the left side of the peephole. On the right, there was a chick's hairline, too short to see. A hairline with a northeast Philly accent. Like Becker's, but tougher, less suburban.

"Mr. Jamison," Philly accent asked. "You ok?"

"Fuck," he warped from Oregon, back to New York, recognizing his own lock again. Two deadbolts plus a quality chain. Not a shitty brass one. This was Brooklyn, for Christ's sake. He wedged his foot to the door as added insurance. The Philly accent seemed to look at the thick dude.

"Yea," he responded, bent awkwardly to line an eyeball with the hole, the agents holding the badges in clear view now. "What do you want?"

"Can we come in, Sir? We have a few questions."

It was real, Brooklyn. Where Carroll Garden meets Red Hook. Squat brick apartment buildings juxtaposed with industrial warehouses and shipping terminals to Gowanus and every point beyond. Connected to the world the old-fashioned way. Not necessarily less expensive than Manhattan. Fuck, he was paying three grand for a one-bedroom garden level. No additional charge for leashed mutts barking in the window, stopping to take a piss. But it worked for L.J., Brooklyn's balance of hip and grit that told him to put down some roots, stay a while. His buddy Becker in Manhattan. Get away from Oregon, put his past in another rearview. That was twenty years ago.

"Regarding what?" he stalled.

The agents looked at each other, contemplating their approach. They were past the moment for weeks-long surveillance, plodding case-building protocol. The country was four days from an attack on our energy infrastructure, the vascular system of our economy. The FBI needed to interview and re-interview every possible suspect, anyone even connected to a possible suspect. "Sir," McMannis gave it a shot. "There's been a rash of eco-terrorism events."

"So?

"Mr. Jamison," Roberts explained. "We could use your help."

"I don't know anything."

"Were you an active member of Earth First!?"

L.J. paused at the door, not sure if he should slide an additional bolt across, or turn the knob open. "So?"

"We can get a warrant if we have to," she suggested, although no one on either side of the door was fully confident of that statement.

The second hand of a watch echoed in L.J.'s head as he contemplated a thousand scenarios. He moved the chain out of the way, turned the deadbolts, reluctantly opened the door. "I was just a kid. In college. I told you guys a million times." L.J. walked back into the apartment scanning for incriminating material. He tugged at his afro, pulling a knap out of shape.

"You told other agents?" McMannis asked as they walked in behind him.

"Yea, I told other agents," he exhaled with exasperation and answered the next question before it was asked. "But I gotta explain everything to you, right?"

"I'm afraid so."

"I'm a sophomore at Redwood State, right? I sat in on some meetings, a few weekends. Music and speeches and dope. What can I tell you? I was a kid. Just hoping to get laid, really."

"You participated in the Williamette Forest blockade?" Roberts tried to corner him.

"So?" L.J. questioned. "Isn't that past the statute of limitations?"

McMannis changed course. "Mr. Jamison. We're actually investigating recent terrorist activity. Are you familiar with the King of Clubs events?"

L.J. nodded. "Isn't everyone?"

"Can you identify your daily whereabouts this past Sunday, April 16th?"

"Easter? I work at a church. In the soup kitchen. Holy Redeemer on 39th in Manhattan."

"And the prior Monday? April 10th?"

"At work. All day." Before they could ask, he pulled out his badge and flipped open the leather case. "I'm an EMT. Car accidents. Falls. Heart attacks. You name it. I drive the ambulance. Check with my dispatcher."

They eyed his badge, the apartment, some EMT apparatus: an extra stethoscope and paddles to re-jump a coronary. Three African masks above the couch. CDs and a traditional receiver and speakers. A picture: L.J. holding baby Zoe, flanked by Becker and Amy laughing at the bundle screaming bloody murder in his arms. An ashtray with a half-smoked joint on the wooden coffee table that doubled for dining if folks didn't mind sitting on the floor, Indian style. "Do you mind if we sit down," Roberts asked, bouncing crumbs off the couch, writing his company and badge info down.

"My shift is in 20 minutes."

"Are you friends with David Becker of Manhattan?"

"We've been friends for years."

"You were at Redwood State together?"

"That's right."

"Both part of Earth First!?"

"Yea. I told you," his jaw muscles clenched. "It was a long time ago."

It wasn't much, but L.J. carved out a decent little niche for himself the past couple of decades. The job was steady, good crew of friends. Never a problem meeting the ladies. OK, things got out of hand a couple of times with Theresa, the way her brothers would show up packing heat. But nothing to throw it away over, that's for sure. Instead, it was the news that day, the follow-up visit to the hospital, when the blood drained from his face as the prognosis came through the fog. He thought he was in the clear. He got the stroke before it got him. Dodged a bullet. But when Dr. Rosen, the brain specialist, took a closer look, he realized there was a mini volcano in L.J.'s cerebellum, an eruption in waiting. Several of them actually, a Ring of Fire, faults swimming above, tectonic plates grinding ominously below. L.J.'s brain was when, not if, the big one would blow, short-circuit all of his God-given wiring, sparking like the pop of bacon, unforeseen, grease exploding out of the pan one day.

"Do you have any reason to believe he may be currently active in eco-terrorism?"

"No," L.J. shook his head. "Do you?"

L.J. never shared that info, the ring of fire in his brain, the bacon grease ready to crackle. Never wanted Becker's sympathy in that way. He'd conjure up an awkward smile, change the subject. What was the point?   Becker was suicidal as it was. Now it was L.J. entertaining such thoughts. He motioned the agents to the door.

"Don't wanna be late to my shift."

"You mentioned," McMannis tugged at his forehead in thought. "One more question, Mr. Jamison. You mentioned you volunteer at a church?"

"I get paid. Not much. But yea, it's the soup kitchen. Why?"

"Run into any characters there?   You know, anti-establishment types?"

"It's just homeless. Guys down on their luck."

"No discussion of illegal activities?"

"Not that I'm aware of." The agents thanked L.J. for his time. He watched them leave, out the apartment, down a block or more before turning out of sight. He turned on his phone and started typing. He pondered out the window the duration of a 4th quarter commercial break. Something amiss, the way no one was coming or going from the Ben Franklin Electric van across the street. L.J. erased his screen, put his uniform on, and went to work, the EMT on the front lines. He was two hours early for his shift.

# Chapter 46. How'd You Know That

The buzzer vibrated through the apartment on 22nd Street. Zoe and Amelia were home from school, cooking brownies, music in the background. On Thursdays, after an extended Language Arts class, they'd get an early release from the place they called "the correctional facility." The buzzer hummed again.

"Sounds urgent. I bet its Travis and River." Amelia said with excitement as Zoe finished off a bong hit. "They skip last period all the time."

"Can I help you?" Zoe answered with frog-like baritone, the bong-hit remnants filling the intercom speaker.

"This is Agents McMannis and Roberts with the F.B.I. Is David Becker home? My partner and I would like to ask a few questions." The agents planned to get there when Becker wasn't. He has a daughter, Zoe, 17 years old, a junior at Rachel Carson High School. Maybe she could answer some questions about Dad: visitors, strange phone calls, a change in the financial situation, that sort of thing.

Zoe smirked at Amelia and released the button. "Travis is the worst actor!" She held the button and baritoned again, "Uh, sure, come on up." Zoe buzzed them in. The girls ran to the rounded staircase and peered over the banister. McMannis and Roberts climbed half a floor and gazed up to Zoe and Amelia looking down at them. "Holy Shit, are you really from the FBI?"

"Really, really," Roberts offered, an homage to Shrek.

"My dad's not home. Is he in trouble?"

"Not necessarily. We just want to ask a few questions," as the agents panted to the fourth floor. "When does he usually get home?"

Zoe introduced herself as casually as she could, inspected their business cards and badges. Then it dawned across her gray matter: the bong, the computer, her phone. The universe just a few feet away. Like the crowd at a tennis match, her head tacked back and forth between the federal agents and the open apartment door.

"We don't mind waiting," Roberts leaned into the jam. "Can we ask about your Dad?"

Zoe scrambled inside, positioned the bong under the sink, wiped the weed crumbs off the counter. And just like that, McMannis and Roberts sauntered in, scanning as they go: the glass piece, still off-gassing, being tucked from view, the nervous gather of hair. McMannis turned left, surveying the long bookshelf on the wall. Edward Abbey, the Vonnegut collection, the golden buddha statue on the bookshelf. He paused at a picture, Becker and Amy in the Williamette Forest, L.J. and other hooligans in the background.

"Would you say your Dad is an environmentalist?" he asked.

"Definitely. He works for the Sustainable Pathway Fund."

"This is your mom?"

"Yea. She passed away when I was 11."

"They were in Earth First! together?"

"How'd you know that?"

"We didn't," they lied. "Does he maintain contact with anyone else from that organization?"

"I don't think so," she lied back. "I know all his friends."

"What about religion?" Roberts asked, strolling toward the office nook. "Is your Dad religious?"

"Well, we're Jewish. But not very. My dad is kind-of a Bu-Jew." Roberts looked back blankly. Zoe waved her hands, trying to hit undo. "He's not really religious." She froze, staring at Amelia as if *rigor mortis* had begun. Roberts thumbed through a pile of papers. McMannis peered into Zoe's open backpack for anything incriminating.

A voice stabbed the door opening. "What's going on?"

Zoe screamed with relief. "Dad!"

"Mr. Becker? We just have a few questions, Sir. Are you familiar with the King of Clubs eco-terrorist activities?"

"Do you have a warrant?" Becker asked with indignation. He grabbed McMannis by the elbow, guided him to the door. "If not, I'm gonna have to ask you to leave."

"Mr. Becker," Roberts reasoned, "you filed an investigation request with the FBI about six months ago? Regarding the death of Amir Abassi?"

Following Abassi's death and the forced entry into the Faith and Freedom Foundation's computers, Becker contacted the FBI, hoping to help them connect the dots. But the FBI turned it around and questioned Becker's mental stability. He dropped the issue, increased his medication dosage, and began binging on re-runs of Survivor.

"Yea, that's right. But it was closed, ruled a suicide." Becker looked at the Agents sternly. "I could sue for a warrantless search. My daughter is a minor and isn't fully aware of her rights. But I am."

He shoved them out of the apartment, slammed the door, and slid the bolt into place.

Becker, Zoe, and Amelia glared at each other in silence, hearts beating out of their chests, not quite sure what just happened.

"I should get going," Amelia offered.

"I think that's a good idea," Becker replied.

\*\*\*\*

McMannis and Roberts crossed the street and looked back at the fourth-floor apartment on 22$^{nd}$ Street. Roberts stuck a piece of gum in her mouth, concealing her lips from view.

"Is he hiding something?"

"Definitely."

"And the daughter? Covering for Dad?"

McMannis turned back to their car, parked a few blocks away. "Looks like it," he replied.

Things were pointing to this corner of the world. Recent internet traffic from the area: computer searches for Georgia power plants, aerial views of Texas drill pads, auto dealerships in Erie Pennsylvania. And now, a former eco-terrorist was looking rather culpable, perhaps emotionally unstable. At one point, he claimed a research scientist was murdered.

"Do we have enough for a warrant? Probable cause?" she asked doubtfully.

He shook his head no. "Connection is too tenuous."

"Maybe we can get StingRays in position," Roberts offered. "Close in on phone activity."

"Need a warrant for that as well in New York," McMannis followed. "I think I can lever someone from his past."

"Yea?"

"There's only one problem."

"What's that?"

"This guy, the lever."

"Yea?"

"He's just getting back from Africa."

# Chapter 47. Africa

Two days earlier.

As it lowered to the ground, the Vietnam-vintage Huey created a sonic blast. Even shouting, it was difficult for Shrink to communicate with Frannie or MBolo and his team of guards. The copter blades—nearly 60 feet in diameter, spinning at eight revolutions per second—had Shrink in their vortex, simultaneously shoving him to the ground and pulling him into the air.

"He's only under for another hour or so," he screamed. MBolo's team nodded and moved quickly. The subject: male; 2 years old; 2,500 pounds; head concealed in heavy cloth, the horn jutting past, to keep the massive beast calm.

They tied its feet in fist-width straps and connected it to heavy-gauge carabiners and cable dangling ominously from the bottom of the aircraft. Shrink was too in the moment for his usual anger, the rage that could build just chatting over a beer in the cinderblock village bar with Frannie.

The helicopter strained as the juvenile Black Rhino and a westerly wind toyed with its aerodynamics. The pilot fought the controls and the copter captured a few feet of altitude. Shrink and his colleagues protected the animal's head and neck as it floated shoulder high, before ascending, gaining elevation, clearing the treetops. They whooped in celebration and ran to a smaller chase vehicle. It quickly took off and there they were: two antique whirlibirds in tandem over the African savannah. The morning sun, still low in the sky, cast bands of crimson and rose across rocky outcrops and arid roadless terrain.

"How many are we down to?" Shrink asked Frannie. He was tall and lean, red hair in a ponytail that hung half-way down his back, the bald spot covered with a dirty baseball cap, a freebie from his friends at World Wildlife Fund. His blue eyes sparkled behind ruddy, weathered skin.

"You mean to relocate or total?" she asked. Frannie was fighting the good fight as long as anyone could remember. Bright brown eyes behind her glasses matched her knit cap. She wore it even in the middle of summer, reminding Shrink of his grandmother when he was a boy in eastern Washington. It seemed fitting since he and Frannie spent so many holidays together. She pulled out a small orange and started peeling it.

He took a section. "To relocate."

"That was number four this week."

"And total?"

"Blacks?"

"Yea."

"5,500," she answered hesitantly.

"That's a small town in America."

"They should consider themselves lucky. Javas are in way worse shape."

"I'll let them know." Shrink leaned into the window, dejected. "It's only fuckin' keratin. The same ingredient as our fingernails!"

"I know," Frannie reminded him gently.

"It doesn't have any medicinal value. It can't make your dick hard regardless if it's smoked or snorted or ground up into a tea."

"I know, Nils. I know."

"But the stuff is still worth about $65,000 per kilogram on the Asian black market. Just myth and greed, the selfishness of man..." his voice trailed off, watching the sparse vegetation pass underneath.

Frannie and Shrink were wildlife biologists. Last month, it was Rothschild Giraffes, with just over eleven hundred remaining around Uganda. Today, it was Black Rhinos.

"You headed back to the states soon?" she asked.

"Yeah. Tomorrow. When I'm there, I want to be here. When I'm here, I want to be back there, not knowing."

Frannie shook her head with understanding. She knew how emotional Shrink could get, the time in jail, being caught on the wrong side of a police club. He had seen far too much, though he never shared more than a drunk snicker at the concrete block village bar.

The small helicopter began its quick descent to the landing pad at the Nairobi National Zoo. The animal was lowered gently to a small mound of old mattresses. The hitch to heavy chain dangling from the helicopter was released. Mbolo's men unbound the legs. Then, last to go, the blindfold. The animal twitched with diminishing sedation and jerked to its feet. They backed away to give him room, slipping from the enclosed area, dropping a bundle of hay across the chain-link fence.

The handlers congratulated each other on a job well done. Shrink stared at the rhino, pensive, not believing the compliments. He still had to be de-horned and re-settled in a permanent locality with enough healthy rhinos to ensure genetic diversity. Frannie put her arm around him, attempting distraction. "Buy you a coffee? I bet the beans were picked within 10 miles of here. Can't say that back home."

They walked into the dining hall, tourists to the national park zoo, milling about. It was made of large timbers, a thatched roof, the walls open to the savannah around it. Frannie sat at a table, suddenly not feeling well.

"Just relax. I'll get us some breakfast."

Shrink pulled out a tray and walked along the cafeteria line. Eggs, cereal, hash browns, yogurt, coffee. His famish suddenly hit him. He paid and led back to the table, lost in thought.

Shrink held up his fork, overcooked eggs rolling off. "The scrambled look awful today." Frannie, slouched in her chair, puffed a little laugh. Shrink dove in anyway, the hash browns nice and crispy.

"I don't know how those helicopter pilots do it, ya know?," he continued. He finally peered up from self-conversation to find his colleague slumped like a lethargic zoo animal. "Frannie? Frannie!" The wildlife biologist popped to his feet, eyeballing across the dining hall. "Is anybody a doctor? I need a doctor!"

Two men ran over. "I'm a veterinarian with the zoo," one says. "What's going on?"

"I don't know," Shrink responded. "She was fine one minute. And now, she looks pretty ill." Her skin turned ashen.

"Is she on any medications?"

"I'm not sure. Perhaps something for cholesterol. We were just in a helicopter, coming in from the savannah. Would that matter?"

"It could actually." They laid Frannie on the floor. The vet listened to her heart, took her pulse. Shrink was standing behind, watching intently, as a circle of onlookers deepened, eyes peering over shoulders pondering the commotion. A tap on Shrink's shoulder.

"Not now, I think she's in shock," Shrink dismissed the interruption. The person tapped again.

"Are you Nils Jensen?" a voice asked. Shrink turned to see who knew his real name.

"Yea, that's me."

"Sir, I'm an assistant manager with the Zoo."

"I haven't checked in yet," Shrink explained. The zoo had a room for him so he could spend the night, fly out the next day.

"No, I'm sorry," the man illuminated, "we got a call. They said you need to phone back right away." He handed Shrink a piece of paper with the Zoo logo on it.

"Who was it?" Shrink asked.

"The FBI."

"They c... called from Africa?"

"No, the United States."

Shrink read the handwritten note. *'Agents McMannis and Roberts. Urgent manner. Call U.S. - time unimportant. +1 705-223-2567'*

"I see."

"They said not calling them back could be a punishable crime," the assistant manager added, his suspicious tone not very well hidden.

"I'll take care of it. Thank you," Shrink said and glanced back nervously at Frannie on the ground. He folded the paper and put it in his pocket, surveying. *Good*, he thought, *they were all focused on Frannie.*

Frannie seemed ok, a bit dehydrated, the morning overwhelming. As she sat up, the crowd was asked to provide room. Shrink slunk away, got his room key, closed the door, and dialed the number provided.

"Agent McMannis," the voice across the ocean said. Shrink froze. "Agent McMannis, FBI," the voice said again.

"Uh, hi. My name is Shrink. I mean, Nils. Nils Jensen. You c... called me. I'm on assignment in Africa."

"Thanks for calling back, Mr. Jensen. You're in Africa on behalf of Africa Wildlife Fund?"

"Yes. Others pay my cost. It's a bit complicated. Is this why you called?"

"No. You're wanted for questioning. There's been a series of eco-terrorism activities in the U.S. The FBI is investigating. Calling cards—the King of Clubs—have been left at three distinct events."

Just a few hours ago, he was darting a gigantic rhino from a helicopter as the sun was rising across the African landscape. Now, someone was inferring he had connection to recent eco-terrorism. "I don't know anything about that. I've been in Africa for nearly a month."

"Can you verify that with flight info and witnesses?"

"Yes. Of course."

"Does the King of Clubs mean anything to you?"

"No. Why?"

Like postcards from the edge of the solar system, it came back to Shrink. The tree stands, building those pathetic barriers to stop the logging, the gang back in Oregon. Then there was Seattle, wreaking havoc for the World Trade Organization, back in '99. But he paid his debt to society, three months in a Fed lockup with hundreds of others, gathered up by the busload. Since then, he got his shit together, kept his head down, finished his Masters in wildlife biology, focused on his fieldwork.

"What do you want?" he probed.

"The FBI would appreciate your cooperation."

"I told you - I don't know anything." Shrink muffled profanities into a hotel bed pillow.

"Mr. Jensen, when will you be back in the United States?"

"I fly back tomorrow."

"On the 17th?"

"No, on the 18th. It's the 17th here already."

"Then how about the 19th?" Shrink stayed silent. "Wednesday the 19th, then. Your cooperation will be thoroughly weighted in any action against you."

Shrink's head spun in unnatural orbits. "I need talk to my lawyer first. Ca... Ca.. Can we get back to you?"

"Yes. But ignoring this request could put you on a very dangerous list. For your sake, please make sure your counsel contacts us."

"Understood," Shrink said in a trance.

"Mr. Jensen?"

"Yes."

"Any further questions?"

"No," was all Shrink could muster. "I can't think of any."

# Chapter 48. Wednesday

April 19th, 2017. Three days to Earth Day. Washington, D.C.

"Let's go, everybody," Leun Jiang demanded. It was 7:30 in the morning, well before sunrise for the poor bastards on the left coast. 32 people from 9 different organizations crammed into the SIOC's Executive Operations Room. Two rows of black leather chairs arranged in a semi-circle. Jiang sat at the front reviewing half a yellow legal pad of notes as officers filed in, taking their seats. On the phone: Pennsylvania State Troopers, Georgia State Patrol, Texas Rangers—the FBI's Texan cousin, 5 regional field commanders and subordinates.

They've met every day since an attack on the largest power plant in the country sent the southeast into darkness for nearly 24 hours. Jiang closed the door as they did a quick roll call.

"April 19th, everybody."

"Yessir," they responded.

"Appears quiet for now."

The room nodded in agreement. Twenty-two years earlier—in retaliation to the disasters at Waco and Ruby Ridge—Timothy McVeigh and Terry Nichols detonated a truck full of fertilizer outside the Arthur P. Murrah Federal Building in Oklahoma City. The explosion carved out the front of the building like a giant ice cream scoop, killed 168 people. It was the worst terrorist event in U.S. history. Until 9/11, of course.

Sara Roberts checked the wire at 5:00 this morning. Just the usual random murders and school shootings, echoed by cries for sanity and gun control. No attacks on infrastructure. She fell back to bed, unsuccessfully, for a couple more hours before finally giving up. The real attack, she was quite certain, would happen on Saturday, April 22nd.

"So, where the hell are we on King of Clubs?" Jiang asked. "Ballistics? ATF, what's the status?"

"The .50 caliber leads are identical across the attacks," someone from the Bureau of Alcohol, Tobacco, Firearms and Explosives. "It's the same gun. It was tracked to a dealer in Little Rock, Arkansas, and reported stolen."

"Just great," Jiang rubbed his head with frustration.

"The gun was purchased by one Edgar Nyro, age 62, in Arkansas back in 2014. It traded hands illegally. Last purchased by a Jarrett Jacobs of Ozark, Missouri, age 31. Mr. Jacobs ran into money trouble and unloaded it in a private sale. $2,900 cash. He said it was purchased by a man: 6'3", 240 pounds, shaved head, large beard, and a second individual: 5'7", 145 pounds, short brown hair, sunken eyes. He confirmed it was likely the two guys caught on the video feed."

"Bring him in to develop a composite sketch and get that out to law enforcement."

"Yes sir."

"An AR-15 was also used in the first attack, the Pennsylvania car dealership. It was never registered. Possibly manufactured from replacement parts."

"Homemade? Fantastic. What about the vehicle? Whose jurisdiction is that?"

"This is Troy Gayton from the U.S. Marshalls office," another voice spoke up. "We're leading on that. The Tacoma was wearing plates stolen in Odessa, Texas, back near the site of the second attack. We spotted the truck, a red 2002, on highway video surveillance traveling north through Tennessee. Then it seems to have disappeared."

"Well, find it!" Jiang replied. "That's what we pay you for."

"Yes sir. We're down to about 400 candidates with a red Tacoma, a military background, 6 feet 3, 240 pounds. Should have him ID'd by today or tomorrow."

"Tomorrow is no good."

"I mean," Gayton corrected himself, "by the end of the day."

"That's better. FBI profilers, have you made any progress?"

"Sir," McMannis spoke up. "We believe the individuals in the field may not be fully aware of the plot."

"What do you mean, McMannis?" Jiang asked angrily.

"We believe the attacks are being implemented by transients. Limited roots or family bonds. They only need money and a limited comprehension of the plan. We assume that was arranged beforehand or they're getting directions through secure communication."

"They might not know each other?"

"It's quite possible," McMannis swallowed on his words.

"A middle man?"

"We have several suspects in New York, Maine, Oregon. Mostly former activists. We're conducting interviews and surveillance in public places."

"You better set a ton of Stingrays. I want every cell tower near a potential suspect simulated. Someone is communicating these instructions."

"Sir, we've had difficulty arranging warrants in New York. The courts there are far stricter," McMannis explained the legal complexities created by our Bill of Rights.

Jiang scowled at the excuses. "What about the biblical reference?"

McMannis looked to Roberts. She walked to the front of the room, opened a cardboard box, and handed out faux-leather volumes. "Book of Revelation is the last chapter," she instructed. The officers flipped through their bibles hesitantly, almost afraid of its power. Key phrases were highlighted. "Chapter 11 is called Two Witnesses. They were prophets, essentially, with the power to strike the earth."

Jiang's head shuttered as he read. "Have any past eco-terrorist movements had a religious tilt?" he asked.

"Not like this," Roberts answered, waiting for Jiang to finish.

"Its an apocalypse," Jiang concluded, still mouthing the passages. "*Destroy those who destroy the earth.*"

"Yes sir. There were lots of apocalypses in ancient literature. What we think of as *the* Apocalypse is also in the Book of Revelation, several chapters later.

"So," Jiang proposed, "they see themselves as martyrs."

"Essentially," Roberts admitted. "With very powerful friends."

"Dig into those leads," Jiang demanded. "Someone knows these nutjobs, is directing them, funding them, something."

"Yes, Sir. That's our plan."

"*Destroy those who destroy the earth,*" Jiang muttered again, turning the bible over. "Who wrote this thing?"

# Chapter 49. Schackman and Schackman

"McMannis," he answered the phone, forty-five minutes after the morning briefing.

"Agent McMannis?"

"Yes."

"This is Arthur Schackman from the law firm of Schackman and Schackman."

McMannis was punch drunk with exhaustion. "Seriously?"

"Yes, seriously. I represent Nils Jensen. You contacted Mr. Jensen while he was working in Africa. He's updated me on the initial conversation."

"Of course. Are you and your client able to meet today?"

"Mr. Jensen's plane was delayed," Schackman said. "He's still in the air."

"Tomorrow then."

"Yes, but we prefer to meet in a... a neutral location. Perhaps my office. We are in downtown Arlington, a couple blocks from the Metro station."

"That will work. My partner, Agent Roberts, and I will be there."

"2:00?"

"The country is under threat of terrorism. Every hour counts. 7:00 a.m.?"

"How bout 8:00?"

"Excellent."

"Can you give me more information on evidence held against my client?"

"Not at this time. Tomorrow."

"How about your request of him... to cooperate, as you put it?"

"At the meeting."

"Or about connections that were referenced? Let me guess: at the meeting tomorrow."

"That's correct," McMannis clarified.

"We will see you then, Agent. Thank you very much."

Arthur Schackman hung up the phone. "Prick," he muttered. Shrink sat silently across the mahogany desk from his lawyer, chewing on a thumbnail. "Don't do that," Schackman said.

"What?" Shrink switched positions and dug a divot into his forehead.

"Don't do that either. Listen, body language is important. Almost as important as the words you say. You've got to remain calm and collected. Got it?"

"I get it."

"So tell me everything. Assume I'm your therapist. Nothing is off limits. Drugs..."

"Drugs?" Shrink said with alarm. "Where do I start?"

"Prostitutes..."

"Prostitutes?"

"Don't bullshit me. Yes, drugs, sex, every bad decision, friends with bad breath. Everything."

Shrink held his head in his hands. "Fuck."

"I know. We'll get you some coffee. Listen, they don't want you. They want someone else. But it sounds like they might have you by a few short hairs. If you play ball, they let go. If not, they pull tighter."

"Tell me about Earth First!"

"Fuck." Shrink contemplated performing the first self-lobotomy without tools or anesthesia. "Sorry, I've got a lot of anxiety."

"That's ok. I can work with anxiety. Deep down, we're all fucking nuts, kid. Anybody who claims otherwise is probably a liar or a bigger lunatic than you or me, that's for sure." After 35 years in business, Arthur Schackman knew how to appease a client—offer just the right amount of self-confidence.

The rap at the door was almost apologetic. "Mr. Schackman, you wanted more coffee," the attorney's assistant, Barbara, offered.

"Yep, make it strong too," Schackman said, rolling up his sleeves, tossing a fresh notepad on the desk. "Ok, tell me about middle school. Did you get in any trouble?"

Shrink's head fell back to his hands. "Fuck."

"Good, let's start there. Did you ever get arrested? Perversions? Suspensions from school?"

"It's gonna be a long day, huh?"

"Sure is. Barb, where is that damn coffee?" Schackman hollered into the next room.

## Chapter 50. Zoe

Zoe watched the broadcast with little emotion. She had a few minutes of downtime—post-classes, pre-shift at D'Antonio's—channel surfing to nowhere in particular. She paused at the news, now running round the clock

*They've now hit sites in three states*, anchorman Wesley Brandt .chattered in the background, grim CBC News video in foreground, panning the ashen power plant wreckage. *The King of Clubs eco-terrorists have the country in a state of fear and panic.*

But her mind was a million miles away, recalling that first time she heard the word Adenocarcinoma. It sounded like something Daffy Duck would say. Her mom and dad turned off the Looney Tunes she'd watch on Dad's computer after school. Zoe sat on Amy's lap, her mom's eyes swollen, lower lip trembling with reality. It didn't start well, and Zoe spent the first moments trying to pronounce too many syllables past her missing front tooth.

"It's lung cancer, sweetie," her Dad rephrased. "Mom has lung cancer."

"That's impossible," Zoe argued. "Mom doesn't smoke."

*Law enforcement officials are bracing for another attack on Saturday, April 22nd, Earth Day*, Wesley Brandt explained. The footage panned a line of pickups ablaze in a corner of Pennsylvania, oil wells in west Texas, a coal plant in Georgia.

The shadow of a reflection flashed in her mind's eye: climbing out of the crib, Panda Bear in hand, finding her favorite spot in the world: between Becker and Amy, still groggy with sleep. She'd brush Amy's hair like a life-size Barbie and tell Panda not to be so loud because her parents were still sleeping, Dad rolling over to get another hour of sleep, Zoe's toes always finding his ass crack until he finally gave up and relocated his pillow to the living room couch. Mom rolled over, pulled Zoe and Panda in close, and kissed the back of her head. Zoe brushed Panda's fur over the seam that was coming loose and a bit of the stuffing was showing through.

It felt like yesterday, before Adenocarcinoma ever interrupted Bugs Bunny and Yosemite Sam and all their buddies or the large dinner parties her Mom and Dad hosted, moving the furniture out of the living room so they could add the extra leaves to the dining table and surround it with folding chairs or someone could sit low on the ottoman pulled to the corner. She'd help her mom cook all day, learning to sharpen the knives with the machine they kept over the microwave and chop vegetables without cutting off a finger. She'd hide under the table with the other kids or crawl up on an adult's lap or finagle a few dollars to get a Coke from the corner store, her mom watching from the fourth-floor window as they crossed 22nd Street.

Later she would take refuge in her bedroom like any normal pre-teen, her mom's distinctive cackle recognizable above the headphones, especially when Amy and Becker tangoed in the middle of the room, minimal apprehension once the tequila kicked in, muffled echo of laughter and encouragement trickling through. She'd pay any price to create one more of those files in her fading hard drive; one more walk with her mom exploring the perfect space of Central Park, a last lick to clean the spoons as they bake one more birthday cake together.

*Dozens of Federal and state law enforcement agencies are coordinating the manhunt. Two men, seen here driving a red Tacoma, are being sought for questioning.*

By the time she was ten, Zoe knew more about lung cancer than the average adult, let alone a 5th grader. She could draw from memory the age distribution bell curve and spout nation-wide statistics. "Lung is the deadliest, representing 25 percent of all cancer deaths," she expounded without being asked. "Colorectal," she would follow, wrongly anticipating their next question. "...is the second most deadly cancer." Becker brushed her hair back as she spoke, proud of the precocious kid with the oversized new tooth.

"Amy Becker," the chart read of a woman with three bouts of cancer in two years; the chart Zoe stole from the nurses' station, studying the diagnosis and the long list of treatments in the visitor bathroom. She'd take notes so she could look up the words when her Dad wasn't using his computer. She knew he was just protecting her, those concepts not *age-appropriate* for an eleven-year-old, but hated him for it anyway.

Zoe would be a doctor one day, she was certain, waiting for her mom to wake up for a few minutes to see who the flowers came from or watch her eat a dinner of rubbery chicken in Sloan Kettering's Lung Cancer ward. But by the time she was registering for high school classes and her mom was dead for almost three years, Zoe's teenage angst was in Stage IV formation.

She stared through the TV as Wesley Brandt turned to an impromptu interview with Homeland Security's top officer, Leun Jiang. Jiang: short, Asian, and intense, described a hundred thousand citizen tips, a million hours of video feed under review, countless metadata of phone, text, email conversations.

Zoe watched his lips move but only heard a metallic rebound, the harsh welcome she gave her Dad on her 15th birthday. He walked into her room, his hands sheepishly following, holding a gift-wrapped bag with a bow on it. She peered into the bag it to find a bicycle helmet in pink and white. Becker envisioned them sharing Sunday morning rides in the park. "Try it on," he said.

But Zoe was less than excited. She offered Becker the disappointment of countless generations. "Why do kids have to wear bicycle helmets?" she asked.

His face declined from *Happy Birthday!* "Huh?"

"Why do kids wear bicycle helmets, and adults go to fat farms, and... moms show up with oxygen masks, and we have gigantic hospitals to make us better... when we poison the air and the water and make ourselves sick? When we have a government that openly accepts bribes we call campaign contributions from corporations they supposedly regulate so they can keep polluting until enough people get sick they finally put an end to it? Why," she asked again, "do kids have to wear bicycle helmets?"

Becker grimaced with apprehension, pulled the gift bag back, and muttered something about trying again.

*Citizens are being asked to call the FBI with any information regarding the King of Clubs' identity or motives, and warned not to take action independently.*

Zoe bemused with a slight chuckle as she turned off the TV, that deer-in-the-headlight look her poor dad gave that day, caught without response. She walked out of the apartment, down the staircase, out onto 22nd Street.

She wandered east contemplating the twists and loops and eventual knots she had tied in her life's rope, withdrawing from her larger circle of friends, tightening the radius. Among the few she could relate to, of all people, was one of her Dad's college buddies. She and L.J. drew closer. What started as an agitated joke evolved to distracted illusion, supernatural realization. Now a tether seemed to be tightening. She wasn't high, but almost felt as if she was, the broadcast like déjà vu still in her head.

Somehow, her feet found D'Antonio's. She put on her apron and started her shift, happy for a few hours to occupy the time.

# Chapter 51. Carry the Torch

Early December 2016. About four months earlier.

L.J. made his way to Alphabet City late one afternoon, stopping for a slice at D'Antonio's. He contemplated for what seemed like an eternity and finally ordered the mushroom.

"You got a break soon?" he asked.

"In like 10 minutes," Zoe responded.

"Meet across the street?"

"Ok."

Zoe hung up her apron, donned a jacket and a cup of coffee from the pot brewed too many hours ago, and found L.J. checking out the mountain of cameras and laptops in the window of an electronics store. The Christmas buzz seemed to last longer than usual. Decorations were still going up, the jingles and hummers of holiday playlists on endless rotation, the country attempting to shake itself free of its own discontent.

"I got your text," L.J. said as they wandered south. "How's your dad?"

"I'm worried about him. Our neighbor called the police. She thought he was going to jump off the roof. They evaluated him for two days in the hospital."

"I'm sorry. I owe him a visit."

"He's home now, on a lot of meds. Between the election and Abassi's death, and meeting his colleague..." her voice trailed off.

After Becker and Zoe met Shelly Dessev in Boulder, they flew home in silence. Becker was talking to the plane window and appeared to develop a tick. Zoe held his hand and seethed, powerless against the corruption they've uncovered. She wished her mom could be there, to put it all in perspective the way she did. Zoe reached out to the only person she could think of, someone she's known and trusted all her life: L.J. They met for coffee to discuss how to help Becker, fraying at every nerve ending. By the bottom of the second cup, they shared dozens of untold secrets: the phishing endeavor, the revelations in Penny Archer's computer, the ring of fire in L.J.'s brain, the Bitcoin fortune Zoe had made. They sat for hours, contemplating reality and fantasy, perhaps turning the whole thing into an off-Broadway musical. Anything, to relieve the stress. Now, L.J. was back with an urgent text from Zoe.

*Meet me at work tomorrow*, she messaged him.

The past nights, Zoe had succumbed to feverish apparitions. Vivid dreams kept her body floating in a shallow sleep-state. She saw the picture of her mom and dad in Oregon, smiling in rebellion, almost challenging her to join. Then her mom in the hospital and the funeral, a few of the ashes scattered in Central Park under the giant oak where they loved to picnic. She dreamt of Abassi, he and his brave cry to alter course before the ship runs aground, snuffed out, and the Congressmen and their partisan backer, holding the country back from moving forward, our path decided in smoke-filled back rooms.

The vision would repeat and re-form. She conjured being a little girl as her dad tucked her in, deviating from a bedtime fable. He would murmur how it reminded him of Lincoln, one of his heroes and ultimate trickster. Lincoln had to deceive Congress before southern legislators could return from succession in order to rid the country of slavery and pass the 13th Amendment. High crimes worthy of impeachment under ordinary circumstances. Abe was killed for acting upon his beliefs, a rarity in any time period. In the exact span of one painful century, a man named Martin would march on Selma, lurching us forward another step, before being taken to a better place himself. Her dad would tell her the tale in bed as if it was ancient scripture, to be read from scroll.

She'd forgotten it all until it recapped this past week. She'd stir awake, panting, unsure what the vision meant, before drifting back to restless sleep. She didn't understand, and asked her mom to explain. Our division was a continuous weave of argument, her mom described, braiding her hair, shiny-clean after a bath. On one side, petitions for open commerce, individual freedom, and the interpretation of God's intent. On the other, equality and the greater good. From slavery to its motherless child, Jim Crow and the racism that still permeates our society; women's rights; worker's rights; sexual orientation; unnecessary war; corporations and government so big, it's hard to tell who's who. Then the Earth and everything in it appreciated for its own divinity, whatever her mom meant by that. If we believed something, knew it was virtuous in our hearts, we would have to fight for it. Her mother looked directly in her eyes, and spoke through the dream. *Virtue doesn't fight for itself. It needs someone special to carry the torch.* Three nights in a row, the vivid imagery repeated until she was certain of its meaning.

Zoe and L.J. walked along Avenue A, no destination in mind, before she broke the silence. "You know our screenplay?" she asked.
"Yea," he laughed a bit.
"The Congressman?  The targets?"
"Yea?"
"What if we could really do it?"
"Not the screenplay?"
"The real-life play," she said, turning to him. "You know, to carry the torch."
"Carry the torch?" L.J. asked.
"For Dad. For Mom."
The way L.J. figured it, it was the sanest thing he's heard in a while, the crazy-ass idea Zoe just shared with him. An alternate reality in the land of alternative facts. Like the old days, with Amy and Becker in the forest, fighting for something larger. To do something himself before it was too late, a last hurrah, of sorts. He looked deep into her eyes and found conviction beyond her years.
"Let's do it," he said.
"You sure?"
"Yea, I'm sure," he muttered softly, as they continued the stroll with a pensive pace. "You can't tell your Dad."

"No problem. It would send him to the looney bin." She stopped again and peered deep into his soul, see if he really meant it. "Do you know anybody who can implement it?" she asked.

He nodded with affirmation. "I think I might. They'll need some money."

"I have it," she assured him.

\*\*\*

The west side of Manhattan can be a strange place. Just blocks from the overindulged advertisements and marquees of Times Square and Broadway competing for tourists' attention, the city gives way to unexpected industrialization: bus depots, construction sites that consume whole blocks, highway overpasses, stores that specialize in fake plants or the fabric of a scattered army of manufacturers across the globe. Amidst the rabble, a modest catholic church.

For the past four years, Lorenzo Jamison worked in the basement kitchen of Holy Redeemer Church, under the nave of the sturdy red brick structure. The tall black man believed in the power of a properly picked afro. Old school. He had a brilliant white smile and quiet, almost too soft of a voice. But when he shook one's hand, the recipient would invariably lean in and listen intently to hear his perspective. "Please," he would tell them, "call me L.J."

It was probably a Wednesday when the church serves macaroni and cheese. Or maybe it was Friday, fish night. It's hard to remember. The two men seemed to share a bond unexpectedly. L.J. was serving. A large man with a shaved head, full beard, and fatigue pants was receiving.

"You can call me Mo," the bearded one said. He held his plate to receive the food L.J. spooned out, and slid his bible to the far end of the tray to stay clear of the mashed potatoes spilling over. Mo mentioned he was the only radical environmental Christian homeless guy in New York City.

"I thought I was the only one of those," L.J. laughed although he admitted the good fortune of an apartment in Brooklyn he calls home. "It's not much," he said with a bit of guilt.

"This is my friend, Ian," Mo introduced the two. Over the next week, when L.J. wandered to their table, Mo would offer up a conversation on the environment or scripture, and the need to reimagine our connection to God and His creation. The three men shared a bond, a common credo, as well as a few run-ins with the law, as it were.

Mo revealed his military background. It was only 15 months in the Marines, but he learned a lot. "I kind of screwed that one up," he laughed, contemplating his bender-filled leave.

As the days shortened and the chill of winter set in, the dispossessed spent more time in the protection of the church basement. Ian was a quiet little guy, offering his gap-toothed grin, listening mostly as Mo would recall an epic tale as if around campfire. It reminded L.J. of his former self, when uncompromising purpose filled his days.

A week later L.J. invited them to his apartment for a homemade Christmas dinner: spiral ham, roasted vegetables, pecan pie. They accepted readily and felt at home as soon as the cold beers cracked open.

"This may sound a little crazy," L.J. altered the conversation.

"Crazy's ok," Mo reassured him, slugging his beer and glancing at Ian to go along.

"I've come across some powerful information."

At that exact moment, Mo became certain of his fate. He was the messenger the larger *He* conjured up in the chapter the smaller *he* now read on a daily basis. The lampstand and the olive tree. Why would God test him with pride and anger and sloth, pass him through the adversity of alcohol and homelessness, and then send him to New York City and to Holy Redeemer Church? To meet L.J., of course. To fulfill the prophecy. It was all there in Book of Revelation, Chapter 11.

And it was then, less than a week before one of our holiest of holidays, in L.J.'s apartment, that the three men agreed to join forces. They would expose a hidden truth, the evils of unchecked power. More instructions would come. And the money, of course, to cover expenses, perhaps a small incentive for their cooperation.

Mo looked over at Ian, now on his third beer, eyes aglow with scheme and relevance. The second witness was willing and able.

\*\*\*

Less than four months later, after the attack that left Georgia in biblical darkness and the F.B.I knocked on his door and scared the living daylights out of him, L.J. found himself serving meals again in the basement of the Holy Redeemer Church on west 39th Street in New York City's borough of Manhattan.

L.J. removed his apron, asked one of the homeless to spoon out the mac and cheese, and ran across town. He arrived at D'Antonio's just in time, his lungs in desperate search of oxygen. Zoe's shift was just ending. On edge herself, eyes in continual search mode, she spotted L.J. running and turned the other direction, hoping to camouflage into the crowd. But he found her elbow a few doors down and told her the news. He was out. It was a mistake, a ridiculous mistake.

They turned past the threshold of a noodle shop for sustenance and debate. Mama, her tattoo and spiritual advisor, had talked to her in the night, told her to keep going.

"We have to carry the torch, remember?" she said.

"We did carry it. You should be proud."

"But the job's not done. No one's been caught."

L.J. couldn't be swayed – he had to get out. When he went to the bathroom, Zoe grabbed his phone from his coat pocket. She knew his passcode, borrowing the phone before. She logged onto What'sApp.

*Meet in OK City Airport.   Tomorrow at 1300. Sending a new contact person. Too dangerous for me.*
*Our dog is hungry*, came the reply.
*We'll bring dog food*
*75 kibbles*
*50*
*OK, 50*
*Last meal*, she typed out.
*Last meal*, it confirmed.

Zoe wiped clean the conversation, logged out, and put the phone back in L.J.'s coat. When he returned, she supported his decision, and they slurped their noodles in quiet, halfway between calm and torment.

Early the next morning, she stopped at her bank, cashed out $9,900—just under federal reporting requirements—took an Uber to LaGuardia, transferred in Denver. Final destination: Oklahoma City, where she found two men she had only met through a grainy photo on TV.

# Chapter 52. Numbers

Mo was in his boxers and one of Ian's extra t-shirts, two sizes too small. The machines were spinning behind them, the room heavy with excess heat and the smell of dryer sheets. Sammy wandered the laundromat hoping for an offering, alms for the hungry. Or at least for someone to scratch his butt.

It was a day of cleanliness and contemplation. The men dismantled and cleaned their rifles, pulling apart the action from the barrel and the shoulder stock, disassembling the trigger, applying a light cleaning fluid to remove the residue of recent activity, reuniting the components into well-oiled machines. Literally. Phase 1: complete. They turned to the Tacoma, picking up empty Burger King bags, four fries, lettuce, and a revered onion ring scattered under the seat rails where Sammy couldn't quite fit his muzzle; a mound of mostly-empty Mountain Dew cans collecting on the floor in the back; a dozen or so bullets rolling around the truck bed, chattering like crickets in summer every time the baldish tires hit a pock in the highway. After weighing their options, they kept the dirt-covered exterior and the current license plates for another day or two, but decided to complement the Tacoma with a new bumper sticker: Fowler 2020. *Try to fit in.* Phase 2: check.

Then they turned to the sentient beings. Sammy was given a proper bath, then teeth brushing. Annoyed by this unnecessary ritual, the cantankerous Westie bit down hard on human flesh whenever given the opportunity until Ian declared the dog's teeth clean enough. Ian's turn. After consecutive showers, Mo bandaged the dog bite on Ian's hands. Ian unwrapped a new toothbrush and scrubbed. Mo timed him for compliance, then handed him a flosser. Ian's gums were bright red with blood until the sting of mouthwash mitigated the flow. *The Tacoma was complaining of his stench*, Mo explained. Ian wasn't sure whether to believe him. Phase 3c, the large man himself. The beard needed a good trim so he could see the steering wheel again. Head shaved to a beacon, triple showered—Ian conducting pit odor assessments between rounds—followed by thorough dental scouring. Like Ian, he bled like a stuck pig as the flossers made new pathways between tissue and enamel. The sting of mouthwash gave him the satisfaction of self-flagellation. *It hurt because it was supposed to.* Phase 3: mission accomplished.

Phase 4: clothing. And it was there, in the Scrub-a-Dub Laundromat in Springfield, Missouri, Mo found himself in boxers and Ian's extra t-shirt, sitting on one of the collapsible metal chairs, the cushion having long gave way, reading from his favorite book. Ian and Sammy wandered over to survey the progress.

*"And you shall wash your clothes on the seventh day and be clean, and afterward you may enter the camp."* Sammy peered up, whiter and cleaner than Mo could remember, and seemed to wonder if that meant dinner was soon to come. Mo realized the dog

was clueless and looked back at Ian, standing in his boxers and a long-sleeve flannel shirt, also oblivious.

Ian's flannel—broad green stripes crisscrossed with lighter gray ones reminded Mo of his first day in the marines, standing in his underwear waiting for the two sets of XL standard issue camo fatigues to be provided by his Corporal. After a battery of tests, the U.S. Marine Corps realized Maurice Harbaugh wasn't particularly good at anything. He wanted to be a Sniper Scout, one of the key Marine personnel. It harkened back to the Marines very founding. Mo loved the imagery, the Revolutionary War, Corps' marksmen holed up in the crow's nest, supporting their Navy brethren by picking off enemy commanders to sow confusion as the wooden hulks passed close enough the gunners could see the sores in each other's mouths as they screamed, 6 and 8 pound cannonballs shot into the wooden masts, giant splinters of wood and iron ricocheting across flesh. Unfortunately, for a Marine, Mo was just an average shot.

After Sniper Scout, Mo would have preferred being an Amphibious Assault Vehicle (AAV) Operator, an M1A1 Abrams Tank Crew, a fixed-wing (jet) or rotary-wing (helicopter) pilot. Even a Counterintelligence Officer or a Military Working Dog Handler. But the Marines had bigger plans for him. He was designated a Logistics Chief. This translated thusly: Mo Harbaugh of Company C had the awesome role of ordering for, preparing, and serving meals. He was a cook, and quite a disappointed one. Should've been a sniper, he fumed.

A lack of discipline followed, reduced leave, drunken excursions during such reduced leave, and the desperate cry for help that only a cocaine-fueled bar fight can truly provide justice to.

"Not everyone is a fit for the Marine Corps," square-jawed Commander Brigham told him. Mo stood at attention, acquiescent, while Brigham signed the Dishonorable Discharge papers at his desk. It was, in part, a relief. The Commander was right. Not everyone is a fit, especially to cook Beef Stroganoff and Lasagna for 72 guys in Company C. But it was also a giant embarrassment, a scarlet letter on his re-issued civilian uniform. He would take his only real possessions: his pride, his Tacoma, and his bible on a nine-year journey, meandering through jobs, sobriety, and the edge of financial security. Now, his camo pants from Walmart were in spin cycle while his buddy and their 'adopted' dog searched his soul for a clue to when their next meal might occur.

"That's from Numbers," Mo explained. "You shall wash your clothes... 31:24"

"We're kinda hungry," Ian said, speaking for both himself and Sammy.

"I think I saw a Burger King around the corner."

"Perfect," Ian said. Sammy waved his tail in full agreement.

A message from Shaggy came through WhatsApp. Mo read it aloud, amid the tumble of washers and dryers. *"Meet in OK City Airport. Tomorrow at 1300. Sending a new contact person. Too dangerous for me."* The three individuals, dressed a bit strangely, weren't sure how to take the news.

"You think it's a trap?" Ian wondered. Mo gnawed at his lower lip. He typed back, testing for authenticity.
*Our dog is hungry.*

After a confused pause, Shaggy responded.

*We'll bring dog food.*
*75 kibbles*, Mo required.
*50*, came the response.
*OK, 50*
*Last meal*
*Last meal*, the sniper confirmed and logged out.

"New contact?" Mo asked Ian as he scratched at his nuts, reflecting in his boxers, inside the laundromat. Another fork in the road. He shrugged at Ian and Sammy, hoping it would all work out.

# Chapter 53. Thursday

April 20th, 2017. Two Days to Earth Day.

The door to Schackman and Schackman opened promptly at 8:00. FBI agents in dark suits entered. Credentials came out, business cards exchanged.

"And this is my client, Nils Jensen," the attorney facilitated.

It was all too surreal, as if Shrink scrutinized the movie biography of himself, sitting in the dark, large popcorn in lap, while this guy Nils Jensen play-acted on screen, trying not to look at the camera. Jensen's blazer cut him oddly in the armpits, accentuating awkward appendages. He shakes hands with the unlikely Federal agents—an overweight guy with a combover, a pixie of a girl. Jensen's jaw muscles clench as he scans the federal insignia on the business cards.

Schackman tugged at Shrink's blue blazer, as if to turn off the TV and pay attention, and motioned to the conference room. Shrink slunk into the meeting, praying for a plane to fall out of the sky and hit their exact location, to wake up in a small pond of his own sweat, this all a dream weirded by overzealous pours of vodka, mussels that didn't agree with his system.

The conference room overlooked Arlington circle in D.C. suburbia. Traffic fought for position, a line snaked out of Starbucks, a biker pedaled bravely for his life. The center of the table was stacked with legal pads and pens. The agents sat on one length, the attorney and his client on the other. A sidebar overflowed like Eden; orange juice, coffee, danish, fresh fruit, bagels and cream cheese, and a steam tray with eggs and hash browns. *Never hurts to make people feel welcome*, Schackman internalized.

"Help yourself," he offered. McMannis wandered over to the table obligingly.

"We'll just have water," countered Roberts. McMannis pulled his hand from a steam tray and put the plate down. He poured a glass of water for himself and Roberts. Nobody ate the food, a sign of weakness.

"Before we start," Schackman initiated, "I'd like to say my client, Mr. Jensen, is a model citizen, a proud member of the environmental community, working to protect endangered animals. Something we should all aspire to, wouldn't you agree?"

As seniority dictates, McMannis responded first. "Understood and thank you, Mr. Jensen. This is a confidential conversation. No information provided is to leave this room."

"We know the ground rules," Schackman countered. "Mr. Jensen is willing to be cooperative for the benefit of the country."

"The FBI appreciates your candor, Mr. Jensen," Roberts replied.

"And your assistance," McMannis added, trading pleasantries before stunning him the way a fisherman dynamites a reef. Shrink conjured an awkward smile. "Mr. Jensen, we have credible evidence that connects you to a network of individuals and a series of terrorist incidents."

Shrink stuttered in fragments before Schackman put his hand up. "Please show us the evidence, Agent."

"These are photos of Mr. Jensen, in 1986, with members of Earth First!." In several pictures, Shrink can be seen sitting in a tree stand. In others, drinking with a motley crew of friends, barely in their 20s. Becker, L.J., and Amy among the dozen or so, American flags cut and resewn into capes and kilts and underwear, heroic poses and all, laughing in the wilderness. Then Shrink's mug shot from an arrest, one of several: 6'1", reddish hair and beard askew, pale blue eyes squinting with uncertainty.

"Not much to go on here, officers," Schackman retorted. "Do you have pictures of him shitting in the woods?"

"The tree stands are illegal. Your client is clearly engaging in that activity."

"I paid my debt to society," Shrink mumbled to himself.

"I think the statute of limitations would limit any ability to prosecute," Schackman argued

"Not true in cases of terrorism, including eco-terrorism," Roberts added.

Schackman shifted his weight, contemplating the information. "What else, agents?"

"These pictures of social gatherings show Mr. Jensen was connected to several people of interest for the FBI. The tall black gentleman is Lorenzo Jamison, often referred to as L.J. And this man is David Becker. Have you been in contact with either individual?" McMannis asked.

Shrink looked at Schackman, who nodded for him to answer.

"Not in years. I can't remember when…"

"These are from 2011," McMannis said, placing more photographs on the conference table. The pictures showed Shrink, LJ, Becker, and Becker's school-age daughter, Zoe, in a café in New York City.

Shrink focused on the photos, realizing he's been followed for years. He remembered going to that café after visiting Amy in the hospital, meeting Becker and L.J. for lunch. The FBI must be across the street, he processed. "Shit."

"What my client means is, this doesn't really mean anything. You have three men and a young girl eating sandwiches."

"Actually, it looks like burgers."

Schackman began repacking his briefcase, the message clear: the meeting was adjourned. "We're happy to take our chances in court."

"One more item, Counselor," McMannis offered. He fought off the curl of a smile. "Mr. Jensen, you were a camp counselor for a non-profit called the Outer Wild project?"

"Yea," Shrink responded. "It takes inner-city kids to experience the outdoors. Camping, hiking. Why?"

"We have evidence Mr. Jensen was sexually active with a minor. Alana Rodriguez was 16 at the time. Ms. Rodriguez claims Mr. Jensen touched her breasts and thighs when they during a weekend trip to the Smoky Mountains National Park."

"Fuck," Shrink responded.

"Nils, please," Schackman pleaded. "Has Ms. Rodriguez made a statement?"

"She has. Here it is." Roberts handed him a three-page, single-spaced document.

"There wasn't any sex. We were stargazing."

"One doesn't exclude the other."

"Nils, stop talking," Schackman begged.

"We took some city kids up to the Smokies. We were snuggling under a blanket. Nothing happened!"

"She says you rubbed your erection through your clothes."

"We snuggled," he repeated. "I pointed out the Big Dipper." He realized how that came out. "Constellations! I pointed out different constellations! I got an erection. Jesus Christ. Is it illegal to get an erection?"

"Can be if it's rubbed against a minor. And did you touch her breasts?"

"I may have. I mean, Jesus, they were so..."

"Nils!" Schackman pounced mid-sentence. He paused, recognized the change in leverage, and reclosed his briefcase. "What does the FBI want of Mr. Jensen?"

"We need access to Messrs. Jamison and Becker."

"You want Nils to wear a wire?"

"Yea. That's exactly what we want."


# Chapter 54. Bitcoin

On Coinbase, Shopify, and dozens of other sites, one can buy, sell, trade, and make payments with hundreds of cryptocurrencies. An unimaginable world just decades ago. And it all started with Bitcoin.

The currency was created in 2009 by Satoshi Nakamoto, a phantom of an individual believed to be living in Silicon Valley. The first transfer of the currency yielded $0.003/ Bitcoin in March 2010.

Zoe bought in early 2013 for about $89 per coin with half the inheritance from Max, her maternal grandfather. She purchased slightly more than 702 Bitcoin.

By the time Mo and Ian demanded more money, Zoe's remaining investment in the currency was worth about three-quarters of a million. She cashed out some index funds from the other half of her inheritance and got a morning flight to Will Rogers Airport, Oklahoma City. She'd miss her classes, make up some excuse to her Dad: cold-sweats that kept her up all night, perhaps, or a menstrual cycle so painful, he'd terminate the inquiry with guilt in less than a minute.

She changed planes in Denver, an old backpack between her knees the entire flight, and arrived in Oklahoma City in time for lunch. At the tables shared by Gordita's Mexican Kitchen, Tucker's Onion Burger, and Moe's Southwest Grill (no relation), she found two men she recognized from TV footage. One had a shaved head, a long beard, camouflage pants, and a T-shirt with the Dalia Lama, Jesus, and the Indian God Ganesh embracing in what appeared to a technicolor forest. Next to him sat a shorter man with sunken eyes, petting a small dog as he scanned the crowd.

"Is this seat taken?" she asked, as practiced via WhatsApp. Her hair was bunned under a ball cap, a few strays dangling down, jean jacket and sweatpants, no makeup.

Mo and Ian looked back in confusion. Shaggy said it would be a different person, but they never expected a teenage girl. "We're meeting a friend with treats for our dog."

"I have some treats for your pup."

Luckily, the arcane conversation went unnoticed by nearby travelers: parents speaking Spanish to their children; an elderly black couple squinting into the mystery of their cell phones. In the background, a garbled announcement declared which flight just landed, another was about to board.

Zoe opened her backpack to find a small Tupperware with dog treats on top. She tossed a few kibble under Sammy's nose and slid the backpack to Mo. Under the Tupperware, old t-shirts were wrapped around dense bundles.

"It's only the first 10," she explained.

"We said 50."

Zoe took a bite of Ian's burrito, realizing she hadn't eaten a thing since a stale bagel this morning, Mountain Dew to wash it down.

"Too much cash to carry. I'll transfer the rest in Bitcoin."

Mo stared back blankly. "We also said *no crypto*."

When Zoe mentioned others were interested in the job and reached for the backpack, Mo pulled it back quickly and agreed to the terms.

"You're Shaggy?" Ian asked, stupefied.

"No. I'm Yosemite Sam."

"What happened to Shaggy?"

"He couldn't make it," Zoe said and turned back to Mo. "But he says you're doing a great job. I'm going to send you my What'sApp handle. Go thru that from now on," she said, scarfing the burrito again. "You know the next target?"

"Oklahoma on the 20th. Oil storage."

"That's right."

"Sounds fun. We might go up to Wichita for the night. Jack Straw from Wichita."

She didn't get the reference, but it sounded like something her Dad would say. "Then a refinery," she explained. "The biggest in California."

"And the Bitcoin?" he asked.

"I can transfer it now," she said, pausing with a sideways glance. "Last payment." Mo nodded in agreement. Ian watched, mouth open. "You didn't cash out the first payment fully, did you?" she asked

"Just the first 20k for expenses."

"The rest is up 20% since the payout two months ago. Can't beat an investment like that." Zoe logged into Coinbase and navigated to payment. Mo jotted his account number on a napkin that wasn't soiled with burrito yet, pushed it forward. Zoe typed it in, making the transfer. She leaned down to pet Sammy, waiting for the balance in Mo's account to increase by almost 33 coins, now over $1200 per. She checked her own balance quickly, trying not to look surprised. Zoe offered Sammy a final ear scratch and gazed at her accomplices. Mo produced an old bible for mid-food-court prayer. They reminded her of guys on the street in New York. Perhaps a wrong turn here, a misguided step there. Mo muttered to himself as he read. Zoe studied the lines on his face, his long beard, his mismatched outfit—a strange combination of military and peace worship. She leaned in to catch the passage. It was the Book of Revelation.

Before turning to catch her return flight, she couldn't help herself. The curiosity was killing her. "I'm sor, sorry," she stammered, "how did you meet Shaggy?"

## Chapter 55. Greatest City in the World

A few minutes early, Shrink salivated over the camera and laptop bling in the storefront window. He felt a large hand on his shoulder.

"Nils, is that you?"

"L.J. Great to see you." The old friends caught sight of each other, the deepened creases, the gray that crept north.

"I'd love one of those C... Canons," he pointed to a long-lens beast.

"For all your detective work?" L.J. asked him. Shrink pulled at his beard, facial muscles no longer working. "Just busting your balls, man," L.J. laughed loudly.

Shrink staccato'd a chuckle. "Starbucks across the street?"

"How bout the cafe here?" L.J. pointed next door. "You know, buy local." Shrink peered into the street as he held the door for L.J.

"Location altered," McMannis barked from inside a Ben Franklin Electric van. "Repeat, target has altered locations."

"I'll have two of those eclairs," Shrink said to the young woman behind the counter, pointing at the baked goods. "Those look delicious. You want one, L.J.?"

"No thanks, man"

"Too late. I already b... bought you one." They found an open table close to the window so they could watch New York City walk by: a young couple checking their Instagram accounts, businessmen debating the insanity of Bitcoin. An elderly woman entered with her dog. A homeless man followed.

"I was surprised to get your call," L.J. said

"Yea, been meaning to catch up. I'm probably transferring to New York, wanted to get your take."

"Greatest city in the world. If you don't mind the noise, the traffic, and the trash," L.J. laughed, shaking his head at it all.

"Can't wait. You live in Brooklyn? Close to the bridge, right?"

"Yea, that's right," L.J. admitted, uncertain if he mentioned that before. "By the way, how'd you get my number?"

"I just Googled it."

"Huh. That's scary."

"Yea," Shrink agreed.

"I can't imagine why everyone Facebook's everything. Plays right into their hands."

"Livestreaming their crimes?"

"Millenials." They both laughed at the irony. L.J. and Shrink were used to cryptic ciphers, rendezvous points, hidden meetings. L.J. could still recall the knowing glances they'd share, in the woods, about to dismantle an earth mover, or passing each other at a popular college bar, as if they'd never met, worried about who may be watching.

It had been six years since they saw each other at Amy's funeral, a strange mixture of pride and shame as they avoided the subject of their past. At the time, they focused on little Zoe, just 11. And Becker, the poor bastard, overwhelmed by the loss of his soulmate.

L.J. took Shrink in as they sat at the café: the long red hair, the beat-up baseball cap, the unkempt beard. Just like he remembered. Except for an unfamiliar agitation. "So, moving to NYC, huh?" he asked.

"Yea. Wanted to see if you had any ad... advice."

L.J. was more distrustful than normal, given the circumstances. "You found me on Google, made it all the way to midtown Manhattan to ask me about apartments?"

"I was in town. We used to be good friends, remember?"

"I remember." L.J. gawped the café, the patrons drinking coffee, working away on their laptops. An elderly woman fed her dog K-9 chews. A homeless man with an oversized backpack stared into the corner. A giant construction vehicle drove by the café, rumbling the windows as it passed. "We had some good times," he recalled.

"Yeah. Didn't get into too much trouble, huh?"

"Just enough."

"Some of our brothers, though."

"Yeah. They got into some hot water."

"Keep in touch with any of them?"

L.J. scanned the coffee shop again: over-caffeinated tech geeks, whiling hour after hour, crouched over screens.

"No. Been staying low. How 'bout you?"

"Me neither. A lot of field work in Africa, for me. I just can't believe what's going on in this country. You can feel it in the air."

"Uh-huh."

"You see that King of Clubs stuff?" Shrink probed.

"Crazy, huh?"

"It makes me long for the past. I'd love a piece of that. Open things up again."

"Yea. Me too, I guess." L.J. shook his head, recalling the past.

"Since I'm moving to the city looking for an apartment, I'd love to save a few bucks. Would you mind if I crashed at your place for a few days?"

"I don't know if that's a good idea," L.J. replied. He noticed the homeless man, keeping to himself. Not asking for handouts. He had a hearing aid in his ear. Not a cheap one. Like one of those $2000 jobs. "I might have a friend..." he said distantly, turning back to Shrink, searching for a non-existent steadiness in his eyes.

Shrink held L.J.'s gaze as best he could. Christ, it's easier to stare down a charging six-ton elephant than an old college collaborator. His pupils quivered from the center as he attempted to keep the conversation going. "So, you have a friend?"

"Uh, he may have an extra room..."

"That would be great."

L.J. looked at his watch and got up abruptly from the table. "Sorry, Shrink. I gotta get to work. Late for my shift. Let's talk soon."

"Yea, great to see you. Maybe I can call you about the room?"

"Sure." And like that L.J. was gone, into the New York streets.

"Fuck," they whispered simultaneously. The homeless guy, the woman and her pooch, the agents in the van.

Time to review the operation, mistakes made, something the target picked up on. Eyes and ears followed L.J. home, waiting for a mistake.

# Chapter 56. Shrink

Nils Jensen fell back to his hotel room. Sweaty, full of self-disgust. He took off his shirt, imperceptible microphones sewn into two of the buttons. He never wore a button-down in his life. *How could he be so stupid?* He took inventory of the room for suicide options. Windows: don't open. Shower rod? He removed his belt, wrapped it around the aluminum shaft, and tested its strength. Too weak. *Dammit.*

He consented to live another day and turned on the TV. *This thing will kill me eventually*, he figured, flicking through the channels. He grabbed a Heineken from the mini-fridge, the info screen indicated $15. "Fuckin FBI," he said out loud, opened the beer and slunk to the bed. "Those assholes can pay for it."

He fell asleep to Duck Dynasty, pants unbuttoned, half-empty beer in hand. An hour later, his room phone rang.

"Hello?"

"Its Agents McMannis and Roberts. We're coming up in 10 minutes."

Shrink paused, hoping it was all a bad dream. "I'll be here," and lowered the phone to the cradle. "Fuck."

The agents surveyed the room as they entered. A small explosion of clothes, empty Chinese food boxes on the bed. McMannis grabbed the belt hanging past the shower curtain, stuffed it into his jacket pocket.

"You ok?"

"This s... sucks."

"You're gonna get past it. And maybe even save lives."

"Maybe I actually admire these people," Shrink admitted out loud. "Maybe *they're* the h... heros here."

Nils "Shrink" Jensen grew up the son of east Oregon libertarians. Tall, Danish stock, easily sun-poisoned. Dad repaired reapers, big farm equipment among the rural communities growing onions and potatoes and sugar beets. The five boys followed Dad into the family business. Except for Shrink. The youngest son never quite fit in, completely uninterested in the obligatory dinner table conversations: farm equipment, hunting, Ford vs. Chevy. He could be painfully shy back then. The stutter showed up in middle school, and returned whenever he got nervous.

"A lot of folks in Georgia disagree," Roberts argued. "People got hurt, one pretty seriously. Someone could get killed."

"Well, it was a mis... mistake to go after L.J."

"Maybe. Did he look tense?"

"A little. He kept looking at a homeless guy. Was he one of you?"

The agents glanced at each other without emotion. "Did Mr. Jamison look like he was carrying a weapon?"

"No. N... Not that I saw."

"How about his clothes or tattoos? Any sign of the King of Clubs?"

"No."

"Any sign of new money in his life."

"No."

"But he paused when you mentioned the movement, right?"

"Honestly, I'm not sure."

Shrink got to Redwood State two years before Becker and L.J., practically a religious experience, switching identities, swapping out the shy, eastern Washington, stuttering ranch hand. He can still recall meeting his roommate: tapestries on the ceiling; Wish You Were Here in the background; that first bong hit, completely alien, his roommate filling the bowl, teaching him to release the carb and pull the smoke through. He majored in Psychology, swore he wanted to be a shrink one day, be a meaningful source of inspiration for his clients.

Unfortunately, he grew to hate the idea of listening to people's problems all day. The planet was dying, Goddamit, and Nils Jensen was going to do something about it. By junior year, he dropped out and his life revolved around shifts in the hardware store by day, planning rebellion by night. But the name stuck and he loved the moniker, chuckling at the confusion it caused.

"What was your relationship with David Becker," Roberts asked.

"We were friends. He and Amy would come over, drink beer on the porch."

"Is that all?" McMannis asked suspiciously. "Drink beer?"

Shrink stayed silent.

"Mr. Jensen, if you want to plea out your charges, your cooperation is critical."

"You want me to call him now?"

"The morning is ok."

"Good," Shrink sighed with relief.

"I was being sarcastic. Of course now."

"Shit."

Although Shrink no longer attended Redwood State, he would ply the college bars, looking for like-minded young adults to strike up a conversation with. It was probably in the back of Hungry Joe's playing pool, or happy hour at Dos Amigos, he mentioned the latest forest track up for clear-cut and found a curious Amy Zimmerman and other underclassmen. Amy would bring a classmate, David Becker, to an initial meeting, around campfire to learn more.

"David Becker," a frazzled voice answered the phone. "Nils who? Oh, Shrink. How've you been?"

"Good. I've been good," Shrink said, staring at the FBI agents in his hotel room, attempting what convincing should sound like. "How 'bout you?"

"Good. I'm working for an environmental firm now. It's funny you called," his voice trailed off.

"Yea, how so?"

"Just some crazy shit happening out there."

Shrink couldn't agree more but played dumb. "Can you believe Fowler named his astrologist as Energy Secretary? This guy is our President?"

"Crazy," Becker agreed, pausing before blurting out his thoughts. "Do you remember the sex scandal from last year?"

"Yea. That was awesome."

"Yea. I dug into those emails. They're all on Wikileaks."

"Yea, I remember."

"There was a KOC poker game among top congressmen."

"Uh-huh," Shrink responded, not sure where this was going. "KOC?"

"I think it stands for King of Clubs."

McMannis scribbled on a piece of paper and handed it to Shrink. CAN WE MEET?

"David, can we meet?" Pause. "David?"

"When?"

"Tomorrow? Lunch?"

"Perfect."

"I'll text you details."
"Great."

Becker hung up the phone. He looked around his office, stunned, uncertain of what just transpired. One of the negatives of being a stoner like Becker is most hours of the day: it can be hard to keep shit straight. *Why did Shrink call him? He never even said.*
    Becker picked up his phone and texted Zoe.
    "Where are you? We need to talk."

# Chapter 57. Nathan Culp

When their chartered jet touched down at Reagan National, McMannis and Roberts found a Bureau SUV waiting for them. They were confused when it drove past the Strategic Information and Operations Center. It was diverted to the east entrance of the Capitol building. The C3 Subcommittee wanted answers. Through building security, the agents sprinted past Statuary Hall, down the marble corridor. Cap Little was waiting nervously outside the hearing room, half a dozen file boxes in tow.
    "We did the best we could," McMannis panted.
    "It could be a shit-show in there," Cap gaped. "Hold on to your ass."
    "Yes sir."

The C3 Subcommittee was, and remains, the most secretive of entities. The long version—the Counterterrorism, Counterintelligence, and Counterproliferation Subcommittee under the Permanent Select Committee on Intelligence—the C3 is akin to the deepest ring of the Pentagon, the House's inner sanctum requiring highest possible clearance. Military intelligence, cyber warfare, threats foreign and domestic.

On this day, the C3 waited impatiently for the FBI to report on the eco-terrorism tormenting the American people. McMannis walked in backward, awkward, boxes of information in hand, and surveyed the room. Nathan Culp, the wiry representative from northwest Pennsylvania, sat in the middle of the ornate bench, a not-so-modest two feet above the floor, high back leather chair, embossed metal plaque.     Four other republicans and three democrats watched in silence from the bench wings.

Case Agent McMannis and SAC Little sat at the front table, Roberts behind a row in support.

Nathan Culp offered an oblique nod and the C3's support staff—lacking requisite clearance—exited, closing the heavy, soundproof door behind them.

"Agents Little, McMannis."

"Mr. Chairman," they replied in unison, still getting organized.

Culp dispensed with pleasantries. "This has gone on long enough. My Easter Sunday was ruined by the attack in Georgia. Where is the FBI?"

"Shouldn't Leun Jiang from Homeland Security..."

"There's no time," Culp explained. "Besides, we know who is really in charge of this manhunt."

"Yes sir."

Nathan Bartholomew Culp III always knew his future – a life dedicated to politics, to serve the good people of northwestern Pennsylvania as his father did before him, and his father before him. They were named after the disciple, the one Jesus called a true Israelite, a soul without deceit. Nathan married the plainest girl in Erie, Jodi Leckie. Perhaps not beautiful, she was reasonably handsome once the acne cleared and she cut out the chocolate cupcakes, the devil's food. Plus, she was rich. Quite rich. Her father, Simon Leckie, owned a string of car dealerships in the region including Erie Ford, where just a few weeks ago, un-American terrorists, apparently high on drugs, set upon a plot of environmentalism, communism, and godlessness, or some combination thereof.

SAC Little briefed the C3. Hundreds of agents were burrowed under the J. Edgar Hoover building, less than a mile as the crow flies, digging through the feeds of ten million video cameras, scouring the internet. Hundreds more were in the field, tracking down clues, interviewing potential suspects, setting spiderwebs of Stingray intercepts. Supercomputers wove it all together.

"Do you know who we're looking for?" a congressman rifled from the corner.

"We have a shortlist of suspects, and we're pursuing them vigorously," Little volleyed back. Suddenly, the questions were coming in waves, like platoons landing on the beach.

"Is there a tie to ELF? Are they active again?" *We don't believe so*

"How is this gun not registered?" *It was stolen. The registry is irrelevant.*

"What about the AR-15 slugs found at the first attack?" *We believe it's a ghost weapon, home-made, not traceable.*

"Are the criminals on the grid?" *They're hiding on bi-roads, using cash for all purchases.*

"What does the King of Clubs mean? What is the motivation?" Pauline Bridges, Republican of Maine, asked. "And is my state next?" SAC Little paused like an old fluorescent light, flickering with uncertainty.

"We don't believe so," McMannis chimed in, bending toward the microphone. The room fell silent, paused in confusion. "We don't believe Maine is next."

Nathan Culp watched silently from the center chair. It was just yesterday, at Culp's stately apartment on D Street that he was visited by two FBI agents, asking him if he had any insight on the attack in his home district. Of course, not, he harumphed. Did he know the other Congressmen who's districts were hit by the ecoterrorists: Reid Johnston, the Speaker of the House and Ornette Schlesinger from Georgia's 8th? Yes, they played in a card game with a few others.

"We believe the attacks may be political," McMannis explained to the C3, the Subcommittee members baffled by the agent's vagueness.

"We understand they may be political," Congressman Bridges shot back. "But what is the motivation, in the FBI's opinion?"

"They may be trying to communicate a crime."

"Sounds speculative," Nathan Culp registered. "Is the FBI focused on the manhunt?"

SAC Little nudged back into position. "Yes, Mr. Chairman, the Bureau is HIGHLY focused on the manhunt."

"Who's organizing these attacks? Where's the money coming from?"

"We're working on that, Sir."

"How long will it take to catch these bastards?"

"A week at the most."

"A week?!"

"Perhaps shorter, days. Once they make a mistake on the grid, we will have the information to pounce."

"The attacks are six days apart?"

"Yessir."

"That puts the next attack in two days."

"Yessir."

"That's Earth Day."

"Yessir."

"Make sure they're caught before then."

"Yessir."

\*\*\*

An hour later, Becker was watching Seinfeld, the one where Kramer pretends he works in a midtown office, attending meetings, bringing files home to a lonesome Jerry. Becker's only seen it 50 times. Anything to keep his mind from racing. A text came in: Amelia Levy, Zoe's friend. "Hi Dad, its me. I'm using Amelia's phone cause mine is busted. Working on a ginormous science project. Due tomorrw. Love U!"

Becker stared at his cell, wondering. His imagination must be getting the better of him, the paranoid thoughts he was having. "Love you too," he texted back, grabbed a beer from the fridge, and turned the TV a little louder.

# Act Three: Exodus

*The tree of liberty must be refreshed from time to time with the blood of patriots and tyrants.  It is its natural manure.*

- Thomas Jefferson

# Chapter 58. The Rubicon

The crowd outside the Metropolitan Correctional Center grew as news of the 60 Minutes interview rippled outward on concentric circles of fiber and broadband. Each side, pro and con, attempted to drown out the other. Songs of solidarity and bullhorns and cowbells, now weaponized, echoed off the concrete penitentiary, radiating over the tourists as they journeyed the Brooklyn Bridge, under the massive stone arches, and across the infinite meeting rooms of gothic City Hall looming above.

Zoe's attorney, Stanley Zivitz, suggested a break. Surrounded by stainless steel tables and ward-sized kettles, Zivitz pleaded with her from the prison's industrial kitchen. She nodded in agreement as he flailed, something about self-criminalization.

"Incrimination," Zivitz threw his hands up. "Self. In-Crim-In-A-Tion!"

"Right. I get it," Zoe assured him. Makeup personnel entered with a hesitant knock to reapply her foundation, hide the dark half-moons howling under her eyes. Getting a good night's sleep in the MCC was laughable, unable to ignore the pitter-patter of rats and cockroaches scurrying in the dark, the sharp scent of urine in the air, the echo of demented moans.

Heather Danielson interrupted with a five-minute warning and Zoe excused herself as a butchy guard led her to the restroom to find discolored sinks and grungy tile. She caught the guard's glare, closed herself in a stall, and hoped one of them would disappear. "Little privacy, please?" she said.

"60 seconds," the guard responded, exiting to the hallway.

Zoe stood on the toilet seat and crouched low, fingernails dug into her scalp, rocking back and forth, pleading with a God she wasn't sure she believed in. The pleas turned to mute cries, tears finding the toilet water below. The guard knocked on the door; time's almost up. She wiped her face, flushed, and walked to the tarnished sink, the fading mirror. She washed her hands from a far-off planet, not sure how the fingers knew what to do. She found pupils staring back at her, a thousand variations of green and russet in her iris, a hundred thousand voices in her head, millions waiting to hear what she would say next, an infinite number of ancestors and successors arguing about virtue in the clouds. She saw her father, readily. That schnoz, the shape of the ear, the smile she forced at the reflection. Yep, she was a Becker. Her mother? She hadn't noticed her recently, as if the bequeathed features began to fade along with the memories of her laugh, her smell. She drew closer to the glass, deeper into the coffee and emerald shadows. Apparitions obscured in the recesses. She floated a hand to the glass to test its solidity when the door behind her opened.

"Time," Butch said as she entered the bathroom, motioning to the hall. Zoe pretended she wasn't jolted, discarded some paper towels, and muttered thanks for the privacy. She walked back into the cafeteria, past the producer and crew, the outsized security detail and prison management, and took her place in the white plastic chair. Zivitz and Ethan Webber, the 60 Minutes veteran, sat in their respective slots. They gave one another an understanding nod. The lights queued, Danielson counted down and aimed back to Webber. The recording light glowed bloodshot once more.

"Welcome back, Zoe." Webber searched for her gaze as she twisted at her lip, still deep in thought. "So, you first learned of the King of Clubs by hacking a computer?"

"That's r..."

"I'd like to confer with my client," Zivitz interrupted, frustrating the reporter.

Zoe knotted a bun above her head, the hair a bit greasy, leaning into his counsel. Her orange prison jumpsuit hid most of her femininity, except now the nape of her neck, a concealed elegance, shown through. Zivitz whispered again. She reached between the chairs and found Stanley's hand with her own, reassuring him, like the first time a parent is convinced to hand over the car keys. "I just want to tell the story..." She shook her head as if laughing at a joke only she and dogs could hear, and wiped away a tear. "My dad was right. I've never been a good liar." She turned back to Webber. "Can you ask the question again?"

Webber repeated the query. "Is it true you first learned of the King of Clubs by hacking a computer?"

Looking straight through the interviewer, as if communicating with his shadow, Zoe admitted to a federal crime on national TV. "Yes. That's right." She widened eyes wide with emphasis. "We knew Dr. Abassi was killed. His suicide was impossible to my dad. To me."

"It's been reported Dr. Abassi was on lots of medications."

"But he wasn't suicidal. He had a calling."

"What kind of calling?"

"From God." Before Webber could scoff, she continued. "He told my dad that there's an Arabic word for humans: Khalifa. It also means to be a steward of the earth, that humans are set apart from the animal kingdom."

"But..." Webber tried to cut in.

"And that it's our responsibility to protect it. He really believed that. He hated that we weren't living up to that."

"But you didn't know of the conspiracy fully?"

"No. Not yet," she agreed.

"That was just the first crime?" Webber guessed. " Unauthorized Access of a Protected Computer,", referring to charge number 4 of 14 under the Criminal Fraud and Abuse Act made by the Department of Justice. Among the others, four counts of terrorism, two counts of conspiracy to commit terrorism, two counts of wire fraud, three counts of lying to a Federal agent, and two counts of drug possession. The FBI found a joint and two hits of LSD in her pocketbook when they arrested her. Added together, she faced a potential four life sentences plus another 35 years, perhaps more than any college was willing to defer an acceptance letter.

"We weren't really sure until we hacked the Foundation. We found files that made it clear, that Abassi was killed."

"Why not just tell the press or legal authorities?"

Counselor Zivitz repositioned in frustrated silence. Zoe ignored him. The Rubicon was crossed, she figured. Might as well answer everything.

"The spreadsheet, a snip of what we saw on the screen really, didn't mean anything. Names and congressional bills. How the bills died. Nothing groundbreaking by itself."

"And emails as well?"

"We only saw them. I didn't have time to copy or take a pic before the Foundation shut the computer down. Our access was gone. I was too scared to try it again. My dad brought the story to the New York Times, but it was hearsay. One short article was written, but it never went anywhere."

"It never got the public's attention?" Webber asked.

Stanley Zivitz whispered with desperation in Zoe's ear.

"That's right," she responded, ignoring his pleas.

"So you decided to take the matter into your own hands?"

"I did."

"And terrorism was the method?"

Zoe could only nod in agreement.

"And you felt the need to find larger targets?"

"That's right," she said with a nervous twist of her lip.

"Even bigger than the largest coal plant in the country?"

"That's right."

"To highlight a Congressman with murder on his hands?"

Zoe contemplated the hours of research, learning about Congress, the amorphous gerrymandering to fit partisan ambitions, the committee process, the killing of climate bills. She studied the sources of atmospheric carbon dioxide and methane, the mass of ice stored in Antartica, if broken, never to be put back together again, a hundred million homes or more destroyed if the miles thick frozen layers are untied from their moorings. She stayed up for nights on end, irrelevant exams failed, teeth unbrushed, showered only in the LCD light of her laptop, objectively less effective than water. She studied the maneuvers and shenanigans to protect the status quo, the blatant avoidance of real inquiry by our so-called leaders, bills killed in committee and subcommittee, stymied by debate limits and mystifying mark-ups. If a potential law saved the environment in any shape or form, Committee chairs and Speaker Johnston exterminated it like an unwanted wasp nest.

She Googled our energy usage – electricity, natural gas, coal, oil, solar, wind. The endless mining and production, the transportation, the processing, the storage, the distribution, the combustion, the waste. The transmission lines and rail lines and pipelines cat's cradled across the landscape. Three targets down and three to go.

She contemplated her mom, her work incomplete, and her dad, the nervous tick getting worse. Their life's effort, protecting the trees, vainly enforcing the laws rendered toothless by an unconcerned Congress. Now Frank Fowler would wipe every protection off the books, if given the chance. Something had to be done.

"Zoe?" Webber tugged at the tethers of her consciousness.

"The next site," Zoe mused, wading deep into the concrete's worm hole, past the tears. "It was perfect really."


# Chapter 59. Friday

April 21st, 2017. One Day to Earth Day.

McMannis entered the FBI's Strategic Information and Operations Center by 7:00 that morning, later than he planned. Large screens edged one another along the massive main wall. Dozens of agents filled the desks, heads buried in multi-panel screens. McMannis logged in to a terminal, reviewed his email, new file material, anything to prep for the morning update.

Jiang was in the Executive Briefing Room bearing his usual disgruntled exterior. Representatives across the law enforcement spectrum took their seats. Roberts pulled up a chair next to McMannis, just before Jiang closed the door.

"Mr. Gayton, from the U.S. Marshalls office?" Jiang began, as if in mid-meeting.

"Yes sir," he answered in deep Texas twang from a middle row.

"Have you identified the truck driver?"

"Yessir. The truck belongs to a Maurice Harbaugh from Jeanerette, Louisiana. AKA Mo Harbaugh. Formal weapons and tactics training through a fifteen-month stint with the Marine Corps. Dishonorably discharged in 2008. 32 years old. Last known residence: the Holy Redeemer Church on 39th Street in Manhattan."

"A church? New York City?"

"He was homeless, Sir. Took meals in the church basement."

"Drugs?"

"Cocaine and alcohol in the Marine Corps. He was later picked up on marijuana possession with intent to distribute in Macon, Georgia."

"Near the Scherer coal plant?"

"He used to work there. Fired for tardiness and high blood alcohol."

"Hungover?"

"Yessir. He has a sibling in Louisiana, his sister. We contacted her yesterday. She appears cooperative but we have eyes and ears on her just in case. He also has relatives in Florida and Arkansas, but no contact in years."

"And his accomplice?"

"A man named Ian MacArthur from Duluth Minnesota. Also homeless. Known to be friends with Mr. Harbaugh at the Holy Redeemer Church in New York City. We've talked to the priest there."

"Interview everyone in and out of Holy Redeemer, who they talked to, former employers, landlords, anybody that could be connected. And let's get Stingray boxes up there, at the sister's house, anyone else involved."

"The FBI started deploying them yesterday, Sir," Gayton motioned to McMannis.

"Excellent." Jiang turned to McMannis and Roberts. "What about your BAU profiling?

"Sir," Roberts began. "Mr. Harbaugh is considered a religious zealot, interpreting the bible to meet his own radical beliefs."

"We know that already, Agent."

"Yessir," Roberts said dejectedly.

"He's homeless but has a vehicle?"

"He had it parked in New Jersey, behind a bar he used to frequent."

"But someone is funding this exercise?"

"Most likely, Sir. Mr. Harbaugh and his accomplice were seen conversing with an employee of the church, a Mr. Lorenzo Jamison. Mr. Jamison has been connected with Earth First! while at college at Redwood State."

"Jamison, huh?"

"Yessir. He's under Stingray and direct surveillance. We've brought in an old contact, convinced him to wear a wire."

"Convinced?" Jiang said, chuckling at the code word.

"Yessir. Nils Jensen. It took a little... manipulation. But he's been very helpful."

"Cover everyone from this Redwood State crowd."

"We're on it, Sir."

"Anything else?" Jiang barked, noticing Sara's hesitation.

"Sir," McMannis chimed in. "The sites are very deliberate. As if, there is a message in the attacks. If we can unlock the message, we can predict the next attack."

"Maybe," Jiang sounded skeptical. "How many high-profile targets did you find?"

"A few thousand. Across every corner of the country. Refineries, pipelines, power plants. Nuclear. Hydro."

"Hydro?"

"A massive flood," McMannis suggested.

"Jesus. So how do we prioritize these targets?"

"We believe there's a message in the Congressional districts."

Jiang stared in disbelief. "Congress? You're treading on thin ice."

"We spoke to Nathan Culp of Erie Pennsylvania," Roberts explained. "His district includes the auto dealership attacked. Culp mentioned he plays cards with the other Congressmen who's districts were attacked: Reid Johnston and Ornette Schlesinger."

"Cards?"

"Yes, Sir. Poker."

"Sounds like a Grisham novel. Who else is in this card game?"

"Mr. Culp didn't want to say. But he did mention other top Republicans do join the game."

"You get one of them to talk."

"Yes, Sir."

"The next attack could be tomorrow."

"Yes, Sir.

# Chapter 60. Loose Ends

Zoe woke in her clothes, confused, concerned whispers outside the door. She struggled for recognition. The carpet, the furnishings. Amelia's room? No, it was the spare bedroom in Hannah's apartment.

She exited the bedroom, interrupting the stares and mix of hushed English and Korean Hannah and her parents traded in the hall. Zoe broke the awkward silence and excused herself to the bathroom. A finger for a toothbrush and an old comb from one the drawers, she cleaned up, ears pinned on the conversation.

"If her father is that bad, someone should call social services."

"It's not our place," Hannah pleaded. "It's just a couple of days."

Zoe flushed the toilet, announcing another clumsy interruption, quieting the whispers.

She muttered something about studying for an exam, the need to get to school early, and found herself sorting through more stories as she wandered twenty blocks to school, twenty thousand miles in her head.

She passed a cardboard shanty, the homeless tenants sleeping the morning away. Zoe conjured Mo and Ian at the airport yesterday.

Ian was curious. "Why Yosemite Sam?" he asked.

"Someone I could relate to," as she surveyed the food court for attentive eyes. Now a memory floated through—in her Dad's lap, jamming a popcorn where her front baby tooth used to be, giggling at the silly characters, copying their phrases, making up her own. "Reach for the sky, varmint" she stuck her gun finger into Becker's ribs, sniggering. "And no funny business."

She passed another makeshift abode on the stoop of a brownstone. *L.J. said he met them at church?* Zoe assumed they were parishioners at Holy Redeemer. Or maybe volunteers. Now she realized, Holy Redeemer was their mailing address. *No wonder he wanted to handle the crew.*

Too late now, she realized, catching her obscured reflection as she passed a nail salon, then again in a corner store, lottery tickets hanging like Christmas decorations. Besides, it was going all too well. Were there any loose ends? She produced her phone from the Faraday cage.

*Cushing. Tomorrow,* she typed into WhatsApp.

*Scouting now,* the response came.

She continued her path to Rachel Carson High School, head low in hand, hoping not to be noticed.

# Chapter 61. Pipeline Crossroads of the World

Mo's phone buzzed in his pocket. A message on WhatsApp. It was Yosemite Sam, the girl at the airport.

*Cushing. Tomorrow,* the message reminded him.

*Scouting now,* he typed back, wiped the conversation clean, and turned his phone off. It was a bit of a lie. They were about 50 miles away, in the parking lot of a waffle house.

When Ian asked what they would find ahead, Mo kept it simple. "Oil. Lots and lots of oil." He held the waffle house door for Ian and Sammy. The men were wearing new ballcaps and hoodie sweatshirts, thanks to the local Goodwill.

The cute hostess's outfit said American diner, circa 1950. "Table for two?" she asked.

"Two and a half," Ian motioned to Sammy.

"I'm sorry, no dogs allowed."

"What the heck?" a flabbergasted Ian asked his partner, the human one. Mo just shrugged and Ian bound Sammy to the handicap parking sign out front. They found their table, a booth with a good view of the Tacoma, now a lovely primer white. Except Ian couldn't see Sammy outside the front door.

The waitress wiped the table clean and took out her order pad. Mo requisitioned the Lumberjack. Eggs over easy, bacon (not sausage), waffles (not pancakes), hash browns (not fries). O.J. and coffee.

"Awesome," she turned to Ian. "And for you?"

"Blueberry pancakes, please."

"Blueberry pancakes. Awesome." She walked off to place the order.

"Awesome," Mo muttered, mocking the waitress. "Now, this is awesome," pulling his bible from his hoodie pocket. "Not hash browns."

"Maybe I should check on Sammy."

"He'll be ok. Something awesome should fill you with awe, right?" Mo argued. "Inspire you. Like the word of God."

"I guess," Ian agreed distantly as he stretched to improve his view.

"Ian, he's an old, smelly dog. Do you think people are going to steal him?"

A TV played, volume down, in the corner. Scenes of carnage scrolled behind the reporter. Pickups in Pennsylvania, oil drilling in Texas, a massive power plant in Georgia. Flames licking greasy smoke. Exasperated law enforcement vainly searching the country.

"*The nations raged, but your wrath has come,*" Mo read, lips following his favorite chapter. Ian tapped his arm, shifting his attention to the screen: grainy photos, two men in hats, glasses, and mustaches crossing the abandoned lot outside Erie Ford. Mo and Ian watched in silence. The waffle house crowd took in the news, shaking their heads in disbelief before digging back into sausage links. Then another photo, Mo and Ian, in baseball caps, getting out of a red Tacoma to refill. Georgia, maybe. Or Louisiana. It was hard to tell. The men removed their caps in the waffle house. Mo straightened Ian's hair.

"Let's go over the plan."

"Just tell me what you want me to shoot. I'll shoot it."

"Don't you want to know what we're shooting at?" Mo whispered, perturbed at Ian's disinterest, his own fate, for God's sake. Ian didn't respond, still searching for a glimpse of Westie white. A couple of octogenarians entered the waffle house, seemingly innocent of dog theft. "He's fine, I promise."

The waitress set down water and juice glasses, mugs of hot coffee. Before Ian could take a sip, Mo reassembled the beverages into formation and leaned in. "There are giant tanker farms at the far end of the city, arranged likes cases of beer scattered over a large room."

"Cases of beer?" Ian questioned. "They don't sound so big."

"Well, we'd be microscopic in this situation. Now, over here where the maple syrup is, is a low hill. We may be able to get a clear shot. Then we get out on the highway back this way," laying the knives and forks out like interstates. "We get a few miles out of town before they figure out which direction it came from."

"Ok," said Ian, too hungry to pay close attention. He watched as the waitress approached, through the swinging kitchen doors, her arm holding the tray ear-high.

"Blueberry pancakes?" she asked.

"That's me," Ian said, lifting his arms to make an opening.

"Awesome. And then we've got eggs over easy, bacon, and waffles for the hungry lumberjack." The men ate in silence, relieved the TV switched to Dr. Phil. They paid in cash and waddled out of the waffle house to find a crowd around Sammy. The children petting him commented how sad he looked, all tied up by himself. Mo watched sheepishly from the perimeter while Ian grabbed the leash, allowing everyone a last caress.

Folding himself back into the Tacoma, the prison on wheels. Mo let a substantial groan escape. He turned back onto the four-lane road. After two trips circling the radio dial, they arrived at their destination. At the perimeter of the city, a sign: massive white pipes intersecting one another, a large valve atop like the keystone of an arch.

"Cushing Oklahoma, Pipeline Crossroads of the World," Mo read the black-lettering. "I like the sound of that." They got out to stretch their legs on a patch of lawn. It was 4:00 in the afternoon, the sun in the seventh inning of a clear sky, weeks since it's last rained.

Ian searched the internet. "Let's see. Cushing," he read from a wiki page. "...the largest trading hub for crude oil in North America, connecting Gulf Coast suppliers with northern consumers. Blah, blah, blah," he scanned down. "Cushing holds 5% to 10% of the total US crude inventory."

"5 to 10 percent of total U.S. crude inventory?" Mo questioned. "*Oil that is. Black gold.*"

"*Texas Tea,*" Ian chimed in.

"Let's see," Ian kept reading. "Cushing oil tanks: 85 million barrels of storage capacity. How many gallons in a barrel? 40, right?"

"42," Mo corrected him, stretching overhead yoga-style. First one side, then the other.

"42, wow. And 42 times 85 million? Let's see. That's 357 million gallons."

Mo looked at the calculation. "No, you idiot. That's 3.57 *billion* gallons."

"Oh, yea." Ian punched the numbers into the calculator function again. "We'll never get close to it. It's probably guarded like Fort Knox."

"It's probably worth more than Fort Knox." They stared at each other before spotting the oil storage tanks in the distance. The land, flat as a pancake, obscured the sightline, only a sliver of the enormous infrastructure in view. Mo pointed at a low rise of a hill to the south. "That's probably our best vantage point."

"There's no way we can shoot them all."

"Maybe we could cause a cascade?"

"Exploding dominos?"

"Let's drive around and take a look."

"No harm in that."

They turned their attention to Sammy. The Westie was excited by the look on their faces. "Do you think you're getting fed?" Ian asked in a high-pitched tone. "Do you? Do you?" Sammy barked and did a little pirouette of excitement. "Of course, we're gonna feed you!" Ian picked up the dog, held his phone to arm's length, and took a family selfie to memorialize the moment: Mo, Ian, and Sammy at the Pipeline Crossroads of the World.

They got back in the Tacoma in their usual positions: Mo behind the wheel, a big state atlas from the gas station on Ian's lap, Sammy panting bad breath between them. They drove the area, collecting intelligence for their next attack. Eight hours and counting.

# Chapter 62. Meet Me in the Village

Becker was in the back of the diner, occupying the worst booth in the joint, between the wait-stand and the kitchen. He was checking his email and found one from Rachel Carson School of Science. Zoe missed all her classes yesterday. *And then she spent the night at a friend's? What the hell?* He called and texted but got no response.

Shrink wriggled his way, through the crowded diner, toward Becker's table. "Becks," he called out.

Becker stood up to find ol' Shrink, faded with time. He looked as tired as Becker felt. "Hey Shrink. You look good."

"You too. How you been?"

"Good, good," Becker said, the old friends trading lies, both deciding not to mention their suicidal fantasies.

Then an awkward silence as the waitress placed silverware and water glasses down. They ordered quickly. It's New York, lots of people to feed. Two burgers. Cheese? One with cheese, one without. A ginger ale, a coffee. For all the waitress knew, they could be tech titans ready to make a billion-dollar deal. Or professors or cops or criminals. She was very good at not paying attention. Shrink asked Becker what he was up to.

"Working for an environmental non-profit."

"I remember."

"Then Amy dies. Cancer."

"I'm so sorry. I think that was the last time I saw you."

"Thanks."

"And your daughter? Zoe, right?"

"Yep. You've got a good memory. Awesome kid. 17. Crazy, huh?"

"Junior year?"

"Yea."

"I remember mine. Got into a lot of trouble."

"Me too," Becker recalled with newfound angst. He quickly typed a text to Amelia Levy asking about Zoe. *Have her call me, please.* He changed the subject and queried Shrink about himself.

Shrink brought Becker to the African savannah, with MBolo and his men, and the giant rhino, blindfold on, floating upside down, chained to the '69 Huey. Fighting the good fight.

"Amazing," Becker replied. "I would have loved to have been there."

"It was quite a sight," Shrink beamed, pretty proud of himself.

Black lettering over a plain white van, Ben Franklin Electric, parked a few doors down. In Washington, D.C., McMannis and Roberts listened to the conversation, reviewing an FBI FD-302: *David Stuart Becker. Born: Philadelphia. Abington High School. Rank 426 out of 729. No extracurricular clubs or sports. Redwood State University. B.S. in Computer Science. Graduated in five years. GPA: 2.87. Known to be active in Earth First! with girlfriend Amy Zimmerman and peers Lorenzo Jamison and Nils Jensen. Arrested for disorderly conduct outside Dos Amigos at 2:00 in the morning February 19th, 1985 after fight with girlfriend. Paid $150 fine. Apartment searched in 1986, nothing illegal found.*

"You mentioned the sex scandal?" Shrink prodded. "And the K... King of Clubs."

"Yea?"

"You think there's a connection?"

Becker found himself in the reflection of his knife, the soundtrack of that last phone call with Amir playing in his head. "Someone was killed. It was made to look like a suicide but it wasn't."

"Who?"

"He was a researcher at a national lab. Amir Abassi. He was at Redwood State with us. Do you remember him?"

"Vaguely. He was murdered?"

"Yea. Well, I think so..."

*Mr. Becker moved to New York City in 1988. Attended Fordham Law School 1992 – 1995. Various attorney positions. Currently works for Sustainable Pathway Fund in the Federal Affairs Department. Resides at 217 E. 22nd Street, Apt. 4C, New York, NY. Spouse: Amy Becker (nee Zimmerman), married 1998 – 2011 (deceased, lung cancer). Becker did not remarry. No known current relationships. One daughter: Zoe Becker. On December 1, 2016, Becker filed a report with the Manhattan FBI, claiming a friend, Dr. Amir Abassi, may have been murdered. Dr. Abassi's death was determined a suicide by Washington D.C. coroner's office.*

"Why," Shrink asked about Abassi, "would anyone kill him?"

"He was studying climate change in a way others weren't."

"Two burgers," the waitress brought the food over. "One cheese, one without. One ginger ale. One coffee. Anything else, gentlemen?"

"Looks good," Shrink exclaimed.

"I think we're all set," Becker replied. They dove in, wiping the grease from their chins between bites. He began the tale. "I'm pissed off. Like everybody. It's a giant shit show. Corrupt Frank Fowler could be the next President of the United States? How is that possible?"

"Couldn't agree more."

"When the Paradise scandal hits, I start digging around. Radcliffe's emails say the hookers were paid for by PA. Others refer to a KOC poker game." Becker bit into his burger and raised his eyebrows at Shrink. *You know what I'm saying*, the eyebrows say.

*Mr. Becker was noted for erratic behavior. December 19th, 2016, a neighbor, Louise Goldberg, same address, called 911 stating Mr. Becker was going to jump from the apartment building rooftop. Mr. Becker grew agitated, denied neighbor's account, and was brought in for 48 hours of evaluation. Therapist Martin Feldman confirms Mr. Becker has been a patient for 19 years.*

"And this has to do with Abassi?"

"I don't have hard proof," Becker admitted. "But I think there's a connection."

"Doesn't sound like much."

"Well, I talked to Abassi before he died. He felt threatened not to testify. Thought he might be bugged."

"Based on what?"

"I don't know. But now he's fuckin dead!"

"Take it easy." They ate their burgers in silence, neck hair at attention, not sure what to say next.

*Mr. Becker and daughter Zoe were briefly questioned on Tuesday, April 18, 2017 in connection with the King of Clubs terrorist activities. Mr. Becker claimed no knowledge but suspiciously terminated the inquiry and asked FBI agents to leave the premises. David Becker is currently under several surveillance techniques including...*

Becker stared at his phone when a new text came in:

*Hi, Mr. Becker. It's Amelia. I haven't seen Zoe. Try Hannah.*

He stopped eating, pulled out $25 for his half of the tab, and made up some excuse. "I'm sorry – there's some fire at work. The EPA is trying to get out of the Paris Accord. I gotta go file a brief. Can you get the rest?"

"Uh, sure."

"Good to see you, man," Becker walked out.

"Good to see you too," Shrink said past a mouthful of fries. He swallowed it down with ginger ale.

A low moan crossed the Ben Franklin Electric van. "Fuck."

# Chapter 63. Reid Johnston

"More coffee, Congressman?" Dottie offered.

He lowered the Wall Street Journal so he could see the waitress, still voluptuous in her late 30s. She had been working at the DC coffee shop for 15 years, serving Reid Johnston every Tuesday and Thursday, always at 2:30 p.m., his private retreat just after the lunch rush. The Speaker lifted his cup as she topped it off, and eyed her ass as she walked back to the kitchen. He returned to the paper, checking his stocks. JSI, Johnston Services Inc., was down two-and-a-half points. *Fucking eco-terrorists*, he shook his head.

"A few moments of your time, Sir?" they asked, a man and a woman.

The Journal barely flinched. "I hold my press conferences at the end of the week."

"We're not from the media." McMannis slid his badge under the paper and whispered into the crease. "Agents McMannis and Roberts with the FBI. Could we ask you a few questions?"

Johnston lowered the paper to find business suits staring back at him. "We called your office. They said you were here."

"Is it important?"

"Yes, Sir. Quite. Can we go somewhere private to talk?"

"No one will bother us here."

The waitress placed a steaming omelet in front of Johnston and turned to McMannis. "Should I get you some menus?"

"That won't be necessary, Dottie," Johnston responded, eyes fixed with McMannis. "They can't stay long."

Reid Johnston physically embodied Texas—large, loud, and full of confidence. He made it look easy somehow. The war hero; a chopper pilot in Nam with 62 successful missions. Even got shot down, scuttled back from behind enemy lines, his leg broken in three places. The pentagon loved that story and ran with it for nine months to detract from the body bags. After his decorated discharge, Johnston turned to business. Oil, of course. He *is* from Texas. He rightly predicted the services business may be more profitable than the hit or miss wildcatting game, and he got into leasing equipment, selling supplies. Johnston Services, Inc. doubled revenues and tripled profits every 18 months for the next three decades. Everything from derricks to Doritos for independent drillers and their roughnecks. It was the best days of his life. Until he took it public. Those shareholder meetings full of snot-nosed Wall Street MBAs, enough to make him puke. Once he won and successfully defended Texas' 14th and the twins were released from juvie, he handed them JSI to run, hoping they wouldn't kill each other in the process.

"Sir, have you been following the eco-terrorism activity?" McMannis asked.

"Of course. What's taking the Bureau so long?"

McMannis caught Roberts in the eye. "We're... working on it, Sir. We wanted to ask you about the King of Clubs. Does that mean anything to you?"

"Of course, not," the Congressman said dismissively, the paper winning his attention again.

McMannis leaned across the fold. "Are you familiar with a KOC poker game among members of Congress?"

Johnston looked back with contempt, the inference clear. "You won't be able to get a job at Target once I'm done with you."

"Perhaps," Roberts responded. "But can you answer Agent McMannis's question: are you familiar with a KOC poker game?"

"No, I'm not."

"Do you play poker with other Congressmen?"

"Everybody in this town plays poker."

"You play with Congressmen Culp and Schlesinger?"

"I've played with many people."

"Can you tell us who?"

"I don't recall at the moment. Besides, who I play poker with is not a concern of the FBI's."

McMannis took a chance and unrolled an extra napkin on the table to find the silverware. "I just realized, I am pretty hungry," he pulled Johnston's breakfast plate closer and took a bite. "What is this, Western?"

"Excuse me?"

"Is this a Western omelet?"

"Its ham, onion, and cheese."

"So, like a Western but without the peppers?" Homer took another bite.

"They bother my stomach," Johnston caught himself explaining.

"Agent McMannis, you better watch your behavior."

"You're right, Sir. My hunger got the better of me. It's been a crazy few days."

"That's no excuse," Johnston pulled the plate back.

"But one more question, Sir?" Homer speared a home fry. "Have you ever gotten a hooker?"

For the first time in his life, Reid Johnston was speechless, images bubbling to the surface as he sifted his storage banks. He came to. "I'll have your ass in a sling, Agent McMannis. Are you through?"

"What about Old Man Schlesinger? I bet he likes the ladies."

"Ornette?" the Speaker questioned, a distant smile on his face. Johnston caught himself again. "I'd like you to leave."

Homer slid a business card across the formica table. "If you can recall the other poker players, it could help solve the case."

"Thank you, agent." Johnston tucked the card in his shirt pocket and re-buried his nose in the Wall Street Journal.

On the Capitol steps, McMannis turned to Roberts, wondering if she was thinking what he was thinking.

"Becker's not so crazy?"

"We better get back to New York."

## Chapter 64. Dim Sum

After working remotely in the morning, half-eaten lunch with Shrink, at the office all afternoon preparing a brief, Becker walked home slowly, talking to himself, not sure what to think. He entered the apartment, went to the bathroom, and commiserated with the confused-looking guy already there.

"Where the hell is my daughter?"

No response.

"And was it me, or was Shrink asking some weird questions?"

"You're not crazy," his reflection reassured him. He called Zoe. Straight to voicemail. *Dammit!* He texted Hannah. She hasn't seen Zoe. She's out with her family for a big dinner. Maybe try Travis. Or Amelia. He was going in circles. *Fuck!*

The buzzer hit him like a cattle prod. He stared at the intercom panel, finally pushing the button. "Yea?"

"David Becker?"

"Yea?"

"Agents McMannis and Roberts from the FBI. Can we talk to you?"

"Do you have a warrant?"

"No sir. But we think you may be in danger." Becker paused at the door, contemplating the chess match. *Could that be true?*

"You were here the other day?"

"Yes, Sir."

Time was running short. The FBI was one day from a massive attack and normal protocol was a luxury they couldn't afford. Crazy or not, when Becker threw down his cash and walked away from Shrink and the diner, McMannis knew that source had dried up. It didn't help that Shrink was the worst actor in the world, his stutter like a scale's needle, measuring how much bullshit was coming out. Homer decided to come clean, or at least pretend like he had.

"Mr. Becker? We're aware of your concerns."

"What concerns?"

"Sir, Nils Jensen is working with us."

Becker released the button. *Shrink? Of course.*

Becker crept down the stairs, head angled into the concentric pattern of stairwell, baseball bat in hand as if that might help somehow. From the last landing, through the obscured glass block, he recognized the agents' silhouettes. The weeble on the left, balding, a bit overweight. The pixie on the right. Looks like they're in business suits. He put his face to the glass block, searched for retinas.

"Mr. Becker?" she asked through the security door.

"Yea?"

"If you open the door, we can explain, Sir."

"So, Shrink is working with you?"

"We encouraged Mr. Jensen to call you."

*Encouraged?* Becker conjured a dozen scenarios. *Jail? Possibly. Never heard from again? Wait a minute? That's CIA. FBI, they just rough you up, stick you in the trunk, drive you to the dock, behind the tall fencing...*

"Mr. Becker," he heard again.

"He was wearing a wire when we met?" Becker asked, the answer pretty obvious.

Just then, the lock turned, the door opened. It was Mrs. Goldberg, home with new tins of cat food and ice cream. Fancy feast and pistachio. Friday night.

"David," she greeted him.

"Louise."

The hush was deafening as Mrs. Goldberg passed. Becker ineptly tried to act natural.

"Mr. Becker..." McMannis edged into the open door before it closed again. "Can we discuss this inside?" Becker found himself in the hall, a baseball bat in hand, an FBI agent's foot in his door. He waited for Mrs. Goldberg to turn the stairs and leaned his head out the crack.

"I really don't know anything."

"Mr. Becker..."

"They're just crazy theories."

"If you have information regarding the King of Clubs, it's against the law to withhold that." Becker grudgingly led them up to 4C. As he climbed the stairs, a text came through, a number he didn't recognize. *"Hey, Its Z. oN hannah's sisters phone. Gonna hang heer tonight. Love you"* Heart emoji. Becker wasn't sure if that was good news or bad.

Three hours and a large container of food from the steam tins at the corner store later, Homer's hand cramped from the continuous notes, the long intense conversation with Becker, the improbable story of a scientist, his models predicting doom for the planet, the nervous phone call to Becker. Roberts ran next door for food, all of them famished from the day as Becker retold his tale. He explained it all: Redwood State, the late nights causing mischief in the Williamette, his friendship with Amir and the angst they both felt.

"Mr. Becker, in your first report to the FBI, back in December?"
"Yes."

"You said there was a Christian organization involved?"
"That's right."

"The Faith and Freedom Foundation."

"That's what Amir told me." Becker got up to take a leak, hoping to keep the story straight as he conjured it.

McMannis strained to make sense of it all. "And you say Abassi was threatened not to testify?"

"That's right," Becker said, standing at the toilet, the long stream in the background. "Well, he felt threatened. That's for sure. People following him home, that sort of thing. He'd never kill himself." *That's more my thing,* he reconciled in the mirror. "It didn't make any sense," his voice pointed back to the living room.

"No," McMannis admitted. "It doesn't." McMannis never noticed the creep of the stairs, the foot patter in the hall. But Roberts did. Her head angled back as the sound drew close, coming down the hall. As the bolt turned, Roberts shadowed the door, back to the wall, unclipping the leather holster, raising her weapon slowly. McMannis lowered his conversation, Becker gave it a last shake, both realizing the tension in the room.

The door creaked open, an arm peered through the opening, searching the wall in silence. Roberts re-sheathed her gun, took hold of the arm, raised a knee for leverage, and jerked the hooded assailant, body flying, landing with a perfect thud. Roberts stomped on a foot, gun drawn at the hooded intruder. "Freeze!" Only the sound of heartbeats and lungs refilling.

"It's me! It's me!"

"Zoe!" Becker screamed. He forgot all about her. "Aren't you staying with Hannah?" Becker asked.

Roberts quickly holstered her gun, caught McMannis in the eye, relieved. They helped her up like a pet on its hind legs.

"I'm not here," she sniggered, a cloud in the air. "Just picking up a things... few." She slanted toward her room.

"Zoe?" Becker gazed at the agents, mortified.

"Dad," she called from her room, "y'know the dim sum place I love?"

"Zoe?"

"They have the best happy hour. Sake shots for a dollar..."

"Zoe!" Becker screamed.

She stammered out and finally took notice of the FBI agents, the ones that just threw her to the ground and pulled a gun inches from her skull. The same FBI agents from the other day. "Oh, hey," she said. Her head oscillated on its axis.

"Zoe, this is serious."

"I know. I mean, sorry."

Becker grabbed her elbows to hold her up.

She tried her best, staring at Becker, the gravity of the situation taking hold. The ominous text, the change in vocal tonation as his eyes grew wide with every word. But it started in the nostrils, a tiny snigger. A small vibration, a quick flight of phlegm, a flutter of lips like horses chattering on the open prairie. Then it came, the second wave, back out the nostrils, larger, uncontrolled. An embarrassing, drunken, ill-timed giant snort, accompanied by a small, almost imperceptible poof fart.

She stared at Becker. His eyes pulled at hers, drawing his bravest, most sober daughter he knew was there, somewhere. Her facial muscles tightened, all 43 of them, almost in tears, holding in gas at either end.

"I'm sorry," Becker explained. "I think my daughter's drunk."

"Mr. Becker - you've been very cooperative. You should get her to bed. We will type this up and bring you an affidavit tomorrow. Could we finalize and get your statement on record tomorrow?"

Becker paused. Until now, it was a fable, the perceptions of a nobody stumbling across an expanse of imagination and paranoia.

"It could be very helpful to the country," Roberts said.

"It will give us more resources to protect you as well, Mr. Becker." McMannis added. "You and your daughter."

"Ok. Do I need to get a lawyer?"

"That won't be necessary," they said simultaneously.

"We'll be back in the morning to get your affidavit," Roberts explained.

"8:00," McMannis said. "We'll see you then, Mr. Becker."

# Chapter 65. Earth Day

April 22, 2017, 12:04 a.m.

The Tacoma and its inhabitants rolled forward searching for any rise in the horizontal landscape, about a mile and a half east of Cushing.

A few hours earlier, as dusk was fading, they were driving these same roads to inspect the target, the terrain, the various pathways to the interstate, the potential for watchful eyes. Now, they were back, just after the clock struck midnight. Six days since the last attack.

From this low angle, Mo could make out the perimeter of massive vessels, platoons of squat cylinders—the largest oil storage facility in the country—in the distance. He climbed to the top of the truck to improve his vantage point. Only the tank farm at the southeast end of the massive complex offered a clear line of sight. Dozens more spread west and north, but improved proximity was too dangerous a prospect, too complex an egress route, their lifeblood, in the aftermath. This southeastern corner would have to do.

"I can't hit that with the AR, right?" Ian asked.

"You'd have to arc it like a mortar. We'll just use the 50 cal," Mo responded. He passed the spotting scope to Ian, kept his voice to a whisper. "You see the lights that go up the tanks? The metal staircases? Those are the containers."

"Yep," Ian whispered back, imagining the explosion through the scope.

"Ok. Time's a-wasting," Mo said as he climbed down.

Ian noticed the dog pacing in the back seat. "I think he needs a walk."

"He's fine. Just help me set up and keep watch."

They lowered the truck gate, slid the suitcases and dog food out of the way, and started unloading. Mo popped the Pelican and ogled the beast, its matte finish leaden and infinite. No light escaped. He set up the bi-pod, screwed on the suppressor. Mo handed Ian the Tacoma keys while he played with the scope.

"Turn the truck east, ready to roll."

"Which way is east?"

"That way, you idiot. Where we came from."

"Got it." Ian did as instructed and got back out to help with the preparations. Sammy watched from inside.

"Time?" Mo asked.

"12:09"

"Five quick shots and the car repacked in 90 seconds, ok?"

"Yep."

Mo climbed back on top of the Tacoma, readied his prone position. Ian handed him the 50. The target vaulted in the optics with each heartbeat.

Dog barking broke the silence. Sammy was calling for Ian.

"Jesus Christ," Mo said. "Can you shut him up?"

Ian put Sammy on a leash. "He needs to pee."

"Don't move a muscle," Mo whispered through clenched jaw, steadying the rifle. "And SHUT. UP."

Ian looked down at Sammy and put his finger over his lips, letting the leash go, allowing Sammy a little privacy. Mo fought his heart rate down, like holding an enemy combatant underwater. With a final breath, he pulled the trigger. A second later, they heard the bullet hit its target.

"Did it pierce the tank?" Mo asked

"I can't tell. I don't see anything."

A sound of sparklers, the incendiary came in low and muffled. Mo pulled the rifle back into position and shot at two other massive tanks 26 football fields away. The first tank caught fire where the bullet pierced the steel skin, flames shooting sideways like a volcanic eruption on a distant planet. Two more quick shots at the last tankers visible over the scrub. Far off explosions indicated success.

Then the sirens, gaining volume as they fanned out in every direction for miles. Ear-splitting sirens.

Mo scrambled down, half-assed disassembled the 50, and tossed it into the back seat.

"Gather the cartridges!" Mo shouted, flipping the spotting scope next to the rifle. "Get in," he shouted, behind the wheel, engine on, rumbling down the dirt road with the lights off.

"Shit! Sammy!" Ian exclaimed. Mo hit the brakes, forcing the Tacoma to a dust-filled stop.

"We'll just leave him!" Sure, he was cute. And loyal. A savior to Ian. But he was an old dog. Expendable. He put the Tacoma back in drive.

"His tags!" Ian shouted. "Your cell is on there!"

Mo hit the brakes again, reversed the Tacoma, skidding back to the crime scene, lights off, searching the darkness. They got out and called for Sammy in hushed tones.

"Jesus Christ," Mo muttered. "Sammy?"

Suddenly a bark from the far corner of the dirt road. Sammy's leash tangled in low brush. Mo watched as Ian freed the dog, shaking his head, not sure who to kill first: Ian, Sammy, or himself.

They drove the hell out of dodge, lights off, screaming down 760, south onto Route 99.

"The cards!" Mo suddenly remembered. "We never marked the site."

Ian grabbed a fresh pack from the glove box, searching the deck, organized Ace to King: Diamond, Spade, Hearts, Clubs!

"King of Clubs! I found it."

"Just throw it out the window. They'll find it." Ian tossed the card, detritus to keep the beer cans and burger wrappers company. Another mile down, the ramp to I44, blend in on the Interstate. West, back to Oklahoma City.

Cop cars, sirens blaring—every unit in the state, it seemed— passed in the opposite direction. To the chaos in Cushing. Mo kept her in the right lane, as slowly as his adrenaline-filled veins would allow, desperate not to hit everything that passed. Now miles away, the carnage escalated. Ian watched as the first tank exploded. Full bedlam, a giant fireball pillowing over the topography.

"Holy shit, that was close!" Ian screamed.

Mo whooped with primal satisfaction.

"Sammy!" Ian picked up the dog, shaking him over his head. "We almost lost you!" The dog stared back blankly, uncertain how to respond.

# Chapter 66. The Situation Room

From every corner of the room, commotion. Hands waving at imaginary subordinates as they retold the tale, where they were when they heard the news, awoke by a phone call in the night, reporters knocking on doors, bedside text messages buzzing to life.

For Leun Jiang, Homeland Security Special Agent in Charge, it was a phone call, 2:29 a.m. "Fuck," Jiang whispered in the night. On the toilet for the fourth time tonight just trying to get a good stream. The landline handset was about 11 inches from his ear, just outside the little toilet alcove where he sat, too fucking narrow. He always hated that toilet alcove. The ring pierced his ear.

"Jesus," he flinched, lifting the handset. "Leun Jiang," he answered

"AGENT! SECRETARY OF DEFENSE DONALD GRAHAM," Graham shouted. No time for intermediaries.

Jiang pulled the phone a safe distance from his ear. "Yes, Sir."

"Where the hell are you?!!"

It was like enemy fire, the flash of rounds, the shells falling too close for comfort. Jiang paused, covered the phone's mouthpiece, and reoriented in his bathroom of 17 years. "At home, Sir."

"WHERE?" the Secretary, 83 years young, shouted.

"YOU CALLED ME AT *HOME*, SIR," Jiang yelled, still inside the toilet alcove, jammy drawers around his ankles.

"JIANG! OUR COUNTRY IS UNDER ATTACK! THE NATIONAL SECURITY COUNCIL WANTS AN IMMEDIATE BRIEFING."

"Yes, Sir."

"ITS THOSE KING OF CLUBS ECO BASTARDS."

"Yes, Sir."

"GET TO THE SITUATION ROOM. WE HAVE A SERIOUS FUCKING SITUATION!"

"Yes, Sir!"

Jiang gave it a last few shakes and ran back to the bedroom. In 34 minutes he showered, changed, barked at seven subordinates, brushed and gargled.

The waiting Suburban hit 70 through the suburbs, past Secretary Graham's home, entering his own large black SUV, shouting orders at an aide, finding 120 MPH on the highway before squealing off the ramp for the E Street Exit to the White House. Past two sets of armed gates.

Buried deep under 1600 Pennsylvania Avenue, behind six-inch steel doors, guarded retina scans, weapons check, cell phones surrendered: 5,500 square feet of intelligence infrastructure. Past more security, Jiang was escorted to a mahogany-paneled space for only the highest clearance individuals in the country; where Reagan observed Gorbachev's fall, W surveyed the shock and awe to hit Saddam, and Obama watched Osama slip to a watery grave.

"It was international," came from one corner of the room. "I bet Iran is behind it."

"Eco-nuts," more speculation came from another corner. "They're trying to spark a war!"

"Gentleman," Secretary of Defense Graham announced, "please take your seats." The room came to a quiet hush as chairs we're filled according to rank, the country's toppest brass: the Joint Chiefs of the Army, Navy, Air Force, the Homeland Security Department chief, the heads of the FBI, CIA, NSA and the Department of Energy.

"SAC Jiang, you have the floor."

Jiang found infuriated stares seeking answers. "Thank you, Sir. Five tanks were hit. One exploded and had a catastrophic failure. Limited damage to the other four. No cascading explosions, as we believe was the intention."

"We may have dodged a bullet."

"Yes, Sir."

While the physical damage was contained, the emotional toll was significant. The country was on high alert, obsessed with news feeds and phantom sightings. Gasoline prices increased 100% overnight. Long lines started forming at gas stations, more price escalation expected.

"What is our plan?" an army general interjected. The questions poured in like ants invading a picnic.

"Yes, what is our plan?"

"When will they strike next?"

"How many are there?"

"What is taking so long?"

"Gentleman!" Jiang reigned in control. "Homeland Security is asking for Defense personnel and assets to guard national infrastructure, purely in a Civil Defense security posture."

"Like the cold war?"

"We will be prioritizing all energy production sites. Our directions will be available by noon today."

# Chapter 67. Bad Hombres

*We've got some bad hombres causing chaos in the U.S. Don't worry America. They will be caught and convicted, never to be seen or heard from again.*

@PresidentPOTUS, April 22nd, 2017 07:58:01 am.

# Chapter 68. Have it Your Way

"Mr. Becker?" the voice came through the intercom panel.

"Yes."

"This is Agent McMannis."

Becker came down the stairs and saw the agents through the block glass. He opened the door, surprised to see they had lots of company. "I'm ready for the affidavit..."

They pushed him to the ground, showed him the warrant, zip-tied his wrists, and read him his Miranda. A dozen agents in cheap FBI jackets filed past, large empty boxes in hand, two-stepping it to 4C. Twenty minutes later, the jackets and boxes descended the staircase. Laptops, external hard drives, work files, bills, notes, the Vonnegut collection. They emptied the office nook, the bookshelf, anything with words, pictures, scribble, fingerprints. McMannis approached Becker, Indian-style on the ground, bending forward at the waist, wrists knotted behind him.

"Mr. Becker?"

"Am I under arrest?"

"We're bringing you in for questioning. Do you know where your daughter is?"

"She's not in bed?"

"No, Sir."

"She may be at work. D'Antonio's. How long can you detain me?"

"Without charges, 72 hours." McMannis picked up Becker's phone. "Care to tell me the passcode?"

"I'm gonna need a lawyer."

"Have it your way, Mr. Becker."

Eleven boxes of Becker's life left the FBI van and were scurried to the agency's Manhattan office. Digital scans were conducted on the laptop and hard drives. Two hours later, they found an unexpected file. A .png document, a screenshot. Appears to be a spreadsheet called the King of Clubs. Down column A: Reid Johnston, Texas; Nathan Culp, Pennsylvania; Ornette Schlesinger, Georgia; Norman Radcliffe, Oklahoma. The FBI agents struggled to make sense of it—legislative bills, status updates.

"Radcliffe is from Oklahoma?" Roberts asked.

"Yep."

"Bet he represents Cushing?"

"I'd take that bet." There were two names they didn't recognize: Chad Droburn, Jr. and Landry Muldoon. They Googled their districts. The next attack was either in southern California or northern Louisiana.

"But where'd that file come from?"

"And how did it get on Becker's laptop?"

"Becker smart enough to break into a computer?"

"I doubt it. Maybe the kid?"

"What next?"

"I've got a hunch," McMannis grabbed his suit jacket. "Becker's lawyer should be here soon. Find out what you can," he told Roberts.

"Where you headed?"

"Gonna pay a little visit to the Faith and Freedom Foundation, maybe a few congressmen."

# Chapter 69. Go West Young Man

Ian unwrapped the dirty bandages around Sammy's paw, the stitches were miraculously gone. A quick trim seemed appropriate. Something was coming to a head, Sammy might as well look his best. Ian worked the scissors deftly. Pull a tuft and snip. Pull and snip. "Hold still, darn it," he complained, "or someone's gonna get hurt."

The old dog looked back in concern, tongue displaced. His rear legs trembled with fear, an evolutionary aversion to scissors, it appeared.

"You know how he hates gettin' his hair cut," Mo reminded him.

"I know, but Mr. Sammy can't see past his bangs."

"He looks even more mangey than before."

After the fireworks in Cushing, they hugged the byroads. North on 81 through Enid, Oklahoma, west on 64, through the panhandle, to Campo in southeastern Colorado. They parked behind an old auto repair, blending in with the other junk, a few hours' shut-eye. Flat, brown, and covered with thorn. You'd never know it's the same state as heavenly Telluride or the majestic Maroon Bells.

Mo planned a quick breakfast, get back on the road. Then Ian decides to start grooming the old dog. Mo eyed his watch, the third time in the past 5 minutes. "Car's packed. Just need the passengers."

"Almost done. Just gotta clean up this tail. And then this belly looks a bit..."

"Ian!" Mo shouted before tapering his volume. "I don't think you understand the gravity of the situation. Please," his hands shook in frustration "... we need to get moving."

"You said you were going to work on your anger."

"I am, Ian. This is *me* not killing *you*. That, I think," as he led Sammy to the Tacoma, spilling the dog into the backseat, "is pretty good progress."

"Where we headed?" Ian asked as he jumped in.

"West. Like the saying goes, *Go west, young man*."

Ian thought that sounded familiar. "Like, California?"

"I'm not sure, we haven't gotten instructions yet. But I figure, as long as we're averting the law, we might as well see some of the country."

The Tacoma drove north and connected with I-70, a hundred miles from Denver as the Rocky Mountains start to take shape. The Holy Mountaintop. Past the city's brown cloud and intersecting snarl, the road began to climb. Ian was filled with awe. Morrison, Indian Peaks, Georgetown; mining towns that fill a narrow crack in the mountains, small planks of level ground where hearty individuals found riches in the ore they pulled out of the earth. Or, barely eked out an existence before an untimely demise.

Ian bemused about the prior day. "That young girl delivering the money was..."

"Careful, Ian. I think she was not exactly *of legal age*." Mo noticed the embarrassment he caused. "Of course, if this was biblical times, or even well after, when these old mining towns were settled, she would've been perfectly suitable for courtin'."

That made Ian feel a bit better but then reminded him of the gap-tooth grin he may have scared her with. "Yea, biblical times. I bet we would've fit in real well back then," Ian surmised. "Two witnesses, that's what we are."

"Ian, I've been meaning to share something." The truck strained to climb higher, to cross the Continental Divide at the Eisenhower-Johnson tunnel, elevation 11,158.

"This is some hill," Ian said. "You were saying..."

"Yea, about the biblical times. You see, the two witnesses go through... How shall I put this? A difficult journey. We better read it together." Mo handed Ian the bible, his leatherette-bound future. Mo gave him a solemn stare. "It's Revelation, Chapter 11."

"I remember."

"I think we just finished the 6th verse." More powerful SUVs and pickups serpentined past the Tacoma as it geared down, the engine revving louder, struggling to maintain speed as highway and sky converged.

"Ok. Revelation 11:7. Let's see..."

*'Now when they have finished their testimony, the beast that comes up from the Abyss will attack them, and overpower and kill them.'*

Ian looked over at Mo, mouth agape.

"Yea, that's the part I've been meaning to talk to you about."

Ian read on. *'Their bodies will lie in the public square of the great city—which is figuratively called Sodom and Egypt—where also their Lord was crucified. For three and a half days some from every people, tribe, language and nation will gaze on their bodies and refuse them burial. The inhabitants of the earth will gloat over them and will celebrate by sending each other gifts, because these two prophets had tormented those who live on the earth.'"*

Mo puffed out his cheeks in silent admission. "So, it says the beast—that's the people, of course—they kill the witnesses and then exchange gifts, it seems, and have a big party for three and a..."

Ian grabbed Mo about the neck and gave a squeeze of biblical proportions. The larger man struggled to stay on the road and fend off his friend. He pulled over to safety, just below the tunnel, the engineering marvel. Late-season skiers honked at the erratic driver, annoyed by the delay.

"Why didn't you tell me that?!" Ian demanded. He paused and loosened his grip, allowing air to pass again.

"It's not an easy subject to raise," Mo gasped, as his coloring descended hues of tangerine and lavender. He looked over in shame, got out of the car, and came round the passenger side to comfort Ian. "I'm sorry. I really am, little buddy."

Ian got out of the car and shook his head in disbelief. Mo gave him a firm embrace, the traffic inching past them as three lanes merged into two, the vehicles gasping for oxygen, forward through the Eisenhower, the orifice to the west. Ian's eyes moistened and a tear dropped down his cheek. He never imagined it would end like this.

"But read the next part," Mo said. "It gets better."

Ian took a deep breath, wiped his nose, opened the book, and soldiered on. He raised his voice so Mo could hear him over the passing traffic. '*But after the three and a half days the breath of life from God entered them, and they stood on their feet, and terror struck those who saw them. Then they heard a loud voice from heaven saying to them, "Come up here." And they went up to heaven in a cloud, while their enemies looked on.*'

"*Come up here,*" Mo repeated, eyes lit with the holy spirit. "Everything's gonna be ok, Ian. We're headed to an extraordinary place."

Ian looked around, verdant evergreen and snow and rock jutting into the sky from every corner of their vista. Below to the east, the traffic ascended the hill, attenuating hidden peaks and flats to approach the tunnel. "It sure is beautiful here."

"It gets even better," Mo said. "You gotta see Utah."

# Chapter 70. One More Thing

Zoe is in the rear car of the subway, pants down, sitting on a child-size toilet in a tiny bathroom, cold air scooting up her hole, as it starts spinning in unnatural directions, sideways across the rails, horn blaring. Through a small window, she spotted the oncoming headlights of a tractor trailer carrying far too much speed to stop in time. Just before the fiery crash, the all-night surgeries in the intensive care unit, she jarred herself awake, covered in sweat. Reeking of sake and strange memories, she peered past the window shades. The sun fringed the horizon.

She raced out of the building before her Dad's third degree, stuffed her phone, an extra pair of panties, makeup, and a t-shirt in a backpack. She walked to the Brooklyn Bridge and back, hands flailing, battling demons of her own creation. An hour and a half later, she edged the corner of 3$^{rd}$ Avenue, and witnessed her greatest fear coming to life: FBI agents hauling boxes out of 217 E. 22$^{nd}$ Street.

She turned south, west on 18$^{th}$, south again on Park, down the subway stairs, eighty blocks north to 96$^{th}$ street. Across Central Park and the throngs of Earth Day protestors gathered, organizing their chants, talk of the Oklahoma attack bouncing from conversation to conversation. Every other sign exalted the King of Clubs. Counter arguers rallied from an encircling perimeter, their faces filled with violent objection.

Down more subway steps, Zoe jumped on the #1 to Manhattan's southern edge. With slight variation, the loop was repeated five times, passing hour after hour in a state of panic. She searched the crowd of carnival gazes and nonexistent stares for suspicious activity, hidden in plain view.

A quarter to 4. She pulled her phone hesitantly from the Faraday Cage. They could probably lock onto her signal in minutes. She logged onto WhatsApp and typed out a message.

*Washington Square Park, 5:00.*

*Thumbs up*, the emoji response came back.

Zoe stowed the cell again and traced maze patterns in the streets for 75 minutes. They met next to the white marble arch; the interior, less-ornate side, surrounded by tourists and the screams of children as they played, the large fountain arcing behind them. Zoe scanned the crowd but the long-range cameras and boom microphones were too distant to be noticed.

"Dad was arrested," she said.

"Christ," L.J. responded. "The shit's hitting the fan. Does he know?"

"He must. I've been avoiding him for days. The FBI have been back twice to ask questions. Then I see them hauling boxes out of our apartment this morning. I got out of there just in time." They caught each other in the eye.

"Should've just written the screenplay," L.J. joked.

"It would've made millions." Zoe shrugged a tearful laugh, then clutched him tightly. "I'm so sorry..." L.J. brushed her hair as she confessed. "I used your phone to contact them. I gave them more money, told them to keep going. I'm... I'm sorry."

"It's ok. I'm the one who should be sorry. I never should have let it get this far." He chuckled uneasily.

She released her hug and wiped the mess her face had taken on. She shook her head no. "It was my crazy idea. It's not your fault."

"But I'm supposed to be the adult."

Cloaked in a dirty wool blanket, a homeless man walked by. A small laugh escaped Zoe's lips. "Is he working for us, too?"

"I meant to tell you about them."

"They seem like... interesting characters."

"Yeah," L.J. said distantly. "They had their own reasons. Doesn't matter now. You can still fight this, ya know. You're just a kid."

"You can as well. You never actually threw a bomb, pulled a trigger."

"Maybe." They turned away from each other, not sure how to say goodbye. L.J.'s head throbbed in pain, a strange smell of bacon on the wind.

"One more thing..." she called back, wiping another tear, narrowing the distance with a couple of skips, searching for the words. "You know... I love you."

They hugged again, Zoe's head against his chest, finding his heartbeat.

"I love you too," L.J. said, exhaling as if he forgot how. "Like you were my own." He paused with a knowing stare. "You're gonna be o.k."

"You too."

Then separate directions, Zoe east, L.J. south.

A block later, Zoe pinged Amelia on WhatsApp. Amelia was getting off work soon; she'll pick her up in an hour. *Can't wait to party!*

*Not my apartment*, Zoe responded. *Meet me in Bryant Park, just behind the library.*

*OK*, Amelia texted back.

One last message, this one to Mo: *Next Target-Southern CA. 4/28.*

# Chapter 71. Don't Get Fired

Within hours following the attack, squadrons of news teams descended on chaos's unlikely new epicenter: Cushing, Oklahoma. They set up their video cameras—a distant backdrop of scarred oil tanks, offered their audience super-zoomed views of bullet holes and the residue of fire retardant. The town's two diners were packed full with rental cars and east coast accents. Police lights and law enforcement's black SUVs flashed for miles on every farm road in three counties.

TV's talking heads discussed the resiliency, or lack thereof, of the country's nuclear fleet, the oil refining portfolio, of bridge safety and dam security, of the countless pipelines and high-voltage transmission lines that pattern across the continent. Overnight, the populace became cereal-box experts in infrastructure and energy, security and manhunts.

Leun Jiang was there as well, in Cushing, touring the damage and the presumed strike location. Agents crawled the dusty roads, sifting the soft shoulders of county roads for inklings of information.

"SAC Jiang," he answered his cell.

McMannis was on another flight, back to D.C., a daily occurrence as he tightened the ambit. "It's Agent McMannis. We've had a break with the Becker lead. The next targets are southern California and northern Louisiana."

"It's too late, Agent. Forces are being deployed across the country."

The wheels were in motion: national guardsmen escorted oil delivery trucks to neighborhood gas stations; video cameras added to highway ramps and bi-way stoplights; drones lofted; first responders returned from vacations, double shifts until the terrorism threat abated. Army reserves were called up and shipped out to the Baaken, the Marcellus, the Anadarko.

"Sir," McMannis protested, "it's critical we focus resources wisely."

"I'll handle the resources, Agent."

"Yes, Sir."

"California and Louisiana?"

"Yes, Sir. California's 50th district. And Louisiana 8th. Do you need the counties?"

"We'll look it up, get more assets in place."

"Thank you, Sir."

"More Congressmen involved?"

"I believe so."

"Oklahoma? That was part of the plot?"

"Norman Radcliffe."

"From the Paradise Scandal?"

"Yea. That's the one."

"Interesting. Don't get fired."

"I'll try not to. Thank you, Sir."

\*\*\*

As law enforcement and national defenses fanned across the country, additional surveillance took root. Covert, unauthorized. Police scanners and chat rooms. Would-be lawmen tracked official evidence, created a parallel manhunt. They shared potential sightings and visions of glory, to hang those eco assholes from the highest tree.

One individual was particularly engaged. Eleven tattoos and a red mullet under a trucker hat had been following the ecotage for three weeks.

# Chapter 72. In the Land of Moab

"The Kingdom of Moab," Mo extolled, "the land where Moses is buried." He tapped the gas nozzle against the Tacoma. Every drop counts. "One day we'll get to the real one. Utah will have to do for today."

Ian wrestled the wedge of the door for a restful angle. Sprawled on Ian's lap, belly up, Sammy found a comfortable position with greater success. "This is Moab?" he squinted out the open window to find low angled rays on beige flatness and squat, function-over-form buildings. "Not what I expected."

"No," Mo explained. "This is Loma. Colorado. Nothing special. The promised land is coming up. Another hour or so." Ian closed his eyes and pet Sammy's tummy as the dog instructed. He crossed his chest, praying for a few hours of decent sleep.

Mo's phone buzzed with a new WhatsApp message. He logged in: *Next Target-Southern CA. 4/28*. The objective: one of the largest refineries in the country. No need to reply. He stuck his phone back in his pocket.

"*From my father.* That's what Moab means," Mo continued, settling behind the wheel again, pulling at his beard a bit. "Moab ruled a powerful kingdom east of the Dead Sea. I think it's Jordan now."

Ian tugged at Sammy's ear, not paying attention.

Two large helicopters flew low overhead. Dust and bass-filled thump kicked in all directions. The Tacoma hid under the high gas station awning. "Did you know Moses camped on the plains of Moab. God told him to climb the Mountain of Pisgah..."

"Mo," Ian interrupted. "We should probably get going."

"These are true stories, Ian. We're talking Moses," Mo scoffed. He scanned the gas station and the surrounding buildings and muttered underneath his breath. "Well, true for the bible." A pale man with lots of tattoos and a red mullet was on his cell phone, staring intently at the Tacoma. He gesticulated in frustration.

Mo looked knowingly at his partner. "Ian... its time." Ian looked back, stammered a bit, and quickly realized Mo was right. "Do you still have those plates you stole from the Tesla?"

"I think they're under your seat." Ian picked Sammy up and looked him in the eye. "Mr. Sammy. You're gonna be ok," and they met forehead to forehead in primal comprehension. As Ian walked the dog into the gas station, Mo found the license plates and the screwdriver. The gas station attendant's blue vest hung loosely over her white blouse and matching beads. Her name tag read Nelly.

"What a cute little boy. What's your name?" she asked bending down on one knee.

"His name is Sammy," Ian responded.

"That was my husband's name," as she found his favorite spot: under the chin, just behind the jowl, tail wagging with approval. "He had bad breath just like you," as the dog stretched to kiss her.

Ian smiled. "My friend and I...," he paused. "We're headed into the desert..."

"Uh-huh," she said as if she knew where this was going.

"...for a few days. And I'm worried Sammy may be... uncomfortable. Would you... mind watching him?" He offered two hundred dollars cash, and she relented, excited to find a bowl and some food. He offered a quick over-the-shoulder thank you before she could change her mind.

Ian walked past Red Mullett—crouched toward the powdered doughnuts, whispering into his cell phone—then past a pyramid display of windshield washer fluid, out the door, and back into the Tacoma. Mo finished changing out the plates and assumed his position behind the wheel.

The two men nodded as Mo drove off. "She seemed like a real nice lady," Mo contemplated.

"Yea," Ian agreed, his eyes welling up with tears. He knew that was the last time he would see Sammy. Perhaps they'd find each other in the next life.

The last few buildings gave way to broad horizons of low desert shrub, wooden posts, and uninterrupted wire.

Back at the gas station, four large pickups pulled up, horns blaring. "They went west," Red Mullett said in frustration. "What took you so long? Keep your damn radios off. Cops will be listening," he instructed. "I want these assholes myself."

Sunset turned the landscape campfire red. Mo raced ahead, 100 miles an hour. Two antelope flitted away over the low pink Desert Phlox and clumps of Mountain Pepperplant. The full-sized sign read: Cisco, 128. Next to it, a much smaller sign Mo felt fortunate to spot given the speed and diminishing light: Moab. The back way.

He pulled off the highway, up the steep embankment ramp, and turned left back over the highway. Looking down the interstate, Mo spotted a curious formation: five sets of large headlights barreling west at breakneck speed in the remaining scraps of the day.

"I think we have company."

"Dammit," Ian said with realization, "the guns are in the back."

"That's ok." Mo clasped Ian's hand and gave it a quick squeeze. "No human life, remember?"

"No human life," Ian recalled.

"It's up to God, now."

The column of oversized pickups followed the Tacoma up the off-ramp. The Tacoma's tires squealed as it cornered hard over a short rise with the G-force of an old-time roller coaster. The men's eyes, wide with uncertainty, peered around each escarpment as it passed.

The eroded natural fortress of Fisher Towers came into view. Monoliths of sandstone, stacked and sculpted by rain and the eons, glowed bright crimson and ochre; mystical silhouettes as if prisoners were escaping in the dark.

A few turns behind, the truck lights grew closer, oversized tires kicked up a giant rooster tail of dread. The Tacoma struggled to stay ahead. Mo tilted the mirror down and handed Ian the bible for safekeeping.

A sharp left turn and the Tacoma descended into the river valley, twisting and turning. They could hear the roar of the posse's modified engines. Three gunshots whizzed past the car, dirt exploding high into the air all around the Tacoma, the first kernels in a kettle full of popcorn. Both men screamed bloody hell, their fate realized before them.

## Chapter 73. The Bait

It was the end of a crisp day in the nation's capital, the afternoon light fading as McMannis entered the white marble building on 14<sup>th</sup> Street. The Faith and Freedom Foundation occupied the entire top floor.

"Thank you for meeting me," he shook her hand.

"Never a problem to support our nation's law enforcement." Penny Archer's circuitous smile said otherwise.

McMannis took in the surroundings while the chit chat began. Dark wood paneling, pictures of Penny with dignitaries across the globe. Nelson Mandela and President Frank Fowler. Of course, she knows Reid Johnston, Ornette Schlesinger, Nathan Culp, she explained. She wouldn't be an effective advocate if she didn't.

"Does the King of Clubs have any significance to you?" he asked.

"A horrible pestilence on the country."

"But no direct connection?"

"Of course not, Agent McMannis!"

He produced his laptop from his briefcase and shared a file with her: a screenshot of a computer screen.

"Does this look familiar?" he asked.

"No," she said behind a frozen smile.

"A man was arrested today. This file was found on his computer. We believe the screenshot may have been taken while hacking a computer."

"There's a lot of crazy people out there," she tisked, her head rotating with doubt.

"The file appears to be called the King of Clubs. All the Congressmen affected by the eco-terrorism are listed, status in various committees..."

"I'm sorry. I don't recognize it."

"OK," he snapped the laptop closed. "I'm sorry to waste your time."

McMannis rode the elevator down to the first floor and stepped onto 14th Street. He crossed at the corner and passed a van: Ben Franklin Electric. They seem to work in D.C. too.

On the top floor, Archer made a phone call. Her cell took a split second longer to find a signal, passing the FBI's StingRay.

"Reid Johnston," the Speaker announced himself.

"Reid, we have a problem..."

"Let me guess. Agent McMannis."

"Yea."

"Shit. You shouldn't be calling me."

McMannis caught sight of the van driver, flashing a thumbs up. He called Roberts, beaming. "We got her!"

"I know!" she replied, elated.

"How do you know?"

"Wait, how do *you* know?"

"Who are you talking about?" he asked.

"Zoe, of course."

"The daughter?"

"She contacted Lorenzo Jamison through WhatsApp. They met in Washington Square park. We've got all of it recorded. Then she contacted Maurice Harbaugh. He's on the Colorado-Utah border."

"Wow. Great job," McMannis congratulated his partner.

"Thanks," she replied back. "Who were *you* talking about?"

"Penny Archer. I've got one more stop to make. I'll call you in a few."

McMannis' steps echoed down the marble-lined halls of Congress. It was 7:00 p.m. on Saturday, the building usually quiet as a morgue. This evening it was buzzing. Reporters jockeyed for position. Congressmen, heeled by their staff, *Grande* Starbucks cup in hand, frenetic texting in the other, shuffled through. Reid Johnston stepped to a bank of microphones, a quickly-scheduled press conference to assuage the country about the latest attack in Oklahoma.

McMannis stepped past the dog and pony show, dodged a late-arriving TV crew, and made his way to a back office. "I'm here to see Congressman Culp."

"I'm sorry, the Congressman just stepped out," his secretary responded.

"I can wait," McMannis replied as he sat on the leather reception couch.

"It could be a while," the secretary said, as if McMannis shouldn't get too comfortable. Just then, Culp slid back into the room, still peering out the cracked door.

"Congressman? This is  Agent McMannis with the FBI."

"Yes, of course. Nice to meet you…," Culp offered, checking his watch.

Homer stuck his doughy hand in for a shake. "We've met, Sir. The other day at your apartment."

"Yes, of course."

"And at the C3 meeting."

"Yes, of course. Evora, please hold my calls," Culp instructed uneasily. They grabbed briefcases, entered the office, and closed the door. "Are you close to catching those eco fuckers?"

"It's our top priority, Sir," McMannis responded, perusing the décor. Obligatory photos, memorabilia. An award: Champion of Freedom from the Faith and Freedom Foundation.

"Great organization." Homer offered, taking in the scroll lettering, the gold leaf trim.

"What exactly can I help the FBI with today?"

"It's funny. The Foundation… Do you coordinate with them regularly?"

"I listen to their views," he offered the standard line. "They represent my constituents."

"And back at the townhouse, the one on D Street, we were talking about poker. That's a beautiful place, by the way."

"Thank you. You were saying."

"Yes, poker. Now, we have four congressional districts that were hit. We believe all four affected Congressmen play poker together. And a murder may have been planned, in part, during that poker game."

"Are you accusing me of something, Agent McMannis?"

"I'm merely suggesting..."

"Yes?"

"That your lawyer calls us. Monday morning, no later, if you want to make a deal." He handed his card to the Congressman and walked out. Thank you, McMannis offered the receptionist, quite pleased with himself. He passed the press conference bulging at the seams, Reid Johnston easing the tension with his folksy Texan manner. Out the Capitol and around to Constitution Avenue, past an unassuming van, Ben Franklin Electric. Hard working electricians.

Culp gazed at the FBI agent's card and contemplated his next move. He picked up his cell and made a call.

"Hello?" she answered.

"Penny, we have a problem."

"Did the FBI contact you? Agent McMannis?"

"How did you know?"

"Shit," she responded. "You shouldn't have called me."

# Chapter 74. The Incident at Goose Creek

Mo used the entire road, skidding the little pickup into each turn. He cursed himself. When he bought the truck new, he assumed his post in the marines was a lifetime opportunity. Nonetheless, money was tight, first-year recruits barely paid. To save a few bucks,

Mo made an economic and thoroughly rational decision, and opted for the mid-tier engine: a 2.7 liter four-cylinder. Deep down, he really wanted the growl and power of the V6, but his practical side got the better of him that day.

Fifteen years later, as dust billowed behind, five oversized truck revved in chase. They were close enough Mo could hear the whoops of the drivers and passengers, quite literally, riding shotgun. High-beams and spotlights were trained on the Tacoma in the last glints of the Western day. As bullets echoed past, the shells bouncing off the red rock escarpment Utah 128 was carved into, Mo Harbaugh realized he made a very bad decision that day. He was losing ground, the Tacoma clearly outmatched.

Bouncing up and down in the passenger seat, Ian fumbled with the bible, searching for fate.

"*Now when they have finished their testimony, the beast that comes up from the Abyss will attack them, and overpower and kill them.*"

"That's all it says!" Ian complained.

They turned once more, a sharp right, and rode the ridge just above the sheer red rock walls of the Colorado River valley. The sinewy flow flickered softly below, its imperfections catching a last glimpse of salmon-colored sky. The Tacoma's engine wailed up over a rise, the lights of the pickups behind them. Three more shots echoed in the canyon, one hitting their vehicle. The men ducked as the bullet ricocheted in the Tacoma's bed.

"They're getting closer, Mo."

"I know some back roads in this area. We just need to get through town, and I can lose them." Suddenly, the flapping of giant birds, the whomping of helicopters over the rock rim. Two of them in formation, midnight blue with white U.S. Marshall insignias.

"HOLD YOUR FIRE," they commanded the trailing vigilantes. A voice from above. "DO NOT IMPEDE LAW ENFORCEMENT." Mo kept his speed, tires squealing on the ridge road, across the double yellow line, using every inch of available asphalt, dirt kicking from one soft shoulder to the other.

Large spotlights trained on the Tacoma from above. "IN THE TACOMA. MAURICE HARBAUGH. IAN MACARTHUR. WE KNOW WHO YOU ARE. STOP THE VEHICLE AND COME OUT WITH YOUR HANDS UP. STOP THE VEHICLE!"

Mo looked at Ian. It was not supposed to end here. A sheer rock wall opened across the river. 500 feet of sculpted fortress, the flowing artiste meandered peacefully below. A hairpin turn to the left nearly forced them into the river below. The engine revved louder still. A giant outcropping forced the helicopters off course. The road dropped lower, closer to the river, the carver. Ian squeezed the bible tight, his finger a bookmark to the fateful passage. Revelations 11. The Two Witnesses.

\*\*\*

"Jonah, put your helmet on," his mom told him again. "And keep an eye on Rachel."

"OK," the 10-year-old agreed with exasperation. The freedom of the bike path called him. "Come on Rachel," he commanded. She grabbed her bike, hoping to keep pace with her older brother. The family was camping at Goose Creek, just across the starlit Colorado River from the sheer red rock walls of Arches National Park. "We're going to Utah for spring break!" Jonah shouted to his friends last week. They feigned jealousy, not sure of what Utah was.

They hit top speed, the bike path a perfect asphalt ribbon, up the slight grade following the river west, wondering if they could meet the sea where it ends. A moment later, they couldn't hear each other anymore. The echo of helicopters throbbed through the canyon, blanketing their screams. Eerie luminescence submerged them. Confused, Rachel turned into the road and fell near the double yellow line. Jonah noticed and instinctively turned back, trying to pick his sister up.

\*\*\*

Omnipotent spotlights followed the Tacoma like silent actors on a state-sized community stage. The vigilante posse barreled just behind, screaming with excitement as they pulled almost even to the old truck. Mo checked the speedometer. The needle flickered at the 90. The engines roared. The tires squealed. The helicopters thumped. Bathed in light and shadow, Mo and Ian could barely hear the chaos around them.

Something sparkled in the road. Pinwheels of reflection. The eyes of angels.

"Deer!" Ian cried.

"Worse," Mo shouted. "Kids!" He pulled the wheel hard to the right. The car flew. Silence. It dismounted the road, edged an outcrop, and flipped into the river. The Colorado swallowed the Tacoma. Only the rear tires, the back bumper, and the upside-down Virginia plates—GAZ SUX—showed itself above the riffle, swollen and ice cold from the snowmelt of the La Sal mountains, watching the scene stoically in the distance.

Red Mullet and company pulled to a dead stop. The children, their eyes filled with dust, rolled their bicycles to safety, screaming for mom to make sense of it all.

Divers bravely endeavored the rescue.

As word of the incident spread: the infamous men, the chase across the undulating desert, the helicopter spotlight along the canyon's tenuous crest, people flocked to the scene. They brought their binoculars and took pictures with long-range lenses. They came from far and wide and set up grills and charcoaled bratwurst and hamburgers and covered the meat in mustard and pickles and ketchup. They exchanged gifts of cold beer, macaroni salad, and best of all, their stories: the hellish sound and light overhead, the uncanny déjà vu as they stowed the kids in a safe place, and packed for an unknown celebration. Hours later, after counting the morbid tally, Moab police and firefighters winched the Tacoma unceremoniously to the rocky shoreline.

They watched in awe as the ambulance angled past the police barriers and backed to the water. The dead men, gray and bloated with river water were placed on gurneys and slid into the ambulance, the pulse of the siren flash keeping ominous time to it all. One of the men still clutched a bible, his finger bookmarking the last passage read. Revelation, Chapter 11.

# Chapter 75. The Rager Upstate

Two thousand miles east, Travis waived them in. "A few inches more," he instructed, his third beer in hand. Amelia edged the car over the uneven dirt. "Good," he shouted as he walked over to the passenger side. "I thought you'd never get here."

"It was a shit show leaving the city," Zoe explained.

Travis handed her an unopened can, sweating its cold out. "I brought you a fresh one."

"Thanks," she said, sharing a knowing look with Amelia. Zoe cracked the beer open and took a big slug until it spilled down her chin. "I needed that."

They slammed the car doors closed and followed the lights of the farmhouse, the thump of electronic music. High school seniors drank on the porch. Behind them, a faint whinny called from the dark; Zoe paused and turned to spot an old barn on the far side of the property.

As they entered, Amelia apologized for taking so long. River offered hugs and shots. The clamor came into focus. Yelps of hard-fought beer pong echoed through, guys in an epic battle. In another room, teens swayed in the dark to pulsing music and strobe.

Zoe and Amelia edged back onto the porch, past a sloppy make-out session, girls pouting in endless selfie. They sat on the porch floor, legs dangling over, taking in the night sky, the contrast of quiet farmland in front, raucous party in back. Travis and River joined them, bragging how wasted they were. "You want some molly?" Travis offered, as he opened his hand: white pills in a small plastic bag.

"Not tonight," Zoe replied.

"What's with you lately?" Travis grilled. She pretended not to understand.

"Zoe's gonna save the world," Amelia explained. "She told me on the ride up."

"Don't listen to her," Zoe scoffed.

"Like an eco-terrorist?" River questioned.

"Those people are so stupid," Travis countered. "It's not gonna do anything."

"So, we should do nothing?" Zoe asked. "Wait for the bridge to fall down before we repair it? Let the cats shit all over the house, never cleaning the litter box?" Travis and River looked back in confusion.

Zoe slugged down the rest of her beer. "It's a bad metaphor. I need another beer," she explained and River retrieved some cold ones. Three beers later, they were still in heated discussion. When Zoe took a walk, Amelia joined and they wandered into the airy barn to find two chestnuts and an appaloosa. Zoe walked closer, one of the chestnuts meeting her above the paddock wall. Zoe stroked the horse's soft muzzle and leaned in to touch cheeks. The chestnut stared at her with infinite wisdom and Zoe broke down into tears.

"You ok?" Amelia asked.

Zoe shook her head no. "I need to tell you something..."

\*\*\*

L.J. was waiting, watching TV, strangely calm, when he heard them pull up. It was about 11, he was finishing up a Seinfeld rerun—the one where George converts to Latvian Orthodox—pretending not to think about it. They blocked off half of Red Hook, set up a couple of unmarked vans across from L.J.'s garden apartment. Two dozen came to the door in FBI jackets, another dozen in the alley behind the building. Roberts rang the bell.

"Who is it?" L.J. asked dumbly, cocking the trigger.

"Mr. Jamison, it's the FBI. Please come out with your hands up."

"I just got out of the shower. Hold on a second."

"Sir," Roberts spoke as they readied the battering ram. "We have a warrant for your arrest, Mr. Jamison. Mr. Jamison?"

Roberts stepped aside and counted down in silence as they practiced the swing of a battering ram. The ram bashed where the bolt meets the frame. A second swing, the door flung open, and the agents poured inside.

"Freeze, hands up!" they screamed in the darkness. A slam from behind the bedroom door. They approached, battering ram still in hand.

"Mr. Jamison?" Roberts screamed into the bedroom, testing the knob. It turned, and they entered with military precision. No sign of Jamison. The fire escape, Roberts realized, was outside one of the windows. She looked up the metal structure, found L.J. climbing to the roof, and pursued.

When Roberts got to the roof, the other agents setting up shot angles, she found L.J. atop the knee wall, five stories above unforgiving sidewalk. He held a .38 in his hand, pointed at his temple, and a slight smile on his face.

"Mr. Jamison!" Roberts screamed. "Please don't."

"It doesn't matter," L.J. screamed back. "I'm dead anyway. Only the mode matters now."

"Mr. Jamison? The gun, Sir."

L.J. eased the .38 from his temple and pointed it at Roberts. Two dozen FBI agents tensed, rifles and pistols cocked. Roberts raised her hand for calm. "Please, Mr. Jamison, drop it gently to the roof."

L.J. did and stood straight up on the knee wall.

"Good. Now, come on down," Roberts suggested.

"OK," L.J. said with a grin. He raised his arms and began a conversation with a higher authority. "I'm sorry," he whispered, "if I let you down."

"Mr. Jamison," Roberts tried again.

"I hear you," L.J. responded distantly and he fell back like a swinging door, slowly with dreaded anticipation. Roberts peered over the knee wall before recoiling with nausea, blood splattered on the pavement in all directions.

She climbed down the fire escape, back through the apartment, and out to the sidewalk. "Time of death?" Roberts asked.

"11:09," someone responded, as they cordoned off the area with yellow tape.

\*\*\*

About 12:45 on Sunday morning, Zoe collapsed in the master bedroom upstairs, the party still thumping. 50 officers quietly encircled the farmhouse. They thundered through the front and back doors simultaneously, badges extended from FBI and US Marshall jackets, ordering everyone to the floor.

"Zoe Becker! Where is she?" From the beer-sticky floor, the teens pointed upstairs, the parent's bedroom. They found her sprawled out, dwarfed by the mound of coats piled on the bed. Zoe woke to thick static: 20 lawmen screaming, guns drawn. One shouted her Miranda rights above the din as she was shoved to the floor.

She walked down the stairs, hair in all directions, metal cuffs ahead, Federal agents behind, with an expecting calm. She mouthed *Sorry* to Amelia and Travis and River, and was led outside to an awaiting Black Suburban. A hand guided her head, the back door closed, the siren went on, and the Suburban drove away.

The teenagers were held for hours, answering questions about connections to Zoe, their whereabouts this month. Travis and Amelia were taken in for further inquiry. All said and done, the rager went very different from planned.

# Chapter 76. You're Welcome America

The Next Day.

Among his 17 tweets before day-break, President Fowler offered this to his flock of followers and the nation:

*Evil eco-terrorists were stopped by the best law enforcement agencies in history. You're welcome America. We will immediately prosecute #ZoeBecker and her delinquent father. Lock her up!*

@PresidentPOTUS, April 23, 2017 02:03:17 am

# Chapter 77. I'm Bad With Names

Ten days later.

Large vans, adorned with satellite dishes and ad hoc antennae, filled the street. A large press corp waited in folding chairs for a statement.

Ornette Schlesinger, the Fossil of Congress, walked outside his suburban Atlanta home, a perfect replica of Tara from Gone With the Wind, flanked by his lawyers and children, themselves nearly old enough to claim social security. They pulled up to the sidewalk to proclaim his innocence, subdue the media sensation, refute any evidence linking him to the King of Clubs poker game and murder of Dr. Amir Abassi, the scientist from Colorado. Unfortunately, Team Schlesinger was not fully informed.

Schlesinger's lawyer initiated the press briefing with historical context. "Congressman Schlesinger is currently the longest-serving member of the House of Representatives, having served under 9 U.S. Presidents."

"The whole thing is preposterous," Ornette Schlesinger added, clearly disgusted by the unnecessary fuss, as his counsel unsuccessfully tried to rein in his outburst. "I don't know anything about this poker game or any Faith and Freedom establishment." "Mr. Schlesinger," a female reporter cut in. "Are you aware Nathan Culp of Pennsylvania has just made a public admission? He said he attended the King of Clubs poker game, that it was organized by the Faith and Freedom Foundation, and that you, Reid Johnston, and other specific Congressmen attended."

Ornette and his lawyer faltered for control.

The reporter looked back at her notes. "Oh, and that the gathering including prostitutes on occasion, paid for by the Foundation."

Another reporter shot in. "Is it true Mr. Schlesinger accepted subsidized rent from the Foundation? His residence on D Street in Washington, D.C.? Isn't that against Congressional policy?"

The Georgian's eyes rolled back, past the coke bottle glasses, desperately searching for a way out of this mess.

"Congressman Schlesinger is currently the longest-serving member of the House of Representatives," Schlesinger's lawyer reminded the gathered outside the stately home. The hands of sixty-four reporters shot up with questions. "Nothing further at this time," and he pulled Schlesinger and family inside, shut the door, and adjusted the shades.

\*\*\*

"Yea, I remember the little guy," Bonnie Del Rio told the interviewer when asked about Ornette Schlesinger. The long-legged ginger was ready to tell her story. She agreed to go on Dateline three days after Nathan Culp's public admission. "He was kinda cute. Like a tree frog or some nocturnal animal."

"And Landry Muldoon?"

"The fat one? Yep, he was there too."

"And Chad Droburn?"

"Yep. It was six of them. Johnston, Droburn, Radcliffe, Culp, Muldoon, and the little, old guy."

"Schlesinger?"

"Yea. Sorry, I'm bad with names," as she welled up with emotion.

He handed her a tissue. "That's ok. And why did you decide to come forward now?"

"When I heard about the scientist getting killed, and the oceans dying, and that brave girl tried to expose the whole thing. I said to myself 'Bonnie, this is bigger than you.'"

"There are rumors you have a book in the works and this is just a publicity stunt."

"My lawyer told me not to talk about that."

\*\*\*

Two days later, McMannis and Roberts emerged from a room with Graham Bucksworth, his confession in hand. The FBI believed the murder was an accident, the food poisoning too effective. When Bucksworth and Paul Anderson went back to check on him, they found Dr. Abassi dead in the corner. They undid his belt and strung him up to the antiquated piping of the Biltmore's fire protection system, kicked over a chair, and strung him up in faux suicide. The piping creaked under his weight but luckily the good doctor was a slender individual.

Buckworth's plea bargain would save his life. His charge was reduced to involuntary manslaughter, the sentence a modest five years. He could be out in two and a half with good behavior. In exchange, he detailed everything he knew, recalled every conversation: the late night chats with Penny Archer, Droburn's clear direction to go above and beyond for the Foundation, the undeniable threat they agreed to make on Abassi's life.

\*\*\*

McMannis and Roberts approached the park bench in the morning, just outside the long shadow of the Capitol. Penny Archer sat calmly as pigeons fought for an advantageous spot in the arc of bread she tossed to the ground.

"It's a beautiful building," she said, recognizing the footsteps from behind. "A national treasure, really." She stared at the massive columned dome atop the marble structure.

"Ms. Archer...," Homer interrupted.

Penny maintained her awed daze. "That was one mistake the Founding Fathers made, not incorporating God more clearly."

"Ms. Archer, do you understand why we're here?"

"That wasn't their intent. A misinterpretation, really."

"You're under arrest. You have the right to remain silent." Roberts stood Penny up and placed the cuffs on.

"You're Agent McMannis, I remember now," Penny said through the fog, staring closely at Homer.

"That's right."

"It's the Great Awakening, Agent."

"Ms. Archer, anything you say can and will be used against you in a court of law. You have the right to an attorney. If you cannot afford an attorney, one will be provided for you."

Penny kept eyeing the Capitol, one last glimpse, as the FBI turned her around and guided her into the waiting SUV, the siren flashing silently. "Beautiful, isn't it, Agent McMannis?"

"Yes, Maam. Do you understand your rights?"

The SUV drove off, Penny craning her neck to get a last glimpse.

\*\*\*

Two more days and the FBI showed up at the Tara replica Schlesinger called home in suburban Georgia. They escorted the old man past the over-manicured lawn and faux Grecian statues, wrists cuffed under a draped jacket, into the back of a waiting SUV. Similar scenes took place in Texas, Louisiana, California, and Oklahoma.

***

The applause echoed through the bar. McMannis and Roberts sat together. She and her margarita. He and his beer. Their colleagues milled about, congratulating each other for solving the biggest eco-terrorism case in U.S. history. Took down a few crooked politicians as well. A table piled high with nachos and wings, commendations to all. Cap Little came over and shook their hands. Told them he always believed in them.

"An incredible accomplishment," he said.

"Thank you, Sir," they said in unison. Cap turned to accept acknowledgements from the Bureau's top brass as they entered the tavern, the revelry getting louder.

McMannis watched the screen, beaming, as the news replayed scenes of Schlesinger's SUV driving away, the old man slumping with guilt in the backseat. "Nothing more satisfying than that."

"A Congressman in handcuffs?"

"It could be a statue outside the Capitol."

"No specific names, of course," Roberts suggested.

"No," McMannis agreed, "To our unknown brethren..."

"Past, present, and future," she laughed as their glasses met in celebration. "Be careful with your power."

"Or you'll keep us employed for generations."

# Chapter 78. Anklet

Sunday, June 4th, 2017. A few hours before 60 Minutes would air.

"No. No. Of course, not," Becker shook his head, just outside the front door on 22nd Street. "I'm not ashamed of my daughter." He was with his lawyer, Arthur Schackman of Schackman and Schackman, recommended by his old friend, Nils Jensen. He had been on house arrest the past few incredible, hectic days. Electronic anklet in place, he was no longer considered a risk of flight, to society, or himself. He and the whole world, it seemed, would watch his daughter talk to 60 Minutes in a few hours, a week before her trial.

Outside his apartment, microphones and cameras swirled in hysteria.

"Did you know Zoe masterminded this plan?"

"Did you hack into the Foundation computers?"

"Should she be tried as an adult?"

"Will you testify against her?"

Becker shook his head no as if to repel the verbal attacks with his schnoz. It was all much more than any human being could take, a father especially. An hour earlier, inside the apartment, up the four flights, the drapes closed, Becker checked in on the soldiers at attention, at the ready, at the back of the bathroom cabinet. The pill bottles looked at him blankly, waiting for their orders. He closed the door. Not today. His daughter will need him soon. Now, more than ever.

An SUV pulled up to shuttle him away from the chaos. He gazed the crowd. Pruned faces, heads nodding in disgust. Among the discord, a pair of compassionate eyes framed by a braid of shiny black. It was Empress from the Jade Dragon. They caught each other as acrobats might, Becker in mid-air, his bearings askew. She gave him a reassuring look, an understanding beam. *Maybe he wasn't the worst parent ever.* He offered a sheepish smile back, silent gratitude for her support.

Schackman opened the door and Becker lowered his head into the SUV's back seat. Schackman got up front and the driver rolled through the crowd, slow enough not to crush an overzealous cameraman. They drove to the FBI's office on Federal Plaza, just a few blocks from the MCC, the prison Zoe apparently just opened up her soul from.

Becker entered the building ready to tell his tale, as best he could. If Zoe was going to cooperate fully, so was he. No more cryptic answers. No more half-truths.

# Chapter 79. Family Business

Back at the Metropolitan Correctional Center, Zoe and her attorney returned from a small meeting room. She wanted to continue, against all of her counselor's advice. Zivitz frantically called the Federal prosecutor at the Department of Justice, asked if a plea deal was possible. But as expected, Zoe would have no leverage once admitting fully to the crimes, especially on national TV. Zoe begged Zivitz to relax. *The truth will set me free*, she insisted.

They returned to the plastic chairs and the ad hoc studio at the center of the prison's dining hall. The interview, starting its third hour, had more than adequate material for a lead segment on 60 Minutes when it would air tomorrow night. But so much of the story had yet to unfurl.

"Because of the exposure, Penny Archer and five Congressmen went to jail," Webber prompted her.

"I'm really proud of that."

"And Lorenzo Jamison committed suicide."

Zoe stared back at him, facial muscles losing composition. "Is there a question?"

"Do you feel guilty about Mr. Jamison's suicide?"

"No." Zoe reached for the Kleenex, floodgates about to burst. "That's not true. L.J. was one of the greatest people I've ever known. He killed himself to save me."

"But it didn't work. You went to jail. Did you know he was going to take his own life?"

"No. But I wasn't surprised. We met in the park that day. I told him I loved him."

"He knew it was over?"

Her lips quivered but no sound came out.

"How did you know each other?"

"He was a good friend of my mom and dad's. He would come over when I was little. He had a way of explaining the world to me.

It was never varnished. He just knew a child could understand the truth if you explain it to them right. Then Dr. Abassi was murdered, and we realized no one would ever know the story. It was just make believe at first. We were writing a screenplay. Then one day, I said I wanted to do it for real. He said he might know someone, someone who could actually do our plan in real life. They shared our philosophy."

"That was Mo Harbaugh and Ian MacArthur?"

"Yea, that was Mo and Ian."

"Did you know those men?"

"No. I never met them. At least, not until the end."

"Authorities think they may have been deranged. Seeing messages in the bible, as if they were prophets..."

"Perhaps."

"Attacking the country every six days."

"That was my idea," Zoe said, wadding her tissues into an oversized golf ball. "God gave us this amazing gift..."

"And it was your money? You funded it?"

"That's right. When my grandfather died, I got an inheritance. I bet on a hunch. Luckily, I didn't really know a lot about investing."

"You made millions in Bitcoin?"

"Something like that."

"You've maintained your Dad was not involved."

"That's right. He didn't know."

"He should've figured it out, wouldn't you say?"

Zoe had read the papers, saw the talking heads on TV. *How could a 17-year-old orchestrate this?... And her Dad not know? ... Puh-lease, all the clues and he takes no action? He stifles the FBI's investigation. He's as guilty as the child!* She searched the concrete's wormhole for guidance.

Zivitz tugged at her for response, but it only drew her further. To 22nd Street, to her dad: screaming over the traffic; laughing as they smoked from the hookah they bought in the Tel Aviv market; burning his mouth as he dug too eagerly into the shrimp dumplings at Jade Dragon; the sacred pinky bond. She knew, somewhere, her

Dad would be watching, drowning in recrimination. The pain she must have caused him, must still be causing him.

"I never told him. He was going through a rough time. After the election, he could barely cope."

"He looked away while you executed his extremist ideology, isn't that right?" Webber taunted her.

"No, it's not true!"

"You carried on the family business, probably under his watchful eye."

"Ethan!" Zivitz jumped in as Zoe wept, tremoring. "Zoe is not on trial in this interview. And neither is her father."

Webber offered a modest shrug of guilt. He moved on. "Teenagers, little girls and boys are going to be watching this broadcast tomorrow night. Millions of them from every corner of the country. What would you like to tell them?"

Zoe rubbed inky raccoons around her eyes and contemplated a response. She threw her hands in the air searching for meaning to it all. "Don't give up," she offered.

"Don't give up?" Webber repeated.

"Don't give up. Don't give in. Demand that your opinion matters. It's the adults who should be listening to the children."

"Is that it?"

"Everything in nature is a gift. Every forest, every coral reef, every species, every insect."

"A gift?"

"We need to treasure these gifts. Save as much as we can for every future generation, and pass on the gift that God gave us. It would be rude of us not to."

"Treasure God's gift?"

"That's right," Zoe offered, certain it would be misconstrued somehow. She shook her head with grief, simply exhausted by the process. She looked at Zivitz, her attorney, and offered an exhausted smile. She hadn't made his job any easier.

They called it a wrap, and the crew broke down the lights and camera equipment, coiled the oversized cables, and dismantled the catering tables, all in deafening silence.

\*\*\*

The next day, at 7:00 Eastern, Americans turned off their Netflix and their video games. They finished making supper and filled their plates as they gathered, movie night style, in front of the TV. Not the little one in the kitchen or the old one in the bedroom. The good one in the living room, with the lights lowered a bit for dramatic effect, and the dog already walked so it didn't bark for attention during the broadcast. They stopped their gardening and the weak attempt at doing bills, cut their bike rides and car washes short, soap scum still in the door handles, Armor All still in spray pattern on the passenger side dash.

They heard the familiar stopwatch and the reporters as they introduced themselves. "I'm Ethan Webber, those stories tonight, on 60 Minutes."

As Zoe Becker broke down physically and emotionally on their screens, so too did they, these Americans, with bikes strewn across the front yard, the wheels still spinning, wobbling in space. Frozen with contemplation, they listened to the story of the teenager and her rage.

A collective sigh could be heard across the land, the smell of fear dissipating. The terror and the mystery were gone, the tale known. Sentencing remained uncertain. But they could go about their day, their lives, again. Collect their bicycles from the front lawn and finish the car wash, wipe the Armor All into the faux leather until it brought out its original luster. They looked at each other, these Americans, caught one another in the gleam of the eye and saw something they hadn't before. When they spoke, phlegm surfaced first before being cleared.

"Did you watch 60 Minutes?" they asked.

"That sure was something."